Gregory Benford is a professor of physics at the University of California, Irvine, a Woodrow Wilson Fellow and a fellow at Cambridge University, and an advisor to the US Department of Energy, NASA and the White House Council on Space Policy. Dr Benford is also one of the most honoured authors in science fiction. His many novels, including the classic *Timescape*, have won two Nebula Awards, the John W. Campbell Award and the United Nations Medal in Literature.

Find out more about Gregory Benford and other Orbit authors by registering for the free monthly newsletter at www.orbitbooks.co.uk

D0332673

Beyond Infinity

Gregory Benford

www.orbitbooks.co.uk

An *Orbit* Book

First published in Great Britain by Orbit 2004

Copyright © Gregory Benford 2004

The moral right of the author has been asserted.

ISBN 1 84149 188 8

Typeset by Palimpsest Book Production Limited,
Polmont, Stirlingshire
Printed and bound in Great Britain by
Mackays of Chatham plc, Chatham, Kent

Orbit
An imprint of
Time Warner Books UK
Brettenham House
Lancaster Place
London WC2E 7EN

To Arthur Clarke, without whom . . .

CONTENTS

Beyond Infinity

I
Growing Up Original

Thought shall be harder,
heart the keener
courage the greater,
as our might lessens.
—'The Battle of Maldon'
Tenth Century A.D.

1
Cley

At times Cley thought that she was, well, a bit too intense. She seemed to have too much personality for one person and yet not enough for two.

Perhaps the cause lay in her upbringing. She had been most attentively raised by her Meta, an ancient term for the meta-family. Hers had several hundred loosely related people clustered in ever-shifting patterns. It provided an overview, a larger vision of how to grow up.

The Meta had spotted her as a wild card early on. It made no difference. Though hers, the Hard River Meta, was entirely, deliberately populated by Naturals – those without deep-seated connections to external machine intelligences – not many were Originals. Cley was an Original of particularly primordial type, based on genes of great vintage. Other Originals carried genes that had passed through revisions so many times that, by comparison, Cley's genetic suite was a fossil.

This gave her a kind of status. Not many true Originals walked the Earth, though the historians who pestered her early education said there had once been billions of them afoot. Billions! There were hardly a tenth that many now in all Earthly humanity. Not that she cared much about such numbers. Mathematics was a fossil art. Few in her time bothered to scale those heights of analysis with their majestic, abstruse peaks that the ancient civilizations had climbed, marked as their own, and finally abandoned as too chilly, remote, and even inhuman.

She cared far more for things close by, not abstractions. That was the gift of living in Hard River Meta — the natural world, custom-made for Naturals. They had enough technology to be comfortable but did not waste time tending to it. Nobody much cared about events beyond the horizon.

She had dozens of good friends and saw them daily. Children had jobs that meant something — farming, maintenance, big-muscle stuff — and nobody lorded it over others. Leadership rotated. Kids tried on jobs like clothes. Her life was one of small, steady delights.

She was happy, but— The filling in of the rest of that sentence would, she knew quite early, occupy the rest of her life. And she knew even then that the things she sought in life could disappear even as she reached for them, the way a fist went away when she opened her hand.

She suspected her antic energy came from a heavy genetic legacy. She belonged to the narrowest class of the Ur-humans — a genuine Original, and as such, something of a puzzle to her Meta of Naturals and much-revised Originals. A rarity.

She knew herself to be something of a hothouse plant. Not an orchid, no. More like a cactus, feverishly flowering under the occasional passing cloudburst. Anyone who showered her with attention got her one-plus-some personality, ready or not. She wore people out.

Especially, she tired her fellow Naturals in their orderly oatmeal lives. She secretly suspected that she also carried some Supra genes, or maybe some of the intermediate breeds of human that had been in vogue through the last several hundred million years. She tried to find out if this might be so, but hit the stone wall of Meta security, whose motto in most matters genetic was 'Best not to know.'

So she watched herself for telltale signs of intermediate forms. Nobody would help her, and she was too close to herself to be objective — and who wasn't? A stutter she developed at age nine — could that be a sign? She worried endlessly. Bit off fingernails, even when they were part of her extendable tools. Chewed her lip. Then the stutter went away. Another sign?

She felt as though she might very well spend the rest of her life with her button nose pressed against the glass of a room where she should be, only she couldn't find the door.

Her Meta never told her exactly who her parents were. There were Moms, which stood for *mother of the moment*, who tended to her upbringing for years, then handed her off to another Mom. All her previous Moms stayed in the background, ready to help.

She only knew for sure that some pair among the sixty or so in her Meta had given birth to her genetically. But which pair? She had often wondered. It was usually reassuring that the genetic parents sometimes did not themselves recall — and sometimes it was not reassuring at all.

But then, growing up was not supposed to be easy. One Mom remarked offhandedly, 'It's the toughest work you'll ever do.' For a long while Cley had thought this an exaggeration. Now she was not so sure she could even do it.

The troubling question was, when was growing up over? Maybe never.

So she took her earliest Mom as a model. That Mom was a stocky, affable woman of wide smile and high cheekbones. Cley had good, trim cheekbones like hers but had grown to be slim, tall, muscular, small-breasted. Were these differences clues to her father's genes? She wished she had gotten more cleavage and an easier manner. But even Cley knew that gene combinations were not so simple.

In late childhood, when she first started to fret over such matters, she had mentioned her vague ideas about her father to her then-nominal Mom, who said, 'You don't need to know, dear, and anyway, he's far away.'

'How far?'

'See the horizon?'

'Beyond those mountains?' She had never been that far.

'You're looking at the wrong part of the view.'

This she did not understand at all, and so she pestered Mom for days. Only once did Mom's patient smile fade. 'You've had something caught crosswise in you all week, my girl.'

'But I need to know—'

'You need to get inside there and turn it right-wise. Go meditate a bit.'

She liked meditation, the feeling of lifting off the stolid, solid Earth and soaring up a solemn mountain of herself. It was satisfying. Three members of her Meta did little else. But it wasn't for her. It made her feel wonderfully at peace, but eventually even peace got boring. She felt a restlessness that she hoped reflected the horizon-hopping aspect of her father.

'Was he like me?' she would ask Mom.

Mom gave her an arched eyebrow, no more. 'Oh, yes, he was plenty self-full.'

To be full of self the Meta discouraged. Naturals were supposed to embody the primordial art of merging with the ancient world of forests and animals, to lose themselves in it. Naturals were to stay where and what they were, merging with the ample lands being reshaped by higher folk.

The word stung Cley.

'Self-full?' she fretted to one of her girlfriends. They were lying out on a fused stone parapet, lazily watching piping work-birds build their cute layer houses. It seemed a good time for gal-pal talk. 'Really?'

'Um,' the friend said tactfully. 'Maybe a little self-absorbed; could be, yup.'

'But is that really bad?'

'Y'know, worrying about it is self-full in itself.'

'Uh . . . Oh.' Caught in a logical trap. 'Let's talk about something else, then.'

Privately, she thought that having the spirit to leave the Meta was, well, a way of making oneself . . . better. Different. Another idea the Meta discouraged.

But then, there were Supras around, glimpsed as they passed through the Meta's territory on their mysterious, important business. Supras were reminders that some people really *were* more than you. Worse, Supras were better in ways that were not even easy to put a finger on. Even the Supra children of her age were daunting. They ignored her, of course.

Cley had no more species politics than a bird, and not even one of the smart birds, either. Still, being snubbed went beyond theory, straight to the gut. So she inverted the snobbery, in her mind making Originals the true, secret elite, and the Supras into just afterthoughts. That worked, for a year or two.

The whole subject — sociogenetics, her inboards classified it when she went to them for background — was far too complicated. And ancient, as well. The torrent of information from her inboards made her think about it with a curious, dispassionate distance. She guessed that was how real grown-ups thought. It was a bit sobering to know that so much wisdom was buried in her spine somewhere, ready to leap into her head whenever she prompted the inboard summons.

The means of making a fresh person were so complex, she learned, that old ideas like simple parenting, with strictly assignable designer DNA, were useless. The Meta loved her, brought her to the verge of first maturity, and so fell heir to the usual blame for the traumas everyone suffered just in getting that far.

Many women in her Meta Mommed Cley, as their time came available and their interest allowed. Some years it was smiling, big-breasted Andramana, and other years it was lean, cool, analytical Iratain. Others, too, maybe half a dozen — each fine in their moments, then receding into the background as others came to the fore.

The Meta's men provided fathering, too, but here the usual Meta scheme went awry. Her friends liked this, and it seemed to work for them. Like them, she was supposed to gain judgment from these multiple fatherings, to see what men were like in general, and work on her attachment strategies in light of this.

Instead, she just got confused. They were all so different, each with pluses and minuses and no clue to how Cley could ever choose what worked best. So much for theory.

By accident, and persistent questioning thereafter, she

learned that her genetic father had left the Meta for undisclosed reasons when she was three years old. She consulted her inboards, learned some techniques for memory mining, and plumbed her own childhood. She recalled some dim sensations of him: a dark musk, deeply resonant voice, and scratchy whiskers (an affectation, apparently quite ancient). That was all, but it was enough.

So, thinking it absolutely natural, she awaited his return. She dreamed about it sometimes – a weighty presence descending from the sky, usually, like angry thunderheads brimming with ribbed light. She worked on making herself wonderful for him, anticipating his grand homecoming, their reunion as a family. Occasionally, a new male would join the Meta, and she always wondered if maybe this new set of smells and sounds was her one true father.

She could not be sure, of course, because the Meta kept genetic fatherhood and motherhood quite secret. Not so much because it was hugely significant, though. Just policy. People would put too much weight on those old, simple connections, so best be done with them. Mothers, though, were usually too close to disguise; the Meta didn't even try. Everybody needed a Mom, a daily presence, essential as oxygen, but a father could be vague. Better for a young girl to view all men on an equal footing and learn to objectively assess men's abilities as fathers. She would probably choose a new Meta, and her own pairings, using those standards someday.

Her Meta felt that genetic details were totally beside the point anyhow. What mattered, truly, was the Meta and its work. The Meta was the family of all. Humans did not reproduce like animals, after all, anchored in primordial musk and pairings.

Cley wasn't having any of this, though she never said so. Her gut feelings won out over all inherited wisdom. She simply kept making herself wonderful for her father, sure he would show up. And of course, when he did, she would know.

Her true genetic mother might be within arm's reach at any moment, in the milling Meta culture, but that had no claim on her attention. Her mother's identity was a conventional puzzle, dulled by overuse and close familiarity with all her Moms. Father, though – now there was true, singing mystery.

He grew daily in her imagination, as the placid Natural males around her all fell short of what she felt a father should be. She loved him; she worshiped him; she built whole stories around his exploits. 'Dad's Dangerous Days'; chapter thirty-seven.

By this time, no man who ever came into the Meta matched up to the specifications of her father, so she was quite sure that he had never returned. He was off somewhere over the forested horizon, having Original adventures.

She sat dutifully through the ritual experiences of a Meta upbringing, honestly enjoying them but knowing deep down that they were preliminaries to the moment when she would really know, down deep – when her father returned.

She did wonder, as her years stacked up, why this yearning never fastened upon her mother mystery. To raise it brought an odd pang of disloyalty to her nominal Mom. But the issue did not have heft, did not wrap itself in the shadowy shroud of the father. Obviously. Though she sometimes wondered why this was so.

Was the uniqueness of his puzzling absence, affecting only her of all her Meta, part of her own Originality? Was this oddness part of what made her not just another Natural? No one else seemed to long to go over the horizon.

When she spoke about this with any of the adults in her Meta, they carefully reasoned with her, taking ample time. And it all seemed straightened out, crystal clean . . . until she left the room. Then she would run free again, down the hallways of her mind, banging on doors, eager to explore, ready with her latest father story to tell, a story that was somehow about Cley as well.

She had noticed early on that everyone had some sort of story to tell, not about fathers but about themselves. So she got one, too. Fashioned from oddments, nothing too fancy. She was just an Original after all, no more, a genetic form roughly close to the variety that had started civilization off so long ago that to express it took an exponential notation. Not much material to start with. So she stuck to emotions.

Her story was about the father, of course, only cloaked in Meta language. Yearnings, feelings of a destiny lying ahead of her. Fairly common stuff, she thought. Her life story did not quite seem to belong to her, though. She used it to get close to people, and she did care about them . . . but relating ostensibly personal substories about herself seemed to be like offering them for barter. In return for . . . what? She was not sure.

So people — first from her Meta, then from allied Metas — came into her life, shaped it, and departed, their bags already packed. She wondered if everyone experienced life this way — if others came in, introduced themselves, exchanged confidences, and then milled around in their lives until they found an exit. She valued them terribly at the time, but they left only smudged memories.

After a while she started dining out on the delightful details of people she knew, things they did. Other people were so much easier to talk about. She had sharpened her powers of observation while looking for her father. The step from watcher to critic was easy, fun. People were the most complex things in the world, ready-made for stories. Exotica like the slow-walking croucher trees and skin-winged floater birds were fun but, in the end, had no stories. The natural world usually didn't. It was just there. She suspected that civilization had been invented to make more stories.

And after a while, she came to feel that most others deserved her implied tribute: They really were more interesting than she was. Sometimes she felt like saying to strangers, 'Hello, and welcome to my anecdote.'

The electric leer of artfully crafted memory guided her. People remembered each other because they recalled stories, for stories made the person. With the myriad ways to remember, from embedded inboards to external agent-selves, there were endless fertile ways to sort and filter and rewrite the stories that were other people's lives. At times, she soon noticed, people constructed stories that were missing parts, as if the business of being themselves did not hold their full attention. Shoddy work. She was much, much better at it.

She was intent upon the sliding scale that people showed her. Boys her age would rise from arrogant to impressive in the span of a single sentence and then ooze back down that slope again — and she was never sure just why.

At times she was not quite certain who she was. When she was with the boys she knew growing up, she often thought that she was more alive for being with them: *He thinks; therefore, I am.* Afterward, she would enjoy the feeling of having been with a boy and come through it all right, free of awful, embarrassing moments.

Still, she had the odd feeling of being disconnected: *This will be fun to remember;* not *This is fun now.*

She had the usual simple sexual adventures. Kissing was sometimes like devouring the other person, savoring the sweet, swarthy head meat — no sauce, please. Bright grins, dark excesses. So healthy, everybody said.

Even then, though, she came to feel that lust lacked, well, depth. Amid the mad moment, she would sometimes think, *This reminds me of the time I felt déjà vu.*

But if you couldn't learn from experience, what was left? Theory. She talked about this with one of the older women in her Meta, who said dryly, 'The best definition of intelligence is the ability to learn not from your mistakes but from others'.'

Cley went away puzzled. She needed not advice but a road map of life.

So she resolved: Until she knew where she stood, she would continue lying down. Good ol' sex. It certainly beat running away. That way she had tried, too: hard him, hesitant her.

There was no cure for such bewilderments. Cley endured them. Get through it, her girlfriends said. But she also endured because she assumed that after the ordeals of adolescence were done, she would get her reward: the clear, smooth calm and blithe confidence that adults surely had. After all, they looked self-assured, didn't they? Especially the Supras, who were more than adults.

Soon enough, she was big enough to mistake for an Original adult (smaller than Supras, of course, but more muscular). She had a growth spurt and loomed over her girlfriends. 'You're kinda Supra-sized,' they taunted, not knowing that they were just giving away their envy.

Then she realized that the Supras didn't even worry about matters that preoccupied her Meta. One day, three Supras came to talk to her Meta about their ongoing restoration of Earth to a moist, green world. Unfailingly courteous, they spoke of ideas that played out over many centuries. That impressed her enormously. The Supras passed through the forests, nodding politely at the Naturals, the Originals, even taking opticals of them. Of her. She preened and pranced for one, and he grinned. Her heart nearly stopped.

They were also there to look for something that had fallen from the sky, or so some said. They had assumed that the strange play of lights in the sky, witnessed by all her Meta for over a year, were descending craft from the spaces above. On the mere suggestion, Cley studied up on her inboards about the whole meaning of the myriad lights above. She learned the planets, the many lesser lights, the lot. Even history – not her best subject. There was about the huge landscape of the past an enduring sadness, a note of things known but now lost, that made her pause. So much order built up, so many lives well lived, only to be rendered into dust. That was when she learned what a billion really meant.

The Supras searched for many days and found nothing. She watched them react to this, peeking from a tree perch she had made at night to get a better vantage on them. They murmured, worried, ignored the Ur-humans. She got bored, even with these supermen. And superwomen, but she ignored them.

Then one night she woke in her perch. The Supras below were shouting. The sky was alive with twisting luminous shapes. Fire descended from these, igniting the forest down the valley. Helical angers worked across the sky. The Supras trained instruments on these. A fork came down and twirled in the nearby air and skewered one of them. It was a spindly woman. She died noisily.

Cley did not sleep after that. The next morning the Supras left, stopping to tell the assembled Meta that something wrong was afoot. Something dangerous. That the Supras needed them all to keep on as they had before, not to be concerned with matters they did not understand.

Cley's girlfriends thought this was boringly self-evident, but what could they do? Cley found the bare fact that Supras could die, bleed out their lives on the ground, ripped from throat to gut — well, it was at least enlightening. She felt for the first time the electrifying sense of actually living in an important time.

Then the days simmered down, and she relaxed. She was coming into her womanhood, after all, a more pressing issue.

So she persisted in her faith, which was, of course, not a dry slate of dictates but a story: that first thing of all, she would pass through schools, then find something she loved doing, meet men and mate with them (no genetic contracts implied, though), experience raptures and delights unknown to mere young people, survive those and learn from them, and then generally move with growing serenity through the ever-expanding world.

She did manage to finish school. That was as far as her life game plan worked.

2

Being Natural

Adolescence came upon Cley unannounced.

The various shades of humanity above Naturals had dispensed with such sudden advents and halts in the body's evolution. 'Nature's unwanted punctuations,' they sniffed. They could orchestrate their tides and rhythms like an artfully managed story. So she had not heeded warnings of the Natural progressions, especially the firm events of an Original such as she. Menstruation arrived with startling, well, frankness. She had senso-ed about it, of course, but the sudden flow made her think of a wound, not a grand overture to heart-stopping romance.

When it first happened, she dipped her head as if in prayer to natural forces, knees knocked together to hold in the embarrassment. As if this were not a blossoming, but punishment for a transgression. She fell to her knees, hands linking fingers, head tilted up to a God she did not believe in. Whatever God made of this, He/She/It did not help. The dark, hot, leaden burn refused to go away.

There was a simple pharmaceutical cure for all this, of course, and one of the Meta women offered it. Cley automatically rejected it without quite knowing why. And paid the price of discomfort and awkwardness for four months before doing the standard thing.

One Original frontier crossed, she awaited the virginity event. The Meta was easy-going about sex. With other nearby Metas it gave scrupulously clear classes and instructional aids. These were carefully not erotic, but in their clinical cheer also did not give any good reason to do the thing at all. Abstraction prevailed.

At this time she invented her own, interior theory of virginity. In her model, virginity was not a single thing, abolished by a single act, but a continuum. She could give away parts of it. After all, wasn't she a many-sided person, even if a mere Natural?

With other Naturals she had tussled quite agreeably on lounging chairs, preferring the outdoors. But she had not dispensed any of the fractions in her V inventory, as she termed it to her girlfriends. Knowledge, call it K. Then the equation went, V lost equals K gained.

Such thinking enlivened her mathist inputs, at least. Her inboard math abilities seized upon any chance to exercise themselves. An array of equations glided before her left eye; tutorials offered themselves; a learned voice whispered. She knew she should take her major inboards out for a romp every now and then, to keep them fresh, but the mathist parts were boring.

Not that her friends felt that way. 'You have to think precisely,' one of them said, 'or life's just a muddle.' But at the time Cley sensed life as swampy and sexy, so muddle seemed about right.

She had avoided the company of most young women in her Meta. They seemed more attached to the trappings of the world, most of them on their way to being trapped into an attachment, already approved and ordained by the Meta. For Meta reasons, of course: Types naturally attracted each other, as the conventional wisdom had it.

But Cley never got much of a buzz from the men of her supposed type. Nor from those in the nearby classes of human. She had an arranged meeting with a man of the Sigmas, once, which stood in her mind for the whole round-Cley-square-men puzzle. Sigmas were a rare inter-mediate rank of human who usually went nude. As she bandied nonsense with this one, she noticed that he had no apparent genitalia. There was nothing there at all, not even hair.

He caught her glance and said blandly, 'It's inside.'

'It?'

'The ancient apparatus had several parts, true, but ours is integrated into one shaft.' He smiled, as if describing a mildly interesting toy. 'The Original design was not elegant. Um, *is* not . . . and the danger!' His eyebrows shot up.

'I thought the, uh, older gadget had at least two uses.'

'Of course, but we do not excrete through ours.'

'Uh, you . . .'

'Use the rear exit for both.'

Demurely put, she thought. 'And the machinery comes out to play only at recess?'

He laughed quite easily. She was blushing and wished she could stop it, but such control was not available to Originals. 'Only as needed, to prevent damage. The shaft generates the semen as well.'

She kept her eyes resolutely on his. 'No need to have those messy add-ons dangling out in the air?'

'In you Originals that was a design feature to keep the

semen cool. We simply adjust our blood flow, lowering the internal temperature in their vicinity.'

She kept a purely dispassionate expression on her face, afraid to let her lips move for fear they would lapse into a deranged leer, an O of astonishment, or something even worse. Shouting, *Show me your plumage!* for example. Or, *Design feature? Seems more like a bug.* But firmly fixing her face, she said instead, 'Is it the same . . . otherwise?'

For the first time he displayed a knowing grin. 'Larger.'

'Where have I heard that before?' Though in fact she hadn't.

'To give us an advantage.'

'At?'

'Social and biological.' His tone was bland, but the grin stayed put.

'I'm just all atwitter.'

Absolutely flat: 'You should be.'

'You're too sure of yourself.'

'And you, too unsure.' With that he evaporated, turning away and into the spongelike crowd.

She felt put down, and also lucky, not to know what his next line was.

So it came to be with the other classes and orders of greater-than-thou humans. They were almost jaunty in their arid certainty that their variation on the grand theme was the best, or at least better than the first. Their men plainly felt that she should be bowled over by the chance to enjoy their obliquely referred-to talents, endowments, or superior wiring diagrams. Their women twisted luscious true-red mouths (no cosmetics!) in sour amusement, sure that she was an upstart tart who had wandered out of her rightful level.

Even if they were all scrupulously correct and had pots of advanced abilities, charm was not one of them. The best aspect of their company was that at least it was not addictive.

3

First Love, Of Sorts

For a long time she was terribly aware that everyone knew.

They knew, she imagined, that she, as an Original, was going through the primordial fever pitch of oncoming sexual urges and could do nothing about it. Helpless, swept down the hormonal river.

Plenty of Supra art suggested that they thought Naturals lived close to the deep, musky human sources. Cley didn't feel all that swept away. Mostly the idea just embarrassed her.

Other times, she was proud of it. She wanted to shout in crowded rooms, 'I'm following Nature! Watch!' – and then do nothing, just stand there brimming with primitivo life.

She never did that, of course.

What she did was an intellectual version, in a way, of declaring her Naturalness. Her Originality was steeped in ancient times, so she sought out and took an underling position at the Library of Life. In the Vaults.

They deserved the capital letter — vast, forbidding underground repositories of human history. Though the continents continued to grind and shove away at each other, the Ancients (a collective noun covering more time than linear thinking could encompass) had chosen below-ground burial for their legacies. An unconscious repetition of the habit of burying the dead, probably. Primitivo.

And there, amid the claustro-corridors far from sunlight, she met Kurani. He loomed large – physically, mentally, in sheer presence.

Their first job was to unearth a slab that carried intricate data encoded in nuclear spins – a method Kurani termed 'savage nouveaux.' The team of eight trained bright beams upon the flinty surface, and machines tracked across the slab, clicking, measuring, sucking up history.

As Kurani passed before one of the spotlights, she felt herself momentarily eclipsed by his shadow, a chill stealing over her suddenly prickly skin. He was, of course, bigger than anybody else in the team, his gait gliding. They had just opened a new Vault, and technology hovered in the air like flies. These microreaders would snap up any data dust that escaped the slab. Amid the buzz he skated on rippling legs, the Supra carriage gliding smooth and sure. Level, hydraulic, supple. 'Are the indices noted?' he asked of the air.

Nobody seemed sure who was addressed, so she said, 'Done already. Dates unclear—'

'A specialty scheme?'

'It seems so,' she managed.

He orbited toward her, his size bringing full night to shroud her. Craggy, heavy-eyed, the planes of him flat and solid. She wondered how they would rest against anything soft and comforting, and – and did not let herself think any further. 'Why did so many of the Ancients think they should redate everything? That some birth or death or collapse of a civilization was so important?'

She ventured, adding to his sentence, 'That of course,

all human history would ever after be marked from that time.'

'Exactly.' His smile brought the sun back to her shadowed self.

'So what all those eras have in common is the automatic assumption that they are special.'

'Our fault as well.' He smiled slightly, turning his full-bore gaze upon her, and it was like a second spotlight in the narrow Vault.

'You think time begins with you?' It was not a very bright comment, but she had to say something – his eyes were not letting her slide away from them.

'When we meet people, we can't see them – because we are so busy looking at ourselves to be sure we look all right, in case this should be an important somebody we are just meeting.' He smiled with one raised eyebrow, a common Supra signal that meant *idea jump coming up.* 'The same with meeting deep history.'

To this avalanche of astonishing self-revelation (or was it, with the 'we'?), she shot back, 'Me, too. I'm thinking that I really suddenly *see* this person, when what I'm seeing is me reflected in their eyes. Me, proving yet again that I am quick and fascinating and that I *can*.'

And then, of course, she saw that he had been speaking aloud what he had noticed in her. Very Supra. But still . . .

He laughed, sunrise again. 'So you almost envy people who are meeting you? Because they're getting the full you?'

She nodded furiously, not giving herself enough time to see that she was sledding downhill without a clue. And picking up speed. Supras were notorious for jumping from public to personal and back again without warning, but this was over the top. *Okay, then* . . . 'I keep wanting to meet somebody who is completely on, the way I can be maybe five minutes in a year.'

He turned just slightly, as if a shot had nearly winged him. 'The way you are right now.'

How could he know so much? 'Oh, this is just warming up.'

A lie, and his quizzical lift of a lip conveyed that he knew it. She was not just downsloping now, but plunging. Maybe big, black rocks up ahead, but . . . it felt glorious.

Still, she couldn't let him have the last word, even an unspoken one. 'I always wanted to be somebody,' she said. A pause. 'Maybe I should have been more specific.'

To his credit – even if he did have a huge account with her already – he laughed. Loudly. Big.

The trick in talking to Supras, she saw, was to have anything to talk about that was wholly hers. To dress up the dumb stuff she had believed or done, to make it seem at least ardent and naive, not just boneheaded and Original.

Then, too, there was the toiling, earnest quality, even to conversation. Some elegant Supras, far over the horizon somewhere, might spend their vast days on haute fluff, yes. But here in the Library all was earnest. This was the whole human heritage, after all. Even laughter had a purpose: relieving stress.

From him, weirdly, she learned to relax. To smooth the stress, at least. Her nerves jumped; she talked too fast, eyes darting. An Original working among Supras was a mouse foraging for seeds among elephant feet.

And there were the elephants. They supervised a lot of the heavy manual work. More supple than machines, savvy in the ways living things carried in their guts, they worked joyously, singing, dancing late into the night. Their conversations were a bit, well, ponderous. She worked with them and thought they were an excellent, unlikely creation. She was astonished to find that they were more ancient than humans, and not invented at all.

The team even went to an elephant dance, and there unwound. Kurani had methods of soothing the jangled nerveworks. Technical ones: inboards, flex triggers to the neuromusculars — tricks even the Supras found necessary. She was shocked to find he did not even know the chemical Original methods, some as ancient as alcohol. Those particular molecules locked agreeably into his receptors, he found, with a sizzle and a shake.

This broke the ice between them, and then the pattern was straightforward. Flirting became a second language between them. The inevitable came. Between breeds and castes there is always a certain fascination, longing looks cast both up and down the staircase of genetic gradient. He was the primary, she the satellite. He knew centuries; she was not full-grown. She learned to relax even more.

Right away he took command of the situation, of her. A Supra utterly at ease, a king. Deep bass words that rang like bells in her hollow heart. His face, a smile in it somewhere. So many nuances crowded into that classic expression, it was hard for her to make out the significance of a slightly arched eyebrow, the flashing of his earlobes as they recorded her image, smell, glandular secretions — all for a processor sitting somewhere maybe on the other side of the world, but feeding Kurani all he needed to know to assess the situation. To assess her.

He had her. They both knew it. So they then filled the rest of their first intimate meeting, and then a drink, and then a meal, with fodder talk. Facts, data, life trajectories sketched out in names of cities and schools and Meta connections. Sniffing.

All through it she felt as if he were saying something else, or rather *more* – that subtext flitted through his words like birds, lofty and quick, beings of the moment, gone if not glimpsed.

Uneasily and yet, she supposed, quite naturally, she sensed that he had arranged all this. Had stalked her, maybe. But in an offhand fashion, seemingly without effort, invisibly – and she knew then that he would have her.

In that moment she felt another fraction of her virginity inventory vanish, though there had been not a jot of the physical, no act beyond a lifted corner of his ample mouth. She could not take her eyes off that mouth.

He knew it, too. He reached across the table to take her hand. 'Simple fingers.' His voice resonated deep notes down to her toes.

She blushed – another Natural response she made a note to get edited out immediately, if possible. She extended three of her tool augmentations through her two shortest fingers, saying lightly, 'Not entirely.' The web sensors that wrapped around her thumbs went without saying.

'Do they feel as supple?' He watched her eyes, not the finger display.

'As . . . ? How would I know?'

'You could try a repcant, you know. Experience what the higher adaptations are like.'

Yes, he had actually said 'higher,' even though it was very rude. Or maybe because it was.

After the meal they walked the corridors, made narrow by Kurani. Their boots rang against the walls like snapped fingers, calling her to attention. The Library air hung clammy with time beyond knowing, humid with the pungent breath that she couldn't quite get enough of. With him beside her the long avenues shrank, as though seen down the wrong end of a telescope. When he stopped and drew her to him, it was entirely like being gathered up. She felt herself blown up a mountainside, driven by an overpowering wind.

'Wait,' she said, and instantly disliked herself.

So much of him, so little of her. With a rich, velvety sound he slid his hand down her back. He asked where she lived, but it was a formality, of course. He could get it in an eye flick from his inboards. But she whispered the truth back to him in words gone moist. When they got to her spare, scrupulous room, she was paralyzed with dread and hope and fever dreams.

She sent a quick spurt to turn on the lights – dim – and he caught it, said no, and countered her signal to the room with an electromagnetic tweak. A command from the king.

His pushing through the door into the next room, into her private spaces, sent her fever rising thick and warm into her throat. He reached down and unslipped the side of her suit. It peeled off, and she said, 'Prehistoric,' hoping it would come over as a joke, but as the word left her, she meant it.

'So you are,' he answered, moving all over her.

Stress fell away like a filmy dress. As if she had one on.

The next thing she felt was his hot breath between her legs, and an answering 'Oh' from inside her. *Oh, oh, oh, yes, yearning to be a zero. I'll be O and you be . . .*

A fraction, soon gone. Well spent.

4

The Semi-Infinite Library

S he went to work in his division. There was a useful
role even for Originals.

The essential trait all types of humans relied on was
time binding. To work in the Library meant laboring in
the shadow of time itself, after all. So to get a grasp at
all took knowing how humans saw the word. Humans of
whatever vintage.

Her days passed in an aura of sultry air, short of breath,
high, excited trills echoing in her. The work was good.
At meals she ate with many varieties of humans, though
here they were mostly Supras. She enjoyed the food and
the talk, and sometimes she was allowed to speak.

She caught fragments of the unspoken, which seemed to
comprise most of what was getting said. She caught the
phrase '. . . manages to be naked with her clothes on . . .'
About *her,* the verb signifier said. It came with clear Supra
uptones but was obliquely a compliment. Or she took it so.

So she worked to fit in. This was easier than she had
expected.

The span of a single life was quite great, taking into
account the contacts with the old and young, who
extended one's reach fore and aft in time. Even among
the ancients, in fragile bodies unaided by technology, the
span was a few centuries.

Now it was many millennia. Prehistory, back when life was astonishingly short — a few decades! — still had spanned ten thousand generations. In years, that was not much. In generations, it was respectable, comparable to the lifetimes of the advanced societies, where people lived for eons and had plenty of time to get bored with their relatives. With their friends. With, sometimes, everything — exit, stage left, in haste.

Prehistory had been the great shaping time of primordial, first-form humanity — the Naturals. No surprise, then, that Naturals' own opinions about what was important in life had been molded far more by prehistory than by their trivial experience of early, simple civilization.

From that vast early era Naturals got their basic perceptions. Their leaders, who understood this, rang down through their history. Naturals felt best in groups of a hundred or so, and even better if only a few dozen were involved. Hunting parties had been about that size, for the long-extinct big game. Many important institutions were of the same rough scale: the ancient village, governing councils of nations, commanding elites of vast armies, teams playing games, orchestras, family fests. All human enterprises that worked were of that size, and nearly everything that failed was not.

So the Library had to be organized using this bedrock wisdom. Otherwise, it would fail.

Civilization had long maintained the appearance of such communal closeness, in small units people could manage. Societies had evolved that could stack such social nuggets into vaster, larger arrays. A squad of ten worked well together and, united with ten other squads, could do far more. Those ten who commanded squads could then meet in a room and make up a squad themselves, and so on up a pyramid that could sum the labors of billions.

All this was built on the firm foundation of primate bonding patterns. If the pattern broke down at the bottom, it made a rabble. Loss of scale at the top led to dictators, who always fell in the long run. Democracy emerged and worked because it let people form groups they could actually manage and like.

The Library was democratic, but . . . After all, there were dozens of variations on the great human theme in the staff. The Library needed them all because their forms had all contributed to the Library. Fathoming what Library records meant demanded intense cooperation. Every form of human had to be respected. Acknowledged.

Democratic, but . . . The Supras were still, everybody agreed, the very best.

She started working in serial languages. Easy stuff, suitable for Originals. She could almost hear Kurani thinking that.

Serial writings were a persistent human tradition. Many Library workers felt them to be somehow more authentic than the later methods that directly integrated with the nervous system. Cley had little experience with serial writings, though. How quaint, she thought at first, even for a Library: to set down symbols one after another and make the eyes (or in one case, the fingers, and in another, the nose) manufacture meaning from them, seen one at a time. Piecework.

Nobody did that anymore, though of course, speech was still serial. No subspecies had ever tried to make the throat and vocal cords perform in the way the eyes could, ferrying vast gouts of information at a glance. Making sound waves do that faced both a bandwidth problem and a fleshly one.

The throat was a stringed instrument, resonant but limited. Humans could not drink and speak at the same time – a design flaw not shared by the other ancient primates. Yet it was one that nobody had ever overcome. People still strangled at banquets, and were appropriately dressed in their formal best for their funerals – all due to a faulty collaboration between eating and speaking.

Not Supras, of course; they had bigger, supple tracheae, to slip food by the windpipe. Inevitably, Originals made up a dirty joke about the *real* purpose.

She got interested in serial writings and delved back into the very earliest. The most ancient, the Arbic, notation had a mere twenty-six letters, whereas even the ancients knew that something around forty speech-sounds and phonemes was optimum. The earliest forms even used something she had to struggle to understand: letters with two cases, big and small, with almost no value added to the doubling of symbols.

Later languages dropped these cultural carbuncles. Down through the myriad millennia, letters assumed shapes to show the position taken by the vocal organs (which varied) in articulating the sounds. Those quickest to draw evoked the most frequent sounds.

She got the idea of serial writing right away. Humans liked the step-by-step nature of stories, of narrative momentum, and sentences carried one forward in a pleasurable way.

Still, she was glad to get back into the hohlraum. It was a wondrous tool that shaped itself to her (in)abilities.

Supple, subtle, sly. Deftly it brought her intense, layered knowledge. After reading the serial languages, the hohlraum was like the experience of *having read*. The memories of the serial texts were there, but reachable instantly at many levels.

The hohlraum flew like a bird over a rumpled landscape, spying all. It could see the geological layers beneath that bore in massive strata the assumptions, histories, and worldviews that slumbered beneath the surface text. It could sense the warp and weave of time, as well. Like conceptual lava, information flowed up to the surface, seeping hot and new, there to cool and congeal into ravines of reasoning and mountains of conclusion. In the long sweep of time those peaks and valleys would in turn crumble, their continental wisdoms collide, rumbling into dust.

All this came into her mind in the slow pace of gravid change, its majesty impressing her. This was the lot of being human over the long eras, in which whole grand cultures were mere mayflies.

5

Growing Up Fast

She taught herself not to mind when he vanished for days. Supras did that.

It was as if, on leaving, he turned out the light. Supra-style sex, having come rushing to her out of nowhere, rushed away. So she worked.

Then he would return, send her a quirky smile. His tide came roaring back in.

Supras had other concerns, matters lying well beyond her conceptual horizons. Yes, yes, she understood that. But . . .

She understood that her father fascination was a bump in the roadway of life, and Kurani's absences called up deep resonances of being left behind. So much for conscious knowledge. For the first time she got it that conscious understanding — the kind that came from her Meta upbringing — had to be used to overpower the blind-siding emotional lurches of life. Or so the litany went.

Still, when he reappeared, it was always first things first. First, as in Original. Was this his first affair with an Original? He seemed to savor the simplicities of her body.

With him, she felt less like a verb in his vocabulary, more a noun. An object for his attentions, even at work. When they were discussing some fine point of translation

— his voice low and precise, hers skittering higher, quicker — and his hand drifted over her leg, she did not know what to do with this reference to their other life together. Except that the wry joke of the gesture, touch tasking them to the basics of their species, made her smile.

She liked his taste, and not merely his skin. He had kept the Original cock, a handsome wick indeed. No efficient Supra rig for him, no. Nor the off-putting earlier Sigma engineering, which she — though not some of her stunned girlfriends — had avoided.

She had seen it all before, of course, literally. There was to the entire act, up close, the quality of being attacked by a giant, remorseless snail. The whole arrangement seemed on the face of it unlikely, a temporary design that had gotten legislated into concrete.

But it worked. Somehow. Wisdom of the ancients. Snail and swamp, who could have guessed?

Kurani paid attention to site selection for their trysts, too. Nothing was more Original than what humans of all brands called, with unthinking arrogance, 'the out of doors' — as if all creation were defined by its location just outside where we lived. Amazing, when you recognized the meaning.

Kurani never used the term, but he certainly used the feelings.

He liked weather — the more, the better. They always slept with his room opened to the outside when a storm of swollen, angry purple clouds came muscling over the horizon. As the heavens tore at each other, so did the humans. One powerful night, the thunder and lightning came closer and closer together, each booming roar like a commandment, which they followed to the letter.

Afterward they lay exhausted and warm and delightfully sweaty, listening to the storm shoulder its way off into the mountains to command someone else. A cleansing rain began to patter down on the balcony outside with the indescribable rich aroma a good rain brought to a fine moment. She close-upped her vision and watched the teardrops plunge to their deaths, pearly in the fine light.

'Whoosh! Enough to make you believe in God,' he said.

As if anybody did, except maybe Originals. She whispered, 'Or that we and the weather are geared together.'

'Same thing.' He grinned.

It wasn't all about sex, either.

She firmly believed that people had, as a species, an innate drive to mesh with others – that the sense of self emerged from a web of intimate relations. The Supras seemed to feel that all humans were the outcome of impersonal drives like sex and envy, plus others they could not speak about very well. Maybe they didn't want to reveal too much, to keep the Supra nature shadowy. Kurani sometimes shrugged, that most hallowed of gestures, as if to convey the gulf between them.

She clung to the precipice of that gulf and sometimes threw herself across. Or tried.

Yet she knew already that love could fade. Not so much on its own, but from the efforts of the people experiencing it – so intensely as to, well, to kill it. Love made many naked, unsettled by longing. The pressure was always there. And oppositely, some felt too safe in a relationship and fantasized about something more racy. It was terribly confusing.

Famously, Naturals longed for the touch of Arts, the earliest artificial forms. She felt some of this herself: the lure of the Primitivo. The earliest human artifice lay in self-decoration — the attraction of the human assembly. Kurani termed this the allure of simple skin. She had always been tantalized by the externals, particularly the styles of cocks, but rumor had it among her Meta that the internals were the truly amazing portion of Art anatomy.

The longest-running human game lay not in self-ornamentation but in relationships. Kurani taught her a calmer way of looking at these things. This was his way of explaining what Cley and he were about under the covers.

In his view, the true deep human fantasy was the conviction of safety. Men believed their women were devoted; wives felt that their men were dependable. Both ignored contrary evidence. Each acted to fulfill the other's belief. When the whole collusive contrivance collapsed, each cried, 'This is not the person I thought!' They had merely gotten trapped in the quicksand of protective gray that each laid to trim the rampaging velocity of romantic love.

Even sex could develop this deadening, out of self-defense. Without a dull patina it was too vivid to sustain for long — dragging one into surrenders, losses of self, immersion in the rhythms and sensations of another. 'Same reverse twist for aggression,' he added cryptically.

She nodded. Love scared anyone. Primates reacted to threat with anger, so they got into fights without knowing why. Or just ran away.

Cley countered this with her simple sense that the inscrutable other should be an ideal mate. She felt better when she let herself see Kurani as more handsome and valuable than others thought him to be. Her dream man, personified in Kurani, would not let time or routine lessen the intensity of authentic experience: 'You keep building sand castles even though you know the tide's coming in.'

Their days were simple: work, study, love, sleep, then back to work. Sometimes love came right after work, even before dinner. And sometimes she thought that her need for love was really a mask over her desire for, well, sex.

But when she was in that moment, it was not so much like lust as it was like worship. Maybe what she sought in love was only symbolized by sex, and at the same time made real – something far more powerful: completion.

Whether Kurani saw the emotional landscape this way, she was unsure. Most people routinely lived for several centuries, and Kurani was even older. He had literally forgotten more than she knew.

One day he took her by the hand and led her into an unused corridor of the Library. He stood at one end far away, a tiny figure, and whispered words of unexpected tenderness that roared along the walls, amplified somehow by ancient acoustics. Into her ears came cherished phrases, ones she was sure she would remember all her life. The secret of these acoustic amplifiers had long been lost. But he knew just how to use it.

He was vast, yet he loved her, too – she knew this with granite conviction. She knew also that to him she must be a familiar type. Electrically primitive, but exhausting. She used that. She seduced him with her intensity, her one-plus-some personality. But she also unnerved him with the instant intimacy she offered, able to turn it on in the pivot of a second.

Their days were electric for her, in the vast Library, laboring in the long, dry valley rimmed by snowcapped peaks. Her world was crisp and sure for the first time. Intoxicating, just to breathe the cutting air.

First loves were the fiercest, she realized. So it couldn't last. Fair enough. But there was nothing stopping her working on that.

And she was, right up until the attack.

II
A Universe In Ruins

The years teach much that the days never know.
—Emerson

1

Allies and Evil

From high above, the naked woman seemed to be dead.

The four-winged bird concluded this as it gyred down through a pale afternoon sky. It wheeled in lazy eights with the woman at the cross point, keeping the unmoving body under its precise gaze. The forewings flapped easily, letting the longer hind wings luxuriate in the warm loft of thermals that rose from the rocky bluff nearby. Its forewings canted wind into the broad, gossamer-thin hind wings, bringing an ancient pleasure.

But then directives ingrained in its deepest genes tugged it back to its assigned task: to find the living humans in this area and summon aid.

The analytic portion of its oddly shaped intelligence decided that this woman, who evidently had not stirred for long hours, was certainly dead. It made this decision not by reason but through the sour smells that rose from the body, a mere few molecules bringing news of corruption and decay.

Once this creature had been a carrion eater, its senses set long before it had come to know reason. It judged automatically the brown stain on the pebbles around her head and the massive bruise that blossomed over her left ribs like a purple sunrise.

Already the bird had seen over twenty dead humans among the trees, most of them charred to ashes and none living. The four-winger had much rugged territory to cover and was running out of time. It glided for a long moment, indecisive as only a considerable intelligence can be, forewings rising as hind wings fell.

A life could hang upon this decision. The organic molecules were few, their message of dried blood and wounds strongly suggesting death. Vexed, it decided not to report this body as a possible candidate. That would take valuable time, and members of this curious, unimpressive subspecies of humans were notoriously fragile. The four-winger peeled away, eyes scanning every minute speck below.

The afternoon shadows lengthened considerably before the woman stirred, her weak, gasping lost beneath the chuckle of the nearby stream. Her breath whistled between broken teeth. She rolled fitfully, moaned, and the brown stain spread further.

This sound attracted a six-legged, furred mother making her way with her two cubs along the muddy bank. The woman's dying might have gained an audience then. But the sleek creatures saw that the woman distinctly resembled those who truly ruled here, though she smelled quite different.

The mother instructed her cubs to note and always warily respect that human form, now broken but always dangerous. She used a language simple in words but complex in positional grammar, inflections giving layers of meaning. She augmented this with deft signs, using her midlegs.

The family's quick flight downstream sent a tang into a crosswind, and this in turn roused the interest of a more curious creature. This strutting shape was distantly descended from the raccoon, its pelt a rich, symbol-laden swirl of reds and auburn. Behind darting eyes a crafty intelligence quickly assessed the situation from the cover of stingbushes.

It was cautious but not afraid. The revival of its species many millennia ago had built upon an ancient design, with considerable added intelligence. Such human engineering, already ancient, had rendered with fidelity a creature in many ways superior to the pitiful figure it now watched intently.

To it, the most important issue here lay in interlacing the dying woman's jarring presence with an elaborated meaning of its own life. From birth it had integrated each experience with its innate sense of balance and appropriate scale – indeed, this was the sole purpose of its conscious being.

Suddenly, it felt a cusp moment, a branching of possibility that carried weight and tremor. Somehow, this event was crucial. It did not know why, but *why* was a late kind of knowledge, often illuminating but arid, coming long after the intensity of experience.

Surely the violent, vibrant clashes in far valleys, days before, had set the stage for this meeting. The twisting cylinders of acid glow in the sky had seemed to point its padded feet along this path. It could but follow. It sensed that this moment was like a blossom ready to open, to bring into the world a fresh flowering.

At last, and with a proper anticipation of the pattern of events that might spread from its actions like the branches of an infinite tree, unending, the raccoonlike beast padded forward.

It sniffed the woman – sour. The body was evaporating

away the pungent waste molecules that came of its futile attempt to heal. Sniffing again for clues, it caught the dull thread of death in the trees beyond. And the sharp bite of fresh dung nearby. It took some satisfaction in this blend: the immediate overlaid the eternal.

It trotted over and explored. The dead were Natural humans. The dung was less interesting but told a small tale of a reptile predator that had passed some hours before. It had hesitated a moment and then decided that the woman was a better prospect for tonight, when she would be safely dead.

The shaggy creature sniffed and smiled, black-lipped. The reptile would be surprised, for the woman could live — with a bit of help.

This information rippled atop the usual background flavorings of sunset: a crisp aroma of granite cooling, the sweet perfume of the eternal beckoning flowers, a musty odor of fungus drawing water up the hills from the muttering stream.

It set to work. The woman's swollen skull was the worst problem. The optical disk now bulged in both eyes. With long, tapered hands that echoed only faintly their origin in claws, the creature felt the unfamiliar cage of bones beneath the skin and muscle. This early hominid form had antiquated struts and pivots, clearly a preliminary design. The right arm skewed unnaturally awry. Several ribs were cleanly snapped.

Plainly, from the simple body plan — archaic, a patchwork of temporary solutions to passing problems — an Original. Yet long ago, on a middle-aged world, evolution had sanctified these cumbersome measures with success in the raw, natural world.

The creature set about healing the body. It did not know how the woman came to be here or why she was in any way special. But whoever she was, she deserved the service of an allied species, also of some antiquity.

Gingerly it used techniques that were second nature, massaging points in this body that it knew triggered restoring hormones. It used its elbows – an awkward but unavoidable feature still not bettered in nature – to generate healing vibrations. The soft, swollen contusion in the right temple responded to rhythmic squeezing of the spine. It labored on.

The creature could feel pressures slowly relent and diffuse throughout the woman's head. Her glandular imperatives sluggishly closed internal hemorrhages. Stimuli to the neck and abdomen made her internal organs begin their filtering of the waste-clogged blood. Straightening and setting the arm, temporarily securing the snapped ribs so they would not puncture lungs, perking the bones' regrowth – all took time.

Dusk brought the rustle of movement to the creature's large ears, but none of the telltale sounds implied danger. It sat comfortably beside the sprawled woman and slept, though even then with an alertness the woman could never know. At midnight the reptile returned, expecting a dead human. It made a surprised, tasty snack. Fit reward for good labors.

When the woman began to mutter, the creature realized it could understand the slurred words.

'Ah . . . it sliced, sliced . . . him . . . get way! . . . Keep down . . . down . . . no . . . see us . . . fire . . . from the air . . .'

Much of her talk was garbled fever dreams. From brief

moments of coherence the creature came to understand that the woman had been hunted remorselessly from a flyer, along with her tribe, as they fled a library.

Her tribe had not escaped. A dry night breeze coming off the hotter plains to the west brought the scent of charred, ashen flesh. The creature closed its nostrils to the smell.

It was pleasantly surprised that it could understand the woman's words. The lands here were filled with life forms drawn from two billion years of incessant creation. Some could not fathom the languages of the others. This woman must have been taught, perhaps by genetic tuning, to comprehend the complex tongues more advanced creatures used.

The creature felt that to ingrain such knowledge was an error, a skewed and perhaps arrogant presumption. An early human form such as this might well be confused by such complex, disorienting craft. Language arose from a worldview. The rich web of perceptions that had formed her present tongue could scarcely ride easily in her cramped mental confines.

Normally, it did not question the deeds of the advanced human forms called the Supras. But this badly mauled woman, her skin lacerated and turgid with deep bruises, raised doubts. Perhaps her injuries stemmed directly from . . . her knowledge?

The killers had gone after all the Naturals. Did they possess some quality the fires sought to exterminate?

After some contemplation, however, it relied on its innate sense. That life was a dusty mirror, reflecting only passing images of truth. Such reflection told it that this woman was here for no ordinary reason. So it sat and

thought and monitored her body's own weak but persistent self-repairing.

The woman lay beneath a night that gradually cleared
as cumulus clouds blew in from the west and went on
beyond the distant hills, as though hurrying for an
appointment they could never meet. The creature sensed
rising plumes of water vapor exhaled by the dense jungle
and forest. These great, moist wedges acted like invisible
mountains, forcing in-blowing air to rise and rain out its
wet burden.

A great luminous band rose on the horizon, so bright
and varied that it did not seem to be composed of stars,
but rather of ivory and ice. Vast ragged lanes of dust
sprawled across swarms of piercing lights. It knew this
lustrous glory well. These were the shreds of the galactic
arm, a last rampart shielding this world from a full view
of the galactic center.

It gazed up at this splendor, as enthralled as ever. It
knew that Earth had been deflected toward this central
hub long ago, before its own kind had fully evolved, when
Earth was verdant for the first time. The scope of such
an undertaking was beyond the creature's comprehension.
It dimly sensed that the humans of that time had made
the sun pass near another star, one that refused to shine
in the night.

It knew those events through legend. Since that era,
the galaxy had rotated about its center four times. In that
far time, a sharp veer around that dead, dark mass had
sent the solar system plunging inward toward the great
galactic bulge.

The sun had crossed lanes of dust as the galaxy rotated,
its spiral arms trailing like those of a spinning starfish.

The constellations in Earth's nights warped and shifted. Ages passed. Life performed its ceaseless self-contortions. Fresh intelligences arose. Strange, alien minds came from distant suns.

The purposes of that time were shrouded in ambiguity. The sun followed a stretched ellipse that looped close to the galactic center. On Earth, a shimmering sphere of light gradually grew in the heavens. To remain near this wheeling bee swarm of ten billion stars, yet another gravitational encounter had proved necessary.

In that time, legend said, the sun had brushed by a giant molecular cloud. Gravity's tugs rearranged the stately glide of the planets. The precision of those soft collisions had been of such delicacy that the new orbits fit the needs of humanity's vast engineering enterprises — the dismantling of whole worlds. Such had humans been, once.

Reflecting, the creature found a few planets — the survivors of that epic age of boundless ambition — among the great washes of light that hung above. The sky worked with enterprises unknown. Innumerable comet tails pointed outward from the sun toward gossamer banks of dim radiance. Feeder clouds glowed with dull red energies, dotting the plane where the planets dwelled. Arcs of emerald vapor flowed among the clouds, going about their chemical business. In such a crowded symphony of sky the slow gavotte of worlds seemed a minor theme.

But tonight the heavens stirred with more.

The creature recognized luminous trouble. Staring upward, it watched ruby spheres and perfect golden pyramids flare and dodge and veer. Soundless and involuted, these were the scribbles of swift combat. Without the slightest idea of what they were – though surely they were not ships – it sensed the jagged geometries of war.

Bright traceries faded slowly. Abruptly, fresh abrasions scratched across the sky's serenity. Soundless, darting violences pursued and died and flared again.

They were the first acts of hostility written on this broad sky for nearly a billion years. Did they arise from the conflicts inherent in the minds of humans – that uneasy anthology of past influences?

The creature sighed. *Ah, humans.*

Their reptilian sub-brains, tucked around the nerve stem, preserved a taste for ritual and violence. Surrounding that, other facets of their brains brought an emotional tang to all thoughts – this an invention of the early mammals. Together these two ancient remnants gave humans their visceral awareness of the world. Such simple elements, yet they worked together in ways that stunned the mind.

As the furry creature watched the flowering night, it wondered if the battle above marked the emergence of something fearsome and strange and not human. Those coiled maneuvers were not from minds it knew.

Could it be sure? Humanity's neocortex wrapped around the two animal brains in an unsure clasp, to be sure. In some eras that grip had slipped, unleashing powerful bursts of creativity, of madness, of squandered energy. The neocortex did hold sway with its ancient gray sagacity, directing its reasoning power outward into the world. But always the deeper minds flowed to their own rhythms.

Some forms of the human species had integrated this divided brain after heroic struggle. Others had reengineered the neocortex until it mastered the lower two levels with complete, unceasing vigilance. In human history, all manner of contrivances had seemed to be the answer. In the end, the species had decided to keep all its major variants. It now preserved all the human variations, including Originals.

The creature that wondered at the night had a very different mind. It came from nearly a billion years more of design beyond this Original's, forged both by Darwinnowing and by careful human pruning. Misgivings stirred in that mind now. The broad face wrinkled with complex, unreadable expressions. From its feral legacy it allowed itself a low, moaning growl colored with unease.

It had little guidance. Very little of humanity's history had survived the rub of millennia. In any case, much of that tangled record, shot through by discordant voices, would not have been comprehensible to the creature.

Still, it sensed that it was witnessing in the streaked sky not a mere passing incident, but the birth of a savage new age. The vast flashes and ugly contortions that worked across the silent sky could not be the mere trails of space craft. Forces struggled to be born up there.

Something vast was coming. Yet the creature knew also that some of the night's furious energies came from human machines and intentions.

Since the Primordials, who came even before the simple Ur-human form that labored to live nearby, humanity's greatest adversary had not been the unthinking universe, but itself.

Now the sky worked with strangeness. A fresh evil had arrived. But from where?

2
Lessons of Pain

The woman dreamed for two days.

She thrashed sometimes, calling out hoarsely, her words slurred beyond comprehension. The creature carefully moved her to the shade of some tall trees whose branches formed curious curls like hooks at the very top. It foraged for simple fruit and held slices to the woman's mouth so the juice would trickle down her swollen throat. For itself, meals of small animals sufficed, after the first night's reptile feast. It caught these simply by keeping still for long periods and letting them wander within reach. This was enough, for it knew how to conserve strength while never letting its attention wander from the woman's weak but persistent rhythms of regrowth.

The uses of fantasy are many, and healing is not the least of these. She slept not merely because this was the best way to repair herself. Behind her jerking eyelids, it knew, a thin layer outside the neocortex brain was rerunning the events that had led to her trauma. This sub-brain integrated emotional and physiological elements, replaying her actions, searching for some fulcrum moment when she might have averted the calamity.

Nothing worked. It sensed that there was some comfort in knowing, finally, that nothing would have changed the outcome. When she reached this conclusion, a stiffness left her. Her body softened into deeper sleep. Some memories were eventually discarded in this process as too painful to carry, while others were amplified in order to attain a kind of narrative equilibrium. This editing saved her from a burden of remorse and anxiety that, in earlier forms of humanity, would have plagued her for years after.

In the second day she momentarily burst into a slurred song. At dusk she awoke. She looked up into the long, tapered muzzle of her watcher and asked fuzzily, 'How many . . . lived?'

'Only you, that I can sense.' The creature's voice was low and yet lilting, like a bass note that had worked itself impossibly through the throat of a flute.

'No . . . ?' She was quiet for a time, studying the green moon that swam beyond the sharp mountains. She cried and finally said weakly, 'The Supras . . .'

'They did this?'

'No, no. I saw something strange. Distorted air. Refractions, I guess. Then . . .' She shivered.

'A murderous fire.'

'More . . . more than fire.' Another shiver. 'Most of the Supras were engaged . . . far away. I thought they would help us.'

'They have been busy.' It gestured at the southern horizon. In the twilight's dim gleam a fat column of oily smoke stood like an obsidian gravestone.

Her eyes widened. 'What's . . . ?'

'It has been there for days.'

'Ah.' She closed her eyes then and subsided into her curious, eyelid-fluttering sleep. For her it was a slippery descent into a labyrinth where twin urges fought, revenge versus survival. These two instincts, already ancient before the first hominid walked, rarely married with any security. Yet if she did not feel the pinch of their competition, she would not be, by her own judgment, a true human.

The next day she got up. Creaking unsteadily, she walked to the stream, where she lay facedown and drank for a long time. Ribs firm, arm supple and whole. One finger was missing from her left hand, but she insisted on helping the creature forage for berries and edible leaves. She spoke little. They took shelter when silvery filigrees flashed across the sky. She flinched. But this time there were no rolling booms, no searing bolts, as she remembered from before. She did not speak of what had happened, and her companion did not ask.

In the undergrowth they came upon three humans crisped to ashes. She wept over each. 'I never saw such weapons before,' she said. 'Like living flames.'

'Your enemy took care to thoroughly burn each.'

She sifted through the shattered bones. 'They were like geometries, polygons. They cast down bolts, explosions . . .'

At the evening meal she sang again the hypnotic slow song she had pushed up out of her dream state before. There were phrases about her Meta, about a Supra (male, from the case-form of her sentences, but unnamed). Her somber voice hung and wavered on the long notes. Then her eyes abruptly filled, and she rushed off into the night. Later she sheepishly returned, her mouth attempting a crooked smile. The need to cover emotion was a quirk of humans, pointless to the raccoon-creature.

*   *   *

On the morning of the third day she broke a long silence with 'I am Cley. Do you use names?' She guessed that the creature did not use names among its own kind; it was not among the animals who mimicked men.

'I have been called the Seeker After Patterns.'

'Well then, Seeker, I thank you for—'

'Our species are allies. Nothing need be said.' Seeker dipped its large head. The movement seemed unnatural to it, awkward. Cley realized with a pang that Seeker had studied humans enough to attempt this gesture, invoking humbleness.

'Still, I owe so much.'

'My species came long after yours, though based upon a small creature of equally ancient origin.'

'You are . . . ?'

'We are formally referred to as procyons. A later variety of human shaped us. I believe my kind benefited from your struggle.'

'I doubt we did you much good.'

'Life builds upon life. You Ur-humans were but fossils when we first walked.'

They gathered berries in silence. Seeker could stand entirely on its hind legs, using its forepaws as nimbly as Cley's hands. It bulk deceived Cley at first, so she was startled by its speed. With single-minded zest it scooped many small fish from the cold, giggling stream that rushed over black pebbles. They ate the yellow-green fish without using a fire and stayed well back among the trees.

Cley ate with relish. She had processed her deep sense of loss through several nights now, and the searing pain of it ebbed. Color returned to her cheeks. The sad tug of memories slowly lost its immediate grip on her mind.

Her life, so wondrous before, was now brutally spare.

A thousand questions rose. How was her Meta? The Library?

If only she could truly remember. She sensed that her undermind was blocking memories, to ease her recovery. She had flashing images, framed in fear and burning dreams.

The attack had come in a savage, fire-bright moment.

It began with strange droplets coasting on the air, shimmering, murmuring. Floodlights ringed a gray, chipped slab where she worked with Kurani. Recently opened passages far into the Library labyrinth had yielded complicated new puzzles in data slabs. They were reading out a curious string of phrases in a long-dead language, from a society that had reached the peak of mathematical wisdom – or so the historians said.

The floating, humming motes distracted her. Unlike the familiar microtech that pervaded the Library, performing tasks, these shifted and scintillated in the hard spotlight glare.

Kurani ignored them. His powers of concentration were vast and pointed. He had just discovered that these ancient people had used numbers not as nouns or adjectives, but to modify verbs, words of action. Instead of 'see those three trees,' they would say something like, 'the living things manifesting treeness here act visibly as a collection divided to the extent of three.'

She remembered Kurani's furrowed brow, his quizzical interrogation of distant resource libraries as he struggled with this conceptual gulf. These Ancients had used number systems that recognized three bases – 10, 12, and

5 – and were rooted in the body, with its five toes and six fingers. Being so grounded in the flesh, what insights did the Ancients reach in far more rarefied pursuits? Scholars had already found a deep fathoming of the extra dimensions known to exist in the universe. The slab before Cley and Kurani spoke of experiments in dimensional transport, all rendered in a strangely canted manner.

Cley kept her focus as tightly wrapped around this problem as she could. She found such abstractions engulfing.

But the motes . . . and suddenly she looked up at a new source of light. The motes were tumbling in a field of amber glitter. Sharp blue shards of brilliance lanced into her eyes. The motes were not microtech but *windows* into another place, where hard radiance rumbled and fought.

She turned to Kurani to warn him—

And the world was sliced. Cut into thin parallel sheets, each showing a different part of Kurani, sectioned neatly by a mad geometer.

But this was not illusion, not a mere refraction in the air. He was divided, slashed crosswise. She could see into his red interior, organs working, pulsing. She stepped toward him . . .

Then came the fire, hot pain, and screaming. She remembered running. The motes swept after her, and she was trying to get away from the terrible screams. Only when she gasped for breath did she realize that the screams had come from her.

She made herself stop. Turned, for a moment that would haunt her forever. Looked back down a long, stony corridor that tapered to infinity – and Kurani was at the other end, not running. Impaled on blades of light. Sliced. Writhing.

And then, to her shame, she turned and ran away. Without another backward glance. Terrified.

The memory came sharply into her. The bare fossil outlines of later events swelled up, filling her throat, the past pressing to get out.

Finding a dozen members of a neighboring Meta cowering in a passageway. Fidgeting with fear. They had to shout themselves hoarse in the thundering violence.

Then the booming eased away. Crackling energies came instead.

The other Naturals said the attacks raged through all the valleys of the Library. They were being pursued by a rage beyond comprehension. Let the Supras fight it if they could.

They would be hunted like rats here. She agreed – they had to get out, into the forest.

The seething air in the passageway became prickly. A sound like fat frying grew near. No one could stand and wait for it.

She went down a side tunnel. The other Originals fled toward the main passage. Better to run and hide alone than in a straggling rabble. But the tunnel ceiling got lower as she trotted, then walked, finally duckwalked.

She cowered far back in the tunnel, alone in blackness. Stabs of virulent lightning forked in the distance and splashed the tunnel walls with an ivory glow. Getting closer. In one of the flashes she saw tiny designs in the tunnel wall.

Her fingers found the pattern. Ancient, a two-tiered language. A . . . combination? Plan?

She extruded a finger into a tool wedge and tracked

along the grooves. It was telling a tale of architectural detail she could not follow very well, reading at high speed through the tool. She sensed a sense-phrase, inserted in the middle of an extended brag about the design. It referred to an inlet — or maybe outlet. A two-valence, anyway. Okay, okay, but where?

More snapping flashes, emerald now. Nearer. Could they *hear* her?

She inched farther into the tunnel. Her head bumped the ceiling; the rough bore was narrowing. In another quick glimmer, followed by an electrical snarl, she saw a web of symbol-tracks, impossible to follow. *So damn much history! Where's the door?*

She scrunched farther in. The web tapered down into a shallow track, and she got her finger wedge in. *Ah! Codes.* She twisted, probed — and the wall flopped open into another tunnel.

She crawled through, trying to be quiet. A glowing brown snake was coming after her down the tunnel. She slammed the curved hatch in its face.

Pitch black. At least the lightning had shown her what was going on. She sat absolutely still. Faint thunder and a trembling in the floor. This tunnel was round and . . . a soft breeze.

She crawled toward it. Not even height to duckwalk. The slight wind got stronger. Cool to her fevered brow.

Smells: dust, leaves? A dull thump behind her. She hurried, banging her knees—

And spilled halfway out into clear air. Above, stars. A drop of about her height, onto dirt. She reversed and dropped to the ground. Scent of dry dirt. Flashes to the left. She went right.

She ran. Snapping crashes behind her. Dim shapes up ahead. Trees? A rising sucking sound behind. A brittle thrust of amber fire rushed over her left shoulder and shattered into a bush, exploding it into flames.

Trees — she dodged left. Faint screams somewhere.

The sucking sound again. Into the trees, heels digging in hard.

Another amber bolt, this time roasting the air near her. It veered up and ignited a crackling bower of fronds.

Screams getting louder. Up ahead? Glows there. She went right, down a gully, splashing across a stream. Not deep enough to cover her.

A spark sizzled down from the air into the trees up ahead. She went left and found a wall of brambles. Distant flickering gave her enough light to pick her way along, gasping. Around the brambles, into thick trees. She crossed the stream again. Deeper here. Downstream went back toward the open, toward the excavated tunnels. She ran upstream. The sucking rush came stealing up behind. She dodged, ducked, dodged. *Stay near the stream.* If the water got deeper . . .

The pain swarmed over her and pushed her into blackness.

3
Aftermath

Later, as she healed, she and Seeker set out to search the forest further for bodies. To do something gave her strength, despite what she dreaded finding.

She had enjoyed no other steady lover, male or female, but she had known all the other Originals who worked in the Library. They had sported an ironic humor about their roles as Originals among the Supras, playing the role of the least gifted but well-honored surviving strains of Primordial humans. There had been many wry jokes between them.

Not that she had been immune to it all. She had gloried in her affair with Kurani, been whispered about and envied and criticized, even insulted. Enormous fun.

The anonymous charred remains they found were a blessing, in a way. The Furies, as the Supras called them, had been quite thorough. None had been left to rot. She could not identify them.

They searched systematically through the afternoon, finding only more scorched bodies. Even as she worked, she knew this was helping her. Better to act, not think.

Finally, they stood looking down into a broad valley — tired, job done, planning where to go next.

'I trust you are all right,' a deep voice said behind them.

Cley whirled. Seeker was already dashing with liquid

grace among the nearby trees. A tall, blocky man stood on the outer deck of a brass-colored craft that balanced silently in the air.

He had come upon them from behind without even Seeker noticing, and this, more than his size and the silent power of his craft, told Cley that she had no chance of getting away. Blinking against the sun glare, she saw that this was a Supra.

Another. It all came rushing up into her again, the smothered pain. *Kurani.*

And she put it away. There would be a time to feel it, and that time was not now. The longing and passion had been part of becoming a young woman, a time she would treasure. Wondrous. That was over, and she knew with a leaden suddenness that it would not come again. She could not let it.

And this Supra – why did he survive? When my love died?

Her head spun with wild emotions. She hated this Supra; she needed him; she wanted him to fold her in his long arms and take away the anguish.

Then she made herself put all that away, as well. *Concentrate, the way Kurani did. See what is before you.*

He carried all the advanced signatures: big glossy eyes; scalloped ears that could turn to capture sound; enlarged trachea to help food bypass the windpipe better. Forward-tilted upper torso, lessening pressure on the spine. Backward-curved neck with bigger vertebrae, counterbalancing the close-ribbed chest. His casual amble along the deck of the flyer told her that his knees could bend backward, muting the grind of bones in sockets. Heavier bones, thicker skull, an angular, glinting intelligence in the face.

The sight of him brought her memories of Kurani

flooding back. This man was slightly different – muscles lean and planar, but of the same design era. She gazed at him, the yearning welling in her, and she forced it down. And after what seemed to her like forever, forced out some words. 'I . . . yes, I am.'

He smiled affably. 'One of our scouts finally admitted that it was not sure all the bodies it saw were dead. I am happy I decided to check its work.'

As he spoke, his ship settled gently near Cley, and he stepped off without glancing at the ground. Despite his bulk he moved with unconscious, springy lightness. She noted abstractly that he used 'I,' which Kurani seldom did. Until now she had never wondered why.

She gestured behind her. 'My friend saved me.'

'Ah. Can you induce it to return?'

'Seeker! Please come!'

She glimpsed a bulk moving through the nearby bushes, coming opposite from the direction Seeker had left. It must be quicker than it looked. There was scarcely a ripple in the foliage, but she knew it was there, still and cautious.

The man smiled slightly and shrugged. 'Very well.'

'You came to bury my kind?' Cley said bitingly.

'If necessary. I would rather save them.'

'Too late for that.'

He nodded as several emotions flickered across his face: sadness, regret, firm resolve. 'The scouts reported some bodies, but all had been burned. You are all I have found – delightfully alive.'

Delightfully? The word was almost flirtatious. His calm mildness was maddening. 'Where *were* you Supras? They – it – hounded us! Tracked us! Killed us all!'

Again his face showed a quick succession of emotions, each too fleeting for her to read before the next crowded in. Still he said nothing, though his mouth became a tight line and his eyes moistened. He gestured at a pall of smoke that still climbed on the far horizon.

Cley followed his movement and said severely, 'I guessed you had to defend your own, but couldn't you have, have . . .'

Her voice trailed away when she saw the pained twinge constricting his face as her words struck home.

Then his mouth thinned again, and he nodded. 'All along the Library valleys they attacked new work and old alike. We could not divine what they were about – killing Originals – and when we did, it was too late.'

Her anger, stilled for a moment by his vulnerability, returned like an acrid burn in the back of her throat. 'We had nothing to defend ourselves!'

'Did you think we had weapons?'

'Supras have everything!'

He sighed. 'Few were useful. We protect through our laboring machines, leaning on the genius of our past. These failed.'

'There was fighting in the past. I have heard—'

'The far past. Well before your time. We—'

'*They* knew how. Why didn't *you*?'

His expression changed again several times with a speed she found baffling. Then a grave sourness shaped his mouth with a sardonic twist. 'Tell me who they were, and perhaps I can answer you.'

'They?' She felt sudden doubt. 'I thought you would know.'

'I do not.'

She dammed up the bitter torrent within her and said quietly, 'I saw nothing that looked human.'

'Nor we.'

She studied him for a long moment. He was twice her size, with an enormous head. Yet his nose was stubby, like an afterthought. Kurani had been a variation on the Supra theme, taller and more muscled. This other variation she found less appealing, but the focused intelligence in this man was reassuring now. 'We, we depend on you, we Originals—'

'Ur-human,' the man corrected absently, distracted.

'What?'

'Oh, I am quite sorry. We term your particular kind Ur-human, since you are the earliest form available of all Originals.'

Her lips whitened under pressure. 'And what do you call yourselves?'

'Ah, humans,' he said uncomfortably.

'How can you tell which I am?'

'Earlobes, teeth narrowly spaced. Those were later modified in even early Original forms, I gather from my studies with the Keeper of Records.'

'Look, I—'

'Large spacings prevent food from accumulating and decaying. Even we use that design, as you can see, but also regrow a set every century to compensate for wear. If—'

'You don't know what to do next, do you?'

The man's raptly studious expression vanished as he blinked. 'I merely hoped to enlist your aid.'

'You people run the world, not us.'

Soberly he said, 'No longer.'

'What were those, those *things,* those Furies that killed my people, my . . . ?'

He paced, his energy barely contained. 'We do not know. You possess mostly those skills appropriate to tending the forests. None of us has mastered warring technology – it is ancient beyond measure.'

He gazed apprehensively at the sky, rubbing his shoulder as though he were stiff. She noticed that his light, loose-fitting jumpsuit was stained and torn.

'You fought them how?'

'As we could. We were surprised. Many died in the first moments. You say you saw humanlike forms in those fast geometric displays? It could be they were humans in warcraft. I saw only flame out beyond our shields – which soon dissolved.'

Seeker spoke from beside them. 'The lightning returned here, later, to burn the dead humans more thoroughly.'

Both humans were startled. Blinking, the man said, 'That fits.'

Seeker shrugged. 'You found no bodies unburned, anywhere?'

The man frowned. 'Not yet.'

'I doubt you will,' Seeker said. 'I believe they were crisping to destroy even the DNA.'

They stood without speaking until Cley asked, 'The, the Library?'

'Come.' He gave the order without taking his eyes from the sky. His mouth echoed a quick flurry of emotion, and he held a palm up to Seeker. 'We gather now, those who remain.'

This seemed enough for Seeker; it had made up its mind to go, and told her so with an arched shrug, close enough to a human gesture to convey meaning. The brass-bright craft tilted momentarily on its electromagnetic cushion as the procyon boarded. Cley went through the wide hatchway and into a simple, comfortable control cabin. The ship lifted with scarcely a murmur.

'I am Rin,' he said, as though anyone would know who he was. His casual confidence told her even more than the name, for he was well known. She responded to his questions about the last few days with short, precise answers. She had rarely seen Supras, growing up. Kurani had come as a revelation. This one was not winning her over.

But as they rose with smooth acceleration, Cley gaped, not attempting to hide her surprise. Within moments she saw the lands where she had lived and labored reduced to a mere spot in a vastly larger canvas. As a young girl she had dreamed of flying like this. Now the magnitude of the Supras' latest labors became obvious. She watched the mountains she had admired as a girl reduced to foot soldiers in an army that marched around the curve of the world.

Her Meta had known well the green complexity of the forests. Below, many fresh, thin brown rivers flowed through narrow canyons, cutting. These gave the mountain range the look of a knobby spine from which many nerves trailed into the tan deserts beyond. A planetary spinal axis, as though the Earth itself had a mind. She wondered if in some sense this could be so.

Brilliant snowcaps crowned the tallest peaks, but these were not, she saw, the source of the countless rivers. Each muddy rivulet began abruptly, high in a canyon, swelling as it ran through rough slopes. The many waterfalls and deep gullies told her that each was busily digging itself in deeper, fresh and energetic.

Cley pointed, and before she could ask, Rin said, 'We feed the new rivers from tunnels. The great Millennium Lakes lie far underground here.'

This land sculpting was only millennia old, but already moist wealth had reclaimed much of the planet's dry midcontinent. Rin sat back as he silently ordered his ship to perform a long turn, showing them the expanses. She caught a brilliant spark of polished metal far away on the very curve of the planet.

'Sonomulia,' Rin said.

'The legend,' she whispered.

'It is quite real,' he said, running his eyes over the display screens that studded the space around them.

'Did they go there, too?'

'The attackers? No. I have no idea why not.'

'Does Sonomulia's name come from an ancient word for *sleep*?'

'What?' His lip twisted. 'No, of course not. Who said it did?'

'It was a joke we made,' she said to unknit his eyebrows. 'That you Supras had been walled up in there so long—'

'Nonsense! We saved humanity, holding on against the encroaching desert. We—'

'And that green spot? Far beyond Sonomulia?'

'That's Illusivia.'

'Illusive? As in hard to pin down?'

'No! Those ancient terms do not apply to the purpose of our cities.' Rin's eyes blazed. 'Look, I do not know what you Ur-humans do for amusement, but I do not find—'

'I was merely recalling some primeval humor.'

Rin shook his head. His eyes never left the screens, and she realized he was looking for a sign that the attackers might return again. How they could vanish so readily and elude the Supras, she could not fathom. But then, the Earth was large, and in these sprawling lands there were many places to hide. But perhaps not, for humans.

4

The Library of Life

They descended along the spine of snowcapped mountains. The craft was silent, save for the strum of winds at its prow.

Cley was surprised to find that seen this way, the soaring peaks were like crumpled sacks carelessly thrown on a tan table, all other detail washed away. She did know that in the long duration of humanity on Earth, even mountains had been passing features, froth stirred up by the slow waltz of continents.

These particular proudly jutting spires had first broken through an ancient ocean floor as the seas themselves drained away. The birth of the first peaks had been chronicled in a ledger, now lost in the recesses of ornate and useless detail that Sonomulia still hoarded. These groaning ridges had risen during a time when the greatest of all human religions bloomed on their flanks. That faith had converted the entire world, had plumbed the philosophic depths of the then-human soul, and now was totally forgotten. Only the Keeper of Records knew the name of that belief, Rin commented, and he had not bothered to unveil that dusty era. The furious causes and grand illusions of the past were like the ghosts of worn, vanquished mountain ranges, too, now sunk beneath the seas of sand.

Cley gazed across the broad plains of desert. For so long they had been like the winding sheets of Earth's corpse, and now were being forced back by forest. Sandy wastes still lapped at the jewel of Sonomulia. She saw as they swept southward that from distant Illusivia a long finger of a river valley pointed into the desert, reaching crookedly toward Sonomulia.

The green reconquering of the planet proceeded around its girth, and at this sight a sensation swept over her of sudden lightness, of buoyant hope. The loss of her Meta fell away from her for at least one moment, and she basked in the spectacle of her world, seeing for the first time its intricate wholeness.

Something moved on the far curved horizon, and she pointed. 'What's that?'

'Nothing dangerous,' Rin answered.

At the limits of her telescope vision she could make out a long, straight line that pointed nearly straight down. Her eyes followed the line up into the dark vault of space, dwindling away. So large! The Supras certainly could work miracles. It seemed to move, and then she lost it in distant clouds. Rin ignored her, his brooding eyes flicking among the many dense thickets of data that the ship's walls offered him.

'Where are we going?'

He blinked as though returning from some distant place. 'To hell and back.'

When she frowned, puzzled, he smiled. 'An ancient phrase. Come, I'll show you where hell does dwell on Earth for the moment.'

They plunged down through a storm wrack that was speeding around the equator. Clouds, fat and purpling with moisture, speckled the air's high expanse. In the last few years she had felt their winds and rain more often as moisture spread through the parched ecosphere. Orange spikes forked upward, tapering fingers stretched toward the stars. The planet was acting like a vast spherical capacitor, endlessly adjusting its charges between soil and sky. The ionosphere's shell would disperse these energies – a dynamo the Supras tapped, she knew, though she did not know how.

The craft swooped through dappled decks of fog and down, across vistas of windswept sand. Seeker put its tapered hand in hers and murmured, 'Wait.' She shot it a quick questioning glance. Its bandit-mask markings around the large eyes seemed to promise mischievous revelations. Rin apparently noticed nothing except the walls' sliding arrays.

'See?' He summoned up a continent-wide view of the desert. A network of red lines appeared slowly, images building up like pale blood vessels pulsing beneath a sallow skin. 'The old subway tunnels, leading to cities that once lived.'

'When?'

'More years ago than you could count if you did nothing else throughout your life.'

She stared. The display showed wispy lattices of streets beneath the shifting sands, the shadows of cities whose very names were lost. 'So many . . .'

'I had a hand in excavating those subways,' Rin said wistfully. 'In each, there were cryonic jackets filled with the corpses of their greatest, the luminaries who had earned passage into the future. They thought it would be better, more suited to their talents.'

She blinked. 'But — these subways are long! Some pass through mountain ranges, crossing continents.'

'Yes, and each corpse represented the best minds of whole eras.'

'Such potential!'

'So many wild cards.' Rin grimaced.

'If we could revive them—'

'Oh, we can.'

'Then we should!' She could not stifle her enthusiasm. 'So much talent—'

'And release energies we cannot know in advance?' He smiled. 'These ancients may be dictators of enormous charisma, prophets of vanished religions who will seek to reinvent their faiths, inventors who can bring forth engines of destruction that later human variants erased as too dangerous, artists who can throw our very worldview into crisis — and we cannot tell them apart! The records are long lost.'

She felt crushed. The stretches of time implied by the problem were numbing. And she knew so little. The cities that now lay beneath the sands, their very shadows implying whole histories . . . 'The subways . . .'

'There were vast alternatives to Sonomulia then. Great cities devoted to crafts we abandoned. We did not seize them.'

'And now?'

Rin laughed. 'Precisely because we have lost so much, there is so much to do. Uncountable! Infinitude!'

'Because . . .'

'We are casting off lethargy at last.' He waved a hand at the screen. 'The bots. The dead hand of this static past.'

To her surprise, Seeker spoke, reedy and melodious.

'There are more breeds of infinitude than of finiteness.'

Rin raised his eyebrows, startled. 'You know of trans-finites?'

'You speak of mere mathematics. I refer to your species.' Seeker had not spoken to Rin since they entered the ship. Cley saw that the beast was not awed by this sleek, swift artifact. It sat perfectly at ease, and nothing escaped its quick, bright eyes.

Rin pursed his lips. 'Just so, sage. Did you know that your kind evolved to keep humans intellectually honest?'

Cley could not read Seeker's expression as it said with a rippling intonation, 'So humans think.'

Rin looked disconcerted. 'I . . . I suppose we Supras, too, have illusions.'

'Truth depends on sense organs,' Seeker said with what Cley took to be a kindly tinge to its clipped words. Or was she imposing a human judgment on Seeker's slight crinklings around its slitted eyes, the sharpening of the peaks of its yellow ears?

'We have records of the long discourses between your kind and mine,' Rin began. 'I studied them.'

'A human library,' Seeker said. 'Not ours.'

Cley saw in Seeker's eyes a gulf, the spaces that would always hang between species. Across hundreds of millions of years, and chasms of genetics, words were mere signal flares held up against the encroaching night.

'Yes, and that is what burns,' Rin said soberly. 'We know what humans thought and did, yes. But I am coming to see that much history passed outside human ken.'

'Much should.'

'But we will regain everything.' Rin slapped a palm down. 'You cannot regain time.'

'We can make up for it.'

Seeker said slowly, with infinite sympathy, 'Now time and space alike conspire against you.'

Rin nodded with wan fatigue.

Cley felt that she had missed much of this cryptic exchange. She had learned with Kurani to keep her respectful silence, as one both of few years and earlier origins. But this Rin . . .

She had realized earlier that she knew fragments of his history. Even among Supras he was famous. Of course, all other human orders knew the Supras better than any other variants. Rin had changed in the several centuries since, as a daring boy, he had altered human fortunes. He had pried the Supra forms from their sequestered city, Sonomulia. The Supra Breakout, as some termed it, was in large part his creation – done with youthful zest, over-powering inertia. Some of that still smoldered in his darting eyes.

All other human variants were but witnesses to the sudden reemergence of Supra ambition, after their kind had slumbered in their crystal city for uncounted millennia. Once again, Supras thought they could do anything. It might be so. Certainly regreening the world was a good beginning.

Still, Cley watched him with trepidation. An Original would have passed through wisdom and died in the time this man had enjoyed – another sign of the unknowable distance between the subspecies.

But he felt the range of human emotions, still – and visibly. Rin's spirit ebbed, his face clouding, as if this flight had taken him momentarily away from a fact he could not digest.

The ship was landing beside a wall of black that she at first took to be solid. Then she saw ash-gray coils rising through sullen clouds and knew that this was the smoky column she had seen for days.

'The Library of Life,' Rin said. 'They attacked it with something like smart lightning. Bolts that struck and burrowed and hunted.'

She saw the black-crusted gouges and ruptured vaults, polished clean by electric fire. Something had found the treasure that ages of wearing winds had not discovered.

'All the underground library?' Cley asked. She remembered that her tribe had once shaken their heads at a Supra who told them of this practice, the attempt to imprison meaning in fixed substance. People who lived and worked in the constant flux of the deep woods saw permanence for the illusion that it was.

'Not all, luckily. Some legacy survived,' Rin said. 'The Ancients knew its storehouse would not be needed in my crystal city, Sonomulia. The urge to preserve was profound in them, and so they buried deep.'

'A recurrent human feature,' Seeker said. 'Sealing meaning into stone.'

'The only way to understand the past,' Rin countered sharply.

'Meaning passes,' Seeker said.

'Does transfinite geometry?'

'Geometry signifies. It does not mean.'

Rin grunted with exasperation and kicked open the hatch. The wall of soaring smoke bulked like a dark, angry mountain. The smoke's sharp bite made Cley cough, but Rin took no notice of it. They climbed out into a buzz and clamor of feverish activity. All around the ship worked legions of bots — ceramic and metal, and some of the plasma-discharge swirls. A few Supras commanded teams that struggled up from ragged-mouthed tunnels in the tawny desert, carrying long cylinders of gleaming glass.

'We're trying to save the last fragments of the Library, but most of it is gone,' Rin said, striding quickly away from the guttural rumble of the enormous fire. Smoke streamed from channels gouged in the desert. These many thin, soot-black wedges made up the enormous pyre that towered above them, filling half the sky.

'What was in there?' Cley asked.

'Frozen life,' Seeker said.

'Yes,' Rin said, his glance betraying surprise; an animal knew this? 'The record of all life's handiwork for well over a billion years. Left here, should the race ever need biological stores again.'

'Then that which burns,' Seeker said, 'is the coding.'

Rin nodded bitterly. 'A mountain-sized repository of DNA.'

'Why was it in the desert?' Cley asked.

'Because there might have come a time when even Sonomulia failed, yet humanity went on,' Rin said. 'So the Keeper of Records says.'

'I . . . see.' She could scarcely follow his words.

She had never seen the full panoply of the Supras at work. Iron-dark clouds raced low before a wind that boomed in the valley and whined through the wrecked galleries of the Library. Dust swirled into the cracked caverns that had been kept crisply sterilized for longer than any single species could remember. Stenches — carbon fires, open graves, smoke ripped ragged out of smashed vaults, rotting bodies thawing from the foggy liquid nitrogen, sweaty fear – seemed to coat the very sounds of this hubbub with rank odors. Metal clangs of slinking gray snake-bots, hammers thudding, joints popping, wheels creaking, leaden footfalls of ceramic diggers, voices raised in anger, sobs, whispers, silken pleas, ritual song, hushed prayer.

Cley turned, looking at the unfolding drama. Women wrapped ancient bodies, kept for rebirth after their freezings and now permitted to thaw out, dead forever. Survivors, blinded by the Furies, staggered to their tasks, unwilling to sit idle. An elaborately gowned matron screamed that she sought her family's stored bequest, hammering at a burned compartment. Animals trotted by, speaking in their slanted tongues of horrors none could explain, tongues hanging between guttural words. Grim attendants exploded dangerously teetering arches, slamming the architecture of antiquity into powder.

'So much . . . gone.' She instinctively stepped nearer to Rin.

'Not all, we hope.'

The teams of ceramo-bots moved in precise ranks, so methodical that even the hubbub of fighting the fires could not fracture their lines. They surged on wheels and legs and tracks, churning the loose soil as they pushed large mounds of grit and gravel into the open troughs where flames still licked. She could see where explosions had ripped open the long trenches. The Furies had scoured out the deep veins of the planet's accumulated genetic wisdom. The bots were like insect teams automatically hurrying to protect their queen, preserving a legacy they could not share.

Cley could scarcely take her eyes from the towering pyre of rising, roiling gray smoke, the heritage of numberless extinct species vanishing into billowing wreaths of dead carbon.

The machines automatically avoided the three of them as they walked over a low gravel hill and into an open hardpan plain. Rin did not bother to move aside as battalions of bots rushed past them. Cley realized that this was an unconscious tribute to the static perfection he knew in Sonomulia, where such error did not occur. The machines came shooting past, deflecting sidewise at the last instant before collision, then reforming their precise columns as they sped away. Seeker flinched visibly at the roar and wind of the great machines, dangerously close.

Cley saw that the dead sands had already advanced here, drifting across the smoky remains of humanity's efforts. Supras hurried everywhere, ordering columns of machines with quick stabs at handheld instruments.

'The fight goes no better,' Rin said sourly. 'We are trying to snuff it out by burying the flames. But the attackers have used some inventive electromotive fire that survives even burial.'

'The arts of strife,' a woman's whispery voice came, sardonic and wistful.

Cley turned and saw a tall, powerfully built woman some distance away. Yet her voice had seemed close, intimate.

'Rin!' the woman called, and ran toward them. 'We have lost a phylum.'

Rin's stern grimace stiffened further. 'Something minor, I hope?'

'The Myriasoma.'

'The many-bodied? No!' Creases of despair flitted across his face.

Cley asked, 'What are they?'

Rin stared grimly into the distance. 'A form my own species knew, long ago. A composite intelligence which used drones capable of receiving electromagnetic instructions. The creature could disperse itself at will.'

Cley looked at the woman uneasily, feeling an odd tension playing at the edge of her perceptions. 'I never saw one.'

'We had not revived them yet,' Rin said. 'Now they are lost.'

Seeker said, 'Do not be hasty.'

'What?' He cast Seeker an irritated glance.

'This is not the only place where life brims.'

Rin ignored it, his gaze boring into the tall, stately woman. 'You are sure we lost all?'

The woman said, 'I hoped there would be traces, but . . . yes. All.'

Cley heard the woman and simultaneously felt a deeper, resonant voice sounding in her mind. The woman turned to her and said slowly, enunciating the words so that they came through the echoes in her mind's ear, 'You have the Talent, yes. Hear.'

This time the woman's voice resounded only in Cley's mind, laced with strange, strumming bass notes: We – or as you would say, *I* – I am Kata, a Supra who shares *this*.

'I, I don't understand,' Cley said. She glanced at Seeker and Rin but could not read their looks.

We Supras recreated you Ur-humans from the entries in this Library. We further augmented you so that you could

understand us through this direct Talent. Your skull contains
a processor that receives compressed, filtered messages from
my own mind's speech center.

'But Rin didn't—'

He is of Sonomulia and thus lacks the Talent.

She raised one finger as a prompt. Her small smile
played briefly. Here . . .

Cley staggered. She took in an assault of images, side
paths, ideas, histories, jokes and puns, and a strange
sadness.

She had no choice. It demanded that she swim in a
torrent hot off the heart, flooding through her. She could
not even tell if these were ideas, emotions, or something
beyond that. Moods came surging up from something
deeper that sponsored them — currents from the woman
Kata's depths. Cley felt sliced moments slip through her,
entries being lodged in her memories. She was swimming,
trying to breathe through a deluge. Darting, fevered
chunks of knowledge glanced off her, unable to penetrate
— and then more, slanting in, slamming into her mind
like silver shards.

She gasped. 'Stop!'

Sorry. We presume too much. You are, after all, Ur-
human . . .

She tried to think simply, to get her footing again.
'You say "we," not "I"—'

We use 'we' because we are linked, and so share.

'How?'

Only we from Illusivia have the threads of microwave-active
magnetite laid down in skull and brain. They twine among
your — and our — neurological circuitry. When stimulated electrically, these amplify and transmit our thoughts.

The linear sentences were clear, but the rushing river of other sensations drowned her again. A mere moment of direct contact filled her to the brim.

She gasped, the world's whirl slowed, and she grasped the layers below the simple sentences. *This* was how the Supras thought? She felt the yawning gulf beneath her feet. *They lived so intensely.* Deeper than her Original verve, more somber. How should she respond?

Kata took Cley's hands and held them up, palms facing together, then slowly brought them to Kata's temples. Cley felt the voice strengthen. I am antenna and receiver, as are you.

So I am! Cley sent back.

'I could never do this before!' Cley said loudly, joyously, as if the new Talent made her doubt her older voice.

The Talent must be stimulated first, since it is not natural to Ur-humans. Kata smiled sardonically. It might have helped your species overcome your drawbacks in your first, Original age. We of Illusivia have it because for so long we lived for the whole, for our community. This knits us together.

'And Rin?' She felt dizzy. Asking a simple question was all she could manage. Around them swirled work, noise, scents, a clamor of purpose. Yet within this strange, enclosed space of the mind, she could carry on a cool conversation.

His city, Sonomulia, is the vast master of urban mechanism. Mine, Illusivia, championed verdant wooded majesty. Their art escapes boundaries through abstraction, while ours sings of our time and community. Sonomulia rejected the enveloping intimacy of the Talent, though it is an unending pleasure. And we of Illusivia pay the price of mortality for this.

'This Talent . . . kills you?'

Kata smiled wearily. Yes. Stressed so, inevitably the brain loses structure, substance. Diseases find a foothold. Unfixable. This defect of finiteness we share with you Urhumans. Your form is hopeless, alas.

Cley staggered, reeling with this assault of knowledge.

Rin and the others have elected to omit this Talent, and thus live far longer.

Of course Originals knew they were mortal, although to a young woman, the Original span of several centuries seemed ample. But to encounter an immortal Supra who gave it up for this method of intense communication – she could not get her equilibrium, before such an avalanche of facts. Her feet were stumps, her body a log balanced on them, her head wobbly.

She panted, managed to get out, 'I – this means that Kurani – he did not have this Talent, either. He used technology for something like this, though – his inboards, to get and send data, and for other communication. He was always connected to other Supras through that. You aren't?' She felt safer, sticking to acoustic voice.

True. We reject some capabilities that so many have amassed in human history. No one soul can bear them all. To live is to select. To edit from the past.

'There's . . . so much. Hard to get my bearings.'

Do not struggle to know all this too soon. You are only an Ur-human – honored, but limited.

'Yeah, no kidding.' Her breath came fast and hard.

You will come to terms with it in time.

'Uh . . . right.' Cley knew that she was speaking with one of those who had brought her kind back into the world, yet she could not decide whether to be angry or grateful. They were *so* sure of themselves. 'Then why give it to us, if we did not have it before . . . before you cooked us up from your Library?'

Did a quick flicker of caution pass in the tightening of Kata's lips? For now, let me simply say that we know you well enough to savor your kinesthetic joys, your quick and zesty sense of the world. That we lost in Illusivia.

Cley thought, carefully shaping it through her speech center: Lost because of this Talent?

Kata blinked, and Cley knew she had been understood. And the thought had registered as something like an insult in this strange medium.

Cley had a sudden, shooting memory: of being a child, on a Mom's lap, gazing at a simple illoed story. *Mother* – Cley felt a pang she had been suppressing, the abyss of loss of that warm, loving presence, the center of her Meta life. All her Moms – gone now, leaving her alone, alone . . .

And that memory wrapped around another. She was suddenly *there,* beneath the big fern fronds rustling, making the golden light dance across the sheet where the story unfolded. Her Mom's voice murmured; time stood still . . .

She must have been two years old. The moment hung solid and timeless for her, when she looked down at the images and saw in the framed air beside them a notation. She had just been learning to read. Hanging there was the assent symbol, coming in color from a woman character. Suddenly, the two-year-old said aloud, 'Yes. Yes, yes, yes!' And her Mom nodded, murmuring praise. In a single astonished moment it came into her that these incomprehensible marks near the characters were *words,* and the woman was saying *yes.* So all the symbols around her, hanging in the soft moist air, *meant something* – if she could only learn how to figure them out.

The moment stood transfixed in memory because then the power of symbols came full force. The whole world was alive with messages. She had ignored their meaningless scribbles until then, but now they promised everything. They would tell her what the world meant. A desire had flooded her then, a hot yearning to know what the world was trying to tell her.

And now here was a new, sweeping possibility, huge and full of fresh meaning. She could venture not merely into symbol-spaces but into minds, could know them fully.

She gasped with the power and freedom of it, struggling to keep her face from giving way. The Talent was like reading – a doorway to a new world.

Yet around her the routine world went on, clanking and working as though this were an ordinary passing moment, and—

Somberly Kata said, carrying on their conversation as if nothing had happened, We believed the great lie about invaders, yes. Some say that is why we are so named. Sonomulia and Illusivia alike – we slept.

'I . . . I . . . Invaders?' She steadied her breathing. *Calm yourself.* Using this new Talent was labor, and Cley found speaking a relief.

Once both Sonomulia and Illusivia believed that humanity fled the stars, before a horde. But the fact – uncovered by Rin as he ventured out from Sonomulia, to Illusivia and beyond – is that humanity retreated before the knowledge of greater minds. Constructed intelligences. Not merely among the stars, but beyond.

Cley frowned. 'What's beyond the stars?'

Spaces, geometries – beyond infinity, in a way.

Cley sent, Beyond our universe?

Other dimensions, other . . . surfaces, in those dimensions. Membranes. It is difficult to explain without training in the topologies of space-time.

Cley had gotten used to being told there were huge areas she knew nothing about, and by now was not even irked at the mild, unintended insult. Supras never even knew they were doing it, as far as she could tell. 'Okay,' she said aloud, 'what did you do about it?'

We tried to evolve even vaster forces, minds free of matter itself. And succeeded. But the struggle was too much. Exhaustion and fear drove us into a wan recessional as cities died and hopes faded.

An immense sadness ran through these thoughts, long, rolling notes that held in Cley's mind like a soulful dirge. These chords were all counterpointed by the pressing world around her – a medley of crackling distant fires, the acrid tang of oily smoke, the hoarse shouts of orders, the grim grinding of heavy machines, a quiet sobbing somewhere nearby.

'And Rin, his role?' She sent this mentally, but found she had voiced it as well. This method required practice.

She realized Rin was studying her with interest; she had spoken his name. Immediately she had a sense of the chasm that had opened between her and anyone who could not catch the silky speed of this Talent, its filmy warmth and cloaked meanings. They were well worth the effort. But the chasm was their price.

And the Talent brought more still – pure, unbidden sensation. Kata turned to give a spoken order to a machine, and Cley felt an echo of the woman's swivel, the catch of indrawn breath, minute pressures and flexes. Still deeper in Kata burned a slow, sensual fire. The heat smoldered but could be summoned either by setting or by will. Power over emotion. This was a startling capability Cley did not have, and she could not immediately imagine its use. She guessed that the folk of Illusivia had kept the roiling passions of early humanity, the carnal joy and longing that flushed the mind with goaty rut, calling up the pulsing urgencies laid down in reptile brains on muddy shores. They were closer to her forms, the rudimentary Ur-humans, than Rin's more cerebral sorts were. Yet they also ruled their emotions, holding them like caged lions, ready to release.

Kata was an adult in a way Rin would never be. She ruled herself profoundly. Neither way was wrong or right; each subspecies had chosen profoundly different paths. But the effect was staggering when the gap between them spanned the myriad genetic choices of a billion years.

'Ah, yes,' Cley made herself say, jerking her mind out of the hot, cloying satisfactions of this Talent. *To read another truly . . .* 'I, I . . .'

'You need say nothing,' Rin said aloud, smiling. 'I envy you. More, I need you.'

She began to stutter a reply, but noise engulfed them. Ranks of tractor-driven bots roared by them, making talk impossible, slinging pebbles high in the air. Gravel spat over her bare skin, stinging. Seeker nervously shuffled back and forth, eyeing the gargantuan machines. It now had the look of an animal in strange surroundings: wary and skittish. Cley was concerned for it, but she knew she could do nothing for Seeker without the approval of the Supras.

'Need me?' she asked finally. 'For what?'

Rin said smoothly, 'You are a rarity now. That was why I searched.'

'The lightning sought out Ur-humans,' Kata put in. 'Rin himself volunteered to look for the survivors, but . . .'

Cley glanced from Rin to Kata, acutely conscious of their casual ease. They were half again as large as she, their chocolate skins vibrant with health. Cley felt rustic with her thicker, reddened skin bared. Kata, though, showed lines in her face, which gave it a grave, crinkled geometry. The Supras' clothes rippled to accommodate each movement. An air of unconscious well-being hovered around their sleek resilience. She glanced down at herself: nude, bruised from her injuries, scratched by bushes, skin creased and scabbed and dirty.

She felt a flickering burst of embarrassment.

I am sorry, Kata sent with concern. That was an overlap of my own emotion. Nakedness carries sexual and social signals in Illusivia.

Cley asked wonderingly, 'The simple baring of skins?' Her people enjoyed the rub of the world on their flesh, but it meant nothing more. For her, passion rose from context, from people, not attire.

Rin's kind do not feel it, since immortals rarely need reproduction.

'They do not . . . make love?'

Seldom. Long ago they altered themselves – a subcurrent added – (or perhaps the machines did a little pruning, before the long ages of intelligent artifices waned) – with a lilting tinge of tinkling laughter – to avoid the ferment of sexuality. They banished sexual signaling, all the unconscious signs and gestures. Still, I have this trait, and some of my feelings transmitted to you. I—

'Never mind,' Cley said shortly. She ordinarily felt no shame at all about sex and much preferred her present nudity. Clothes robbed her of freedom and a silky sensitivity.

What did bother her was her sudden intense feeling of inferiority. It came welling up, tagged with unsettling embarrassment and riding on her knowledge that her kind was so limited. To the Supras she was a living fossil. A curiosity, no more.

She remembered with some satisfaction that Rin was deaf to the darting Talent-currents and so spoke aloud, though already the thick movements of her throat and tongue were beginning to seem brutish and clumsy. 'Why are you so concerned for us?'

'You Ur-humans are valuable,' Rin said cautiously.

Cley arched an eyebrow. 'Because we can do grunt labor?'

'You know you have crafts that we later adaptations do not,' Kata said evenly, and aloud in deference to Rin.

'Oh, sure.' Cley held up a small finger, which she quickly transformed into five different tools: needle, connector, biokey, pruner, linkweb. 'This wasn't your add-on?'

'Well,' Kata said carefully, 'we did modify a few of them. But Ur-humans had the underlying capabilities.'

Cley's mouth twisted with ironic humor. 'Good thing you gave me this Talent-talk. I can feel that there's something you don't want to tell me. That would have breezed by your ordinary Original.'

'You are right.' Rin had missed her tone; he swept his arms to take in the wall of roiling smoke that stood like a solid, ominous barrier. 'We're concerned now because we could lose you all.'

'Lose us?'

She caught thoughts from Kata, but the layers were chopped wedges, fogged by meanings she could sense but not decipher. In the instant between 'lose' and 'us' she felt a long, stretched interval in which gravid blocks of meaning rushed by her. It was as if immense objects swept through a high, vaulted space that she could see only in quilted shadows. She felt then the true depth and speed of Kata – knew that through this luxuriant Talent she was floating like a dust mote in a tiny illuminated corner of an immense cathedral of ideas, far from the great transept and unaware of labyrinths forever shrouded. Passages yawned far away, reduced by perspective to small mouths, yet she knew instantly that they were corridors of thought down which she could never venture in her lifetime. The hollow silence of these chilly spaces, all part of Kata, held unintelligible mystery.

These people looked human despite their size and odd liquid grace. But now she suddenly sensed that they were as strange as any beast she had seen in the swelling forests – and more dangerous. Yet they stood in the long genetic tradition of her kind, and so she owed them some loyalty. Still, the sheer *size* of their minds . . .

'We could lose you Ur-humans,' Rin said with what Cley now saw was indulgent patience. 'Your species records were obliterated in the attack. Gone, lost. And all other Ur-humans were burned to a crisp. You, Cley, are the last remaining Original copy.'

5

A Larger Topology

She worked long days in the shattered ruins. It felt good. Simple, hard, sweaty, so that a hot meal and a shower sent her tumbling into bed. Seeker worked alongside, silently learning bits of dexterous craft. In salvaging, scraps become triumphs.

Bots cleared the heavy wreckage, but there were innumerable places where human care and common sense could rescue a fragment of the shattered past, and she was glad to help. The severed finger on her left hand had regrown but was still stiff and weak, so she wanted to exercise it. And she needed time to clear her head, to climb out of a gray abyss of grief.

The attack had been remorseless, grinding. Livid electrical bolts had assaulted one wing of the Library with particular attention, she learned. Shafts had lanced again and again in brilliant skeins of color, hanging for long moments like a malevolent rainbow whose feet shot electrical arrows into the soil.

That wing had housed the Library of Humanity. The Ur-humans had been the oldest form lodged there, and now they and all the many varieties of humanity that had immediately followed them were lost — except for Cley.

The impact of this was difficult for her to comprehend. The bots gave her awkward, excessive deference. The

Supras all paid her polite respect, and she felt their careful protection as she worked. In turn, without being obvious, she watched the Supras commanding their bot legions, but did not know how to read their mood.

Then one day a Supra woman suddenly broke off her task and began to dance. She moved with effortless energy, whirling and tumbling, her feet flashing across the debris of the Library, hands held up as if to clasp the sky. Other Supras took up the dance behind her, and in moments they were all moving with stunning speed that did not have any note of rush or frenzy.

Cley knew then that she was watching a refinement of Ur-human rituals that went far beyond anything her tribe had used to defuse inner torments. She could glimpse no pattern to their arabesques but sensed subtle elements slipping by in each movement. It was eerie to see several hundred bodies revolve and spring and bounce and glide, all without the merest glance at one another, without song or even faint music. In the total silence she could pick up no signals from the Talent; they were utterly quiet, each orbiting in a closed curve. The Supras danced without pause or sign of tiring for the rest of the day and through the night and on well into the next morning.

Cley watched their relentless, driving dance without hope of comprehending. Without meaning to, the Supras told her that she was utterly alone. Seeker was no company, either; it gave the Supras only an occasional glance, as if tired from so much exposure to humans in all their confusing forms, and soon fell asleep.

She longed for her own people and tried to leave the Supra compound, but as she approached the perimeter, her skin began to burn and itch intolerably. While the tall, perfect figures whirled through the night, she remembered loves and lives now lost down death's dark funnel. She tried to sleep and could not. The Talent-speak would not let her alone.

And then, without a sign or gesture, they abruptly stopped . . . looked around at each other . . . and wordlessly returned to work. Their bots started up again, and there was never any mention of the matter.

Cley sang to herself the next day as she worked. Her Meta had taught her the sing-therapy, a kind of meditation that transfixed the mind in a simple rhythm while allowing the rest of life to go on its ordinary way. It helped. It would take time to recover from the shock of all that had happened.

Then she knew what she needed now. She found Rin and arranged a quick flight to the forests where her Meta had lived. The reports had been dire, but she wanted to see for herself.

The tawny hills were blackened. Tree stumps jutted on the hills like broken teeth. A giant had stepped on the artful adobe buildings at the Meta center. Farther away, the dwellings were cut and seared. The playground where she had leaped and played was a curious dark color.

The flyer set down there, and a bot sampled the soil for her. The stain was blood. At least someone had cleared the bodies away.

She walked for hours through the woods and along the streams. This was as close to saying good-bye as she would ever get, she realized. The trees absorbed her singing, and no voice came forth in answer.

She flew back to the Library in silence and said nothing for two days more.

At work soon after this, Kata took samples of her hair, skin, blood. For the Library, Kata explained.

'But there isn't much of one anymore.'

Come.

Kata led her and Seeker down through a shattered portal. Cley had lived nearly all her life in the irregular beauties of the forests, where her people labored. She was unprepared for the immense geometries below: the curling subterranean galleries that curved out of sight, the alabaster helicities that tricked her eye into believing that gravity had been routed.

Already we rebuild.

Teams of bronzed bots were tending large, blocky machines that exuded glossy walls. The metallic blue stuff oozed forth and bonded seamlessly, yet when Cley touched it a moment later, the slick surface was rock-hard.

'But for what? You've lost the genetic material.' She preferred to speak now rather than use the Talent, for fear of giving away her true feelings.

We can save your personal DNA, of course, and the few scraps we have recovered here. Other species dwell in the forests. We will need your help in gathering them.

Currents from Kata gently urged her to use her Talent exclusively, but Cley resisted, wanting to keep a distance between them. 'Good. You've read my helix; now let me go—'

Not yet. We have processes to initiate. To recreate your kind demands guidance from you as well.

'You did it without me before.'

With difficulty and error.

'Look, maybe I can find some of my people. You may have missed—'

Rin is sure that none remain.

'He can't be certain. We're forest folk, good at hiding.'

Rin possesses a surety you cannot know.

Seeker said in its high, melodious voice like sunlight dancing on water, 'Rin moves in his own arc.'

Cley blinked. *Seeker had the Talent.* But didn't use it . . . *Was there more than one kind of Talent?*

Kata studied the creature carefully. 'You perceive him as a segment of a larger topology?'

Seeker rose up on its hind legs, ropes of muscle sliding under its fur, and gestured with both its forelegs and hands – signals Cley could not decipher.

'He first resolved the central opposition between the interior and exterior of Sonomulia,' Seeker said in its curious, light voice. 'This, his service, this act, led him outward again, in a starship.'

Kata gaped – the first time Cley had ever seen a Supra impressed. 'How could you possibly know . . . ?'

Seeker waved aside her question. 'Among the stars he found another barrier, the vacant cage of something great beyond humanity. This spatial barrier he now confronts in his own mind, and seeks to turn it into a barrier in time.'

'I . . . I don't understand . . .' Cley said.

'I do.' Speaking aloud, Kata studied Seeker warily. 'This beast sees our motions in another plane. It has pieced together our conversations and ferreted out much. But what do you mean, a barrier in time?'

Seeker's broad mouth turned downward, the opposite of a human smile. Cley suspected that Seeker was conveying something like ironic amusement, for its eyes darted with a kind of liquid, skipping joy. 'Two meanings I offer. He delves backward in time, to evolution's edge, for the Ur-humans. As well, he seeks something outside of time, a new cage.'

Cley felt a flash of alarm in Kata, who stiffly said, 'That is nonsense.'

'Of course,' Seeker said. 'But not my nonsense.' It made a dry, barking noise that Cley could have sworn was laughter carrying dark filigrees beneath.

Cley felt a surf of consternation roll over the sea-deep swell of Kata's mind.

'And next?' Kata asked.

'No cage holds forever.'

'So the . . . thing . . . will escape. Will you help us?'

'I have a higher cause,' Seeker said quietly.

'I suspected as much.' Kata raised one eyebrow. 'Higher than the destiny of intelligent life?'

'Yours is a local intelligence.'

'We spread once among the stars, and we can do it again.'

'And yet you remain bottled inside your skins.'

'As do you,' Kata said with clipped precision.

'You know we differ. You must be able to sense it.' Seeker rapped the cranial bulge that capped its snout, as though knocking on a door.

'I can feel something, yes,' Kata said guardedly.

Cley could pick up nothing from Seeker. She shuffled uneasily, lost in the speed and glancing impressions of their conversation.

'You humans have emotions,' Seeker said slowly, 'but more often emotions have you.'

Kata prodded, 'And your kind?'

'We have urges which serve other causes.'

Kata nodded, deepening Cley's sensation of enormous shared insights, tapering Supra perspectives that led to infinities, and yet that seemed as unremarkable to them as the air they breathed. They all lived as ants in the shadow of mountains of millennia, and time's sheer mass shaded every word. So no one spoke clearly. Dimly she guessed that the river run of ages had somehow blurred all certainties, cast doubt on the very categories of knowing. History held counterexamples to any facile rule. All tales were finally slippery, suspect, so talk darted among somber chasms of ignorance and upjuts of painful memory as old as continents, softening tongues into ambiguity and guile.

Seeker broke the long, strained silence between them. 'We are allies at the moment; that we both know.'

'I am happy to hear so. I have wondered why you accompanied Cley.'

'I wished to save her.'

Kata asked suspiciously, 'You just happened along?'

'I was searching to learn of fresh dangers which vex my species.'

Kata folded her arms and shifted her weight – an age-old human gesture that Cley guessed meant the same to all species: a protective reservation of judgment. 'Are you descended from the copies we made?'

'From your Library of Life?' Seeker coughed as though to cover impolite amusement, then showed its gleaming teeth in a broad, unreadable grin. 'Genetically, yes. But once you released my species, we took up our ancient tasks.'

Kata frowned. 'I thought you were originally companions to a species of human now vanished.'

'So that species thought.'

'That's what the libraries of Sonomulia say,' Kata said with a trace of affronted ire.

'Exactly. They were a wise species, even so.'

'Ur-human?' Cley asked. She would like to think that her ancestors' lost saga had included friends like Seeker.

Its large eyes studied her for a long moment. 'No, they were a breed that knew the stars differently than you.'

'Better?'

'Differently.'

'And they're completely lost?' Cley asked quietly into a stillness that had come over their conversation. She was acutely aware of the shrouded masses of history.

'They are gone.'

Kata asked suspiciously, 'Gone – or extinct?'

'From your perspective, for now,' Seeker said, 'there is no difference.'

'Seems to me extinction pretty much closes the book on you,' Cley said lightly, hoping to dispel the tension that had now crept into the air.

'Just so,' Kata said evenly. 'The stability of this biosphere depends on keeping many species alive. The greater their number, the more rugged Earthlife is, should further disasters befall the planet.'

'As they shall,' Seeker said, settling effortlessly into its position for walking, a signal that it would talk no more.

Damned insolent animal! Kata could not shield this thought from Cley, or else did not want to. Cley was shocked.

They left the Library of Humanity in a seething silence, Kata deliberately blocking off her Talent so that Cley could not catch the slightest prickly fragment of her thoughts.

6

To Dance on Time

That evening Rin presided over a grand reception and meal for three hundred, with Cley as guest of honor.

Bots had labored through the day, extruding a large, many-spired banquet hall that seemed to rise up groaning from the soil itself. Its walls were sand-colored but opalescent. Inside, a broad ceiling of overlapping arches looked down on tables that also grew directly from a granite floor. Sky peeked through spaces above. Spiral lines wrapped around the walls, glowing soft blue at the floor and shifting to red as they rose, circling the room, making an eerie effect like a sunset seen above an azure sea.

Tricks of perspective led Cley into false corridors. Sometimes there appeared to be thousands of other guests eating in the distance. Often holes would gape in the floor, and bots would rise through them bearing food, a process she found so unsettling that for a while she stayed apprehensively seated. Despite the cold night air of the desert, the room enjoyed a warm spring breeze scented like the pine forests she knew so well. Her gown scarcely seemed to have substance, caressing her like water, yet it covered her from ankle to neck. Perfect – and a bot had made it in less time than she took to describe her wants.

They ate grains and vegetables of primordial origin, many dating back to the dawn of humanity. These had already been spread through the emerging biosphere, and this meal was the boon of an ample harvest, brought here from crops across the globe. Cley savored the rich sauces and heady aromas but kept her wits about her in conversation with her hosts.

Often their talk went straight by her. Arabesques of Talent-talk slid among percussive verbal punctuations. The Supras of Illusivia tapered their rapid-fire signals to make them comprehensible to Cley. Those of Sonomulia used only the subset of their language that she could follow. They tried to keep the din of layered cross-references simple in deference to her, but gusts of enthusiasm would sweep their ornate conversations into realms of mystifying complexity.

Her worst adolescent uncertainties came back. She compensated – worse, *knew* she was compensating – by fixing them all with her withering, unspoken judgments.

Supra styles in hair and dress varied wildly. They seemed to do this to provoke not regard from each other, but wry amusement.

Beneath it all, this evening, she felt their remorse and anger smoldering. And underlying that ran a stern resolve to recover what they could.

A woman seemed to embody this. Alone, dressed in black, she argued furiously with three men about the Furies. Cley felt the brittle, edged anger from her, the mollifying replies of the men – all without words, for they were using their Talents to convey something between ideas and emotions, beyond her abilities. Yet their faces remained calm and they sipped a fuming drink from long-stemmed glasses. Utterly tranquil, to the eye.

Still, Rin made jokes, forced lightness, even quoting

some ancient motto of a scholarly society from the dawn of science. *'Nullius in verba,'* he said dryly, 'or, "don't take anyone's word for it." Makes libraries seem pointless, wouldn't you say?'

Cley shrugged. 'I am no student.'

'Exactly! Time to stop studying our history. We should reinvent it.' From an ornate chalice Rin took a long drink of something that steamed blue.

'I'd like to just live my life, thanks,' Cley said quietly.

'Ah,' he said, 'but the true trick is to treasure what we were and have done – without letting it smother us.'

Rin smiled with a dashing exuberance Cley had seldom seen among the other Supras. Except for Kurani, she suddenly thought with a pang. Rin waved happily as what appeared to be a flock of giant, scaly birds flew through the hall, wheeled beautifully, and flew straight through the ceiling without leaving a mark. The illusion was startling.

A bundle of complex comments rattled through her in the Talent, about the dinner. Cley sniffed in disdain. Good food was like sex, one of life's blessings, but they both lost their edge when talked about too much. Better go back to experience, then. She amped up her Talent and ate, feeling to her surprise the synergy between these senses. Down deep, the Talent was not just another way to hold a conversation. It reverberated from other senses, altering the texture of her world.

Her first bite was slow and deep, sinking through layers of thick taste. Onion-sharp, apple-sweet, fishy-rich – but not those flavors, not at all. Something beyond those. Supra food embodied all the feel of both Natural diets, animal and vegetable, and those of manufactured fare. She bit deeper, letting the savors drift through her sinuses and throat. It felt as if she were tasting with her eyes — a startling confusion. Now the salty fish-roe savor did not have to fight for recognition. Then came quick, hot spurts of texture, blending with Talent senses from others. Naturals ate together to talk; those with Talent, to heighten their world through each other. Very well, then.

She inhaled the rest of the cuisine-stack, not caring whether this was correct Supra etiquette. Nor did she allow herself to look at how the others took in the ottoman-sized slices of a cake tower — too tempting. Mingled with the Talent, this stuff was simply too good. To wrap yourself around it required no intellect, but resisting it would take a towering will. Vaguely she remembered something about entire sybaritic civilizations that had ebbed away, seduced by such delights. One of her Moms had told her of a lost year, all memories gone, after the Mom got addicted to a particular Supra gastronomical delight. She decided to leave the Supra treats table for special occasions, since she still intended to retain her ability to walk upright.

Still, it was hard to fight such temptation; she had the nagging thought that it might not come again.

Self-consciousness came tiptoeing in. The Talent buzz was intense, like a migraine hum. She tuned it out. A Supra man glided by with their characteristic smooth carriage, arched an eyebrow with a turn of his upper lip, and they sidled into a conversation. Now, *this* was more like it, she thought. He was named Fanak and was of exactly the same physical variation as Kurani. Something about him made her sing inside — final proof, as if any were needed, that she had a type.

The odd, off-key tone of this party had unsettled her. A pall had hung over their world since the attack, and she suddenly wanted to get out from under the emotional overcast. Do something frivolous and unthinking. So . . .

Fanak said something mild, a clear opening, and she jumped in. Made a weak joke. Got flustered. Blundered into fake profundity. Laughed it off. Concluded with a roll of the eyes and, realizing that she was coming over as rough, obvious . . . 'I'm Cley — sometimes, I guess, the sort of woman who needs a woman's touch.'

To his credit, he laughed anyway.

They spoke of trifles, mannerisms — anything except the Library and Furies — and he shrugged off a small recent bit of gossip with 'Education may banish ignorance, but nothing can ban stupidity.' She thought this was very amusing, and told him so before she could stop herself. She went on about Seeker and Fanak was interested, asking all sorts of questions about the procyons as a species, which she did not know answers for, so she shrugged and just described Seeker alone, concluding in a rush, to her own surprise, 'You need friends to keep you on your feet, and enemies to keep you on your toes.'

'We have plenty of the latter.'

'The—'

'No, we're enemies enough among ourselves,' he cut her off before she could say anything glaringly obvious. 'Supras and Naturals and Compacts and Obscurantists—'

'But we're not enemies. Not *now.*'

A careless shrug, undeniably appealing. 'As long as the Supras run things, of course. But how long will that last?'

A hint of species politics she did not comprehend. 'I, uh—'

'You haven't fully plugged into the Talent yet, my dear. It can eat up your time, I warn you.' A fetching smile. She felt herself wrapping voluntarily around his augmented, extra-sized finger.

'I have a weak Talent, but no other talent.'

'As a unique, you must.'

'Oh, being one of a kind? But you Supras can always make other Originals.'

He gave her a tapered grin, as if making an oblique point. 'Suppose we make an exact copy of you. What's been lost?'

'Nothing, by defin—'

'Uniqueness.'

'Oh. That's just a word trick.'

'It's a metaphor, a symbolic mirror. To reflect on a truth — that we may not get the same Original every time we create one artificially. I'd prefer to stick with one like you, who has grown up in the forest, the old way.'

Wasn't she the only one left? Or was he hinting at something? She saw that he was working around to his point — very Supra. Best to be a naive Natural, then. 'You need more Originals?'

'I gather so. Growing our own seems to be in the air.'

'I intend to, uh, make some of my own, eventu—'

'Not enough time. And how could you, alone?'

Despite her affected gaiety, getting stretched rather thin now, she could not find a light and airy way around this question. It had been wearing on her. No simple Original motherhood for her: the genes would have to be tuned, embedded, policed. She was enough of an Original to feel wistful about it, too. No Supra would, she guessed; they were remorselessly analytical. How to counterpunch, then?

'What would you do in my place?'

He was smooth enough to say, 'I'm sure I cannot imagine. Luckily, we men are still spared such vexing questions. We do have artificial means, some quite quick.'

Cley wished she could get their conversation back into a flirty, easy air. It had veered this way without her seeing the swerve coming — and then she recognized another Supra signature: one-move-ahead thinking.

She laughed, but it came out like a squeak falling down a well. Fanak made a joke about that, and they were back on track, she feeling relieved, his smile saying that he was happy to be in the company of such a charming lady. She began to relax. Then there was more food passing on bot trays, and Fanak had to mingle, and she did, too. Some quick eye contact, body turns, and postures completed the deal: They would be seeing each other again. Her heart stopped thumping only after an annoyingly long while.

She wished Seeker had come to this bewildering banquet, but the quiet beast had elected to rest. Another puzzle: She could not in all honesty see why Seeker stayed with her when the Supras would probably have let it go free. Lately, its laconic replies had antagonized Kata, and that could make Seeker unwelcome. While Supras had never harmed Ur-humans, she was not sure any such convention governed their relations with distant species. In any case, caution outweighed theory, as mice knew about elephants.

Not to seem a complete dunce, she tried to get back into conversation. Rin was the center of attention, but he looked quickly at her when she sat beside him and asked, 'How can you shrug off history?'

He eyed her closely, as if trying to read something

inscrutable. Would he pick up the thread of their previous conversation? She needn't have wondered. He leaned forward, eyes intent and sharp with mirth. 'By studied neglect.'

The day of dancing seemed to have released him from some burden she could not guess. 'History is such detail! Emperors are like the dinosaurs, their names and antics unimportant.'

Someone called from down the table, 'Careful! The Keeper of Records will scold you.'

Rin answered, 'No, he will not. He knows we hold aloft time's dread weight only by keeping a sense of balance. Otherwise it would crush us.'

'We dance on time!' another voice called. 'It's beneath us.'

Rin chuckled. 'True, in a way. The roll call of empires is dust beneath our feet . . . yet we cling to our old habits. Those last.'

'We need some human continuity,' Cley said reasonably. 'My tribe tells its tales, keeps its customs—'

'Yes, a pleasant invention. When we recalled you all, it was apparent we could not let you resurrect the old imperial habits.'

Cley frowned. 'Imperial . . . ?'

'Of course,' Kata said. 'You do not know.' She inhaled a passing fizzy spice cloud, and while her lungs savored it she sent, We took your genotype from the Age of Empire, when humanity plundered the solar system and nearly extinguished itself.

The Talent-voice of Kata carried both a sting of rebuke and the balm of forgiveness. This irritated Cley, but she struggled to hide it.

'My tribe made no . . . war.' She had to pause and let her deep-based vocabulary call up the word, for she had never used it before. Comprehending the definition and import of the word took a long moment. With foreboding she permanently tagged it for ready future use. *War* – the very sound was primitive, raw.

'That was how we wanted it.' Rin smiled as though he were discussing the weather. 'We reasoned that at most you might eventually expand for territory, rather than for political gains and taxes, as in the imperial model.'

'We did not realize we were so . . . planned.' Cley gritted her teeth, hoping that her unease would not leak out through her Talent. This nakedness of her thoughts was proving to be a nuisance.

'We did not interfere with your basic design, believe me,' Kata said kindly. 'I merely activated a latency. Your Meta was left untalented by simply never stimulating its use.' She offered Cley a tart fruit and seemed unbothered at its refusal. 'Your group loyalty is your species' most important way to find an identity. It fosters social warmth. Such patterns persist, from a children's playhouse to a transworld alliance.'

'And how do you work together?'

Rin said, 'We do not struggle against each other, for such traits have been very nearly edited out of us. But most important, we have the dubious blessing of a higher goal.'

'What?' Cley demanded.

'Perhaps "enemy" is a better term than "goal." Until now I would have said that history was our true foe, dragging at our heels as we attempted to escape from it. But now we have met an active enemy from out of history itself, and I must say I find myself filled with eagerness, and a great need, to understand it.'

Rin seemed the youngest of these Supras, though Cley could not reliably read the age of any of these bland, perfect faces. 'Enemies? Other Supras?'

'No no! You are recalling those people who supposedly fired at you, who killed your tribe-fellows, who destroyed the Library of Life?'

'Yes.' Cley's mouth narrowed with the effort of concealing her hate. Primitive emotions would not go well here.

Rin waved a hand. 'They were illusions.'

'I saw them!'

'They appeared here, too. I closely examined our records and' – he snapped his fingers – 'there they were. Just as you had seen. We were too busy to notice, and so we owe you thanks for observing it.'

'They were real!'

'Extensive study of their spectral images show them to be artful refractions of heated air.'

Cley looked blank. The sensation of being robbed of a clear enemy was like stepping off a stair in darkness and finding no next step. 'Then . . . what . . . ?'

Rin leaned back and cupped his hands behind his neck, elbows high. He gazed up at the clear night, seeming to take great joy in the broad sweep of stars. Many comets unfurled their filmy tails, like a flock of arrows aimed at the unseen sun, which had sheltered in fear behind the curve of Earth.

Rin said slowly, 'What heats air? Lightning. But to do it so craftily?'

Kata looked surprised. Cley saw that Rin had told none

of this to the others, for throughout the great hall the long tables fell silent.

Kata said, 'Electrical currents — that's all lightning is. But to make realistic images . . .'

Cley asked, 'All to trick us?'

Rin clapped his hands together loudly, startling his hushed audience. 'Exactly! Such ability!'

Kata asked quietly, 'Already?'

Rin nodded. 'The Malign. It has returned.'

'No!' Kata's mouth sagged.

Rin glanced at Cley. 'History, our true foe.'

Kata said wonderingly, 'I thought the Quandary had . . .'

'Nothing is eternal — including prisons.' Rin grimaced.

Cley opened her mouth to ask a question, and Kata sent a jittery, blindingly fast message to all those around her. Before Cley could form a syllable, a blizzard of Talent-talk struck her like a blow. Supras were on their feet, buzzing with speculation. Inside her head percussive waves hammered home. *The torrent . . .*

Again she felt the labyrinth of their minds, the kinesthetic thrust of ideas streaming past, giant complexes of thought, images, word groups — *Malign, Singular, Quandary* — and following immediately, scenes whose features blurred beyond comprehension by sheer mental *speed . . .*

Whirlwinds.
A black roaring against ruby stars.
Purple geysers on an infinite plain.
The plain shrinking until it was a disk, the black sun at its center.
Stars shredded into phosphorescent tapestries.

Spaces cut into strips, geometries wrenched.

A dead black cleft swam at the rim of the bee-swarm gossamer galaxy.

Sliding slices of vibrant color buzzed ominously at the very focus of the spiral arms.

Furious energies erupting from nothingness.

A dizzying sensation of a giant hand squashing her, of smashing accelerations, hard into the flexing mouth of . . .

She dropped away from darkening thunderheads, fleeing this storm. Withdrawing, she tucked herself into a crevice of her mind. *Too much — I'm taking in too much.*

She staggered away from the dinner party. The handsome one, Fanak, gave her a sympathetic smile. By reflex she smiled back, but her face felt as if it were cracking.

Out, into fresh, cool air. The snowy peaks above seemed to tip toward her, full of expectations. The entire valley lay whispering in pale blue-green moonlight. Fires at the Library sputtered, coiling ropes of black into the silvery night.

She sagged against a pillar. *Face it, young one,* she thought. *You're drowning here, in a sea you can't even name.*

An hour ago she had been hanging on Fanak's every word, hoping to connect. Now nothing could make her go back in there. She was hopelessly outclassed.

Panting with the mental exertion, she wondered what the people of Illusivia were like when they were alone. Or if they ever were.

III

Around the Curve of the Cosmos

Beauty is the first test; there is no permanent place in the world for ugly mathematics.
> —G. H. Hardy, *A Mathematician's Apology*

1
Morphs

Cley sensed them first by their stench.

A tangy reek like old bile curled into her nostrils. Then a flat, metallic smell. She had time to sniff, look around — and there was a gaudy sheen near her head. A slick mix of blues and reds. Mats of it spun in the air, humming, immune to gravity.

Then it was gone — *pop*!

Cley's eyes widened. 'That was alive.'

'Morphs, I am told they were once called,' Seeker said in its curious accent, the vowels stretched as the long, black-ribbed mouth lingered over every word. 'There is an entry on them in the fragments we found days ago. More than passing strange.'

'Not . . .' Somehow, she could not speak the word.

'One of the Furies?'

Cley glanced around, her teeth fidgeting across her lips, edgy. They were working outside in slanted morning rays, and ivory clouds were snagged on the distant peaks. She could not bear the smashed and burned corridors below, so she insisted that she and Seeker tote their smashed 'finds' up into daylight. Not standard method, but nobody was sticking to rules now.

She breathed deeply to dispel her mood. These last ten days had been restful. Originals notoriously liked simple manual labor, classic big-muscle work, and she had used that to smooth over the jangling tensions left after the Supra dinner party. Seeker had suggested, well before a command came down from the Supras, that they search for records about extradimensional physics. The Furies seemed linked to that, though Cley did not see how.

Search results were spotty. By now they knew that the technology for spanning dimensions had been the grand adventure of the Third Fabricant Age. It had come late in the Uranium Age, which was itself embedded in the high period of interstellar exploration.

Such overlappings were common, and the Library date notations had been confusing. A long period of linear dating mysteriously labeled A.D. had a tiny interruption denoted B.C.E. Translators found after much struggle that this stood for *Before Common Era* in the language of that time, a subspecies of Arbic. Nobody knew what A.D. meant. What made the era 'common' was unknown. That they disliked A.D.? In any case, sanity had eventually prevailed. Historians apparently saw the virtue of a continuous system, and the A.D. system returned. But was it truly connected, with no gaps? No one knew; this was a fine point of classical scholarship, a dusty controversy.

Cley had been quite pleased to find that those eras had been the last pinnacle of Original culture. *Her kind* had found the underlying truths about the entire physical cosmos! That triumph was a crescendo of the human symphony, or so she had heard. The Third Fabricant Age had ushered in the later Natural forms, who then gave way to the myriad later human species. Just absorbing all this made her proud. She had read portions aloud to Seeker, who seemed to choose those moments to fall asleep.

Maybe because it was too confusing?

That there were more than the obvious three spatial dimensions – in fact, thirteen in all – struck her as bizarre. Most of the others were tiny, rolled-up tubes. Nobody could ever tell they were there. Rather abstract . . .

'Do you smell oiled metal?' Seeker said.

By now Cley knew this was a politeness. Seeker had picked up a faint scent, and charitably assumed that a human could, too. But Originals had little smelling ability, and Supras even less. Civilization did not seem to reward such subtlety. 'When the Morph was here?'

'Then – and now again.'

Cley tensed. She liked to think that she was recovering from the Furies, but her body knew otherwise. Crossing the central Library plaza yesterday, a bot had suddenly broken an ancient seal with a loud bang. She hit the stones hard and crawled for cover. When she finally got up and brushed herself off, even the bots were staring at her. Luckily, no Supras were present, or she would have turned her Original deep pink and bolted. She trembled for an hour afterward.

Seeker saw her unease and said softly, 'Breathe; sing.' Cley did, in her shaky soprano.

Seeker nodded after Cley had wound down, and said, 'I saw a summary of the Third Fabricant Age last night – quite suggestive. Your breed devised a process which relied on a virulent state of matter termed *quagma* – a pun upon *quark*, a species of basic particle manifestation, when they gather into clouds, becoming *plasma*.' Seeker raised both eyebrows. 'You humans love your terms! Plasma, an angry gas of things far smaller than atoms. I gather part of the pun is that it is hot beyond imagination.' The procyon blinked owlishly. 'The ancient text said that it "seared like magma." The Ancients liked their little jokes.'

Cley chuckled. Seeker had its bookish side, precise as a pedant. 'Look, maybe we should move inside. I'm feeling kinda exposed. "Magma" sounds a lot like the Furies to me.'

'Very well.'

Once they were below, the sour, acrid air swarmed up into her nostrils. Seeker said, 'Perhaps you could discover more about the ancients by visiting an Esthete.'

'Who?'

'A human form developed in the Inward Age. They came after you Naturals.'

'Never heard of them.'

'They are seldom admired but much referred to – as they would have preferred.'

'We have some?'

'No Library could work well without a cadre of them.'

Cley lifted an eyebrow. 'You speak with authority.'

'I have seen other Libraries.'

'Really? News to me.'

'Each of your subspecies had a way to leave its mark. Most were lost.'

'But the Library—'

'A singular success. Most of the ancient repositories held discards, buried to get them out of the way.'

'Were their records dangerous?' It had never occurred to her that the Library's contents could be harmful.

'Indirectly, yes. We know the humans of distant eras mostly by their waste. There were once whole continents of it.'

'Ummm. And here I thought the Library was, well, stories about the past.'

'It is, I suppose.' Seeker lounged back. It was not above lecturing – though from what sources, she did not know. 'Individual recollections of the past are easily shaped by others. After a while they need have little bearing on the once-lived events.'

'So how can we be sure the ideas we get—'

'The intellectual breeds of humans think in terms of abstractions. But most people have emotions and think they are having ideas.'

Cley smiled, enjoying this. Seeker never ceased to amuse, and she needed that now. 'So?'

'Most human repositories intend to frighten people away. Who wants vandals visiting? So they play to emotion rather than to mere cool caution.'

'So?'

'I have seen strewn across this mad planet vast citadels that were once thought to be art. Or objects of reverence. Or expressions of eternal truths – most now unreadable, best knocked down. They were nearly always left on flat, grassy plains, I've noticed.'

'Uh, why?'

'I suppose the prehumans who preferred the savannah prospered; those who preferred swamps or highlands did less well.'

'I like living at the edge of the woods.'

'Those are hardwired preferences – like mine, say, for fish caught fresh and struggling from a stream. Delicious!' Seeker rolled its eyes, its claw-hands clenching.

'You have some pretty obvious buttons there.'

'I am – what did that woman call me? – an *animal*!'

'Well, y'know, she didn't really mean—'

'Oh, but she did.'

'You're a whole lot more than—'

'I am different from most animals – augmented, but not a human, no. Not that I would want to be.'

'Really?' Once the word was out, she wished she could call it back.

But no, too late – Seeker laughed. 'You are so – well, *human.* You always think you are the ultimate.'

'And . . . we're not.'

Seeker inspected the ceiling. 'It seems unlikely.'

'What's greater?'

Seeker sat up straight. 'Do you truly want to know?'

A chilly caution came, which she brushed aside. 'Sure.'

'The thing called the Multifold – you have heard of it?'

'Vaguely.'

'It was – *is,* perhaps – greater.'

The chill did not go away. 'Is?'

'It may persist.'

'Where?'

'Among the lanes of the galaxy, I have heard.' A significant look. 'You do not know this?'

'Uh, no. Should I?'

'You Originals made it. It is your creature.'

She waved a disbelieving hand at Seeker, who peered back at her intently. 'How can that be?'

'How can lesser make greater?'

'Well, right – how?'

'It is the wonder of creation.' Seeker grinned mischievously. 'Every parent stands perplexed by it. You have not taken the time to notice this?'

'Been busy lately.'

'Great can come forth from lesser. Nature wants that.'

'I thought nature didn't want, just did.'

Seeker blinked owlishly. 'In selecting the laws of nature, one seeks those which allow a flavoring of originality.'

Now she knew Seeker was kidding. 'Laws don't *like* originality. My Meta's laws didn't, I know.'

'I meant the emergence of originality. Fresh prospects.'

'Ummm . . . new stories?' Her Meta had a rigorous story time, when everybody showed up, listened, and anybody spoke who wanted – but they had to tell a story, not just rant. Hominid grooming, somebody'd called it. She still remembered some of those yarns.

'Well put. Most human stories have little survival value today. Once these tales were true. They sit down there in your unconscious, ready to spring out and force surrounding events to make sense.'

She wondered where this was going. But then, she was talking to an . . . animal. 'You don't think that way? No procyon sagas?'

Seeker hooped and howled so long, she wondered if something was wrong. It reared back, claw-hands jerking, yelping at the air. Then it barked out in a volley of words, 'Father, mother, authority, self, childhood, femininity and masculinity, gathering food, circles and squares – divine forms! Somehow useful back on the savannah! devil/evil, god/goddess/good – how similar such words, even in advanced languages! Sleep, pain, death, communion, number, space and time and big, bad eternity . . .' And it ended gasping for air, laughing, big shaggy head shaking in disbelief.

'Uh, I guess there's something . . .'

'Sorry, sorry.' Seeker recovered, still chuckling as it tried to keep a straight face. 'Those are the substratum of human experience, how you construct meaning – in myth, language, religion, art, or artifacts.'

She poked a finger at the cracked and seared ceiling. 'Like this Library.'

'A story yearning to be told.'

'Only somebody doesn't want it told.'

'Ferociously so.'

'Something about . . . the Multifold?' A guess, but Seeker's pursed lips told her she had scored.

'It would be best for you to go to the Esthetes now.'

'Where?'

'Somewhere in this labyrinth.' Seeker waved a paw in dismissal.

'Why don't you go?'

'Humans like to talk.' Seeker was nodding now, ready for one of its naps. Animal naps, she supposed – humans just kept on going, bullheaded to the end. Supras could get by on an hour of just sitting still. One of the best aspects of being Original, she thought, was a thorough, delicious sleep.

She chided, 'You don't?'

'The human channels are narrow. I prefer broader ones. The human habit' – it waved its head in all directions, sweeping up the whole Library – 'of stacking its talk into stone and honoring it, I find amusing.'

'It's a Library, devoted to knowledge . . .'

'It is an art. And art often has no function; it is an experience, period.' It closed its eyes, sighed. 'Go and experience your species Library.'

2

The Obscurantists

Cley found the Obscurantist section, where she had been told she could find an Esthete, by going through the Fabricant wing of the sprawling Library.

She had not ventured there before, because some of the wing was alive with ancient intelligences, embedded in the structure, and were said to be of foul demeanor. Suppose you were smart and able, Cley imagined, and yet pinned to one spot forever. Yes, you might get testy. One wall said to her imperiously, 'You come as supplicant?' and when she answered ritually from her deep vocabulary, it rebuked her with 'You have not the capacity to profit from the wisdom lodged here,' and would say no more.

No matter; at least it did not block the way. That role was very nearly played by the walkway itself. She entered a long hall, whose floor was firm enough at the edge, but which accelerated her forward as she walked to the center. A Supra would not even have noticed this transition of the tiles to a flowing yet firm liquid, but to Cley it was a wonder. Alone, she was free to gape and bend down to touch the grainy fluid that held her up and carried her forward about three times faster than she could walk.

She touched it, and a slow ripple spread to the sides, ebbing away as the floor eased into the solid phase at the edges. She was tempted to ask about it aloud, certain that the wall intelligences would respond, but then thought that it might be the same haughty mind that had brushed her off.

At the end of the hall stood the double arch that announced itself as the Factotum Division – with an Esthete, Tuva, on duty. Even as a pre-Supra, Tuva had many internal improvements and variations beyond Cley, sporting rippling muscles and a gleaming skin thick with sensors. The major, jauntily obvious Esthete advantage was the compressed mental processing, all delivered by embedded processors in the brain and spinal cord. Tuva's tribe apparently highlighted this. Her robes exposed her upper back, where the thick disks at the top of the spine had cooling fans extruded and ornamented with jewelry.

They made their introductions, Cley asked simple, leading questions, and Tuva silently gathered her resources. Cley opened her inboard social matrix, feeling the surge of energies in her upper lumbar, where Originals carried most of their storage. Her inboards piped out a quick background sketch, to help her avoid making a rude social blunder. Like many Esthetes, Tuva seldom ventured outdoors, since a mild agoraphobia went with their compact minds. Indeed, Esthetes refused to have offices or living quarters on the outside corridors of the Library and would refuse to sit in a chair that backed on an outside wall. The long room had no screens showing comforting views, lighting was remorselessly uniform, and two large desks dominated.

Tuva sat in a chair that rolled easily from one desk to another, adjusting and compiling as she worked through her inboards. Cley could hear data squeaks shooting through the room, startling high whines that her forest-steeped mind read as mousy cries. A glimpse through a doorway showed a small bunk room and a clothes generator. Cley got the impression that Tuva had been in here a very long time – not unusual for Esthetes. She recalled from her shaky knowledge of history, and darting consults with her inboards, that the extreme Esthete form, the Obscurantist persuasion, had become a species of hermits, forsaking all communal connections – to Cley, a horrifying idea – to swim in their eternal data-streams.

'Here,' Tuva announced. Cley felt a squeal feed into her own simple inboard receptors. It would be available after some unconscious processing, eventually conveying to her memory the same level of information that having actually read and digested a subject would leave. Her inboard devices had been developed nearly a billion years before, to preserve sanity in the avalanche of necessary skills and knowledge that came with civilization itself.

'I shall supplement, while you digest,' Tuva said in a flat tone, staring straight at Cley, unblinking. The searchlight intensity of the woman made Cley look away, anywhere but into that rapt gaze. 'The history slabs report that in the late Third Fabricant, quagma-driven geometric bridges had been a source of great adventures and even commerce.'

'They *traded* with other dimensions?'

Even Tuva registered mild interest at this. 'Apparently. The technology was difficult and dangerous. It figured powerfully in the Quandary, I see.'

Cley nipped back into her inboards. The past was a vast labyrinth of decayed wonders, and she had dozed off often in her history lessons. Time to let her inboard files rummage up a quick background. *Here* . . .

The Quandary was a catch-all name for a shadowy period, when the Fabricants had gone voyaging out into the galaxy – and then come back, shattered. Their culture never recovered from the long, withering conflicts they met out there. A faction of anti-Fabricants had managed to destroy nearly all records of those strange encounters. Some said there were vast battles, well fought but lost, while others held that sheer enormity had finally over-whelmed the Fabricant spirit.

A few scattered records spoke of a construction called the Multifold. A collaboration between humans and other unnamed agencies – aliens, machine intelligences? – it was left as an 'edifice hanging between the spiral arms,' as an ancient text put it. All to unknown purposes. Other records spoke of it as 'the Greatwork,' a 'transfinite ally,' the 'ship that sailed the quagma,' and other equally opaque references. She and Tuva traced these down to info-crevices that shed no further light. Cley began to feel that the world of the past was all allusion.

'Ummm,' Cley murmured, covering up her confusion. Her inboards were giving her a running brush-up review, but it was scarcely enough. 'If things like quagma were involved, no wonder the Quandary was so spectacular.'

'It is a little-known era. There are many such.'

Cley tried to envision a time when encroachments of other dimensions could be ordinary, everyday. Certainly, she had never heard of them among her Meta, and Supras seemed to have no direct experience with them. Apparently, once humankind had.

Trying to be helpful, Tuva said, 'The events were large, and occurred in deep space.'

Cley struggled to conceal her exasperation. 'History is

fine, but — look! — what's concerning us is that recently, we've been seeing odd blobs, hanging like there was no gravity . . .'

'Yes. Atypical.'

Tuva went on with a dry summary of how experiments into higher-dimensional physics could cause momentary overlaps that would drift away from the experiment sites. Since a four-D perspective could move rapidly in three-D, these manifestations could appear in two distant places very nearly at once.

Cley dutifully listened but finally got overwhelmed. She tossed aside the augmentations Tuva had provided. 'That's all the juice we're going to get.'

Tuva said strictly, 'We should review the salients of this event. There have been reports lately of—'

'I saw some.' Cley got up to go.

'Rin believes you should know this.'

'Oh? Why?'

'*Sit.*'

The spare, sure woman had a daunting presence, like the weight of shrouded history. Cley sat.

3

Tubeworld

The next day Cley and Seeker set about their labors again, outside in the cool morning. Cley started clicking microexcavation tools to her hand neurals. Good to get back to honest muscle work, after the dry hours with Tuva.

Seeker suddenly froze, then whispered, 'Morphs.'

They were mere flashes, lasting seconds. Feeling a bit more sophisticated after Tuva's rigorous coaching, Cley took little note, once the oddness wore off.

Seeker kept searching the air. Cley liked how the procyon never lost its unending respectful attention to the twists of the world. Not so long ago Cley had aspired to an automatic airy attitude of *The world is odd, yes? Next question . . .* but had not quite attained it yet. Seeker was a living counterexample this morning, sniffing the air with an expression Cley took for wonderment.

'C'mon, let's get this stuff cataloged.' She waved away the air-dancing blobs.

They both set about their labors again. Cley felt uneasy, though. The 4-D Morphs had smelled *wrong*. She wondered if this was her ancient hunter-gatherer instincts coming to the fore again: automatic fear of the strange. Such responses had been ironed out of later human subspecies; they had caused innumerable pointless wars.

But Seeker's nose had wrinkled at the stench, too, she recalled. She shook her head and concentrated on her work.

Some of the microscopic slabcasts they studied went as far back as the early millennia, though only in what the Library termed 'arrested decay.' They found it exciting to recover genomes and sometimes even whole glassified organisms from Earth's distant past – especially if they came from before the Age of Appetite and the following Era of Excess.

Theirs was a privileged task. It required both careful attention and a certain skewed way of looking at what they found among the ancient canisters and recording devices. This was where Seeker excelled; nonhuman intelligences were essential in plumbing the currents of the ancient ecospheres. Nature was almost unimaginably complex. Different perspectives were crucial to understanding. The mind riding in that procyon body was as aslant from human minds as anyone had yet created.

Seeker took joy in carefully rooting in the ruins of this, the fifteenth subsurface level of the Library, in the southwestern quadrant. Even here the Furies had wrecked great smoky damage. Seeker enjoyed using its finely articulated yet rugged hands to pry up slab entries and discern their contents.

Cley listened to Seeker's mutters and smiled. A cool breeze wafted over them, ruffling its fur, provoking from it an uneasy purr.

Cley had gotten used to its oblique intelligence. She could see that forebodings stirred in that mind now; its black lips twisted, and the broad face wrinkled with complex, unreadable expressions. It allowed itself a low growl as it worked.

How to tell damage from erosion? Over the yawning chasm of eons, meanings altered beyond recognition. Seeker had heard of a team that once labored at a site rich in radioactives, gingerly harvesting the lode to great benefit . . . only to discover that the ancient techciv had thought this richness was a pollutant to be buried, with stern, immense markers to warn off their presumably primitive, ignorant descendants. This had been a source of much comedy.

The present Library of Life told of the vast experiments that had yielded such strange fruit as Seeker, but not how those had been achieved. In a way, working here was an expedition of self-discovery, for Cley herself was not a true lineal descendant of the ancient genomes, and certainly not a scrupulously true Original. Nobody was, in all of present humanity. Those precise genes had been scrubbed, edited, or enhanced long ago.

And what would be the point of reproducing the stubby fingers and blurred senses of the far past? Cley could not imagine working without her extruding fingers, inboards, and sculpted internals. But Original she was, as a point of pride. Of course.

'Something's . . . coming.' Seeker's ears pricked up. 'That earlier incident – the seashell, remember? Several days ago?'

'I wasn't here,' Cley said, looking up. Was that a cool, dry breeze stirring her hair again? In the heat of the day? 'Some sort of vandalism, I heard.'

'I wish it had been something so innocuous. Look—' Seeker pointed.

Blobs and rods floated nearby. Slick, red and white, shimmering. A faint moaning . . .

The cutting stench again . . .

The microlab Cley was working on vanished. She looked up into a hovering mass of sickly green, shot through with glowing crimson dots. It emitted a low moan. 'Morph!' she cried, tumbling backward.

Several more shelves of slabs disappeared. 'Damn! It's taking our stuff!'

Seeker was there immediately, springing at the Morph. In its lean paws it held a gray equipment tarp. It wrapped the tarp around the churning Morph and scampered around the shape, pulling. 'Grab the end!' Seeker called.

Cley caught the tail of the tarp, and Seeker grabbed both ends, jerking them together. It made a bag around the Morph. 'Hold – hold – it!'

Seeker grappled with the tarp. It poked and jerked. Cley got a bear hug around the violently struggling package. The Morph punched her in the nose, and she punched back.

Cley felt a sickening swerve. 'What—'

Something yanked on them . . . The world dwindled dizzily – and they were flying.

It was as if immense objects swept through a high, vaulted space that they could see only in quilted, opalescent shades. An immense cathedral of perceptions speeded by. Passages yawned, beckoned, fell away. No gravity tugged at her, and then a huge force knocked the breath from her lungs, plunged her down and then jerked her aside; something shrieked – and was gone.

Cley shook her head. She felt herself floating. Seeker hung nearby, curled up. Shadows slid by. Ground came rushing up, branches of stubby trees – she snapped off pieces as she plunged, tumbling – and she hit. Hard.

She and Seeker were buried in shredded fronds, branches, and pancakes of fungi. Seeker snarled and snapped and thrashed.

Cley looked around. Purpling growths in a tangled gray-green forest shimmered in the vanilla glow. Light seeped from the ground, not from above. They had fallen through the spotty, lavender canopy that hovered above on snaky vines. Debris like helical fronds, fruit of their plunge, lay around them.

'What the—'

'Later.' Seeker spit out a vine it had attacked.

They got to their feet, checked, found no broken bones. It had been over an hour, by Cley's inboard time meter, yet they had seemed to fall only for frightened moments.

They got themselves in order. She had tears in her unisuit. Seeker, of course, never wore clothes; its fur was an elaborate signaling medium for its species, using codes no human was privileged to know. But the shiny coat was matted and fouled with fungi. It scraped away at its neck with a stick.

'I have wrenched my spine,' Seeker said calmly.

'Lie down. Here—'

'I shall work with myself.' It sat and with great care an extruded a tool from its paw and then inserted the point into its neck. Long silent moments passed as Seeker panted, eyes fixed, delicately carrying out a repair. Then it wriggled, jerked – and smiled. 'Done. Repaired.'

They stood amid tangled vegetation, light gleaming up from the hard ground. A persistent breeze sighed.

'What . . . happened?' Cley asked.

'Maybe we got sucked along when the Morph escaped from our space.'

'So where are we?'

'Ummm . . . This place has a curious curve to it,' Seeker said.

Cley looked at the forest rising to right and left, disappearing into an ivory mist overhead. A drop spattered in her eye from a frond overhead. 'We're in a bowl, I guess. Never mind the sightseeing – what *happened*?'

Seeker chuckled, showing pointed teeth. 'I do not know. My "sightseeing" is the only plausible way we shall answer your question. I do not see anyone who is likely to tell us what this place is.'

Seeker was the puzzle lover, Cley more practical; most archeo teams had such a balance. Cley decided to stick to the practical.

She studied the luminous ground. The light here seemed eternal, seeping through the odd, stony soil beneath them. The soil itself was like ground glass held together with translucent, moist webs. The twisted trees grew in the stuff.

A steady breeze stirred the canopy of limbs, fronds, leaves, and pads. The trees were strange: some rough, others smooth; impossible leaves, improbable branches. Small animals made rustling excursions nearby.

'Evolution finds its convergent ways,' Seeker whispered.

The air clung thick, moist, and milky as Cley drew in breaths. Carefully they explored back and forth along the 'axis' of the tubular forest, away from the upward curvature, but found no large clearings. This took hours, and they learned very little. They both wearied, and finally found some comfort in a bed made of the tree leaves.

'We knew something strange was afoot,' Seeker said, lounging back. It was always good at taking its ease when there was no point in not. 'Recall, one of the big symbols at the Library of Life site entrance was a huge seashell, beautifully shaped into a detailed spiral, of precious luster metal. Then that one day it disappeared. Sheared off from its mount, somehow. Mysterious. You were off exploring the Library's labyrinths days later, I recall, when it popped back into existence. I heard the sound, went running. No ordinary person returned it — the spiral just came back, its connection at the shear point flawless.'

Cley frowned, not getting it. 'I heard there was something funny, yes.'

'More than that. It had been lifted, I believe, out of our three-dimensional — three-D — space. When it returned, it was not quite the same.'

'A Morph took it?'

'The way you could pluck an ant off a sheet of glass.' Seeker gazed at Cley significantly. 'That same ant you could see from above, or below, just by lifting the glass over your head. From such a superior perspective, it will appear differently, yes?'

Cley's frown deepened. Another Seeker puzzle, one of their games with each other. The miasma of advanced physics. Seeker frowned.

Despite herself, Cley tried to live up to Seeker's standards. *Original* had to mean something, right? And how much *did* this beast know? Still, Cley did have a little mathematics, so: 'Ah, the spiral was backwards; that's it.'

'Indeed. None of us noticed it at first.'

Cley brightened. 'I see! Same as the ant on glass. If

you look at a spiral from below, it goes from right-handed to left-handed.'

Seeker looked proud of her – an odd expression, but Cley could read such nuances now. Seeker said carefully, 'I suppose the four-D Morphs took our spiral, passed it through our three-D universe, then pivoted it about their dimension. That left it reversed when they so kindly returned it to us.'

'As a warning?'

'The signature of the Morphs – had we read it right.'

'Which we didn't.'

'They showed us who they were, free of the constraints of language or symbols.'

'Polite – a calling card. But why did they attack us, steal the slabs?'

Seeker shrugged. 'We do not know that they were the Furies.'

'But from a higher dimension . . .'

'Which harbors many things. These morphs – could they be like us? They also study human origins? A mere glancing guess; I apologize.'

'Um. That would explain a lot . . . It's easy to think others aren't like us, just because they're mysterious. Maybe they'll give our slabs back.'

'Why do they not give *us* back?' Seeker's fur swirled in a pattern Cley could not read. 'I suspect our being dropped here was an incidental.'

'Sure didn't *feel* incidental.'

'This seems to be some sort of place between our three-D universe and their four-D one. We may have gotten sheared off into it, while the Morphs were passing through.'

'This place is *between* three-D and four-D?'

Seeker shrugged. 'I reason by analogy – a classic human trick, which I borrow frequently.'

'You're welcome.'

'Thieves do not offer thanks. Nor did our Morphs.'

'What's between dimensions?'

'A space contrived for passage? I do not know. If they have built a roadway between dimensions, perhaps this is the ditch beside that roadway. Forgive the analogy.' It tipped a claw to its forehead and laughed.

'So we're ditched?'

Seeker waved its hands broadly. Leathery and black, they were in their fully deployed posture, tapering to thin fingers of great delicacy. 'And perhaps our slabs are, too.'

'That Morph looked pretty agitated.'

'In a hurry to get back, it dropped us.'

'But *where?*'

'You humans made your reputation by pushing beyond the horizon. I suggest such a strategy here.'

'Huh? There *is* no horizon.'

'An axis, then.' Seeker pointed. 'A preferred direction.'

'Ummm . . . like a tube?'

'Somewhere in this odd world, there must be a place where the connection to our three-D universe gets manufactured. Not necessarily nearby, I suppose. The Third Fabricant era used quagma-driven geometric bridges for trade purposes – this seems a similar construct. We were inducted here by some curious property of the quagma, so I suppose.'

'Quagma? Sounds dangerous.'

'So is all of life. Something made us fall into this, some agency—'

'Or something that lives here.'

'Intelligent life seems unlikely in such a narrow place,' Seeker said distantly. 'Plants, at best.'

'Why? The Morphs have all our three dimensions, plus extra to play with.'

'Ummm. We are fond of carbon, thinking it the root of life. True enough – here, in ordinary three-D. But in four-D, there are more choices for molecules to make, ways to hook to each other. Carbon might take longer to form life-helping compounds.'

Cley shrugged. 'Sure, but there might be more available, too.'

'With that I cannot argue. Then there is the problem of what an intelligent organism might look like in four-D. In three-D the design is obvious . . .'

'Human?'

Seeker laughed. 'You tool users are all alike. No, you and I are both mere tubes. Body bags filled with modified seawater. Food goes in; waste gets pushed out. Not elegant, but it works – always. That is the basic design blessed by our three dimensions.'

'Ugh! I'd like to think we're more than that.'

'I am speaking of basic body design – nothing personal.' But Seeker grinned the mock-fiendish grimace that meant it was enjoying this – as usual, for mysterious reasons.

'What's a four-D tube look like, then?'

'They might well have a greater surface area for a given volume . . .' Seeker screwed up its long mouth, obviously trying to visualize. 'That ratio rises as dimension increases, I gather. Brain and heart – if they have one – could be kept deep inside, for safety, and digestion done on the outside.'

'A gut as outside skin? Ugh!'

'Ours are "outside" our bodies, too, geometrically – simply connected to our skins. Lying along a tube, tucked nicely in the middle, where we can't see them work.'

'That's how I like it.'

'I doubt the design emerged to satisfy our sensibilities.'

'What use would digestion on the outside be?'

'Easier flow of air and fluids,' Seeker said. 'One could treat "the runs," as you term them, directly, inspecting the tissues by eye.'

Cley tried to imagine this and failed. More immediate needs intervened. She sniffed, sampled, and finally, out of hunger, nibbled at some seeds they had found on bushes. Bland, but no bad effects. Pretty soon, she wished there were a lot more of them.

'I think we should determine the geometric properties of this place,' Seeker said decisively.

'How? Measurement?'

'Geometry is a global property, not local. We must travel.'

'Me, I'm more interested in finding some fresh water, getting a splash in the face, a drink.'

'I smell water upslope – there.'

Seeker led her a surprisingly short way to a dense clump – shadowed, moist. Bending over a pool, Seeker quickly fetched a fat fish-creature from the shallows and began eating. Fastidious, it carefully washed each piece of flesh before popping the morsel into its ample, black-rimmed mouth. The fish was a slim tube, a design forced by fluid mechanics and survival, no matter where.

Cley saw that the pool was a pond, curving up under

dense boughs. She stripped and plunged in. Luxury! Cool and sweet.

In the pool she watched Seeker disappear into the snaky mat, moving with surprising speed. The trunks warped behind it into a puckering pattern . . . almost, she thought, as though the things were enclosing and digesting Seeken . . .

No matter. She swam with splashing abandon.

When she came out, feeling far brisker, Seeker was gone.

'Damn!' She never quite got used to the ways of the bright animals. At least the ferrets didn't just disappear. You kept thinking of them as humanlike, but their greatest asset lay in their difference. Seeker needed time by itself, she guessed, and wanted to explore, so it just vanished, and might be gone for a moment or a month.

Cley sighed, feeling suddenly quite alone and cold and friendless. She would not have watched Seeker scamper away into the forest of purple-speckled, knotted trunks, and not then followed. Seeker knew that and, knowing the human propensity to argue, had simply evaporated.

Seeker had other ways of . . . well, of feeling. Cley studied the snarled growths all around her. They seemed to writhe like sluggish serpents, stirred by a breeze she could not feel . . . or else they moved on their own. She kept checking nervously behind her.

Silence. She shivered. Seeker never showed true fear – a talent she wished she could share. She suspected that the creature had accepted death in a way the fretful human mind could not. Ancient animals lived without such foreknowledge, or so the conventional wisdom went. Had their indifference, born of ignorance, somehow carried over into Seeker? Shaped from raccoon genetics, amplified and tuned in countless fashions, Seeker and its many companion hybrids carried a quality humans could not readily attain. Death was only one element in their thinking, not an ever-present background drone. Seeker seemed at times oblivious of danger, even in this frightening place, after nearly breaking its neck in a fall . . .

She stood gazing fruitlessly at the forest where Seeker had vanished. What now? Gauzy alabaster light seeped up from the glassy soil, casting vertical shadows . . . Though the forest seethed and fretted, it made none of the sounds she associated with vegetation – no sighing, creaking, swishes – except, she now heard, a deep, rolling bass note, at the limit of hearing, like a great, slow breath of some immense beast. The Morphs? Looking for them?

The thought made her wary, and she wished Seeker would reappear, where the slow, swaying pucker in front of her was smoothing out—

She jumped. Something had touched her shoulder.

'Interesting geometry,' Seeker said. It stood nonchalantly at the end of a claw track that led back into the forest behind her.

'What?!'

'I suspected that this was an odd place . . .'

'How'd you *do* that?'

Seeker grinned, stretching its black gums. 'I walked in what I thought was a straight line. But this is a cylinder we are in, my friend. I walked around the entire geometry and came back behind you.'

Cley looked up. 'Then above that fog . . .'

'There is more forest, yes. We could see it, if the air were ever clear here.'

'So it's a cylinder . . . How long?'

'Infinite, is my guess. Or maybe it curves around and connects back, eats its tail.'

'If this is just an extra tacked-on dimension, how come my hand is three-D?' Cley waved her hand at the forest. 'And these funny trees?'

'My suspicion – and remember, I am only going from zaps and the like – is that this is what is called a *brane,* wrapped around a one-dimensional space.'

Zaps were whole concept nuggets, electronically induced – constellations of ideas that could be imported into a mind, much as a book could be picked up, consulted, put down. Understanding the zap meant ruminating upon it, letting it get integrated with your own thinking. That took time, but much less than old-fashioned learning through the serial input of reading, or even through the parallel processors of eyes and ears through images. Still, if you didn't 'read your zaps,' you knew effectively nothing. Enough to get by at a dinner party with Supras, maybe, but no more.

'So we appear here as three-D things . . .'

'Because we can move in the brane that folds our three-D bodies into this added dimension.'

'Uhhhh . . .'

'We are in a "reduced space," as the jargon has it.'

'We're *wedged into* this four-D place?'

'In a curious fashion – and only a guess, remember. The Morphs must have known we could fit in this kind of halfway house of dimensionality.'

Cley flipped hair from her eyes, exasperated. 'But for what?'

'Because we could comprehend this way? I do not know.

Given the difficulties of broaching even simple ideas to the Morphs, I suggest we try to discover that ourselves.'

'Why didn't the damned Supras do all this?'

Seeker dipped its long nose. 'Exploration demands courage.'

'But they went out to the stars!'

'And came back, tails between legs.'

'You'd known more about tails than I would.'

Ferocious grin. 'Quite.'

'Um . . . So we've only got one way to go, right?'

'Along the one-D axis of this wrapped-around, three-D space, ummm, yes.' Seeker started that way.

It was a hard trudge. Rough ground, thick air. They foraged for berries, and Cley's stomach rumbled. Forest crowded in on them; at least there wasn't much under-brush. This seemed odd, since the light that apparently sustained these plants came from below. Cley wondered aloud about that, but for once, Seeker – who always seemed to have an answer, even if a bit wrong – just shrugged.

'We could be anywhere in this Tubeworld, right? I don't like the sound of that.'

'This is as roomy a puffed-up one-D world as we could expect,' Seeker said. 'Remember, we experience it through a sort of . . . transform.'

'That "brane"?'

'Short for *membrane,* I gather. Like a film at the edge of a higher-dimensional space.'

'I can't really see that.'

'Nor I – though I suspect this place allows us to perceive a more complex realm, in this tube. It may be like a subway between dimensions.'

'I hope it goes somewhere.'

Seeker nodded ruefully. 'Even so, it could be as long along the axis as our space is across — the radius of the universe entire.'

'You mean it's *infinite* going that way?' She pointed fore and aft along the axis, the two flat directions.

Seeker tut-tutted. '*Infinity* is a term promiscuously tossed about.'

'Okay, okay — large.'

'And note that the breeze always blows the same direction.'

'Right. I wonder if it wraps around this whole cylinder world.'

'Possibly. But what drives the wind?'

'A break somewhere?'

'A disturbance in the geometry? We can only guess. Ummm . . . the quagma could provide that break. It's fierce stuff.'

'Okay. But would it drive the air toward itself, or away?'

'I do not know. This is a three-D manifold, speaking mathematically. Not like the spaces we know. It wraps around an extra dimension, a complex brane, I do believe. I christen it Tubeworld.'

Cley laughed. 'Look, before we go all puffed up, founding new worlds or such, worry about this: If your Tubeworld really is light-years long, along this axis, then we'd *never* find the quagma that brought us here, that's doing all this.'

'Well, yes.'

A long silence. Then Cley said, 'Y'know, that spiral back at the Library . . . if we could use that ability, pop things in and out of the extra dimension . . .'

Seeker's eyes opened in agreeable surprise. 'Ah, interesting.'

'We could reverse the sense of rotation in molecules, make them act differently.'

'Excellent.' Seeker cupped its large, tapered head in a paw. 'There might be biological advantages. Some diseases are left-handed because that matches some of our molecules. If we could switch that sense in our bloodstreams, we would become immune.'

'Great – already we're doctors. Only we have to be sure the Morphs that live here don't kill us first.'

'I doubt they live here. This is a portal, no more.'

'Yeah, a *ditch*. The bastards who dumped us here—'

'May not have even noticed that we had been sucked along in their wake.'

'Even worse!'

Seeker found a comfortable soil and stretched out. 'To be unnoticed? I would think it a blessing, ordinarily.'

'Well, you don't think like a human!'

'That does seem to be a problem,' Seeker said lightly, and went to sleep.

4

The Fleshy Birds

Cley kept waking up in the diffuse pearly glow that oozed from the ground. It made her uneasy, and she wondered what made the light. What drove biological processes here? Were there stars, planets? Hidden offstage? If the Morphs made this, they had command of physics in an extra dimension, transcending everything she knew. Not that they were gods, no — she had wrestled with one in the tarp bag, felt its smooth strength jerk and struggle. But vastly strange, yes . . .

She lay awake and turned these questions over, and then heard odd sounds . . . growing louder . . . something coming.

Cley shook Seeker awake. Long reverberations came, building louder. They both stood up. Cley found a stick of satisfying heft to cover her unease.

The sounds seemed to come from all around. Cley discovered that if they turned perpendicular to the long one-D axis, their bodies amplified the vibrations. Rotating away, the sounds eased. Sound itself was polarized somehow. In their ears sounded a tortured *strooooonnng* that repeated like the beats of a slow, thick heart, its pulses refracted and stretched. She did not like them.

Above the twisted trees, beneath the persistent pearly fog, came a great, flapping shape.

There were no feathers. Instead the dull reddish skin looked like the meat of some undersea creature. Cley thought of historical sensos she'd taken in, of long-ago manta rays, gliding through ancient seas with slow strokes of menace. This thing was larger than any bird she had ever seen. It was at the bottom of a swoop. As it neared them, it coasted back up a lazy, long parabola, disappearing into the mists.

'It's not dangerous, is it?' Cley asked.

'Did you notice the curved talons on the ends of those wings?'

'Yup. Just looking for reassurance.'

'I offer none.'

Another of the things dipped into view, rose away. The echoing, eerie *strooooonnng, strooooonnng* got thicker, louder.

Abruptly one came again, this time plunging along a deeper curve. Its maroon flesh was now livid with red stripes, as though it was excited. It wheeled above the nearby trees and plunged abruptly — toward them.

Seeker dodged away, but too late. The talons caught in its fur, and the thing lofted Seeker up, disappearing with a single flap of its meaty wings, into the fog ceiling above. Cley could hear nothing. Her heart pounded, and breath rasped in her throat. She crouched against a thick tree. Another of the strange birds dipped below the misty deck, glided, went back up.

Strooooonnng! Abruptly one appeared again through the fog deck — and Seeker was with it. But now Seeker had its claws dug into the underbelly of the fleshy bird. They wrestled together in air, descending rapidly toward the treetops. Seeker snarled loudly, and a strangled *strooooonnng* came from the vent slits where the creature's wings joined the tubular body. the creature thrashed, trying to shake itself free. With a shrill, angry cry Seeker leaped away from it, grabbing for a nearby branch — missed — and fell through to the next branch . . . and another . . . finally got a hold.

The bird-thing flapped away, sending a harsh, ragged *Strooooonnng!* as it labored up into the mist.

Seeker was in no better mood when it climbed down the crusty bark and slumped, sprawling. 'I believe I have learned something,' it said, wheezing.

'I'd love to know what.'

'Attack when it approaches. Use a sharp stick. Also, I understand something of the geometry here.'

'You learned that while it was *carrying you away*?' Cley chuckled; Seeker never ceased to amaze her.

'The flyer goes upward because gravity is lesser there. It lifted me to a curious place where the fog cleared and the breeze was strong — and we were weightless.'

'How'd you get away from its talons?'

'I used the weightlessness. Easy to turn, use the hindlegs. Gouged its eyes; it has four.'

Cley thought she saw the point. 'No grav at the center. So we're inside a *rotating* cylinder?'

'I thought as much, at first. But remember, this is another dimension, not a mere artifact.'

'So gravity goes away at the center of this, well, cylinder, because . . . ?'

'Some sort of symmetry principle at work, I would wager.' Seeker checked itself over, rubbing and licking its pelt.

Cley yawned and looked around uneasily. So far there was no night here, making surprise less easy, but sleep harder. 'Those birds couldn't be the smartest thing in here, I suppose?'

'No. Something rather smarter must have made this place. It has access to this curled-up extra dimension, and ours as well.'

'Then something's here, and it's really a full four-D creature? How'll we recognize it?'

'I suspect it will be a morph form that manifests in this geometry as more cylindrical, to match the boundary conditions.'

Cley blinked. 'You were once a mathist, weren't you?'

'All procyons are, as children.'

'I didn't learn words like "symmetry principle." Mathists do.'

'Labels are limiting.'

'Aha! Thought so.'

'I suspect that whatever rules here will be a denizen of a dimension we cannot know – and larger than a bird.'

'Somehow I don't find that reassuring, friend.'

When they next woke up, Cley's fears surfaced again. They had been through a lot, and still Seeker seemed unfazed. Maybe it helped, being a mathist.

More immediately, Cley wondered how they could find something to eat. Even Seeker – who seldom seemed victim to the needs of the flesh, unless it wished to be – had a rumbling stomach as it slept. They got up and found yellow seeds hanging like teardrops from the vines. A tiny sample proved tasty and smelled right, so they indulged.

'Should we wait for the smart Morphs to make a move?'

Seeker shook its thick head. 'Maybe they have lost us.

The intermittent nature of their appearances argues that they do not control the interdimensional access very well.'

'Maybe we should light a fire, or something.'

'Visibility is very short through this fog – though I expect they can see us, if they have overcome the problem of looking down into lesser dimensions. And if they bother.'

'There's some disadvantage to having an extra dimension?'

'Hyperseeing,' Seeker said. 'They see both more and less. First there is the difficulty that for us, light oscillates in a plane and moves forward in the third dimension. In four dimensions, light must oscillate in all three dimensions, then move along a fourth. That makes three-D light hard for a four-D being to sense.'

'Good. I'd just as soon that we're invisible to them.'

'Not so now. They found us in our three-D universe, so they have overcome that problem. Perhaps they have stripped away one of the three directions, so they get a sort of edited version of our light.'

'So they can see, but less than we do?'

'More, I suspect. When we look at a two-D painting, we see everything in it from one viewpoint. A four-D creature can then see everything in a three-D scene, without moving viewpoint.'

'I can't visualize that.'

'Not in three-D, no. But suppose you go to an art exhibit to see a sculpture of, say, a Supra woman. There are ten copies of it, each one rotated a bit, standing against a wall. You stand in one place and can look at the entire Supra without moving.'

'*You* went to an art gallery?' Seeker had always seemed

distantly bemused by human amusements and interests.

'You are surprised? I saw such a sculpture and did not recognize the ten different angles as being the same object.'

'Really? You're losing your air of omniscience.'

'Good. I am but a three-D creature, just as you.'

5

Taking Flight

They hiked on farther, with nothing to show for it. The forest just kept repeating itself, long after it had made its point, as though it just might be infinitely long. It seemed to be made of living modules, as if churned out by a living factory somewhere. The oddity of a one-D add-on to three-D — pasted in, somehow, with space-time glue a mathist would admire, and still being nonetheless infinite — well, it not did not seem amusing to her, not after hours of picking their way through the thick, thorny growths.

Plodding along, hypnotized by the routine, Cley dimly noticed sounds coming closer. And an utter quiet between the notes. Deep bass moans, as if from a huge throat, vaguely familiar . . . She had heard that before. 'Morphs!'

She ran and ducked under a grove of trees. Seeker scampered after. The long, pealing notes got louder. Nothing appeared below the mist level. Louder . . .

'Should we signal to them?' Cley whispered.

Seeker cocked its head, listening intently. 'They may be looking for us, yes — but why? To carry us fully into their four-D universe?'

'Don't think I'm up for that.'

'Nor I. It would be good to recover the history slabs, if we could.'

'If the morphs mean to give them back, sure.' The throbbing notes were louder, like a presence in the air above them.

Seeker said, 'I vote for staying silent.'

'Um. Me, too.'

The long pulses seemed to press down on them in stretching waves – ominous, unending. Were they hovering above? Cley felt a sudden impulse to shout, 'Go away!' It was unbearable.

Dead silence.

This was worse. They studied the slow seethe of fog . . . Nothing.

'Think they spotted us?' Cley whispered.

'I do not think when there is no point to it.'

'Meaning?'

'Best to wait.' The silence around them was unnatural, no animals stirring, nothing. Cley stood alert, nerves strumming. Sleeper curled itself around a tree trunk, looking like a thick fur collar at its base.

'You're going to *sleep*?'

'And you are not.'

Which is what happened. Cley could not even doze in the silence. At least Seeker did not snore. When it did awake, the woods had returned to normal. Small scurrying noises came from the ragged brush. A breeze wafted by again. They marched on.

The humidity seemed worse. Heavy drops smacked onto their heads until she made frond hats for them both. Seeker thought of an experiment and got her to bark out short, high-pitched shouts; its throat was not loud enough, it said. Then they stood and listened to a faint whisper of her voice from the opposite direction.

'Wrapping around the cylinder,' Cley guessed. Seeker had timed them, and also knew how far it had gone to circumnavigate the cylinder. From the time interval they got a rough number for the velocity of sound. It was about half of Earth-normal.

Cley nodded. 'Interesting, but so what?'

'We should gather information and then see if it is useful. At least we know why the birds could fly so well: thicker air.'

They had seen a few more of the manta-birds dipping down through the mist, but none attacked. Cley resumed foraging. The ruby-colored berries were getting quite tedious as her sole fare, which Seeker supplemented with small animals it caught and devoured raw. Cley stopped and stood still. 'Wait, we've been stupid.'

Seeker was on the hunt and did not reply. 'We should be flying, too!' she shouted.

It took another round of sleep-trudge-sleep before they found what Cley wanted.

The spire of luminous rock was like other outcroppings they had encountered, but larger. More to the point, taller. Crystal Crag, Cley named it. Seeker laughed. 'How human, to give a label.'

Seeker laughed again at the large fronds Cley collected, but helped stitch them together with thread made from the tough vines. Cley found some bamboolike trees and used the slim trunks cross-lashed together. The fronds held up well as she fitted them to the frame. The labor tired her and took a 'day' – meaning until her eyelids began to droop. They were both losing weight as well as strength here, too.

Deftly Seeker twisted oily branches and gnawed them off. Cley's embedded tools, extended from her forefingers, proved useful in getting the high-stress connections firmly knitted.

They climbed the rocky spire with care. She could feel gravity weakening as they rose, an odd but welcome sensation. The peak had a rounded, polished crown that made footing tricky. Mist roiled and churned above it.

'No room to get a running start,' Cley said.

'We would find that awkward anyway,' Seeker said, 'being of unequal height.' Though Seeker could stand on two feet, it liked to run on all fours, with its hands foreshortened into the ancient, simple paws.

'I'm glad we thought to put in the handholds.' She fitted her fingers into the tight, glovelike sleeves made of bark. Those had taken nearly as much time to make as the whole wing.

'You are hesitating.'

'Yup. If we fall . . .'

'We will not. Notice that there is a steady updraft from the warmer rocks below.'

'We primates have a big thing about falling.'

Seeker grinned, tongue lolling. 'Time to overcome your origins.'

'Hey, your origins were in our labs.'

'Do not remind me.'

Without another word they got into position. A few seconds' pause, silent . . . then together they took three short steps off the crown. The first moment was the worst — falling, the fronds filling with a rattle, but no lift. Then they caught a current and slowly leveled off. But no better — the mist still hovered just above their heads. And her arms were starting to feel the ache already.

'Left,' Seeker said.

She leaned that way, and their glider canted. Lurched. Fell a little. Treetops zoomed by below their heels.

'If we tip—'

'More left.'

They veered farther over. The fronds protested with clatters. She jerked them farther over . . .

A glance down. Snaggy branches and some cushioning fronds . . . a long way down. If they lost it, started to tumble, best to kick away, curl up—

An ominous splintering crack.

And the left wing came up.

An updraft caught them strongly, boosting them into the mist. Fog everywhere. Now she had no way to judge direction. She was almost grateful for the gathering ache in her arms, because it told her which way was down. Wind whistled around them, churned in her hair. The wing shook, veered, rattled, righted itself in churning currents. A moist tang filled her dry mouth.

Then – light. Dim but clear. They soared above the mist, trailing streamers of it. The turbulence sighed away.

Her arm aches vanished. No weight. She felt giddy, though her stomach still refused to stop clenching.

'We're at the center,' she said.

'I knew it would work.'

'Glad you did. I kinda lost my faith back there.'

'I never doubted you.'

'I was worried about the laws of this Tubeworld of yours. Whether we had guessed right.'

'It was no guess.' Seeker freed one paw and made a

show of stretching its hind legs behind it. Yawned. Stretched. 'Though ingenious, your idea, yes. I should have thought of it myself. Here we sit at the center of a barrel made of mist, in no gravity, comfortable. We move with the wind and so feel no breeze.'

'And to think how we plodded along for days.'

'I would rather not.'

6

Quagma

They had brought food, but not enough.

As Seeker had put it, how to plan for a trip that in principle might be quasi-infinite? They ran out after two days (as Cley's thumbnail inboard reported). Water they got by slurping up rivulets that condensed and trickled off the wings into the slipstream.

There were problems they had not considered. Defecating in zero g was a source of great amusement for Seeker and some embarrassment for Cley. Luckily, she had thought to make a vine rope when they were building it. This she spooled out until she trailed behind the glider. Tying it to one hand, she managed — barely.

Seeker was not so fastidious. It even invented a sort of water-skiing sport with the rope. When its spread legs gathered in enough of the vagrant currents that wafted in the wake of the glider, it could artfully swoop from side to side, cackling with glee, even giving forth a whoop utterly unlike anything a true, ancient raccoon had ever made. Only when its sideways momentum started rocking the entire glider did Cley yell at it. Seeker urged her to try the stunt, but she did not — until she was taking a pee in the wake and got blown to one side, then had to air-skate in zero g to get back onto the glider. She pretended that it was all intentional.

They began to wonder how they would know they had reached anything of interest. If the fog remained in its curious cylindrical wedge, they could glide over what they sought. And what *did* they seek? Seeker's best guess was some research station where the quagma-generated geometric gate would stand.

But how big? Would it poke up above the mist?

They kept steady watch, relieving each other in unconscious imitation of the Ancients who crewed the ships that sailed through foggy oceans. Nothing whatever jutted above the mist tunnel. In a way this was good, since they could easily have crashed into an obstacle. The glider held together, but Cley had no illusions about its ability to maneuver, or survive a solid smack.

They saw the meaty birds now and then. The creatures gave off their brooding *strooooonnng, strooooonnng*s well before coming into view, and slowly overtook the glider. How they fed was never clear. Seeker became alarmed when the first of them flapped stolidly within a few lengths of the glider. It braced itself against the struts, claws out – and the bird labored past, scarcely giving them a glance. So did all the others. Apparently, they hunted ground animals – quite large ones, to judge from the immediate attack on Seeker – but considered anything flying in the weightless tunnel not fair game.

'Maybe they never saw anything else up here before,' Cley guessed.

'I doubt so easy a niche would go uncontested,' Seeker said.

A while later she did see a smaller bird scoot up into the wind tunnel – as she thought of it – and dart around. Their glider startled it, and with wildly flapping wings it ducked back into the fog. Now that she listened carefully, she occasionally caught distant squawks and even one odd, strangled cry coming up through the clotted mists. She also wondered why the light here was not much weaker, since they were farther from the ground, but then realized that they got light from the entire Tubeworld perimeter. She and Seeker listened in their utterly quiet glide, getting hungry.

Seeker was puzzled that it had not seen more of the life below in their hiking. 'We smell strange to them, I am sure, inducing silence in the local life as we go.'

The mutual sense of strangeness grew. A somber alien feeling came stealing into Cley's thoughts: the pressing sense of doom here. The featureless fog gave her the sensation of plunging down through an infinite cylinder, confusing her inner ear and bringing momentary bouts of stomach-churning nausea. She learned to swallow back her bile.

Seeker became uneasy as well. This led it to wonder aloud if they might indeed have set out upon an infinite journey, blown by winds that never ceased, circumnavigating the entire three-D universe in this tacked-on Tubeworld. An idiot's odyssey.

Long ago the Ancients had realized that the full universe had many dimensions, Cley remembered dimly. Arguments about mathematical symmetry and beauty had decided the issue for the physicists. Seeker wryly remarked that this all came from a primate preference, that the mathematical elegance of the resulting cosmology was 'too beautiful not to be true.'

But where were all the extra dimensions? All but three of space and one of time were 'rolled up' like tiny scrolls.

They had been since the first few shaved seconds of the Origin, the grand emergence of space and time together in one creation.

Curled up, they could not be sensed, even by delicate experiments. Wave one's hand and it passed through several unseen microdimensions, with no consequence. In ordinary life, the bonus dimensions meant nothing at all. But rolled up to what size? Far smaller than the diameter of an atom, or otherwise the dimensions would show up in the visible spectra that atoms emitted and eyes saw. The span of a single electron was vast compared with the realm where the extra dimensions lay hidden, sleeping.

All this seemed like abstract fictions to Cley, even when Seeker had explained that the idea had led to mathematics that nicely packaged up the fundamental forces, starting with gravity. In theory, the forces then all emerged 'naturally' – for the mathematically minded. To Cley, this had verged on the theological . . . until she had seen her first Morph.

But even those ancient mathists had not envisioned a place like this Tubeworld, a dimension simultaneously near infinite along its cylindrical length, but small enough across to walk around in an hour. So much for theory.

Apparently, the Morphs had made this place as a sort of construction shack. Seeker tried to explain why, speaking in four-D, but it just got Cley more confused.

The sounds from ahead were almost a relief.

Their ghostly glide turned to surges – building fast, slamming them back and forth, making Seeker grab for its grips. A high, keening *shreeeee* pierced the murk ahead and alarmed Cley. It sounded like a buzz saw meeting something it did not like.

'What's that?'

'The sink for this wind,' Seeker said, holding on. 'I hope.'

The idea of a place where the wind went was unsettling. Their wings rattled and wrenched. To Cley they looked suddenly frail.

The vapor around them began to back away, the ivory tunnel they had plunged through for days now opening like a throat into . . . what?

Suddenly, the mists fell away to all sides, and they shot forward into a lava red chamber. The distant walls glared white-hot. Yellow tongues forked, crackling across the entire expanse, and slammed into the walls with eerie blue-green explosions.

'The quagma factory!' Seeker called over the sudden din – sizzles, roars, percussive blows.

'Where'll we go?' Cley called.

There were winds now, sudden gales that buffeted them. They plunged, recovered. Sagged. Slewed. Cley barely held on. No gravity, but plenty of vagrant, blunt forces. Grasping surges, pulling like smooth hands . . .

Her shoulders ached, wrists popped . . . and on top of it, she was *hungry*. And getting irritable. *One should face one's fate well fed!*

Seeker was swaying like a punching bag, its claws embedded in a bamboolike beam. 'Let us – try to – stay in the – middle.'

They were still streaming down the center bore of this place, but now heat pasted into her face like a slap. And ahead was something turning, revolving about a slow, canted axis. It was a ruddy-brown worm, steaming, spinning, livid with spots of ruby radiance from within.

Cley called, 'What's – that . . . ?'

'A big life form – too big to evolve here . . . must be – one of the engineers.'

'The bastards who dumped us here!' Cley gasped. Her hands locked painfully in their gloves. She was terrified, panting, hot.

At their left a pore grew out of the wall. Sickly white, oily, glistening. It thrust up toward them. Fumes blew off it into her face and bit with acidic pain in her nostrils. Like a swollen wound it ripened. She looked ahead, and the ruddy worm was closer, twisting, much closer, closing with them. Long drum-roll beats surged through the liquid-thick air.

'I cannot tell – if this is – what quagma – would be like—' Seeker was struggling to hold on.

The thing like a pore was almost touching them now, still growing, giving off a fierce heat. Her skin shouted with pain, sizzled, broiling—

A hole opened in the pore. Inside was a dark, sullen blue. The throat of the thing opened like a livid mouth. Greedy.

She screamed. Seeker shouted, but she could not tell what it said. Forces stretched her. Her legs shrieked. Her shoulder joints popped.

Then the pore swallowed them . . .

The Black Brane

. . . and they shot through into blue spaces of sudden, chilling cool . . .

. . . tumbled, twirled about an unseen axis . . .

The struts beside her splintered, popping away. The wing crumbled . . .

. . . and she fell onto a hard black surface. She rolled, gasped, and the air was cool, but *where was Seeker*? – and then Seeker fell on her.

They untangled themselves, got their breath . . . and stared up at a vast ebony roof seething with rivulets of ivory glow.

'Black branes?' Seeker said. 'Perhaps . . .'

'Which . . . are?'

'Sheets of space-time. They can wrap around the hidden, tiny dimensions – those for which creation had no true use.'

'Except to build things like *that*?'

'Point taken. This black brane is expanded, like this tubular dimension itself. We are seeing the infinitesimal exploded into the . . .'

Words seemed to have failed Seeker. 'The monstrous, how about?'

It gazed in openmouthed wonder. 'True enough.'

'A kernel of truth puffed up into chunks of trouble?'

Cley tried to remember what Seeker had said in their long days of cruising. It had been hard staying awake, even though their lives might depend on doing so. 'Things that work like black holes, but with dimensions anchored on them?'

Seeker stood erect on two legs, somber, gazing upward. 'Or so the ancient theorists believed. These are membranes, cloaking the universe's squandering of dimensions . . .' Its voice trailed off.

In a way it was comforting to see Seeker truly impressed. Sometimes she wondered if it had seen everything before. Not this time.

Something was making her dizzy, and it wasn't just the ideas. 'You said . . . back there . . . quagma.'

She sat down hard. Rough bumps in the stony stuff that supported them – against a light gravity, she noted abstractly – rasped at her palms. She inhaled the hot, dry air – but at least it was breathable. The thing above might well be the primordial stuff from which God twisted Everything, but she needed a rest.

She hung her head between her knees and breathed steadily, easily, trying to get some equilibrium in all this. Her heart was pounding, nostrils distended. The air stung. And she admitted to herself that she was terrified.

Seeker began speaking, its voice trembling just a bit. She realized that it was trying to wrap some thin, tattered logic around what was happening. Any world was less frightening if some fraction of it made sense. Seeker spoke, words like balm . . . and she felt her pulse gradually slow. She even began to comprehend some of what Seeker was saying. Or she took some comfort from believing that she did . . .

Quagma: Everything had once been all seethe and jostle, at the universe's birth. Heat beyond any human sense of what that short word could possibly mean – it had burst into space-time in a magma of quarks, tiny particles that supped of all the fundamental forces at once. In that infinitesimal era the fundamentals were one, and that superforce could do anything – even alter the balance between the vagrant forces, shape them to a will that could command quagma.

So quagma was the Stuff of All. To master it – to conjure it up for a similar infinitesimal tick of time – gave the power to redesign some wedge of space-time. To make dimensions snake and blur and coil – space-time spaghetti cooked to order. Fuzzy space-time could be knit, sauce added – and all done, perhaps, by a form of life as it dwelled in dimensions that were themselves subject to negotiation.

Or so she gathered. It was all a bit much: terms tossed in as though Seeker knew realms she could not glimpse. Well, maybe it did. The airy spaces of theory were not her proper province.

And she was so hungry . . .

She said, 'So . . . this is where something from four-D makes a connection . . .'

'To our universe. This curious little microcosm of modified one-D space, our Tubeworld, is a way station of sorts.'

'An easier way into three-D?'

'A guess, no more. One would need to ask those who are doing all this.'

'The quagma engineers? That huge, ugly brown thing we saw – that was one of them?'

'Seemingly.'

'*Why* are they doing it?'

'Resources? Exploration? Those are the traditional motives of expansionist species such as yours.'

'Not like yours?'

'My kind are artifacts. I – *look*—'

Something had come into the space here, without entering. It simply appeared – a writhing blob of fleshy reds and pinks and salmons, turning like a greasy art object . . . and reeking.

Cley wrinkled her nose at the queer aroma that came in sour waves from the thing. 'Hey – I've smelled this kind before.'

'I trust it is not harmful.'

'You trust – it looks like death warmed over.'

'Who would warm it over? Oh, I see, a verbal mannerism.'

'What *is* it?'

'I do not know. Remember that this thing can see whatever we do, from any angle.'

'I wasn't going to attack it.'

'Wise.'

With the black brane hanging above, fuming, this new element seemed just one more entry in the weirdness ledger. Then the thing jittered with fevered energy. As if restless.

In quick flash-images she saw: purple-green limbs and folds, oozing into glassy struts – elongating, then splitting into red smoke. Leathery oblongs and polyhedrons folded over each other. Twinkling, jarring slices of hard actinic light poked through them. And it all moved as though blurred by slices of time into a jostling hurry . . .

'We are seeing some aspect of the true, larger four-D,' Seeker said, voice slow with wonder.

'But we still have three-D eyes.'

'I fear this is why none of it makes sense to us.'

She thought about a two-D being suddenly moving through their own three-D world, seeing only cross sections of trees and rocks and moving cars . . . and trying to stitch it into a coherent view. It could make a two-D symbol or picture, and Cley could understand it as a flat scene. But for the two-D creature it would be the whole object, not just a photograph.

So it now was for her, maybe? Sensing these things moving past and not getting how they fitted together into something extending away, in another direction the eye could not see. But maybe the mind could glimpse . . .

'Listen,' Seeker said.

A strange symphony of booms and clatters and screeches came from the air all around them. Seeker covered its ears. 'We are getting the sounds as they are in four-D, where the waves spread out in a different way, in packets and eddies.'

Cley waved her arms in frustration – the only thing she could think to do. The deeply resonant vibrations were even coming from *inside* her. 'Ah! Ah!' *Playing* her.

'I do not think these waves are harmful.'

'It's like something speaking in my guts!'

'Music? A voice? We must find a way to speak back.'

Cley was still sitting beneath the black canopy, afraid to stand up. 'Look – if Morphs can see us entirely, inside and out, steaming guts and all – well, maybe they'll notice my whole body getting involved. Inside and out.'

She got up – and whirled, tumbled, capered, feeling

like a mad dancer, working off her frustrations. Singing her lungs out, the way she had done so long ago in her Meta. It felt glorious . . . and left her panting – until something caught her eye.

A rippling fleshy knob floated near her. She wondered if *near* meant anything now. Gingerly she reached out toward it and felt only air . . . but in her vision her arm telescoped away, growing long and thin – dwindling into the distance down an impossibly long perspective.

The knob grew, flexed, reddened. She reached again – and connected. *To reach across dimensions . . .*

A slick, warm surface. Smooth turning to sticky as she moved her hand down that long tunnel of perspective. Blue spikes poked through the knob's 'skin' as though they grew from it. Hair? She fingered the spikes – hard, hot, strumming with long, low notes like a church organ – but she could only feel these swelling hums, not hear them.

'You may be feeling its . . . bones,' Seeker said delicately.

'Ooog. I wonder if it minds.'

'When you walk down a street, do you mind if a shadow falls over you? It is a two-D intrusion, of a sort.'

'Look, if this is one of the things that jerked us out of our space, made us do all this, damn near killed us—'

'You wish to be at least understood by it.' Seeker nodded, walking at a stately pace around the strange display, treating it as an art object. But its fur bristled with excitement, too.

'I'm not sure what I want. Maybe . . . payback.'

'I share your dislike of being treated so casually.'

The oily colors reeked like old mausoleums – then,

suddenly, of salty air. None of this made any sense. But then, maybe it couldn't. She was a flitting shadow in somebody else's world. How could she talk to shadows, anyhow? Or imagine fearing them? 'If I ever get a chance, damn it . . .'

'I agree. Let us act back upon it.'

'But how?'

'Precisely. I am not feeling terribly powerful at the moment.'

Overhead, the ominous darkness descended.

Sparks and helical neon-bright fibers shot through the air.

Cley crouched, cringed.

'It must be benign,' Seeker said, its composure getting thin. 'Else it would not have arranged these bare amenities. Air we can breathe — though a bit thick and dry — and heat we can withstand.'

'Me, I'd prefer to be left alone.'

She knew she and Seeker were carrying on a semblance of a conversation — because to talk was the only human thing in this utterly alien place. There had been so much strangeness for so long, she felt consumed by it, encased in a universe beyond human ken entirely, gyrating to its own bizarre laws. And she was *hungry* . . .

'I sense some change coming,' Seeker said. The air shot through with bright color. The plastic-slick, sour-smelling blobs and sticks that drifted in the space between them and the inky-black brane became dense, fibrous, as though drawing nearer.

Pop! 'Hey, the history slabs!' Cley picked them up where they had clattered on the stony black sheet at her feet. 'It's brought them back.'

The black brane was very close now, radiating a crisp, hard heat . . .

. . . a sudden stretching sensation, a sidewise lurch . . .

. . . *pop* . . .

. . . and they were standing on sand.

She lost her balance, hit, rolled. The slick blobs were everywhere, churning, churning. But beyond them . . . 'Look!'

Mountains, blue and snow-topped. She recognized them: the valley of the Library of Life. 'They put us back.'

She sucked in cool air, fragrant, wonderful. Nearby was a branch excavation of the Library. Nobody was around, but the gear was out and working, most of it automatic. They were a reasonable walk from where they had started, and it seemed to be midday. She wondered how long they had been gone. Did time tick forward at the same rate in higher dimensions?

If the universe had only one dimension of time, that meant it was shared, even among higher dimensions. But if there were two, or even more, *time* dimensions . . .

She shook her head. Enough.

Morphs danced in the air. Murmured, droned.

Seeker nodded. 'I would like to get them to stay until we can profit from this experience.'

She laughed crazily, decompressing. 'Profit enough, just staying alive.'

'Nonetheless . . .' Seeker twisted its muzzle in thought. It walked over to the excavation equipment. It stretched up, found a tray of instruments. The four-D Morph blobs and sticks were cascading around them with their slick plastic reds and pinks, white strands weaving. Some followed Seeker; the rest stayed with her. They made her uneasy.

Seeker selected a long, deeply curved tool, a horseshoe arch with one sharp, forked tip. It surveyed the variously shaped blobs for a long moment, then seemed to find what it was looking for. A glossy ring-shaped Morph floated near Cley, pulsing gently. Seeker turned with a quick, deft move and plunged the tool with delicate precision through the hole in the Morph's center. It turned with a quick, deft move and plunged the tool directly through the nearest blob.

Chaos among the four-Ds. Seeker batted away one stick and stepped back to survey its work. Carefully Seeker pushed both ends of the tool into the sand, securing the morph. The blob fluttered and distended. It warped into a rosy plate, then a tube, then a teardrop. Moaning, it eased up the shaft and down the other side of the curve. But its path was blocked there. It oozed around to one side of the tool shaft, then another — but could not break free.

Its companions whirled in a cyclone frenzy. They imploded suddenly, grouping around the anchored blob. Though they strained at it, the shaft would not come free of the hard desert earth.

'I suggest we find help,' Seeker said. It set off at a lope. 'We must arrange some more permanent way to trap this portion of the four-D Morph in our dimension.'

Cley ran after the procyon. After days in zero g the solid slap of shoes on soil was a pleasure. 'How come the Morphs can't get the shaft out?'

'I do not know. But a needle can trap a finger in two-D, so . . .'

'What? You did that on pure hunch?'

'Yes. That surprises you?'

Cley shook her head, grinning in disbelief. 'They might've killed you.'

'The four-D society must want this connection. I doubted that they would act harshly, once they understood things.'

'Um. Big gamble, Seeker After Patterns.'

'They have risked our lives already, then saved us – only to dispatch us? I thought not.'

As if in testimony, a company of wheeling, floating teardrops and sticks followed them. Cley looked back; the blob was still pinned. 'You anchored it in three-D. Like getting your three-D hand stuck on two-D sticky paper.'

'Let us be of speed, to think further. They may devise a way to free that portion of the Morph.'

'So "they" isn't quite right – it's one thing?'

'I surmise. Though how can we tell? We have inadequate eyes.'

She thought it through as she gave herself over to the pure pleasure of running in fresh, clean air, unsullied by dimensional ambiguities. Yes, the dimensionally destitute humans in three-D could not see the dimension above. They had to use a basically two-D retina, even if it was in a spherical eyeball, to process light – then reconstitute in their brains the three-D world. A four-D morph must have a three-D eye, then, she reasoned. A sphere that provided the same service, to image the four-D world. Then one more dimension up, a five-D being needed a hypersphere to see its world.

To her surprise, riding on her elation, she was beginning to think the way that Seeker could. She could *intuit* four-D, even if she couldn't see it. Yet.

Meanwhile, Seeker was barking with pleasure as it trotted.

It batted away a floating stick, which dutifully bobbed away, then came back to hover. Surrealistic bees, in pink and white . . .

'Think of what a four-D mind could tell us!' Seeker said. 'Truths about our space we could never guess, any more than an ant crossing a table knows that a human is doing calculus there.'

Cley said, 'If they care to bother.'

'Why else would the morphs make that incursion into the rolled-up microuniverse, a tube that size? An experiment! All in aid of getting through to us. Travel among dimensions is not easy – that we have learned the hard way, from this journey.'

'Maybe we should keep it that way.'

'There is no going back from this!'

Cley laughed. Seeker never got this enthusiastic. It was rebounding from the long days of fear, though Seeker would not, of course, admit it. 'Suppose there really were a Flatland for two-D beings – what we could tell them! We would be fascinated, too.'

They were nearing a clump of workers, who looked up, puzzled.

'We could get the same richness, literally beyond conception,' Seeker said, 'Would that we could talk to the four-Ds.'

Cley laughed again. Home, and already thinking about fresh horizons. *Ah!* Rapture in full three-D.

IV
The Malign

Damn the solar system. Bad light; planets too distant; pestered with comets; feeble contrivance; could make a better myself. —Lord Jeffrey

1

The Multifold

Fanak made much of their excursion into the Tubeworld. 'This is a powerful clue,' he said earnestly. 'Powerful. That they would take *you* – it must mean something.'

Cley looked across Fanak's workplane, which floated around him in his airy vault. She was trying to read his expression, which was generally a bland blankness. That 'take *you*' – did it mean, why would anybody bother with an Original and an animal? Or was she being self-conscious again?

Probably neither. Supras implied tons of things she never glimpsed. In this moody, hollow room it was easy to misread. She felt hushed masses above her here, deep in the shadowed halls of the Library. Fanak was the most erudite of the Supras she knew, so she went to him first with her story. And he had paid more attention to her at that party . . . which she could hardly remember . . . 'Maybe not. We were outside, easily found. Maybe they were just feeling their way.'

Fanak frowned and got up to pace. His workplane followed, passing through Cley and her chair and reforming on the other side. It seemed to show an ancient map of Earth from the era of human emergence, before the continents merged for the second time. Just incidentally, its glow highlighted the bony planes of Fanak's face from below, lending him an added gravity. When he cast a glance to the side, it lit that portion of its display and focused light appealingly around the rest of the huge room. 'Ummm. Still, every clue is vital.'

'I don't think this Tubeworld we went to was, well, ancient.'

He swerved, pinning her with his gaze. 'How could you know?'

'Well, I don't, not for sure, but . . .'

'This is all quite mysterious.' Impatiently he resumed pacing. The obedient workplane followed, lighting objects as he passed, following the direction of his glance. 'We have all been deriving all substance possible from the ancients. Not that they were clear! The Third Fabricants knew higher dimensional cultures and dealt with them. Clearly. That seems to have intersected in the same era with the building of the Multifold – though just what that name implies is also mysterious. I believe it was a collaboration between humanity and a – there must be many! – extradimensional culture.'

'How many dimensions is the Multifold, then?' Cley liked Fanak's directness, his intensity, and a lot else. She knew how to coax a conversation along, even when she did not really understand much of it. Originals picked up such skills.

'Um . . . more than our three spatials.'

He seemed cautious. 'And?'

'There is a hint, in a single frame-text, of an extra time dimension.'

'How could there . . . ?'

'Exactly. Two times? A difficult conceptual landscape.'

He was wearing an artfully made robe that revealed his body in momentary, tantalizing glimpses. His restless pacing made his muscular calves bunch in a pleasing way. She got up and walked toward the other side of his huge quarters. Glancing up at a movement, she saw that she stood beneath sculpted ceilings that told a complex tale in moving figures. The room seemed to demand attention. Information swirled in the walls. And Fanak paced. His workplane kept shadowing him, but he seemed not to notice. She had to keep up with him, and questions seemed the best way.

'And the Malign?' she asked.

'They are united in the historical record with these extra dimensions, yes. But with much confusion.'

She had the distinct impression that he was withholding, but with a Supra it was hard to be sure. And even harder to interrogate them without being blunt. Which, at the moment, she did not wish to do. Their subleties were beyond her.

'Ah – please wait,' he said.

She watched him receive a silent call and make the pause so many Supras made as they replied. His sudden stillness contrasted with the shifting views of the walls. They were mostly landscapes without people but with foregrounding constructions that seemed alien to her. She knew well the ingrained taste of her kind, for savannahs dotted with trees, ponds, nooks that could shelter – and as well, prospects that promised mystery and wide-ranging movement. Her Original taste was ingrained. She liked canopies and inlets, reassuring shelter. Even better if they stood in contrast to panoramas or waterfalls with nearby openings, yet with cozy spots available.

Fanak's walls were subtly off for her. The very same sort of landscape gave off different signals. Refuges were shadowy without giving reassurance. The horizons somehow did not beckon, yet she could not say just how. Yet Fanak favored these oddly askew renderings. She felt again the unspoken distance between her and the Supras – and, she admitted, her continuing fascination. They were, well, different. Fundamentally so.

He finished his silent conversation suddenly and resumed his pacing, scowling with renewed energy. The drive of the man captivated her, and she was quite sure by now it was not just the close likeness to Kurani. Except in the face – Fanak had a lean and piercing hunger that in Kurani was more blended, distant. She allowed herself a moment to wonder what he was like in bed. Those thighs . . .

She shook herself. *How Original! Try not to be a total slut . . .*

Focus, yes. She ventured, 'I wonder if the extra time axis could be the source of confusion?'

He laughed heartily, a startling roar that echoed from the archways. The room seemed to still after this, as though it were paying attention. 'Good idea. It makes as much sense as anything else I have been digging out.'

'From . . . ?'

'Oh, these are full-sensory historicals. You've seen some? From the era when history was thought to be properly a form of drama? Imagine! And all purely senso-ed. You arrive amid a full story line, take what you wish from it, and life in the historical moves on. Subplots and more.' He shook his large head. 'What could they have been thinking?'

'So you experienced this . . . Multifold?'

'I felt and sensed and thought I understood – and then it was gone. Leaving me with an exposure to the era, but little else.'

She kept her distance from him as he walked about his quarters, seemingly oblivious. No chance encounters, at least not yet.

'And the Malign?'

He frowned, hands behind his back as he paced and turned, paced and turned. 'Something shadowy. The two are wedded somehow.'

'Nobody knows how?'

He turned abruptly, nearly colliding with her, his eyes boring into hers. 'There were librarians much better at this, who knew how to integrate the past records.'

Cley took a step away from him, from his bristling intensity. 'The Furies . . .'

'Killed them all, yes.'

'The Furies, they were . . .' It was easier to let him fill in the blanks.

'Systematic. Just as when they exterminated the Originals.'

She shuddered at the memory. *The burnt, swollen faces of friends . . .* 'Why?'

Fanak let emotions play across his face, most of them tinged with a subtle, fleeting anguish. 'A talent for the thorough? I wish I knew.'

'Maybe they – it, whatever they were – wanted to disable us. Cut us off from . . .'

'The Multifold, yes.'

'Where is it?'

'No one alive knows. Yet.'

'The Library . . .'

'We're trying to make it yield that. From what's left.'

He wheeled away again, his bare feet slapping upon the ancient, warmed stones. She felt a rush of emotion, a need to comfort him, to embrace, to . . . 'Can I help?'

He stopped, his back to her. 'Keep at your work. It is valuable.'

'Seeker and I filed a report on our little adventure. If you need to know more—'

'The scientific types – those we have left – are studying the Morph you pinned. Difficult, difficult. Uncooperative. Capturing that thing was very good work, by the way.'

'Seeker and I did it together.'

'Truly? The procyon? It seems a canny beast.'

'That's an understatement.'

He turned back to her, eyes veiled. 'I think of the procyons as rather like cats.'

'Well, they both like fish.' She kept a blank face; Supras were far too good at reading Originals.

'I meant the air of mystery they manage to suggest in every movement, every glance.'

'With cats it's all acting.'

'Not among the smart ones.'

Her eyes widened. 'There are cats enhanced to our level?'

'To yours, yes, there were.'

'I've never seen any. The ordinary sort, yes. I'm a cat person.'

'They were wiped out, the enhanced ones. Too clever by half.'

'When?'

'Several million years ago. I gather there was a . . . revolt.'

'Over . . . ?

'Art, the Library says.'

'What were they like?'

'No one living has ever talked to one, if that's what you mean.' He blinked at her owlishly. 'The smart cats were large, of course – they needed the brain size – and chose to retain their primordial characteristics.'

'Carnivores?'

'Hunters, yes.'

Cley blinked. She was trying to imagine intelligent hunter cats – their point of view, how they would live. And whom they would mortally offend. Just an intuition, but . . . 'The Elegants did it, then.'

'Of course.' As if to erase the thought, he turned sourly to a wall, which brightened with a stunning landscape of waves churning on a silvery night beach. Not a current view – the moon was a shattered remnant. 'To us, art is the jewelry of history, no more. To them – who can feel what those Elegants did? Never forget, our human varieties change. Still, how could they take such measures? Commit such . . .' His voice trailed off as he stared at the ancient silvery beach's incessant clash against the land.

'Crimes?'

'It is considered too simple to use simple words.'

'Well, I'm simple, so crimes it is.'

He laughed again, a delighted dry chuckle this time. 'I wish I could see it that way.'

She saw this for an overture, and maybe it was, but she was not having any, not right now. Figure out why not, later. If ever. Too much going on here.

2

The Saintly

When she got back to work, Seeker was talking to three spindly figures in stark white wrap-robes. Supras, but of a variety she had not seen. Spindly legs, sharp chins, beady eyes, a sheen on their brows.

'You deem them goodly?' one of them asked.

'Not a category I use,' Seeker said, tight-lipped.

'Foul?'

Seeker shook its head irritably.

'Their purpose?' another probed.

Seeker gave a reasonable imitation of a human shrug.

'These were geometrical objects, in our three dimensions, yet living?' the third asked.

'The way they look to us tells very little,' Seeker said, starting to fidget with its claws and eyeing their throats.

Cley smiled. But these were Supras and probably wouldn't take Seeker's hint.

With these three was a Semisent — a smartdog form, four-footed still, but standing half as high as Cley. Furry, muscular, jutting jaw and leathery throat shaped for speech. Its eyes roved over the landscape, keeping up to date, following the conversation but not, of course, taking part.

She nodded toward it — a protocol she had learned as a child. These were forms halfway conscious, good servants, though for her, semisentience was a troubled idea. There were many tests for intelligence, fastening upon features of the human mind: art, analysis, speech, kinesthetics. Whole eras had focused on these aspects, often to the exclusion of others; it seemed that cultures could not hold two ideas in the collective mind at the same time.

An early example was a kind of test, devised out of an anxiety about artificial minds. Many felt they could intuitively sense an intelligence merely by talking to it. For centuries, people quizzed artificial intelligences, guessing whether they were being fooled by another human. Results were muddy. Then Semisents disproved this test quite readily, for their conversation was a stylized human persona. They were completely plausible conversational partners, able to hold forth for hours. Some people even found them charming. They got sexual overtures, along with the dialogue.

The Semisent kinesthetic senses were equally adroit. They could navigate the landscape better than an animal and were quite humanlike, in a limited range. Rumor had it that their sexual invitations were sometimes answered, in a limited fashion.

But the Semisents did not truly carry sentience. A Semisent could do much, tasks beyond number – but it had no abstractions beyond a list of commands and terrains, maneuvers and obstacles. Yet it certainly had some blunted sense of self, the interior model that made it react to changes outside.

In the vast span of great antiquity, someone had played upon the ancient bond between humans and canines to make this type of Semisent. What ancient hunter did not feel a close connection to his dogs and commune with them? This particular uplifting had no doubt informed many a joyous hunt.

Such tinkerings also left a sobering sense of strangeness. The Semi-dogs were both pet and servant, able to talk in simple, slurred speech. Many liked them.

But as this one stood on its four legs, watching, ready to serve, the skating intelligence behind those eyes seemed to Cley only an amplified version of Fanak's responsive room. The walls had sensed Fanak's mood, known his likes, shifted its images and scents and sounds to fit. So did the Semisent serve its masters. It breathed, felt the strums of living tissue, and so Cley gave it the tribute a living form gives another. A nod, no more.

And Seeker gave it less. Without a word, Seeker turned its back.

The others did not even notice. Cley insinuated herself into the tight circle around Seeker and turned to the strangers. 'You wanted . . . ?' She was getting good results with the unfinished sentences.

'We have come to offer counsel,' two said together.

Cley could not read Seeker's expression. 'Uh, what kind?'

'Moral,' they all said together.

She was picking up scattered Talent-talk, but these three seemed to have a way to shield nearly all of it from her. 'Maybe a little early for that,' Cley said. 'Gotta know more.'

'It is never too early,' the tallest said severely.

'Error comes from inattention,' added another.

Seeker said shortly, 'We have work to do.'

The Semisent caught the edge in Seeker's voice and

padded forward, showing teeth. It growled, low and long.

'Big thunder, no rain,' Seeker said.

Searching for a way to defuse the tension, Cley said, 'I could use some help bringing slabs up from the seventeenth floor.'

'We are here to serve, of course,' all three said.

They tried to lecture her, but she wasn't having any. She put them to some tasks instead. Talk was cheap; sweat mattered here.

They worked fairly well but took a long time to fetch forth the slabs. When a bot team came by, the three gave them stern looks. And Cley still didn't know what was going on. 'Say, who *are* they?' She whispered to Seeker.

'They term themselves the Order. They arrived yesterday — from the other side of the world, they said. A pilgrimage to the Library, to advise.'

This meant little to her. Amid the labor, which took great attention to be sure the more crystalline records did not suffer damage, she found the Semisent padding alongside her. Big, shaggy. 'Whom do you serve?' she asked it.

'All.' Its voice was long and slow, the *A* hollow in its barrel chest.

'No, I mean, who are your . . . companions.'

'Three members of the Order, madam.' The sentence sounded painfully hard to get out, rumbling in its throat. 'Madam,' it said again, when she did not speak immediately — apparently, some sort of protocol.

'Uh, the Order is a Meta?'

'No, kindred souls. They, we, are devoted to principled action.'

'Oh. Uh, thank you.'

'Madam is welcome. I am to serve.'

They came up to the surface on an electrostatic lift, and the three of the Order, in their white robes, were straightening the stacks of records. Seeker gave them curt directions. The Semisent approached, but Seeker would not acknowledge it. When the Semisent asked for orders, Seeker addressed instead the nearest member of the Order, and that woman gave the Semisent directions.

This struck Cley as odd, for Seeker never seemed other than contemptuous of hierarchies and stations in society. But Semisents were different, apparently. When she asked Seeker, it said, 'They are not worth our time. They are – what was the old term? – partials.'

'Partial how?'

'They have part, only part, of what it takes to be an actor in the world.'

'So? That doesn't seem to be a sin.'

'The parts are fitted together wrong.'

Seeker would say no more. Cley turned to studying the members of the Order.

They were a sucking blankness. When they came into a room, it seemed emptier. This she had not encountered before, and they came in the next few days, working nearby, to seem the strangest variety of Supra she had known. She began following them closely, as if they were an exhibit.

She had heard of their long tradition. Over the myriad millennia, philosophers had returned again and again to the two great reasons to pursue moral virtue at all. One could improve the world or perfect oneself. These goals struggled against each other, causing countless wars. One view looked outward, the other inward.

Whole societies had echoed this, for in some ways the

strivings of the lone person echo in larger social dreams, working themselves out as ideas, governments, crusades, whole cultures.

Or so she thought. That evening, labors done, she mentioned this classroom truism, and Seeker snorted. 'The inward journey is dubious, the outer one even more so.'

Cley was surprised. 'They're trying to make a better—'

Another snort. 'Can humans find perfection by forgetting the quest itself and serving others?'

'Well, it might be good for the soul—'

Seeker gave her a twisted-mouthed grimace of derision. 'Soul? Think about your own experience – very limited though it is. How many people have you known who devoted their lives to others? Beyond simple motherhood, say.'

'Well . . . a few.' She did not want to get into her mother, her nonfather, and the whole freight of it. But Seeker wouldn't let it go.

'Did they have beautiful personalities?'

'Well . . .'

'So, did you spent much of your free time with them?' She thought. 'Uh . . . no.'

'Yet they had charity in thought and in deed, yes? And patience, probably, and they worried constantly about helping others, alleviating suffering?'

'Oh, yes, but—'

'But those virtues crowded out the ordinary but nonmoral virtues, eh? Like verve and dash, intellectual curiosity?'

'Now that you mention it . . .'

'Did they ever make a joke?'

'Um, seldom.'

Seeker lolled back against a shattered slab, claws idle, clearly enjoying this. 'In my experience – and if I told you how much there is, you would not believe me – I have met two kinds of such good-works saints. Some simply love everyone else without taking notice of the world's temptations. They are seldom made happy by comforts, art, friends, sports, even family. Their inner lives seem, by what they care about, to be curiously barren.'

Cley had to admit she had known at least two morally earnest people who fit the description. Sincere doers of good works, but . . . somehow blank.

'Very well.' To Seeker, the human comedy was plainly a continuously running feature. 'Then there are the saintly types who like all those things I named. But they sacrifice many or even all of them in the cause of duty. There will always be nuns of either sex, for example, of whatever particular faith attracts such people, in whatever era.'

'Aren't you being a little hard on them?'

'But is that not what they wish?'

They laughed together. Cley's mouth twisted in wry recollection. 'Y'know, the ones like that I knew suppressed or denied their strongest desires. I had a teacher who had no family. She said it would eat into her time spent in service to her students.'

Seeker said, 'Those who teach seem prone to that disorder. They can seem inhuman, after one knows them for a while.'

'Vain, maybe? I knew a preacher of the Apocalypse – don't ask, it's a popular church not far from here – whose nose was always in the air. He gave off a whiff of pride in his sacrifice.'

'They seldom have redeeming vices.'

'Like?'

'A taste for bad music, say. Or jokes about themselves.'

'Yeah, uncompromising zeal doesn't look in the mirror much.' Cley eyed the earnest Order trio, who were talking among themselves as they fitted the slabs into reader sheaths. The impulse to reverence was eternal, as so many Library entries showed. Maybe it was built into the chimpanzee substrate all human variants carried, she thought. Hierarchy extended to the ultimate.

Seeker produced a morsel from a pouch, offered it to Cley, and said, 'I knew a physician who remarked that he had forced himself to become an expert on boils in the rectal area, precisely because he found it so hard.'

Cley grimaced and said, 'That preacher I mentioned – he didn't actually believe in a God or anything. But he said we should all aim to be the kind who would get into heaven, anyway.'

'And every atom of self-irony in his body had long vanished.'

'Pretty much. So what's wrong with the other kind – the ones who seek the perfect self?'

Seeker sat up straight, as if this subject demanded more rigor. 'At least they aren't slaves of the impersonal good. But they veer into beautifully lived lives of minimalism. As if doing without was a good in itself, when logically it leads to death. You starve.'

Cley chuckled and ate another sweetmeat. 'So what's the right way to live?'

'Looking for recipes, are we?'

'What's the moral way to live when there are so many kinds of people?'

'Bearing your fair share.'

'What's that?'

'The amount of sacrifice that, if everyone did it, would give the most happiness and least suffering among all the kinds of humans.'

'Pretty mathematical. And nonhumans?'

'Such as me?' Seeker scrunched its mouth into an archly unreadable smile. 'You may take me for human, but prepare to be surprised.'

'Isn't preparing for surprise a contradiction?'

'Exactly! That sense of the paradox of life will get you further up the moral mountain than striving for perfection.' Seeker sniffed. 'Or for what you suppose is the good of others.'

Cley frowned. 'So why try to do much at all?'

Seeker thought about this a good long while, which surprised Cley. Finally, the creature carefully brushed the long hairs of its glistening russet pelt and said, 'Humility is not open to those who want to bring something fresh into the world.'

'Like you?'

'I suppose I am obvious.'

'Hardly. So you can't be a saint?'

'Scarcely.' Seeker snorted. 'That is a human idea.'

'You're trying to change the world, though.'

'To do the new demands a kind of pride, an arrogance.'

'So what're we doing here?'

'For now, trying to keep you alive.'

'It's all about me? Why am I so special?'

Seeker was through jesting. 'I wish I knew. So do many others.'

'Who?'

'Others of my kind.'

Cley grinned. Verbal play was a daily event in her Meta, and she had missed it. 'So you're pretty selfless yourself.'

'Not really.' Seeker gave her a dour look, eyelids drooping. 'I am following my intuitions.'

'And you hate it when the holy types do the same. When the work is done, people – or creatures – like that enrich the world. Maybe more than the do-gooders.'

'And they pay the price of pride.'

'So if you're going to be a saint, forget about being an angel?'

'If you would stand for something, then you cannot stand for just about anything.'

Cley laughed at this, but Seeker did not.

3
Damage

The Furies came that night.

Cley and Seeker had attended a scent symphony that ran late, among a moderate crowd of mixed humans. They ate and went to sleep. Cley awoke from a dream to find people running past their bunk room deep in the Library. Shouts, crashes, metal slamming into metal — then silence.

She and Seeker crawled into a narrow passageway and stayed silent. Absolutely nothing happened, and then kept on happening. Silence stretched. And she was tired . . .

Cley jerked awake. Seeker was gone. Footsteps. Voices hollow in the distance. A jabbing, hard *rap-rap-rap* like somebody firing an electrical discharge into the sky.

She crawled out and saw Fanak hurrying along, carrying some tubular instruments. 'Can I help?'

He was startled and pointed one of the tubes at her. 'I think they are gone.'

'That's a weapon, isn't it?'

'Oddly beautiful, isn't it?' He hefted it, muscles working against a considerable weight. 'We made some from old designs.'

'Death comes out this end?'

'A ray of some kind. Curious, how any tool properly made acquires a beauty.'

The tube with handles filled her with a chill dread, but Fanak's obvious pleasure in the thing made her hold her tongue. 'You used this?'

'I fired it at the things. Furies. Forks, some call them. I believe we kept them from the Library.' He said this in an ordinary tone, but she could read the pride behind it. He beckoned, and they mounted the slide to the surface. She spent the journey worrying about Seeker.

She knew the forks were long, curling lances of virulent fire. Smoky pyres showed that long, smoldering grooves scarred the Library's skin. 'They came down from the sky and probed up and down the valley. We fired at them.' Fanak smiled agreeably. 'Some blew apart.'

She stood close to him as wind whipped by, howling. In the dark sky skittering joints of light frayed and forked. 'Are they still up there?'

'If this time is like last, there will be discharges high in the atmosphere. Accumulated energies playing out, perhaps. But the crucial directing intelligence – from a higher dimension? – is gone.'

'How much damage?'

'Little.' His attention veered toward the dark forest nearby.

She saw it, too – a shape flitting among the cover, short and darting. Something about the gait . . . 'Seeker!'

Fanak had his weapon leveled. She batted it skyward. 'No!'

The dodging shape was eluding something. A frying hiss came down over the valley, gathering like static electricity. The nape of her neck rose, tingling.

A sharp *crack* – and a finger of blue force crackled down. It hit the running shape. A high, agonized cry.

The energies in the air seethed, then subsided. Cley blinked away the afterimage of the thin, hard line of electrical violence. She ran into the shadows. Ahead she saw the shape. It was shaggy and limping. It struggled forward, its pelt wrestling with stark colors.

Shouts came from behind her. 'Get medical!' she shouted back.

Seeker's voice was reedy. 'I wished . . . to see . . .'

'Lie down!'

It rolled onto its back. Blood caked the left rear leg. She pulled aside the matted fur and found a long black cut, burned to a crisp at the raw edges. 'How?'

'I saw the forks leave. They were not attacking . . . so much as searching.' Seeker paused at each phrase, its breath rattling.

'For what?'

'I followed them. To find out.'

With both hands she held the two sides of the burn together to stop blood from oozing out. 'Let the Supras do that!'

'They were busy. I am small. Hard to hit.'

'Huh! Doesn't look like it.'

'They shot at me. Many times. I was not . . . who they sought.'

'Who, then?'

'More of you.'

'Originals?'

'They revisited your sites. Killed anything . . . that moved.'

'Like you.'

'I suppose it is . . . a compliment . . . to be taken for . . . a human.'

'This compliment's going to bleed you to death unless—'

A big Supra came running up, flashed a strong light. She opened her hands and showed him the damage. He muttered, shouldered her aside, and set to work.

Seeker grinned. 'Please to sew me. And give water. I will do the rest.'

'How about a fish?' Cley whispered in its ear.

'I like . . . the oily ones.'

'You lie still.'

'They want you. They must know . . . not all Originals . . . dead.'

'How could they?'

'Remember two-D. To them . . . our three-D is . . . a picture . . . you see . . . all of . . . at once . . . from a higher perspective.'

Seeker panted as the Supra worked. Its eyes were not glassy, and it seemed to focus all its energies on the space between it and Cley.

'So they can see everywhere in three-D, inside buildings, inside—'

'Inside people . . . even.'

'So why didn't they find me?'

'The Furies are . . . agents . . . I believe. Do not have . . . the perceptions . . . of the four-Ds.'

'So they knew I was somewhere around here.' She glanced up into the bowl of sky, where vagrant energies worked still. She shivered.

Seeker closed one eye, but the other pinned her with its intensity. 'They can tell . . . Originals . . . from others.'

'How do you know?' She put a hand on Seeker's brow – hot and damp. Its breath came ragged but steady.

'They ignored the highers.'

She chuckled. 'Don't tell Fanak that. He thinks he drove them off.'

'They will be . . . back.'

The Supra was finishing up. He closed the wound with a smart tissue, which meant that the wound could go now without further treatment. The tissue would fall off when its job was done.

Seeker said mildly, 'I would like . . . that fish . . . now.'

'I'll go throw a line into a stream as soon as we get you—'

A team ran into the light, coming from the direction of the Library. It was the three of the Order, carrying a sling. They stepped near Cley, and one said loudly, 'We heard there were wounded. But this – it is not of us.'

Cley stood up. 'Put the procyon in the sling.'

The tallest of them gave her a *Who are you?* glance and started to walk away. Cley jumped after them, caught the tallest by her shoulder, and wheeled her around. 'Now!'

'We were told that there are humans, even highers, wounded out here—'

'Now.'

They resumed walking away. The Supra medical stood and watched, doing nothing. Cley saw that Seeker's other eye had closed. One of the Order said, 'We have strict, principled precepts for—'

'Deal with this, then,' Cley said. She extruded a special reading tool she had added a week before. It ended in a hollow data-miner tube.

The three of them froze. The tallest said, 'This is a, a . . .'

'Right. Weapon,' Cley lied.

'Those are not allowed—'

'Pick. Up. The. Procyon.'

'You cannot force us. We do not respond to such as this.'

The Supra medical still did nothing, but she could see in his face a flicker of amusement. She figured he knew the tool but they did not. She stepped forward smartly and pressed it against the forehead of the tallest. 'This will not kill you. But you may find it hard to remember your name.'

'I—'

'For a year or two.'

A long silence. The tallest stared straight into Cley's eyes, and Cley wondered what she would do if this did not work. She could not handle them all in a scramble.

'Very . . . very well.'

Cley and the medical got Seeker into the sling. One of the three ran off, probably to tell tales. The other two helped Cley carry Seeker back to the Library in stony silence.

Cley just smiled. She thought of singing but decided against it. Too Original.

4

The Discovery of Forever

S he took her courage, balled it up tight so it would not stick in her throat, and said, 'How old are you?'

Fanak had been working with her on a deciphering problem from the ruined Library, and he did not deflect his attention for a long moment. Then he raised his large, angular head from the view on his workplane and looked at her firmly. 'We do live longer than you, yes.'

'That's not what I asked.'

'It was not what I answered.'

'Supras don't want to tell us how much longer they live, I've noticed.'

'We do all honor privacy, yes?' He smiled very slightly, as if she had committed a minor social gaffe.

'But the very act of bringing back Originals is a moral decision, isn't it? Knowing they will see the contrast.'

'Would you rather not have been born?' The small smile stayed in place, but the eyes did not join in the mirth.

'Nobody can wish for that! I'm not a simpleton, just an Original. Lowest of the Ur-humans.'

She knew she had irked him somehow, in his strange Supra way, because he got up and started pacing. His heels sent sharp notes ringing from the arched, looming chamber, and his workplane followed obediently, always casting him in a flattering light. In a way she found it reassuring that even an advanced form retained the species' liking for the oldest physical rhythms, found them restoring. 'My expected lifespan is set by accident, not disease or decay.'

'So it's . . .'

'We are far safer than when the first Originals walked. In your time, I have read, the accident rate was so high that you would live only a bit over a thousand years, absent disease.'

'So that's my number?'

'Alas, no – you are a true Original, and so do not have the internal mechanisms I do, to defend against the myriad disorders.' He spoke this crisply, mouth tightening around an uncomfortable fact.

'You're saying I'll live – what? A century?'

He shook his head vigorously. 'No, no – much more. We can use the old technologies to correct many afflictions you will meet.'

'Several centuries, then?'

'At least.'

'What's it feel like? To live that long?'

He stopped pacing, and the sudden lapse of the staccato sound gave a hush to his words. 'I cannot recall.'

'You can't remember being centuries old?'

'No.' Noting her astonishment, he smiled a bit more warmly. 'You have perhaps already felt the effect. As a baby, a year was like a lifetime to you because it *was* your lifetime. By age ten, each year added only ten percent to your store of years. At a hundred, one percent.'

'So at age thousand, a year is like a few hours to a baby, in, in . . .'

'In felt experience.' Abruptly he raised his arms and burst into loud song.

'Heaven gives our years of fading strength
'Indemnifying fleetness,
'And those of youth, a seeming length,
'Proportioned to their sweetness.'

She flinched at the power of his voice, completely unlike his ordinary tone. A Supra, singing? She thought only her Meta did. She felt a surge of emotion at this sudden revelation, even though it deepened the mystery. 'That was from . . .'

'An ancient ballad. I came upon it during the research leading up to the first recreation of Originals. It catches the sense of what it must mean to be . . . well, you.' Then he turned and resumed pacing, his mood shifted, hands now clasped behind his back. *Judicious, guarded,* his body language said.

'I've only got three decades, but the years are flickering by faster, yes. So for you—'

'There is a state beyond a thousand years, when one learns to live in the era itself, without heeding memories.'

He said this precisely and firmly, and she knew she should drop the subject.

So she did. And still did not know how old he was.

Still, the conversation reverberated in her memory. She could not resist comparing his distance with her early years. Those she recalled as an idyll: running through sunlit forests, working to harvest fruit in the tanglewood trees, swimming in chilly streams in the promise of a bright spring. Could nostalgia become addictive?

Certainly she felt in herself a longing for that time. The weight of knowing that she could not return to that life came upon her more strongly then, and for days she worked steadily but with a sadness riding in her heart.

She tended to Seeker's recovery. This was less labor than she had anticipated, because the procyon metabolism was far more advanced than her Original mechanisms.

Seeker needed little help, and got irked if she made a fuss. She was so relieved, she laughed at Seeker's feigned baring of its claws. Still, they looked awfully sharp. 'Here, I'll just—'

'I do have some dignity,' Seeker said irritably, not letting the claws retract.

'Not right now. I'll just—'

'You are my burden, but I do not have to carry you every moment.' Seeker did not seem to be kidding, either.

'Look, you need—'

'I need you to remain safe. Out of sight.'

'Say, now, I'm a free—'

'You are important, but I do not yet know why.' And that was all it would say. The claws stayed out.

She consoled herself that at least somebody thought she was important. At best, the Supras treated her with polite distraction.

Then one day she felt among a trove of undated artifacts – data stores, biosheets, talismans once deemed priceless – and withdrew a human hand. The shock of meeting so directly another person, unimaginably ancient, sent shivers through her. The hand was heavy, masculine, yet the skin was hennaed, the nails skillfully manicured. Time had blackened its fingers. Somehow, its flesh was preserved with supple fidelity.

After a hesitation, she slipped it into hers, shaking hands with antiquity. With only the hand and half the forearm, she then imagined the whole man – one who strode through bright days, loved and laughed and drank, and knew a world she never would.

The Library held only pale shadows of such worlds. But the incident redoubled her resolve to make her work here have some meaning.

Ah, meaning.

To burn libraries was a profound kind of cultural murder. The Library of Life's destruction combined loss of antiquity's wisdom with loss of species – nature's wisdom. In contrast, she thought a lot about short little lives, like those lived by Originals. Hers. For the first time she saw that they had a quality of beauty and tragedy, like waves endlessly breaking to no avail on a golden beach. A shore that would never yield.

Her further work underlined this.

Since far antiquity, societies had saved vast quantities of data, much of it never seen by a human at all. Machines logged information into compressed formats, most of it unreadable except after long detective work. Accessible data, however, led to data mining by historians, making their subject something like a science. Using the Library, they could fast-forward history, cross-correlate over spans that dwarfed human lives, zoom in on critical moments.

Such practices had to bridge what the spatialists called the 'chain of migration' from one recording technology to another. Most valued was meta-data, which set the slabs of information in context. Meta-data allowed the artificial intelligences embedded in the Library to keep their 'digital artifacts' exercised, translating them through the migration chain and into fresh languages. In turn this left the vast banks of knowledge ready for potential human users.

Now that humanity was much smaller in numbers than in the far past, and longer-lived, the vast majority of all data had never been visited by a real human mind. Machines embedded in the walls kept track of matters beneath the notice of people, such as the inventory that documented and linked every named human who had ever lived.

She was astonished to find this. All human names! She pointed it out to Fanak, who just yawned and said in a lazy drawl, 'While a gigantic amount has been written or spoken, culture in the end is the fraction that gets remembered.'

For a full week, she wondered if this was a deep truth or just a joke. With Supras, she was never sure.

Then Fanak invited her to a festivity.

The invitation came out of nowhere, a message on her inboards. Phrased more like a summons than an invitation, but thrilling all the same. Another Supra event! Supras were notoriously not very social. Were they offsetting the aftermath of the Furies? She felt a quickening in herself and did not quite know why.

The 'party' – Supras did not use the term, preferring *fratuung*, implying restrained revelry; Cley had to look it up – was in an ornate structure that rose from the valley floor like a luminous wave about to break. Electrolifts took her up into it, past ascending slabs, precise parabolas of arching orange fountains, a welter of buttresses and columns, some transparent. Sculptures she recognized as vastly ancient hovered in illuminated spaces. Some were empire-style, with noble brows eyeing infinite prospects, while others evoked landscapes that could not be Earthly. Colossal battles were caught frozen at their climax, a huge holocrystal showing the latter phases of the era in contrast. This was time-sculpture, she recalled, a craft sometimes confused with real history. Propaganda of sufficient age became art.

Fanak greeted her with an embrace, signaling that this event was Not Work, in case an Original did not grasp the concept. She gave him a twist of a smile in return and caught from him a musk that told her more than she wanted to know just now.

Frowning, she put the moment aside. They were alone – easy to do in the labyrinth of cool columns and moist recesses – and she saw that the building knew him but not her. A steady radiance followed Fanak, an attendant glow that enhanced him in a ruddy nimbus. Neither Rin nor Kata sported this; was it an honor, or cosmetic? The radiance drew him subtly out of the surrounding gloom as the embedded intelligences here tracked his eye movements. Answering light sprang forth to illuminate whatever interested him. At the moment, that was her. This radiance, she saw, framed him for her as well, making him loom masterfully.

All intended for her. She would have to disregard it.

He showed her the view from a wall that seemed to ooze away . . . showing the plain below, the sprawling devastation of the Library, the ramparts of mountains rising to an azure sky. 'Here,' he said, and in a twinkling the floor, too, seeped away under her feet. Despite herself and her resolve not to be impressed, she gave a quiet gasp.

The plain worked with patterns — shot with light, humming with purpose, alive beneath the sands. She was seeing the dumb physical world above, and beneath, the living intelligences that lay embedded in this ancient valley. All of it was aware, sentient in some sense. And . . .

'Beautiful,' she sighed. 'So much . . .'

'This is how I think of the far past,' Fanak said with a studied, casual air.

'Buried . . .'

'Yes. Patterns laid down long ago, giving forth a view of the world we cannot fully comprehend. Beyond the mere slabs and indices we study. Huge.'

'To know it . . . how can we?'

'I thought to show it to you, just to make plain that there is much the Ancients' — he made the capital obvious with his tone — 'gave us. Things large and subtle.'

'If they could make this, then . . .'

'It is all we can know of them.'

'Another recording.'

'Perhaps. Or an intelligence we cannot grasp.'

She turned to him, close now, feeling his presence like an aroma. 'Do we *know* that?'

He smiled, slow and ambiguous. 'Of course not. Nothing at such a remove, across hundreds of millions of years, can be sure.'

He led her across a plaza, talking swiftly and intently. They approached a pond of water, right to the edge. Cley hung back, but Fanak just strode forward, not even looking down. He did not hesitate, putting his shod foot out and down — and the water firmed up under his step.

'What . . . ?'

She had jerked back and now hastened to catch up, her shoes finding a cushioned surface almost like skin. The surface had a ceramic sheen beneath her foot but, a short distance away, lapped like ordinary water. 'How . . . ?'

Distracted, Fanak murmured, 'Ummm? Oh, molecular lattice response.'

Which meant less than nothing to her, but . . . 'What if we wanted to swim?'

'We would tell it.'

They crossed the pond and stepped off onto stone, and the pond reverted to water behind them. How was it done? She looked back at it, but of course, Fanak did not.

Here came the Supra crowd. As they entered a long hall, a frisson went through the stately figures that were dining at floating tables. Fanak stopped to survey the room, opened his jacket, and put his hands on his hips. She had seen this in her own kind, making the sihouette loom suddenly larger and more forbidding – or so it had been in the forest.

The effect seemed the same here. Fanak was a man of social stature, and lesser Supras, she noted, lingered around the periphery. She immediately guessed why: They were hoping to renew alliances and gain new friends without challenging the Fanaks at the center of the room.

And she and Fanak were at the center, socially and geometrically. She felt a flush of pleasure at the attention she got merely as his companion. Frank speculation worked in the surrounding faces. Pursed lips on the women, especially. Cley was unique but still an Original. Some faces plainly said that; after all, peacocks do not show their feathers for dogs.

Passing a couple, she heard, 'What I cannot create I

do not understand.' A laugh. '*This* I know: Someone cooked up an Original soup, I'm told.'

Followed immediately by 'Isn't it always that way?'

Then, 'Can't let them out without supervision, can we?'

And, 'Domesticated, they are quite nice.'

Cley wheeled on them. 'What I do not create I do not appreciate,' she spat back. And stalked away. Not a bad exit, she thought.

She turned to the food — a welcome escape. Meat without bones, skin, gristle, or fat — because it was made somewhere from elemental compounds, not grown in nature. Eggs innocent of the belly of a bird. She ate a bit, trying to suppress the anxiety seeping up in her. Her Meta scorned unnatural food. No help — she cast aside a delicacy, took a sip of fogwine, fumed, turned back into the crowd.

'Let's . . . let's go back out,' she implored Fanak.

He instantly caught her unease. 'Of course.'

In the darkness above the valley she sighed with relief. 'I'm really not up to all this.'

He slid his arms around her while still looking outward at the view. 'You can be.'

The pulse of him was immediate. She looked into his face and could not get her breath. Only moments before she had seen the Supras as much like her kind, but now the difference between them welled up in her, pulse quickening from both fear and desire in equal measures. She remembered Kurani and the leaping, sudden passion, wanted it to be that way again, to be caught up and carried downstream, sweaty and joyful and possessed by something greater . . .

And she pushed him away. 'I . . . I can't.'

He hid his feelings behind a formal 'I see. I am sorry.'

'No, don't be; it's me, really.' Hands in the air, trying to express something beyond words.

'I assumed . . .'

'Maybe I'm not . . . ready.' That wasn't right; there was something worse brewing in her, but she could not say what it was.

'I am sorry.'

He turned away, and she bolted for the Supra crowd within. Maybe she could just blend in. Her heels clicked anxiously, echoes from the high stone walls taunting her. She hurried into the long hall, steps ahead of Fanak, and abruptly stopped at the entrance.

There was no one in the room she could truly talk to. With these people she would always be on guard, seeking, uncertain. Not safe, not accepted. That possibility had vanished with the searing deaths of the Meta.

Abruptly, flooding into her memory came the experience of reading a word for the first time. That had been a jolting revelation. Hidden meanings had leaped out from the world, forever changing it.

Now she knew something equally powerful but could not say what it was – only that Fanak had all the things that drew her to some Supra men, but the experience was not the same now. And she could not say why.

She stepped without thinking into a crowd of them who were immersed in a pale yellow mist. It clung to her as she passed through them and felt in the air a ghostly silence. It wrapped about her, and she moved among the Supras, who were saying things aloud and in Talent-talk but somehow distantly, as though she were at the other end of the room from them in a fashion she could not quite fathom. They did not look directly at her but knew she was there. She breathed in the yellow fog and felt a gathering tension.

She yawned.

This caught their attention. They looked at her for a long moment as she felt suddenly vulnerable, her jaw wide and mouth gaping like a fool.

Had she ever seen a Supra yawn? No. In school hadn't she read somewhere? And here came the inboard reference seeker, which whispered that *of course a yawn brought more oxygen, but as well yawning seemed to be a way of communicating changing environmental or internal conditions to others, possibly as a way to synchronize behavior, most likely a vestigial mechanism that has lost its significance in selection. Supras have omitted the reflex* – and she shut it off, for now those near her were smiling, some with hands held over mouths, not wanting to laugh.

She turned and fled from the obliging yellow fog, from the ripple of stifled laughter that followed her out of the crowd like a wave.

She breathed in the air, laced with something she had never savored before. All about her, the party swirled. Supras, a few Ur-humans, many variants in between – all from different eras in the eon-long explorations of evolution. She escaped onto a parapet. Below stretched the eroded valley, ancient beyond measure.

She felt it come rushing up at her. This desert plain was a baked-dry display table covered with historical curiosities. What vexed currents worked, when different ages sought to conspire! And she was pinned *here*, firmly spiked by the bland, all-powerful, infuriating, unthinkingly condescending *reasonableness* of the Supras.

Cley pressed her palms to her ears. The din of Talent-talk drummed on. Some point was in contention, laced in logics she could not follow. As soon as they got through with their labyrinthine logic, they might notice her again.

Notice. And talk down to her. Reassure her. Treat her like a vaguely remembered pet.

No wonder they had not recalled the many varieties of dogs and cats, she thought bitterly. Ur-humans had served that purpose quite nicely.

There was no one here who was . . . her. Her people . . . Hard River Meta and all the others. All gone. They had labored under the distant direction of the Supras since far, time-shrouded antiquity, tending the flowering biosphere. The Supras had known enough to let them form tribes, to work their own small will upon the forest. But drawn out of that fragile matrix, Cley gasped like a beached fish.

The Talent-talk drummed, drummed, drummed.

She staggered away, anger clouding her vision. Conflicts that had been building in her burst forth, and she hoped the blizzard of Talent-talk hid them. But she could avoid them no longer herself.

Even Kurani – she had felt with him a near-equality, yes. And that had made her earlier passion possible – born, she saw now, of her innocence. And her ignorance of their differences. An innocence she had lost now.

She was like a bug here, scuttling at the feet of these distracted supermen. They were kind enough in their cool, lopsided fashion, but their effort to damp their abilities down to her level was visible – and galling. Longing for her own kind brimmed in her.

. . . drummed . . . drummed . . . drummed . . .

Her only hope of seeing her kind again lay in these Supras. But a clammy fear clasped her when she tried to think what fresh Ur-humans would be like.

Laboratory-made. Bodies decanted from some chilly crucible. Her relatives, yes, even clones of her. But strangers. Unmarked by life, unreared. They would be her people only in the narrow genetic sense.

And she would be bound to those new lives in a kind of genetic slavery. She and all her kind would be ever more kindly, politely *owned* by the Supras.

She saw suddenly that her Meta, her Mom, her mysterious father who might yet be alive somewhere — they had all been kept in benign ignorance. The Supras clearly felt that Originals could not be actors on the interstellar stage.

And maybe they were right. But she resented the idea. In her gut she felt that Originals could matter, if they had a chance.

And somewhere, maybe some Ur-humans lived. Maybe her father. They would know the tribal intimacies, the shared culture she longed for.

If they existed, she had to find them.

Yet every nuance of the Supras' talk suggested a subtle attitude. Not that they would not let her go, no. That they would not see that it was her freedom to choose. *Domesticated, they are quite nice.*

Could she . . . ?

They were not all-powerful — she had to keep reminding herself of that. They gave Seeker an edgy respect, clearly unsure of what it represented.

Their very attainments gave them vulnerabilities. Immortals were enormously cautious; accident could still destroy them. Caution could err.

And they could have missed some of her kind in the dense woods.

Nobody from the crystal elegances of Sonomulia or Illusivia could be worth a damn at tracking in the wilderness.

She sucked in a chilly breath. Things slid into place, deep inside.

Very well, then. She would escape.

5
Flight

S urprise and diversion are tactics best used swiftly.
In Cley's case the surprise had to come at the perimeter the Supras had erected around the wrecked Library. Yet she had no idea how to do this.

She confessed her thoughts to Seeker. She was sure that it would not betray her. It seemed unsurprised by her news, or at least to Cley the beast showed no visible reaction, though its fur did stir with amber patterns. She had hoped for some laconic but practical advice. It simply nodded and disappeared into the night.

'Damn,' she muttered in their quarters. Now that she had decided to act, the hopelessness of her situation seemed comic. She was, after all, the least intelligent human here, surrounded by technology as strange to her as magic.

She had fled the party, fled Fanak. Still, from across the dry valley came the enticing sound of music and talk. Even this far away, waves of Talent-talk frothed in her mind, making it difficult to think clearly. Her head ached. Shielding herself from the din was wearying. Dimly she hoped this torrent would also provide cover for her plans.

A loud, groaning explosion rolled through the dark. Seeker was suddenly beside her. 'Walk,' it said.

Shouts, flashes of purple radiance, a chain of hollow pops. Luminescent panels flickered out in the distance. Screens of the defense perimeter rippled with amped energies. A babble of confusion. The party was over.

They simply slipped away. Seeker had executed some trick to deflate the screens near the Library. This also, unnoticed and incidentally, deactivated the pain-filled perimeter around the camp. 'How'd you do that?' Cley whispered.

'I have been studying their methods for some time,' Seeker said, 'using their own Library.'

'Oh. Wait . . .' Cley took the time to find a small, lethal projector device she had seen one of the Supras put away after demonstrating it. An ancient weapon, scarcely larger than her little finger. The Supras had considered and discarded it in the days after the Furies.

They moved fast. The night seemed to reach out and fold around them. Her heart sang, *Go!*

Behind them the complex, transparent geometries of the screens abruptly collapsed. A strange, metallic howl of dying forces echoed over the plain. Seeker's trick had worked.

For all their mastery of science, the Supras reacted in near-panic to the noisy folding of the screens. They truncated all standing bot orders and directed every effort toward erecting the defenses again.

Cley watched warily as they trotted across the valley floor, to the side nearest the forest. Cley still marveled that they had gotten away at all. 'How did you know to . . . ?'

'The moment was approaching,' was all it would say.

'But the bots . . .'

'They will not expect this now. They never sense the moment in time.'

Silently they moved out of the Supra camp, keeping to the shadows. Everywhere bots hurried to restore the bulwarks of the Library but took no notice of them.

They reached the forest beneath a moonless sky strung with a necklace of dense stars. Cley tweaked her eyesight to enhance the infrared and bring color forth from the pale glow of a thousand suns. Ahead, a slumbering dark. Behind, noisy luminosities.

They ran steadily for the first hour and then slowed as the terrain steepened. Whatever Seeker had used to gain them freedom would not last for long. As she ran, her sobering sense of desolation gave way to resolve. She had been restless under the lofty and distracted restrictions of the Supras. Not for long could she conceal from them her feelings. She suspected that Seeker had sensed her restlessness and had prepared to get the two of them out.

After all, Kata had the Talent, had awakened it in Cley. So in time Kata could read Cley's simple mind and intentions, and tighten her hold. She had felt the power of them all, back there at the party. They could use her for what they willed. And she would not know the purpose of their subtle moves until it was far too late . . .

After a while all this complication fell away from Cley, and she gave herself over to the healing exuberance of the forest. *Home.* She knew from Supra talk that her kind were not the true, original humans who had come out of the natural forces of far antiquity. Not the actual first denizens of the forest. But that mattered little. Though her body could be easily modified, as the inclusion of the thought-Talent showed, the Supras had kept her kind true to their origins. The simple enfolding of forest could still reach deeply into her. She was *of* the leafy, fragrant canopy.

Seeker did not slow its rhythmic pace. Its four legs seemed to slide across the ground while its hands swept obstacles aside for both of them. 'They must be looking for us now,' Cley said after a long time of silence.

'Yes. My technological trick will soon wear away.'

'What was it?'

Seeker looked at her, opened its slanted mouth, but said nothing.

'Is it something I shouldn't know?'

'A thing you cannot know.'

'Oh. And you?'

'Me, neither.' Seeker grinned madly, quite happy in their shared ignorance. Cley could never be sure whether the big procyon valued knowledge itself; it was certainly energetically curious. But it also looked askance at much of what it learned, its dour eyes becoming heavy-lidded with skepticism. Combined with the grin, the effect was unnerving.

She was used to Supras making her feel stupid. Seeker, though – whose enhanced kind had come well over a hundred million years after Ur-humans – made nothing of its abilities. But its folksy 'Me, neither' somehow made its abilities seem more daunting.

'They can find us, though,' she said. 'Supras have so damned many tricks.'

'We must seek concealment.' Seeker pointed up. 'Something more works in the sky.'

She looked up and saw only a low, pearly fog. She

puffed heavily with the effort of keeping up with Seeker as they plowed through dense thickets. 'Why can't they see us right away?'

'We swim in the bath of life.'

With each step the statement became more true. They moved deep into the embrace of a land bustling with transformation. Fungi and lichens coated every exposed rock. This thick, festering paint worked with visible energy, bubbling and fuming as it ate stone and belched digestive gases into a hovering mist. Where they had done their work, webbed emerald grasses already thrived. The world was being worked over by a technology that must be Supra-inspired.

Cley stepped gingerly through a barren area speckled with bile green splotches, afraid one might attack her feet with its acidic eagerness. Not all the vapors that hung over the fevered landscape were mere bioproducts intended to salt the atmosphere with trace elements. Buzzing mites abruptly rose from a stand of moldyweed and swarmed around them. For a vexed moment Seeker batted them off, and Cley, for once in her own field, said calmly, 'Stand still. They're thirsty.'

The cloud was opalescent in her amped vision, its members each like a tiny flying chip of ice that refracted pale blue starlight. Yet they seemed clever, buzzing with encased fervor and quick skill. They banked in elaborate turns around them. She closed her eyes and inhaled, and sensed that to this cloud they must seem like a mountain of chemical cropland.

Seeker whispered, 'What do they—'

'Don't speak! They'll smell your stomach lining and plunge down your throat.'

Seeker shut up, and Cley closed her nostrils as well. Tiny wet mouths lapped in specks over her face. She pressed all her orifices tight. The clasping cartilage in her nose had been useful in staving off water losses in the desert of an ancient Earth, in a time only dimly remembered even by the Keeper of Records. Now it kept out the drumming, moist mites as she held her breath for long moments, wondering what the succulent scent of her digestive acids was like. Or maybe she didn't want to know. She squeezed her eyes shut, gritting her teeth. Once before she had walked into such a swarm, and it surely could not have lasted *this* long . . . If she could only have the luxury of screaming, just once . . .

The pearly fog hesitated, buzzed angrily, and then purred away in search of more tasty banquets.

'They seek to find and alter?' Seeker said. It had curled up in a ball, its fur pointed outward, each thick hair with a gleaming point – a bed of tiny knives. 'Not merely eat.'

Cley rubbed her exposed skin with leaves from a big fern. The motes had left a glazed finish on her, and her skin cried out in its liberation. 'Brrrr!'

Seeker shook itself with visible relish, as though casting off water after a bath. Its ruddy fur knotted and unknotted itself in rippling patterns, an effect Cley had never seen before. But Seeker was back in familiar form, saying distantly, 'Is it not true that long ago there were many forms which lived by chemical craft? They worked on molecules, transforming crude minerals into elegant usefuls.'

Cley shivered. 'They make my skin crawl.'

'These are obviously designed to aid the lichen in their gnawing. Preparing the ground for life?'

'The Supras have a lot of tricks. I never saw the bugs that bad before.'

'Your kind inhabited the deep woods.'

'Nasty. I hope—'

'No more talk. Quickly, now.'

They ran hard. Seeker stopped often and crouched, listening to the ground. Cley took the pauses to adjust her blood chemistry. The rhythms of walking helped key in hormonal cues to lessen metabolic drains and increase endurance. She chose a voluntary signal to send into herself, concentrated, and made it 'stick' – the sensation of a neurochemical lock firmly closing. *This girl's ready. Bring on your worst.*

She kept glancing at the sky, where the galactic center was rising. Awesome, yes. Yet its gossamer radiance was unwelcome; she felt exposed. Nothing between them and the cold eyes of stars, and things that dwelled between.

Loping along a steep hillside, Seeker said, 'They come now.'

'The Supras?' she asked.

'More than them.'

'You can tell that just from listening to—'

Seeker crouched, its snout narrowing, ears flaring. It was absolutely still and then was instantly moving, even faster this time. She ran to catch up. 'What—'

'*Ahead,*' it whispered.

Her breath rasped as they struggled up a narrow draw. A deep bass note seemed to come from everywhere until she realized that she felt it through her feet. A peak above them cracked open with a groan, and abruptly a geyser shot straight up. Tons of water spewed high in the air and showered down. Fat raindrops pelted them.

She staggered. 'A weapon?'

Seeker called, 'A fresh river. Our cover.'

'I'm getting soaked.'

'The rock strain has grown for days, and so I sought the outbreak. It will afford momentary shelter. Our pursuers cannot see well through moisture.'

Heavy droplets hammered at Cley. Seeker made an urgent sign. Through the spray of water overhead she saw rainbow shards of radiance cascade across the sky.

'Searching,' Seeker said.

'Who is?'

'What, not who. That which destroyed the Library.'

They watched as a filigree of incandescence stretched and waxed. Through the geyser's mist the shifting webbed patterns glowed like a design cast over all humanity. Cley had seen this beautiful tapestry before, seen it descend and bring stinging death to all she loved. Its elegant coldness struck into her heart with leaden solidity. She had managed to put aside the horror, but here it was again. Those luminescent tendrils had tracked and burned and nearly killed her, and she longed to find a way to strike back.

War. The ancient word sang in her thumping pulse, in flared nostrils, in dry, taut lips. A part of her loved the sound.

She stood with her clothes sticking to her in the hard rain, hoping that this momentary fountain had saved them. *War.* How long could the mists shield them?

But now among the flexing lightning darted amber dots – craft of the Supras, spreading out from the Library. *War.* She had long expected to see them pursuing her, but they were not searching the ground. Instead they moved in formations around the gaudy, luminescent ripples.

She turned and saw Seeker looked bedraggled, its coat dark with the wet. 'What—'

'Down,' it said firmly.

They scrambled into a shallow cave. The river-forming geyser spread a canopy of fog, but Cley adjusted her sight to bring up the faint images she could make out through the wisps. Shapes of warped geometry skated among each other, aerodynamically impossible, as swift as a thought. She and Seeker watched the intricate dodge and swerve of Supra ships as they sought to enclose and smother the downward-lancing glows.

'Water will hide us for a while,' Seeker said.

'Are they after the Library again?'

'No. They seem to — there.'

A streamer broke through an amber pouch spun by Supra ships. It plunged earthward and, in a dazzling burst, split into fingers of prickly light. These raced over the mountains and down into valleys, like rivulets of a tormented river in the air. One orange filament arced nearby, ripe with crackling ferocity. It dwelled a moment along the way they had come, as if sniffing for a trail, and then darted away, leaving a diminishing flurry of sharp pops.

Seeker said mildly, 'Quite close.'

The Supras seemed to have caged in the remaining bright lacings. The thrusts broke into colors and roiled about the sky like quick, caged fire. Trapped. The glinting Supra ships banked and turned back toward the Library.

'We are fortunate,' Seeker said.

Cley nodded. 'That was a cute trick with the water.'

'I doubted it would work.'

'You gambled our lives on it.'

'I saw little choice.'

'Good thing you don't make mistakes.'

'Oh, I do.' Seeker laughed, tongue lolling out of its red lips, and then sighed with something like weariness. 'To live is to err.'

Cley frowned. 'C'mon! You have some help, right? Some connection.'

'I am alone, like you.'

'What're you connected to?' she persisted. The Supras were linked to immense machine intelligences far greater than her inboards. Often she had sensed in faint Talent-talk their shadowy messages. It seemed likely that Seeker might have some inboard access to an extended intelligence. Some technologies on Earth were human-crafted and had been made long ago, were embedded in the world with ancient craft.

Seeker lifted one amber shoulder in a gesture she could not read. 'Everything. And the nothing. It is difficult to talk about in this constricted language. And pointless.'

Seeker sat back on its haunches and lowered its head, meaning that it would not budge.

She knew not to press. 'Well, anyway, that'll keep the Supras busy. They've already figured out how to fight the lightning.'

'For a while. It searched for us, plainly, knowing we had escaped.'

'How could it?'

'It is intelligence free of matter and has ways we cannot know.' Already Seeker moved on, slipping on some gravel and sprawling, sending pebbles rattling downslope. But it got back up, fatigue showing in its eyes, and moved on in a way that was once called 'dogged' but now had no such description, for there were no longer any true dogs.

Scrambling over the ridgerock, Seeker added, 'And should not know.'

6
Biologic

They made good time. The geyser sent feathery clouds along the backbone of the mountain range. These thickened and burst with rain. The air's ferment hid them and brought moist, swarming scents.

The parched Earth needed more than the water so long hidden in deep lakes. Through the roll of hundreds of millions of years its skin of soil had disappeared, broken by sunlight and baked into vapor. The sun was hammering ever harder at the planet. Like all stars, it polluted its core with the heavier elements born of marrying hydrogen to hydrogen. As higher elements built, there was less hydrogen fuel at the core. To keep its fires going, a star compressed more under the mass of its outer shells. The burning core raged hotter, and so did the star, and its children, the planets, felt the coming of a heat that would eventually doom them all.

Beside this slow stellar agony, Earth warmed through uncounted millennia. Its ruddy rocks absorbed more carbon dioxide, and humans responded by increasing their release of it. The warmer oceans spun more cloud cover, helping a bit. But the water clouds suffered the arrows of ultraviolet, splitting, their hydrogen increasing its steady leak from the top of the atmosphere.

An ancient experiment had sequestered most of the

world's water underground. This had retained the moisture, letting sandy plains reflect more sunlight than the darker oceans. No doubt it had seemed a good idea at the time.

But now, Cley had learned as a little girl, that strategy was ebbing. Other methods were aloft somewhere beyond view, she knew – but she had not paid strict attention in her classes devoted to such arcane abstractions. The Supras were restoring water to the surface, and the plume that had just sheltered them was one of their staged eruptions. Earth was far too precious to abandon.

The Supras had loosed upon these dry expanses the lichen, which could eat stone and fart organic paste. Legions of intricately designed, self-reproducing cells then burrowed into the noxious waste. Within moments such a microbe corps could secrete a rich mire of bacteria, tiny fungi, rotifers. Musty soil grew, the fruit of microscopic victories and stalemates waged in every handful of mud around the globe. Dirty fogs smelling like sewers layered the air.

Seeker said they should skirt along these working perimeters of the forest. The biting vapors made Cley cough, but she understood that the shifting brown fogs also cloaked their movements against easy discovery from above. They would be just more infrared blotches amid all the ferment.

She could glimpse momentary slices of the night sky, now cleared of Supra ships and the many-fingered lightning. They slipped into the shadows of the enveloping woods, but Cley felt uneasy. They climbed; the air thinned. Panting, hours later, they looked down through dawn's slanted rays on the spreading network of narrow valleys they had traversed. She could see that the grasp of life had grown even since she had observed it from Rin's flyer.

Already some fresh forests followed the snaking lines of newborn streams, growths cunningly spreading through the agency of animals. Such plants used animals often, following ancient precept. Long ago the flowers had recruited legions of six-legged insects and two-legged primates to serve them. Tasty nectar and fruit seduced many into propagating seeds. The flowers' radiant beauty charmed first humans and later other animals into careful service, weeding out all but the lovely from gardens; a weed, after all, was simply a plant without guile.

But it was the grasses that had held humanity most firmly in thrall for so long, and they endured as well. Already great plains of crops stretched between the forks of river valleys, tended by animals long bred for the task. Humanity had delegated the tasks of irrigation and soil care. As the Supras revived species, they recreated the clever, narrowly focused intelligences harbored in large rodents. These had proved much more efficient groomers of the grasses than the prehistoric, cumbersome technology of tractors and fertilizers.

Onward, always. Cley felt more at home now as they trekked through dense woods. She kindled her hormones and food reserves to fend off sleep, just as she had in the Tubeworld. But this would be more grueling, she was sure. Grimly she kept up the steady pace needed to stay with Seeker, who showed no signs of fatigue.

The forest resembled no terrain that had ever existed before. Assembled from the legacy of a perpetually fecund biosphere, it boasted forms separated in their origins by a billion years. The Supras had reactivated the vast index of genotypes in the Library with some skill. Life must not be easy. Few predators found easy prey, and seldom did a plant not find some welcoming ground after the lichen had made their mulch.

Over a billion years, even the seeming constants changed. The rub of tides on shorelines had slowed the planet's whirl, lengthening the day by a fourth. Life had faced steadily longer, hotter days as the crust itself drifted and broke. In the Era of Oceans the wreckage of continental collisions had driven up fresh mountains and opened deep sutures in the seabeds – all as patient backdrop to the frantic buzz of life's adjustments to these immense constraints. All had to struggle and adjust. Species rose and died because of minute tunings of their genetic texts. And all the hurried succession and passionate ferment was a drama played out before the gaze of humanity – which had its own agenda.

Over the past billion years the very cycles of life on Earth had followed rhythms laid down by governing intelligences. For so long had nature been a collaboration between humanity and evolution that the effects were inseparable. Yet Cley, a woman of the woods, was startled when they came upon a valley of silent, trudging figures. Not human.

'Caution,' Seeker whispered.

They were crossing a foggy lowland ripe with the thick fragrance of soil-making lichen. Out of the mist came shambling shadows. Cley and Seeker struck a defensive pose, back to back, for the stubby forms were suddenly all around them. Cley switched to infrared to isolate movements against the pale, cloudy background and found the figures too cool to be visible. Ghostly, moving warily, they seemed to spring everywhere from the ground itself.

'Bots?' she whispered, wishing for a hefty weapon.

'No.' Seeker peered closely at the slow, ponderous shapes. 'Plants.'

'What?' Cley heard now the *squish, squish* as limbs labored.

'See – they unhinge from their elders.'

In the murky light they watched the slow, deliberate pods separate from the trunks of great trees. Stubby limbs peeled away from their parents and found unsteady purchase on the ground. It was a slow, deliberate birth, moist and eerie in its silence.

Cley had a sudden idea. 'Plants led, once,' she whispered, even though she was sure these things could not hear. 'From sea to land, so that animals could follow. Flowers made a home for insects—'

'Invented the insects, in my view,' Seeker said.

'But why this . . . ?' She gestured through the heavy fog at the woody forms that worked their limbs forward with grave slowness.

'Every step was an improvement in reproduction,' Seeker said. 'Here is another.'

'I never heard—'

'These adaptations came long after my time, as I came after yours.'

Plants had long suffered at the appetites of rodents and birds, who ate a thousand of the seeds for each one they accidentally scattered. Yet plants held great power over their animal parasites; the replacement of ferns by better-adapted broad-leaved trees had quickly ended the reign of the dinosaurs. Plants' age-old strategy lay in improving their reproduction. Throughout the Age of Mammals this meant hijacking passing animals to spread their seeds.

Cley could see the logic of the shambling shapes that melted in and out of the fog. When ponderous evolution finally found an avenue of escape from this wastefulness, plants elected to copy the primates' care in tending to their young.

She approached one of the stubby, prickly things. It was thick at the base and moved by jerking forward broad, rough appendages like roots. They looked like wobbly pineapples out for a slow stroll. Each great tree exfoliated several walkers, which then moved onto wetter ground, or to spots enjoying better sunlight. Cley thought of eating one, for the resemblance to pineapples was striking, and reached for one. Standing on hind legs, Seeker dug claws into her shoulder, whispering that their sharp thorns smelled of poison. They moved on, and farther up the valley they found a giant bush busily dispatching its progeny as rolling balls, which sought moist bottomland and warmth. The balls popped out merrily and bounced over obstructions with something like a child's joy.

Onward.

They passed a region where carbon dioxide welled from the soil, a legacy of the slow churn of continents. Silvery bark peeled from trees, leaving the spindly pines stark white. Just beyond lay a blackened forest. Cley stopped dead. 'This . . . I remember. I came here one summer. Hot Creek Meta lived . . . there.' She pointed to a ridgeline where stubs of buildings poked at the sky.

Seeker knelt and sniffed. 'The burning is nearly ten megaseconds old.'

'What?'

'A third of a year.'

The landscape jumped out at Cley, powerful stored memories overlaying visually from her inboards. She had played and laughed and sweated here. 'They're all . . . dead.'

'I fear so. At the same time you were injured.'

'Damn . . . I . . .' Somehow this made it all come rushing back.

Seeker stood and gently put a paw on her shoulder. 'The past is not over. It is not even past.'

There was nothing for it but to go on. They kept to the deep canyons, avoiding exposure to the sky. Cloaking mist gave some shelter from the Supra patrols, which now crisscrossed the sky. 'They do not know this luxuriance well,' Seeker remarked, clicking its sharp teeth with satisfaction. 'Nor do their bots.'

Cley saw the truth in this, though she had always assumed that the mechanical wonders were of an innately higher order. Humanity had long managed the planet, tended the self-regulating soup of soil and air, of ocean and rich continents. Finally, exhausted and directionless, they had handed this task over to the bots, only to find after more millions of stately years that the bots were intrinsically cautious, perhaps even to a fault.

Evolution shaped intelligences born in silicon and metal as surely and steadily as it did those minds that arose from carbon and enzymes. The bots had changed, yet kept to their ingrained Mandate of Man: to sustain the myriad species against the wearing of the world. It had been the bots, then, who decided that they could not indefinitely manage a planet moist with organic possibility. A miserly element in them had decreed that the organic realm should be reduced to a minimum. They had persuaded the leaders of the crumbling human cities to retreat, to let the bots suck Earth's already dwindling water into vast basaltic caverns.

So humanity's servants had for hundreds of millions of years managed a simple, desiccated Earth: the Dry.

'Machines feared the small, persistent things,' Seeker explained that night as they camped next to a heatbush. 'Life's subtle turns.' They had taken shelter under a massive sunflower that, at nightfall, drooped its giant petals over to form a warm tent. Nearby was a bristling bush that gave off warmth against the chilly, fragrant fogs.

'Couldn't the bots adjust those?' Cley asked. She had seen the routine miracles of the bots. It was difficult to believe those impassive, methodical presences could not master even this rich world with their steady precision.

'You can swallow the most fatal poisons indefinitely if they are in a few parts per trillion,' Seeker said in what seemed a neutral tone, considering that it was writing off millions of years of heartfelt labor.

Cley cocked an eyebrow. As she grew to know this beast, it had come to seem more approachable, less strange. Yet a cool, distant intelligence lurked behind its eyes, and she never quite knew how to take what it said. Or what its agenda was. This ready use of numbers, for instance, was a sudden veer from its usual eloquent brevity.

'The bots must know that.'

'True, but consider ozone. A poisonous gas, blue, very explosive – and a thin skin of it over our air determines everything.'

Cley nodded. Through the long afternoon of Earth the ozone layer had been leached away countless times. Humanity's excesses had depleted the ozone again and again. Oscillations in the sun's luminosity had wrenched the entire atmospheric balance. Once a great meteor had penetrated humanity's shields when they had fallen into neglect, and very nearly destroyed civilization. All this lay buried in ancient record.

Seeker yawned. 'The bots worried over managing such delicate matters. So they simplified their problem.'

'No messy oceans to worry about anymore?' she chuckled.

'Great error, seen up close, can look like true greatness.'

'The bots seem in control here.'

Seeker clashed its teeth irritably. 'They fear what they cannot master.'

'But they did master much – Rin made them revive the biosphere.'

'And bring the chaos of biologic.' Seeker yawned and lay back with a strange, thin grin and then with great relish scratched its ample amber belly. Wreaths of jade mist curled ripely over the heatbush. Small animals had ventured into a circle around the black shrub as its steady warmth crept through the air. Few animals feared either Cley or Seeker; all species had for so long been clients and partners. They even seemed to understand Seeker's lazy talk. Cley suspected they were hypnotized by the luxuriant, singing tones of Seeker's voice, reedy yet eloquent. The circle had relaxed as though the bush were a campfire. A true fire, of course, would have risked quick detection by the Supras.

'What's your alternative, eh?' Cley jabbed it with a thick-skinned fruit. She had found bunches of the long, curved food today, and they had eaten many after peeling away the yellow skins. Cley found the mealy shaft pleasant, augmented with sacs of pungent juice. The phallic shape was cause for a few jokes, too.

Cley toyed with one as she listened to Seeker describe the worldview of its kind. Long after the Ur-humans, some beasts had risen to intelligence and had engraved in their own genes the elements of racial memory. To instill in wise species a concern for their fragile world, it had been the custom for many millions of years to 'hard-wire' a respect for evolution and one's place in it. This had become a social cement as deeply necessary as religion had been to the earliest human forms, and even in the Ur-humans.

'Don't think this was news. Many organisms lorded over the Earth, not just you,' Seeker said, 'beginning with gray slimes, moving on to pasty blind worms, and then to giant, oblivious reptiles – and all three persisted longer than you Ur-humans.' Seeker snorted so loudly it alarmed her. 'We do not know if the dinosaurs had religion.'

'And your kind?'

'I worship what exists.'

'Look, our tribe chose not to try to learn all that dead history – we had a job to do.'

'And a good one.'

'Right,' she said with flustered pride. 'Tuning the forests so they'd make it in spite of all this junk in the air, the plants slugging it out with each other – this isn't a biosphere yet; it's a riot!'

Seeker yawned. 'But a fruitful one.' Eyes twinkling, it fished a piece of fruit from some hidden pouch of its fleshy fur and grinned – a ferocious sight. The moods of the beast were easier for her to read now, and she felt its quirky mirth.

And she saw Seeker's argument. In antiquity, knowledge gained from the bots had helped humanity accent its intelligence and ensure the immortality of all in Sonomulia.

But to make the world work, the bots had to run a skimpy, dry biosphere. Moisture troubled them, so they labored over a hundred million years to bring forth a yawning desert. That arid world's sole pinnacle was a palsied, stultified mankind. Now the Supras were trying to change all that, shifting beneath the massive weight of history.

As the night chilled, she felt around them the scurryings of small feet. The animals of the night called to each other, rising in chorus, sounding to Cley horrific — like a chorus of squalling fat babies being thrown one by one off a cliff. These were not her woods, no.

A fat, ratlike thing with six legs ventured nearer the bush. Instantly, a black cord whipped out and wrapped around the squealing prey. A surge dragged the big rodent into a maw that suddenly opened near the bush's roots.

After it closed on its supper, Cley could hear the strangled cries for several moments. Evolution was still at work, pruning failures from the gene pool with unblinking patience.

V

The System Solar

When men do whate'er they can,
Easing work endangers man.
Yet there's glory in our freedom,
Human being is not beedom.
— John Hertz

1
Prey

Next morning the fog began to clear. Seeker kept studying the sky. They had made steady progress climbing the flanks of the saw-toothed mountain range, and now the terrain and rich fauna resembled the territory where Cley had grown up.

She searched the distant ridgelines for hints of lookouts. Hers was not the only tribe of Ur-humans, and someone else might have escaped, despite Rin's certainty. She asked Seeker to tune its nose to human tangs, but no traces stirred the fitful breezes.

Twice they sought cover when flying foxes glided over, their ballooned arm-wings shining against the sky. By this time surely the Supras would have sent their birds to reconnoiter, but in the blank blue bowl above, neither her nor Seeker's even sharper vision could make out any of the ponderous, wide-winged silhouettes.

They watched a vast covey of the diaphanous silvery foxes bank and swoop down the valley currents. Seeker motioned to her. Distant rumblings came, as though the mountains above them rubbed against a coarse sky. The foxes reacted, drawing in their formation like silver leaves assembling into a ghostly tree.

Blue striations frenzied the air. The few remaining clouds dissolved in a cyclonic churn.

Cley began, 'What . . .'

Sheets of boiling yellow light shot overhead. A wall of hard sound followed, knocking Cley against Seeker. She found herself facedown among piney needles without any memory of getting there.

All around them the forest lay crushed, as though an enormous thing had trampled it in haste. Deep booms faded slowly in the sky. An eerie silence settled. Cley got up and inspected the wrenched trees, gagging at fumes from a split stinkbush. Nearby, two flying foxes lay side by side, as though mated in death. Their glassy eyes were still open and jerked erratically in their narrow, bony heads.

'Their brains still struggle,' Seeker said. 'But in vain.'

'What *was* that?'

'Like the assault before on your people?'

'I suppose . . . but this time' – she swept her hand to the horizon of mangled forest – it smashed everything.'

'Impatience, perhaps.' Seeker lifted a snapped wing. 'The foxes took the brunt of it for us.'

'Poor things . . .' Her voice trailed off as the animals' bright eyes slowed, dimmed, then closed. 'They died of electrodynamic overload, I guess.'

'Our pursuer does not know precisely where we are, so it sends generous slabs of electrical energy to do its work. And brute-force shock waves to squash.'

Seeker gently lifted the two foxes and made a slow, grave gesture, as if offering them to the sky. A long moment passed. When Seeker lowered its claws, Cley could not see the foxes, and they were not on the ground or anywhere nearby.

'What . . . ?'

Seeker said crisply, 'I judge we should shelter for a while.'

They climbed swiftly up the rough rise to a large stand of the tallest trees Cley had ever seen. Long, fingerlike branches reached far up into the air, hooking over at the very end, as if blown by a wind on high. Yet there was no breeze at all here. She felt exposed by moving to higher ground, closer to the sky that spat death. From here she could see distant banks of purple clouds that roiled with spokes of virulent light. Filaments of orange arced down along long curves.

'Following the magnetic field of Earth,' Seeker said when she pointed them out. 'Probing.'

Cley saw why the Supras had sent no searching birds. Far away, quick darts of blue and orange appeared – probably, she judged, over the Library of Life. And in her mind she felt a dim sense of frenzied struggle.

'The Talent,' she said. Seeker looked quizzically at her. 'I can feel . . . emotion.' She remembered Seeker's remark: 'You do not have emotions; emotions possess you.' What must it be like not to feel those deep, elemental surges? Or did Seeker sense something utterly different? 'The Supras are fighting . . . worried . . . afraid.'

'The being above keeps them busy while it searches.'

They moved on quickly. Cley wanted to get over the highest peak and then work her way along the broad-shouldered mountains, toward where she had lived. She had the image of it all in her head from the flight with Rin, and she felt a powerful urge to return to the familiar. When she said this, Seeker replied flatly, 'They would seek you there in time.'

'So? They'll look everywhere.'

'True,' Seeker said, and she thought she had won a small point. But it sniffed the wind and pointed with its twitching nose. 'Come this way.'

'Why?' Her home grounds lay the opposite way.

'You wished to find Ur-humans.'

'My people?'

'Not yet.'

'Damn it, I want my kind.'

'This way lies your only hope of eventual community.'

How could it be so sure? 'Seeker, you know what I want,' she said plaintively.

'I know what you need.'

She kicked at a rock, feeling frustrated, confused, exhausted. 'And what's that?'

'You need to come this way.'

They moved at a steady trot. Cley had always been a good runner, but Seeker got ahead without showing signs of effort. When she caught up, it had stopped beside a big, gnarled tree and was sniffing around the roots. Seeker took its time, moving cautiously, and Cley knew enough by now to let it have its way.

A large bush nearby gave off an aroma of cooked meat, and Cley watched it cautiously. A small mudskipper rat with an enlarged head came foraging by, smart enough to know that Cley and Seeker were usually no threat to it. It caught the meat smell and slowed, tantalized. It lingered . . . and the bush popped. Spear seeds embedded in the rat. It yelped and scampered away. Another victory for the plants; the rat would carry the seed, nurturing it in return for its narcotic sap, until it died. Then a fresh bush would grow from the rat's body. Cley had seen this little drama many times, and considered catching the rat for meat, and not incidentally for the narcotic, but Seeker said, 'Come.'

Ruins loomed before them. 'Once a great city,' Seeker remarked as they went quickly through lanes between crumbling majesties. Headless statues stood shrouded in their inky cloisters. Undermined monoliths had been tumbled by burrowing worms and now stretched like accusing giant fingers pointing at the rest of the forlorn city. Weeds sprouted in spaces where once-important people had proclaimed that their presumptions were imperishable.

Cley sucked in a breath and smelled that indefinable dusty air that tells of history. She had learned from one of her Moms the sweet sadness that came from acknowledging the long perspective of human eras. To know even a sliver of the past was to grieve at what had been lost. Here, slow attritions had wasted once-grand prospects. Technologies now lost had erected ramparts slanting valiantly across the air; great leaders had ruled from them; crowds had listened in hushed reverence . . . and later eras had mined their marbles for lime to use in mortars.

'A city . . .' She had heard of them, of course. 'So many people, close-packed.'

'Your kind apparently enjoys the crowding.'

'I . . . I can sort of see why it might be exciting. Like a never-ending party.'

'Um.' Seeker grimaced. 'Just the sort of horror I imagined, yes.'

'Now all gone.'

'There are the two Supra cities, still ringed by desert. I have not gone there in several centuries.'

'Lost.' She remembered one of her Moms saying

ruefully, 'I started out with nothing and still have most of it left.' Had she seen these ruins?

The silent testimony of these bulwarks made her anxious to move on. Melancholy does not come easily to the young. The softened sorrows of the blunted spires blended sweetness with their sours — a taste difficult to acquire on short notice.

She caught up to Seeker as they left the looming presence of the ancient works, dodging among bulwarks. Two paces behind the hastening animal, Cley caught quick movement in the corner of her eye, turned — and a lethal gray wedge launched itself at Seeker. It missed. Seeker had ducked at the right instant. The blur of motion landed, turned. It was the Semisent smartdog.

Seeker ran a few steps. Cley stopped, and the dog leaped at her. She took a blow to the forehead. She toppled backward, smacked her skull in the dirt. Rattled, she tried to roll left, more or less away from the attacker, and felt a heavy blow on her back. A weight pressed her down. Something was standing on her. Facedown, she breathed in dust and the heavy, musky stench of the creature on top of her.

She tried to slip out from under — heaved, butted up, squirmed in choking dust — but the weight stayed. She was helpless, terrified. The dust in her mouth and nostrils was turning to clotting, gritty mud; her head spun . . . *Breathe!* She wriggled around to get a look up and saw the jowly muzzle of the Semisent above her right ear. The enormous dog head drooled on her neck. But it was looking around, not at her.

A snarling ball of energy hit the Semisent. Ruddy fur seemed to swarm all over the back of it. Seeker dug its claws into the hide, giving angry shrieks and chatters. The Semisent slashed back at the furious procyon, then yelped in pain. Bloodied, the Semisent hunkered down, pressing into Cley, but it was too late. Seeker had anchored itself and then threw all its weight to the side, prying up the mass. Cley scrambled out from under. Up on her knees, she hit the Semisent straight in the muzzle. It fell over, wheezing.

'Damn!' Cley got up as Seeker released its hold. 'What was . . . ?!' She spit, trying to clear dust from her mouth. Gingerly she felt her chin, scraped raw when the Semisent slammed her down. Her hands seemed weirdly steady, as if they didn't belong to her. Surely they should be shaking, from the juddering pulse of her heart.

The hulking gray body of the thing lay sprawled, and its eyes flickered. It was not unconscious, only dazed. Blood oozed from the cuts of Seeker's claws.

'It has tracked us,' Seeker said. 'Some doggy traits remain.'

'Those saintly ones.'

'I agree; they must have sent it.' Seeker stalked around the bulky thing, studying it, stopping at the head. With a forepaw Seeker slapped the cheeks until the eyes steadied and looked out. 'You!'

'Uh . . . I am . . .' The dull voice came from deep in its barrel chest. It had big doglike haunches and a broad muzzle with powerful jaws. The muscular legs would be good for speed over open ground, Cley saw. The thick, stinking pelt would keep its heat in and water out – a sturdy design. The big mouth panted, paused, tried again. 'I was ordered to find you. Stop you.'

Cley felt her forehead. No skin broken, but it ached.

The thing must have hit her with its own bony brow. 'You could've been easier.' The throbbing in her head spoke of more pain to come.

'I was told. You would resist. You did.'

Seeker circled the thing, spitting out whispers of anger, its face compressed around a working mouth. It clenched and unclenched its claws, as if it were fighting down the impulse to sink them again into the thick mass. The Semisent started to get up, and Seeker kicked dirt in its face. The smartdog went into a coughing fit and pawed at its eyes.

'And me?' Seeker demanded.

'You I tried to get first. Thought you would run away after I missed you.'

Seeker blinked in surprise. 'You are truly stupid, then.'

'Was to kill you. Not her. Was to find her.'

Seeker asked, 'Why kill me?'

'You are crucial, will take her away from Superiors.'

'You mean the Supras?' Cley asked.

'Yes, so you call them. They need you. To regenerate your kind. Make more like you.' The Semisent gave this information warily, eyes shifting from Cley to Seeker and back again.

'They would keep you under paternal tyranny,' Seeker observed.

'Versus your maternal care? Maybe so.' Cley scowled. 'What'll we do with it?'

Seeker jumped atop the Semisent and stood on it, calm returning to its face. 'It will have some way of telling the holy ones and the Supras.'

'If it hasn't already.'

'True. We will have to make quick time now.'

'What'll we do with it?'

'I see only one course.'

'Yeah, we can tie it to a tree—'

'Do not make trouble. For my masters.' The bulky thing blinked at them. The face seemed to frown, but there were already so many folds in its skin that Cley could not be sure.

'They made plenty for us,' Cley said, 'just sending you.'

'I have another solution,' Seeker said – controlled now, almost pitying.

The Semisent studied Seeker with growing concern. 'Do not harm me. I am just a messenger.'

Seeker stepped back from the thing. It had somehow acquired Cley's little projector. 'And now you shall be my message.'

It shot the Semisent. The head smacked down, lay still.

Cley sputtered with shock. Seeker favored the direct approach, and few words, but this was too much.

'It was intelligent!' she protested.

'It was a bad idea. And it would have enslaved you to a Supra agenda, as it was itself enslaved.'

'But, but . . .'

'I had to choose between its life and yours,' Seeker said carefully. 'It would have sent a signal; the holy ones would track us, take you back. I could not allow that. That would run counter to the direction events must flow.'

'How can you be sure?'

Seeker grimaced. 'You have a quality your kind terms 'intuition.' When the unconscious portion of your mind – by far the larger, by the way – knows something, it pops into your aware mind.'

'Sure, every – you mean you don't?'

'Let us say that I can see more of my own thinking than you do.'

'So you have a feeling for how this whole confusing thing is going?'

'Alas, it is in the portion I cannot see. So I navigate by "feel," as you say.'

'And you feel you had to kill it?'

'It was sent to capture you and kill me.'

Seeker was slicing the Semisent with its claws, now fully extended. Daintily it handed Cley the projector and set to work cutting away portions of the flanks.

'You're going to . . .' Cley could not bring herself to say it.

'I, like you, have a meat tooth.'

'I, *ah* . . .'

'And I, like nature, do not waste life. It is ordained.'

Cley gasped, her head reeling. This was a Seeker she could not have imagined. 'You seem so gentle, so . . . so . . . You were sorry about the little flyer foxes . . .'

'I revere the natural, but this thing is not.' It bit off a slice of raw meat and smacked with relish. 'Its taste is its only redeeming quality.'

Cley turned away. 'I never know what you'll do next.'

'Umm. Refreshing, isn't it?' Seeker swallowed the slice whole.

2

Pinwheel

As a girl, she had gotten used to friendships with other girls that began in intense, shared revelations and moved into comfortable small talk. With Seeker there were some early revelations and a lot of hard talk, none of it small. And she was never fully comfortable. Sometimes she could not read its facial expressions, and when she mentioned this, Seeker said, 'At my age, I have the face I deserve.'

So she stuck to what she knew, as they moved quickly through the shrouding forests, avoiding the flitting ships above. They passed by colonies of plants that had a social life, communicating through pollen sprays their needs and distresses. Cley could read these from childhood on, and was pleased to find that Seeker asked for instruction. Some of these signals her Meta had adjusted and seen propagated around the globe by genetic invader seed. These were the log crafts her Meta had cherished. They were part of a philosophy the Originals had brought to the world and, with Supra help, had been applying to this latest of many revivals old Earth had seen.

Cley knew these lessons deeply. The chant of her Meta had ingrained them:

Fast learns, slow remembers. The quick, small things instruct the slow and big by bringing change. The big and slow control by constraint and constancy. Fast gets all the attention; slow has all the power. A robust system needs both.

They had recited it every day at breakfast. She yearned for those lost days, gone forever, and the next time they slept, she had dreams about her Moms, her lost life, and of her shadow-faced father.

They set out at morning and quickly became uneasy. Both she and Seeker sensed an ominous tone flavoring the air. Cley had perceptions that linked to the forest, unconscious yet alert. Her alarm bells were ringing. 'Stop,' she said. 'Sit.'

Seeker sniffed. 'I agree.'

'Don't move.'

Something was seeking them, and it had seeped into the woods. The only way to hide was to be embedded deeper than it was.

They sat with the sun at their backs, so approaching animals had to squint. Cley shed any clothing that wasn't a natural color, and rubbed the rest and her skin with a sachet of bayberry and pine. She flattened herself against a tree to blend in. Her Meta's ruddy skin color did not stand out, and she knew to make only measured movements.

Birds nearby gave *chip-chip* calls, alerting all to these strangers squatting below. So she gave back *pish* through clenched teeth, an alarm call of a similar species. To introduce a new sound she made an injured-mouse squeak by sucking the back of her hand. A squat reptile predator came running for a meal, distracting the birds nearby. When it found nothing and went away, the area settled down, the traces of her and Seeker forgotten. Only then could she slowly sense the microbial mat carrying a slow rise and ebb of information.

The world took on a gentle, undulating movement. Leaves rode on the swell of the water, and light glanced along their edges with an ageless rhythm. In the world's fluency came a tidal movement, massive and yet effortless. She felt a myriad of linked sensations. *A small death among leaves. A gentle current as a twirling leaf descended to the forest floor.*

Within this flux, she sought only to place accents: to make a moment turn *just so*. Seeker followed, a raccoon thumb articulating from a thick-jointed wrist, an eye swiveling in its socket. Like slits in a silk curtain, the quietly gathering sense of place revealed the momentary anatomy of the world beneath its deceptive sheen.

She felt herself and Seeker merge with the woods. And a mere moment later, an inspecting pressure wave swept through the entire forest — probing, prodding, sensing the slight perturbations of dissonance and movement that would have revealed their presence.

The wave washed on. It had missed them.

They kept their positions for a long time. Gradually, the deeply shuttered parts of the woods opened anew, a pressure passed, and they uncoiled their minds from the immersed state they had reached.

Technology can only do so much. The Supras had used the deeply embedded sensors that wreathed the entire planet, integrating the layers of minute data, looking for the fugitives. And they had failed.

'Time to move on,' Cley spoke at last, stretching.

'I agree. We have a meeting.'

'What? With who?'

'With what — but you shall see.' Seeker would say no more.

As they trotted steadily through dense woods, Cley pondered the enigma that was Seeker. Its killing of the Semisent had shocked her, but in so many other ways she and it seemed on the same wavelength. Maybe more than they should, now that she thought about it. Procyons weren't human, after all.

In the early eras of the many human subspecies, it had been easier. Simpler, Original minds like hers had identified the dark elements of life with the random tragedies that humans suffered, from storm and disease and nature's myriad calamities. That time lay in the unimaginable past.

Instead, later beings like Seeker saw the world as a place forever in flux. Disasters, rather than being blows against life, were inevitable sways, bringing rejuvenation along with death. Wildfires cleared tree canopies, letting in sunlight. Floods swept silt from gravel beds, renewing river plains and deltas.

Nature's nature was change. It was not a museum.

'That Semisent . . .' Cley began, then didn't know how to frame her question.

'Morality is an artifact of human culture, yes?' Seeker said, not slowing.

'I suppose.'

'You invented it to grease your social relations, back when you lived in troops and hunted and squatted around your first fires.'

'Hey, I don't go *that* far back.'

Seeker shrugged – not easy to do while trotting quickly. 'Your codes apply to yourself, not to animals.'

'You're an animal.'

'Quite. To us, most human morality is carefully thought-through self-congratulation.'

'Hey, we have a code for other beings, too. Even aliens out in the stars, the Library says.'

She was rather proud of having turned up this fact in her scattershot imbibing of the Library's trove, and was disappointed when Seeker simply skipped the point, saying, 'Some beings lie outside the moral bounds – abominations, you would say.'

'Like what?'

'The Malign.'

'Never met it.'

'You might.'

'So Semisents . . .'

'To us, abominations.'

Cley let it go. To the procyon's thinking, artifices like Semisents, if they seemed to Seeker out of the flowing channel of nature, had no rights to exist. She was sure that was why the beast left the half-eaten carcass behind, not trying to hide it at all. 'You are my message,' Seeker had said to it. A message left for the Supras to ponder. Seeker played for keeps.

She was thinking about this, enjoying the run, and so went well past Seeker when it stopped.

It had opened the side of a large tree. The horny bark peeled back in curls, and light seeped from within.

This was no surprise to Cley, whose people had often sheltered in the many trees teched for just such use. She squeezed through the narrow slit, and soon the bark closed upon them, crackling, leaving only a wan, phosphorescent glow from the walls to guide them. The tree was hollow. All trees were dead inside, anyway, just big cylinders of past years' cellulose with living skins. Someone long ago had engineered this huge barrel trunk that built an interior from the compacted dead matter.

She looked up. In this variation there were vertical compartments connected by ramps. U-shaped growths grew all along the walls. Some creature had nearly filled the compartments with large containers, grainy packages of rough fiber.

'Storage,' was all Seeker would say in answer to her questions. 'Come.'

Using the U-growths, they climbed up through ten compartments. All were crowded with stacks of oblong, crusty containers. Sweating, Cley hoisted herself up into a large vault, completely empty with a wide transparent wall. Cley thumped the window-wall, and the heavy, waxy stuff gave with a soft resistance. She watched the still trees outside, stately cylinders pointing up into a sky that flickered with traceries of quick luminescence.

The Supras were still searching. Something else, too. A bright flare of momentary combat spoke of a conflict she had seen too much of already. She turned away, glad to be inside thick walls.

This place might be safer; she let herself relax slightly. As a girl she had camped among trees something like this, with some of the Meta's menfolk leading. They had eaten . . .

Suddenly, memory sprang to life. Those men – they were all dead.

All . . . but one, perhaps.

My father. A wanderer, restless, self-full, drawn by his need to see beyond the horizon. If he never came back to a Meta, he might have escaped the Furies.

The impact of this stunned her. He would not be alive if he had come back to the forests – the Furies searched and killed there. He could be somewhere beyond, maybe. He could have hidden; he could have survived, as she had! Maybe . . . Where?

The prospect was dizzying. Her head buzzed with the implications of her idea. For a moment she took refuge in the slight memory that had started the thought – of the long-ago outing, camping in the living trees . . . And she recalled what one practical, dear lost Mom had always said: 'Head's too full? Use your hands.'

She took out a knife and gouged the wall. A piece came off with some work. As a girl, she had eaten this way. She took a tentative bite. It tasted surprisingly good. Once trees had been mere woody cellulose, but Originals had teched this to something far more digestible, if not overly exciting. She ate awhile, and Seeker took some. Patches on the walls, ceiling and floor were sticky, without apparent scheme. The compartment smelled of resin and damp wood.

She chanced to glance out the big window as she chewed, and that was why she saw it coming.

Something like a stick poked down through high clouds, swelling as it approached. Perspective told her that it was enormously long. Coming straight down. Its ribbed sinews were knobbed like the vertebrae of a huge spine. Groans and splitting cracks boomed down so loudly that she could hear them here, inside. Curving as it plunged, the great round stalk speared through the sky like an accusing finger. Her jaw dropped. As she watched, frozen, the very end of it curved farther, like a finger beckoning upward.

'Time to lie down,' Seeker said mildly.

A sonic boom slammed through the forest. The

window-wall rattled. She hastily flattened herself on the resilient green floor of the compartment and gazed up through the big window.

'It's falling on us!' she cried.

Seeker grinned, right beside her. 'Its feat is to forever fall and forever recover.'

'It'll smash these trees!'

'Lie still.'

She realized that this was the thin, distant movement she had seen on the horizon from Rin's flyer, long ago. Something immense, whirling through the air. It rushed toward them. Graphite-dark cords wound across the deep mahogany of the huge, trunklike thing.

A high, supersonic shriek rose. Fingers of ropy vine unfolded from its tip as it plunged straight downward. The vines flung themselves toward the treetops. Some snagged in the branches there.

'Grapplers,' Seeker said over the shrilling howl.

A hard thump ran through their tree.

She just had time to see the thick vines snatch at the branches of neighboring trees, grip, and tighten.

The broad brown nub hung in air for a long moment – as if, she thought, it were contemplating the green skin of the planet below it and selecting what it liked. It drifted eastward for one heartbeat, then snatched upward.

Heavy acceleration pressed her into the soft floor. They were yanked aloft. Popping strain flooded their compartment with creaks and snaps and low groans.

Out the window she could see a nearby tree speed ahead. Its roots had curled beneath it, tumbling brown clods falling away behind. The forest dropped away. Other trees dangled from vine grips beside theirs. On one, the uppermost branches sheared off where several thick vines had clutched together. Unable to take the acceleration, it dropped away to crash into the forest below.

She could only lie mutely, struggling to breathe. A flock of tree trunks rose beside them, drawn up to the great beckoning finger. The stalk now retracted up into the sky with gathering speed. It swept them eastward. Their tree lashed in air turbulence. She saw the other trees outside, flapping. As if shaking themselves free of the grip of gravity, and of dirt.

She watched, flooded with fear. Hopeless to try to get up – and what would be the point? They were helpless.

Seeker was enjoying the ride, its tongue lolling, eyes alight. She grimaced. Did *nothing* bother the beast?

Their tree groaned in long bass notes. She watched the nearby trees to see what was happening. The sight of one falling away had not given her great confidence.

Against the steadily increasing tension the ribbed and polished vines managed to retract. They drew their cargo trees up, turbulence diminishing as they all rose into the upper atmosphere. The trees nuzzled into a snug fitting at the base of the blunt, curving rod.

'What . . . is . . . it . . . ?' Even grunting out a word at a time was hard against the punishing acceleration.

'Pinwheel,' Seeker said. 'The center . . . rides high in space . . . and it spins as it orbits. The ends rotate . . . down . . . through the air . . . and kiss the Earth.'

Seeker's calm, melodious voice helped stave off her rising panic. They were tilting as they rose. Cloud banks rushed at them, shrouded the nearby trunks in ghostly white – and shredded away as they shot higher. She glimpsed the underside of the Pinwheel itself, where corded bunches of wiry strands held the vines in place.

'What . . . is . . . ?'

'We spin . . . against Earth's pull. But will slip free.'

Seeker's words reminded her that this *thing* must be known to the Supras, to the Library. She sent a query to her inboards, and instantly they gave her an image.

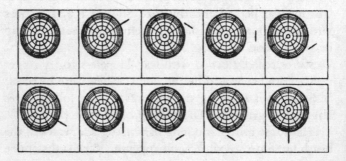

She was looking down on the planet from a pole. An enormous rotating stick orbited it. This rod slowly dipped down into the planet's air, one tip touching the surface when the other end was farthest out in space. It was in orbit but reached down to the surface six times as it circled. At each touchdown, the stick's tip moved backward at a speed equal to the whole shaft's orbital speed.

Briefly, they canceled — its ground-track velocity was zero. As it touched down, it could lift the trees with its vines, making a pickup. And in a few moments move cargo from one part of the globe to another.

And she had seen it before, in her first flyer flight . . . so long ago.

The scale was dizzying. She had thought little about anything beyond the envelope of Earth's air; forest folk lived in the local. The sole Supra craft she had ridden in seemed capable of going into space, and she had supposed that was all there was. But this . . .

This vast thing was far longer than the depth of Earth's air itself. And they were fastened to one end of it, soaring along on an arc that would take them into space.

Still, she could barely conceive of the scale. This creation was like a slender world unto itself. Rolling bass wrenchings strummed through the walls and floor. Her heart thudded painfully, and wind whistled in her ears. Pressures adjusting.

She could see outside that the strain of withstanding the steadily rising acceleration warped the vines. They stretched and twisted in their own agony but held the long, tubular trees tight to the underside. Shrubs and brush festooned the nub. The Pinwheel stretched up into blue-black vistas as the air thinned around them. Hopeless, she realized, to try to see the end of it.

The wind in their compartment wailed, and she sucked in air, fearing a leak. Seeker patted her outstretched hand. It lazed, eyes closed as though asleep. This startled her, and a long moment passed before she guessed that Seeker had done this before, that this was not some colossal accident they had blundered into.

As if in reply Seeker licked its lips, exposing black gums and pointed yellow teeth.

Her ears popped. She looked outward again, beyond the nearby slow buffeting of tree trunks. 'Upward' was now tilted away from the darkening bowl of sky. But their acceleration still lay along the chestnut brown length of the Pinwheel, as they rotated with it. Black shrubs dotted the great stretched expanse of the length that dwindled away, gray laminations making the perspective even starker. Cross-struts of cedar red tied the long strips into an interlocking network that twisted visibly in the howling gale that tore along it. The Pinwheel was flexible, bowing like a tree in a hurricane.

They smacked into the nearest tree, and a big, sharp branch almost punched through the window. But in the pummeling wind their tree wrenched aside, and the impact slammed against another part of the wall. Could the window hold against such impacts? She did not want to find out.

Her ears popped again, and her breath came raggedly. Along the Pinwheel's length great strips of lighter wood rose, with walnut-colored edges. The great shaft canted, sculpting the wind, and the roaring gale subsided; the twisting and wrenching lessened. Pops and creaks still rang out, but she felt a subtle loosening in the coupled structure. It was flying itself.

The last thin haze of atmosphere faded into star-sprinkled black. The floor vibrated. She felt that an invisible, implacable enemy sat on her chest and would forever, talking to her in a language of wrenching low bass notes. Cold, thin air stung her nostrils. She almost panicked but found that there was enough if she labored to fill her lungs.

As she panted, the ample curve of the planet rose serenely at the base of the window. Its smooth ivory cloud decks seemed near enough to touch . . . but she could not raise her arms.

Along the tapering length of the Pinwheel, slow, lazy undulations came marching. The great trunk was rippling. Waves rushed toward her, growing in height. When they first arrived they gave the nub end a hard snap. Cley and Seeker hung on, barely.

The trees thrashed on their vine tethers. Turbulence, she guessed, drove these waves, which dissipated in the whip crack at its ends. Tree trunks thumped and battered, but their cabin pressure held.

Seeker licked its lips again without opening its eyes. They revolved higher. Now she could see the complete expanse of the Pinwheel. It curved slightly, tapering away, like an infinite highway unconcerned with the impossibility of surmounting the will of planets. Vines wrapped along it, and near the middle a green forest flourished.

They were arcing up over the planet. Pale sandy splotches marked the lands where human works had eventually exhausted the soil beyond redemption. The Supras vowed to restore those, in a campaign lasting millennia. One huge, bare continent she remembered from her smattering of history: the ruin of artificial mountains made by the Crafters, an ambitious pre-Supra form. Where once the world's highest peaks had towered, now the rains they captured from passing clouds had ground them into dust. In time, butting continents would probably hoist such ramparts again. The great plates were sliding about as fast as her fingernails grew. Their waltz was the great slow rhythm that played through all the long human adventure, acted out in that thin skin of air.

At the Pinwheel's far end a needle-thin line arced down. The point plunged into the atmosphere — a flare of pink and glaring white. Undulations from this shock raced back toward her. When these reached her, the buffetings were rough but not alarming, for the trees were now tied snugly against the underside of the Pinwheel's nub end.

Deep, solemn notes beat through the walls. The entire Pinwheel was like a huge instrument strummed by wind and gravity, the waves singing a strange song that sounded through her bones.

The Pinwheel now stood out against the whole expanse of Earth, a severe green and brown straight line stretched across the blues and whites. Cley still felt strong acceleration into the compartment's floor, but it was less now as gravity countered the centrifugal whirl. Their air, too, thickened as the tree's walls exuded a sweet-scented, moist vapor.

The spectacle of her whole world, spread out in silent majesty, struck her. They were nearing the top of their ascent, the Pinwheel pointing vertically, as if to bury itself in the heart of the planet.

She wondered what would happen to them next. If they stayed here, their trees would be dropped onto the surface partway around the world. Was that why Seeker had met this whirling machine?

The Pinwheel throbbed. She had felt its many adjustments and percussive changes as it struggled against both elements, air and vacuum, so this latest long undulation seemed unremarkable. Only a short while ago she had thought that the ravenous green, chewing at the pale deserts, waged an epic struggle. Now she rode an unending whirl of immeasurably greater difficulty.

The kinetic whirligig of all these events dizzied her. The last few days had stripped away her comfortable preconceptions, leaving her open to naked wonder. She was beyond fear now, in a curious calm. Ideas floated through her mind like silent fireworks. She looked down and in a glance knew that the Earth and the Pinwheel were two similar systems, brothers of vastly different scales.

The Pinwheel was like a tree, she guessed. Quite certainly alive and yet also, at its core, perhaps a dead spire, cellulose used and discarded by the ancestors of the living cells that made its bark.

'How can this thing be so strong?' she whispered.

'It is made of tiny carbon fibers,' Seeker said. 'They regrow daily and can take more strain than any material.'

'I thought diamond was strongest.'

'It, too, is carbon – but not living, and so evolution has not worked upon it.'

'Who built this?'

'Grew it, you mean? No idea.'

'Ah, something Seeker doesn't know – at last.'

'My order knew these as the Great Trees. Only a living thing has the supple nature to adjust to vacuum and air, and thrive.'

'What a ballet!'

'Its trick is to not let the Earth's spin foil it. Instead, it swims in the atmosphere, propelling itself. More artful than the awkward way your species flails its arms in the water.'

'Hey, I'd like to see you swim at all.'

Seeker gave her its silent, fang-baring laugh. 'Water is where we keep our food.'

She gazed down at the shimmering Earth. It, too, was a thin skin of verdant life atop a huge bulk of rocks. But far down in the magma were elements of the ancestral rocks. In her mind she felt the slide and smack of whole continents as they rode on a slippery base of limestone, layers built up from an infinitude of seashell carcasses. All living systems, in the large, were a skin wrapped around the dead. The Great Tree was an artwork in carbon, shaped like a living diamond.

'Time to go,' Seeker said, getting up awkwardly. Even its strength was barely equal to the centrifugal thrust.

'What! You're not leaving?'

'We both are.'

A loud bang. Cley felt herself falling. She kicked out in her fright. This only served to propel her into the ceiling. She struck and painfully rebounded. Flailing, she hit another wall, and another. Her instincts kept telling herself she was falling, despite the evidence of her eyes – and then some ancient subsystem of her brain cut in, and she automatically quieted. She was not truly falling, except in a sense used by physicists. She was merely weightless, bouncing about the compartment before Seeker's amused yawn.

'What happened?' she called, grabbing a protruding handle and stopping herself.

'We are free, for a bit.'

'Why?'

'See ahead.'

Their vines had slipped off, retracting back to the nub. Freed, their tree shot away from the Pinwheel. They speeded out on a tangent to its circle of revolution. Already the nub was a shrinking spot on the huge, curved tree that hung between air and space. She had an impression of the Pinwheel dipping its mouth into the rich swamp of Earth's air, drinking its fill alternately from one side of itself and then the other. But what kept it going, against the constant drag of those fierce winds?

She was sure it had some enormous skill to solve that

problem, but there was no sign what that might be. She looked out, along the curve of Earth. Ahead was a dark brown splotch on the star-littered blackness.

'A friend,' Seeker said. 'There.'

3
Jonah

They soared away from the release point with surprising speed. The Pinwheel whirled away, its grandiose gyre casting long shadows along its woody length. Splashes of color played where vacuum barnacles stretched their fronds to catch sunlight.

She could see it better now. Despite the winds it suffered, bushes clung to its flanks. The upper end, which they had just left, now rotated down toward the coming twilight. Its midpoint was thickest, and oval, following a circular orbit a third of Earth's radius above the surface. At its farthest extension, groaning and popping with the strain, the great log had reached a distance two-thirds of the Earth's radius, poking well out into the cold clasp of space.

'We're going fast,' Cley said.

Seeker yawned. 'Enough to take trees to other planets, yes.'

'That's where we're—?'

'No, that is not our destination.'

She knew better now than to press Seeker for its plans. When Cley had asked for help escaping the Surpras, the procyon had been following some agenda, and part of it was nondisclosure. Maybe it didn't like to give away its moves and then have them fail; everybody had pride.

Or maybe it didn't want to scare her. Or scare her off. The Pinwheel — who would sign up to ride that? Not Cley, no. Or anybody she knew.

So far, Seeker's mysterious aims had aligned with Cley's. Plainly, something enormous was happening, and neither Supras nor Seeker would explain in bite-sized words exactly what was up. So be it.

But Cley remembered Seeker's answer when she had asked about other Originals. 'They are gone.' Gone from Earth, maybe, but not gone as in extinct. So there might be Originals up in the sky somewhere. Not her Meta, but still her kind. Kin.

And just maybe . . . her father? When you know nothing, you are free to hope.

They shot ahead of the nub, watching it turn downward with stately resolution, as though gravely bowing to necessity by returning to the planet that held it in bondage.

She could not take her eyes from the grandiosity of the Pinwheel. Its lot was to be forever the mediator between two great oceans. Others could sail the skies in serenity, in air or in space. The Pinwheel knew both the ceaseless tumult of the air and the biting cold of vacuum. She wondered if many life forms had dwelled at the border of the ancient oceans of Earth, where waves crunched against shore. Some had to, mediating between worlds — and must have paid the price, beset by storm and predator.

Cley watched silently, clinging to one of the sticky patches on the compartment's walls. There was a solemn majesty to the Pinwheel, a remorseless resignation to the dip of its leading arm into the battering winds. Looking back at it, she saw where they had been held, which was

now the Pinwheel's leading edge. It punched into the
upper atmosphere with a blare of ivory light conjured up
by the shock of reentry. Huge forces worked along the
Great Tree. Yet it plunged on, momentum's captive,
swimming toward its next touchdown.

She saw now why it had momentarily hung steady over
the forest: At bottom, the rotation nearly canceled the
orbital speed. The backward sweep of the Pinwheel's arm
was opposite to the orbital speed. That brief balance of
motion happened just as the tip reached bottom, hanging over the treetops. Craft on such a scale bespoke enormous control, and she asked in a whisper, 'Is it . . .
intelligent?'

'Of course,' Seeker said. 'And quite old.'

'Forever moving, forever going nowhere.' She noticed
that she was whispering, as if it might overhear. 'What
thoughts, what dreams it must have.'

'It is a different form of intelligence from you – neither
greater nor lesser.'

'How old is it?'

'An early artifact of the time well before the
Quickening, as I remember. Though it also made itself,
in part.'

'How can anything that big . . . ?'

Seeker spun playfully in air, clicking sharp teeth in a
disjointed rhythm. It seemed uninterested in answering
her.

'Rin and the others made it, right?'

Seeker yelped in high amusement. 'They could not,
no.'

'Somebody planned that thing.'

'Some body? Yes, the body plans – not the mind.'

'Huh? No, I mean . . .'

'In far antiquity there were beasts designed to forage for iceteroids among the cold spaces beyond the planets – *ooof!* – They knew enough of genecraft to modify themselves – *ah!* – Perhaps they met other life forms which came from other stars – I do not know – *uh!* I doubt that it matters. Time's hand shaped some such creatures into this – *oof!* – and then came the Quickening.' Seeker seldom spoke so long, and it had managed this time to punctuate each sentence with a bounce from the walls, which it enjoyed immensely.

'And the Quickening . . . ?'

'The time when human abilities expanded beyond ordinary perceptions.'

'You mean, my perceptions?'

'Yes. Mine, too.'

'Uh . . . let me mull that one over. Those "beasts" that did in iceteriods – you mean creatures that gobbled ice?'

Seeker settled onto a sticky patch on the wall, held on with two legs, and fanned its remaining legs and arms into the air. 'They were sent to seek such, then spiral it into the inner worlds.'

'Water for Earth?'

'It was needed. Far later, the bots decreed a dry planet. The outer iceteroid halo was exhausted by then, anyway, employed elsewhere.'

'Why not use spaceships?'

'Of metal?' Sad shake of a shaggy head. 'They do not reproduce.'

Cley blinked. 'These things would give birth, out there in the cold?'

'Slowly, yes.'

'How'd they make the Pinwheel? It's sure not an ice eater, I can tell that much.'

'Time is deep. Circumstance has worked on it. More so than upon your kind.'

'Is it smarter?'

'You humans return to that subject always. Different, not greater or lesser.'

Humbled, Cley said, 'I figured it must be smarter than me, to do all that.'

'It flies like a bird, without bother. And thinks long, as befits a thing from the great, slow spaces.'

'How does it fly? The wind alone . . .' The question spoken, she saw the answer. As the other arm of the Pinwheel rose to the top of its circular arc, she could make out thin plumes of white spurting behind it. She had seen Supra craft do that, leaving a line of cloud in their wake. Jets, probably of water plucked from the air.

'Consider it a large tree that flies,' Seeker said.

'Huh? Trees have roots.'

'Trees walk; why not fly? We are guests now inside a smaller flying tree.'

'Ummm. What's it eat?'

'Some from air, from sun-sucking chemistry, some . . .' Seeker gestured ahead, along their trajectory. They shot above and away from the spinning, curved colossus. And Cley saw a thin haze now hanging against the black of space, dimmer than stars but more plentiful. There was a halo around the world, like fireflies drawn to the planet's immense ripe glow. Beyond the nightline the gossamer halo hung like a wreath above Earth's shadow.

One mote grew as they sped near it. It swelled into a complex structure of struts and half-swollen balloons. It had sinews like knotty walnut. Fleshy vines webbed its intersections. Cley tried to imagine the Pinwheel digesting this oddity and decided she would have to see it to believe.

But this minor issue faded as she peered ahead. Other trees like theirs lay fore and aft, some spinning slightly, others tumbling. But all were headed toward a thing that reminded her of a pineapple, prickly with spikes but bristling with slow-waving fur. Around this slowly revolving thing a haze of pale motes clustered.

'All that . . . alive?'

'In a way. Are bots alive?'

'No, of course — are those bots?'

'Not of metal, no. And they do mate. But even bots can make copies of themselves.'

Cley said with exasperation, 'You know what I mean when something's alive.'

'I am deficient in that.'

'Well, if you don't know, I can't tell you.' Sometimes Seeker was deliberately opaque.

'Good.'

'What?'

'Talk is a trick for taking the mystery out of the world.'

Cley did not know what to say and decided to let sleeping mysteries lie. She was just a forest girl, and this leap into space had terrified her. But in these alien voids dwelled more living things than she had dreamed — an exotic biosphere. She was sure there had been talk of this in school, but then, she had nodded off a lot. As a girl she had found indoors dull, outdoors thrilling. Well, maybe her forest-folk skills could get her through here, as well. Space was a really big outdoors.

She sighed and resolved to stop worrying and just live. She could ruminate when they got a quiet spot in their lives. If ever.

'Okay, what's up?' she made herself say brightly. Seeker pointed. Their tree convoy was approaching the fog-glow swathing the pineapple.

Gravity imposes flat floors, straight walls, rectangular rigidities. Weightlessness allows the ample symmetries of the cylinder and sphere. In the swarm of objects large and small, Cley saw an expressive freedom of effortless new geometries. Myriad spokes and limbs, rhomboids and ellipsoids – she got those terms from her inboards. These jutted from the many shells and rough skins, but she could not imagine their uses. Necessity dictates form, she knew.

She watched an orange sphere extend a thin stalk into a nearby array of pale green cylinders. It began to spin about the stalk. This gave it stability, so that the stalk punched surely through the thin walls of its . . . its prey, Cley supposed. She wondered how the sphere spun itself up, and suspected that internal fluids had to counterrotate. But was this an attack? The array of rubbery green columns did not behave like a victim. Instead, it gathered around the sphere. Slow stems embraced, and pulses worked along their crusted brown lengths. Cley wondered if she was watching an exchange, the cylinders throbbing energetically to negotiate a biochemical transaction. Sex among the geometries?

Swiftly their flotilla of trees cut through the insectlike haze of life, passing near myriad forms that sometimes veered to avoid them. Some, though, tried to catch them. These had angular shapes, needle-nosed and surprisingly quick. But the trees still plunged on, outstripping pursuit, directly into the barnacled pineapple. She braced for an impact.

But she saw now that only parts of the huge thing were solid. Large caps at the ends looked firm enough, but the main body revealed more and more detail as they approached. Sunlight glinted from multifaceted specks. Cley realized that these were a multitude of spindly growths projecting out from a central axis. She could see the axis buried deep in the profusion of stalks and webbing, like a bulbous brown root.

She stopped thinking of it as a pineapple and substituted 'prickly pear,' a plant she had seen in the valley where the Library of Life lay. As they came in above the lime green crown at one end of the 'pear,' a wave passed across it. The sudden flash made her blink and shield her eyes. Many facets sent the harsh sunlight back in jeweled bands of color. Her eyes corrected swiftly to let her see through the glare. The wave had stopped neatly halfway across the cap, one side still green, the other a chrome-bright sheen. The piercing shine reminded her of how hard sunlight was, unfiltered by air.

'It swims,' Seeker said.

'Where?'

'Or better to say, it paces its cage.'

'I . . .' Cley began, then remembered Seeker's remark about words robbing mystery. She saw that the shiny half would reflect sunlight, giving the prickly pear a small push from that side. As it rotated, the wave of color change swept around the dome, keeping the thrust always in the same direction.

'Hold to the wall,' Seeker said quickly.

'Who, what's – oh.'

The spectacle had distracted her from their approach. She had unconsciously expected the trees to slow. Now the fibrous wealth of stalks sticking out from the axis grew alarmingly fast. They were headed into a clotted region of interlaced strands.

In the absolute clarity of space she saw smaller and smaller features, many not attached to the prickly pear at all but hovering like feasting insects. She realized only then the true scale of the complexity they sped toward. The prickly pear was as large as a mountain. Their tree was a matchstick plunging headfirst into it.

The lead tree struck a broad tan web. It stretched this membrane and then rebounded – but did not bounce off. Instead, the huge catcher's mitt damped the bounce into rippling waves. Then a second tree struck near the web's edge, sending more circular waves racing away. A third, a fourth – then it was their turn.

Seeker said nothing. A sudden, sickening tug reminded her of acceleration's liabilities – then reversed, sending her stomach aflutter. The lurching lasted for long, sloshing moments, and then they were at rest. Out the window she could see other trees embed themselves in the web, felt their impacts make the net bob erratically.

When the tossing had damped away, she said shakily, 'Rough . . . landing.'

'The price of passage. The Pinwheel pays its momentum debt this way,' Seeker said, detaching itself from the stick-pad.

'Debt? For what?'

'For the momentum it in turn receives back, as it takes on passengers.'

Cley blinked. 'People go down in the Pinwheel, too?'

'And cargo. The flow runs both ways.'

'Well, sure, but . . .' She still could not imagine that anyone would brave the descent through the atmosphere, ending up hanging by the tail of the great space tree as it hesitated, straining, above the ground. How did they jump off? Cley felt herself getting overwhelmed by complexities – and quiet fear. She focused on the present. 'Look, who's this momentum debt paid to?'

'Our host.'

'What is this?'

'A Jonah.'

'What's that mean?'

'A truly ancient term. Your friend Fanak could no doubt tell you its origin.'

'He's not my friend – we're cousins, a billion years removed.' Cley smiled ironically, then frowned as she felt long, slow pulses surge through the walls of their tree. 'Say, what's a Jonah do?'

'It desires to swallow us.'

4
Leviathan

'Swallow us? And we want that?'
 'We could return to Earth.' Seeker grinned wickedly.

'I . . . on the Pinwheel? No.' Her nerves were not up for that.

Crawly creatures were already busy in the compartments. Many-legged, scarcely more than anthologies of ebony sticks and ropy muscle strung together by gray gristle, they poked and shoved the bulky cargo adroitly, forming into long processions.

Though they were quick and able, Cley sensed that these were truly not single individuals. This might be what smart ants became without gravity's grind; insects the size of people.

She and Seeker followed the flow of cargo out the main port, the entrance they had used in the forest only two hours before. Swimming in zero g was fun, though she had quick moments of disoriented panic, which she managed to cover. They floated out into a confusing melange of clacking spiderlike workers, oblong packages, and forking tubular passages that led away into green profusion. The air was fresh, like that in the tree. This place was tuned for humans, she realized, and she relaxed a bit.

Cley was surprised at how quickly she had adjusted to the strangeness of zero gravity. Like many abilities that seem natural once they are learned – like the complex trick of walking itself – weightlessness reflexes had been hard-wired into her kind. Had she paused a moment to reflect, this would have been yet another reminder that she could not possibly represent the planet-bound earliest humans.

But she did not reflect. She was as Original as anyone in existence, and that was enough. She launched herself through the moist air of the great, noisy shafts, rebounding with eager zest from the rubbery walls. The spiders ignored her. Several jostled her in their mechanical haste to carry away what appeared to be a kind of inverted tree. Its outside was hard bark, forming a hollow, thick-walled container open at the top and bottom. Inside sprouted fine gray branches, meeting at the center in large, pendulous blue fruit.

She hungrily reached for one, only to have a spider knock her away with a vicious kick. Seeker, though, lazily picked two of them, and the spiders back-pedaled in air to avoid it. She wondered what musk or gestures Seeker had used; it seemed scarcely awake, much less concerned.

They ate, ruby juice hanging in droplets in the humid air. Canyons rimmed in shimmering light beckoned in all directions. Cley tugged on a nearby transparent tube as big as she was, through which an amber fluid gurgled. From this anchorage she could hold steady and orient herself in the confusing welter of brown spokes, green foliage, metallic-gray shafts, and knobby, damp protrusions.

Their tree-ship hung in the embrace of filmy leaves.

From the hard vacuum of space the tree had apparently been propelled through a translucent passage. Through a membrane Cley could see a slow pusher-plate already retracting back toward the catcher's mitt that had stopped them.

Around them small animals scampered along knotted cables and flaking vines, chirruping, squealing, venting visible yellow farts. Everywhere was animation, purpose, hurry. Momentum.

'Come, please,' Seeker said. It cast off smoothly, and Cley followed down a wide-mouthed olive-green tube. She was surprised to find that she could see through its walls to green layers beyond.

Sunlight filtered through an enchanted canopy. Clouds formed from mere wisps and made droplets, and eager cone-shaped emerald leaves sucked them in. She was kept busy watching the slow-motion but perpetual rhythm of this place until Seeker darted away, out of the tube. She followed hand over hand into a vast space dominated by a hollow half sphere of green moss. The other hemisphere, she saw, was transparent. Not glass – something tough yet flexible. It let in a bar of hot yellow sunlight that must have been reflected and refracted far down into the living maze around them.

Seeker headed straight for the mossy bowl and dug its claws into a low plant. Cley awkwardly bounced off the resilient moss, snatched at a spindly tree, and finally got a hold. Seeker was eating crimson bulbs that grew profusely in grapelike bunches. Cley reached for some, and the bulbs hissed angrily as she plucked one loose. All bluster – the plant did nothing more as she bit in. She liked the rich, grainy taste.

But her irritation grew as her hunger dwindled. Seeker seemed about to go to sleep when she said, 'You brought us here on purpose, didn't you?'

'Surely.' Seeker lazily blinked, tongue lolling.

Angered by this display of unconcern, Cley shouted, 'I wanted to find my people!'

'They are gone.'

'You say that; all-powerful goddamned Rin said they're all dead – but I want to look for them.'

'Rin and his kind are good at a few things. Among them is acquiring information. I believe their search was thorough.'

'They missed me!'

'Only for a while.'

'You said I could find people like me if I followed you.'

'If any remain, they have gone here, into the solar-sphere.'

'I still want to see for myself!' She pressed her lips together in what she hoped was a stern look. 'Alone, maybe – how'd you like that?'

'The price of such seeing will be death,' Seeker said quietly.

She blinked. 'We've done fine so far.'

'A numerical series can have many terms yet be finite.'

'But – but . . .' Cley wanted to express her dismay at being snatched away from everything she knew, but pride forced her to say, 'Something in the sky wants to kill me, right? So to get away we go into the sky? Nonsense!'

'You are unsettled.' Seeker folded its hands across its belly in a gesture that somehow conveyed contrition. 'Still, we must flee as far and as fast as we can.'

'Me, sure. But why you?' She jutted out her chin, thinking, *I can fend for myself,* and knew immediately that she was lying. Adolescent bravado was not going to work here.

'You would be helpless without me.'

Cley's mouth twisted, irritation and self-mockery mingling. 'Guess so, up here. In the woods we'd be even.'

'Perhaps. But against the entities who live in higher dimensions, we are equally powerless.'

Cley shook her head. 'We nabbed that one, right after we got back from the Tubeworld.'

'I believe they are from the other "brane," as humans term it. They wish to intervene in our struggle, clearly, but still have trouble manifesting here. I think they will learn quickly, and we will lose whatever small advantage we had.'

'Intervene why?'

'To affect the flow's pinch point – you.'

'Huh? Because I'm Original? There may be others.'

Seeker smiled. 'Out here? Not with certainty. No one keeps an inventory anywhere, except the Supras, of course.'

'And if I don't make it to this big party somebody's planning, what happens?'

'We all die, I imagine.'

Cley blinked. 'The Malign? It'll—'

'Lay waste to the system solar, and much else.'

'Me? I . . . wish I . . .' She let it trail off, not knowing how to finish. She had almost said, *had my Meta. Had my Moms . . . someone who'd make this right . . .* Or an even older longing: *had my father.* That last she could maybe do something about – look for him, at least, out here in this wild place. Somewhere. Even if it hurt to hope, she could look.

Seeker said nothing, and Cley realized it was being

diplomatic, letting her have her moment to reflect. They weren't on an equal footing here. Cley had woodsy lore, but Seeker had moved through these strange spaces with an unconscious assurance and craft she envied. The procyon had direction, somewhere it believed they needed to be, and clearly had an idea about how they should get there. *Well, at least that makes one of us.* 'Where do we go, then?'

'For now, Earth's moon.'

'The . . .' She had unconsciously assumed they were arcing above the Earth but would return to it along some distant trajectory. Seeker hadn't said they were going to the planets, after all. She knew the Supras voyaged to other worlds, too, but she had never heard of her own kind doing so. The Meta didn't venture much beyond their woods and plains. That's why her sudden idea that maybe her father had done so was, well, a thin reed . . . She shook herself from her reverie. So . . . 'For what?'

'We must move outward and be careful.'

'To save our skins?'

'Your skin.'

'Guess you don't have skin, just fur.'

'It does not seek my fur.'

'And who is it?'

'What, not who.'

Seeker leaned back and arranged itself, all six muscular limbs folded in a comfortable cross-legged posture. It began to speak, softly and melodiously, of times so distant that the very names of their eras had passed away. The great heavy-pelted beast told her of how humanity had met greater intelligences in the vault of stars and had fallen back, recoiling at the blow to its deepest pride.

They had tried to create a higher mentality, and their failure was as vast as their intention.

So they had tried another approach.

'I know about this,' Cley offered. 'I got a holoform of it.'

'How?'

'In the Library.' She shrugged. 'In off-hours.'

She had thought that dipping into the chilly pools of antiquity would help her figure out her time-steeped world, so she did unassigned homework, after Fanak had finished with his pontificating. She recalled the holoform and told Seeker about what she could see in moving forms of ancient vintage.

The story echoed with things unsaid, sorrows unnamed.

In the distant era known only in the Library's holdings as the Quickening, some had left the conceptual space of humanity entirely. Nothing was known of where they went, either mentally or physically.

As the Quickening had approached, human minds that had amplified a billion times thought their way through to a destination unknown. They were said to have been as much beyond ordinary intellects as a woman was beyond the bacteria that flourished in her gut – and the comparison was deliberate in both magnitude and status.

In the final, bittersweet moments of detachment, as the Quickened vanished from human ken, some ordinary people received spotty impressions of what lay beyond. They reported what they perceived, to the limits of their understanding. These gave rise to legends of remarkable persistence.

At first the Quickening ones made a playground.

There the traditional ills of man got erased. Death went

first, forever banished. Even boredom died. Life prolifer-
ated into uncountable worldscapes. Ideologies ranging
from the devouring collective all the way through to the
rigidly, rabidly free — all found their scripts performed.

If necessary, the ever-elusive human nature got tinkered
into compliance with the demands of belief. Populations
lived joyfully under crushing control. Skeptics found their
every doubt confirmed. Believers dwelled in ecstasy, bonding in rapture with their God. Sybarites lounged in pleasure palaces sustained by unflagging energies and desire.
Revolutionaries got to try their experiments upon themselves.

In the telescoping moment when ordinary humans
could see down the dwindling bridge, there flowed
images, ideas, and fidgeting torrents of information. Those
who were left behind witnessed a circus of rapt play.

Ideas exploded in minds unbound by the soft, wet
chemistry of a kilogram of gray meat carried in a hard
skull casing.

Then the Quickened vanished from view.

Where it/they went, no one knew.

There were endless speculations, of course, layered in
the Library down through endless millennia. But no data.
No one had ever heard again from those who went, or
knew what physical form they had adopted. Or even if
they had one.

There were a few scattershot attempts, in both directions. But the transmissions could arrive as floating balls
of humidity, of frantic luminosities, of voices shrieking in
the empty air. The quickened were trying, but they almost
seemed to be moving away at high acceleration.

One day, known for ages as the Loss, the Quickened

simply stopped communicating. Before, their bodies had been living in various space habitats in the outer solar system. Those habitats were found vacant. How the Quickened had left lay in great obscurity.

'Where are they?' Seeker asked, eyes sharp.

'Nobody knows.'

'I am sorry, I thought this was a mystery story.'

'Hey, come on. I only know what I take in.' Thinking, *And how long will it take to digest just what I've already got? I used to think adults were so certain, understood how life was supposed to work. It just gets more confusing and complicated!*

Seeker slid its black lips up over its teeth, sucking abstractly, eyes distant. 'Some of this I did not know.'

'Now, there's a first.'

'You think me arrogant.'

'Just a know-it-all, is all.'

'Then let us share our ignorance.'

Seeker lolled back, eyes half closed, and wove her a tale. Of a time after the Quickening – it was quite sure of at least that – and of another, far later era.

Humanity had encountered alien minds out among the stars. Some collaborations had proved possible, but much one would expect – trade in ideas, art, philosophy, science – was not. The gulf yawned. Minds bred of different evolutions proved too distant to grasp.

And too often, the aliens died away. Ceased to voyage. Ceased to care, to communicate. Sometimes, ceased entirely. There were ancient accounts of vast species suicides. Others vanished without any explanation.

One large grouping of aliens had proved to be the most inscrutable. They dwelled near the galactic center. They had something resembling religious faith, but the very concept is only a rough fit to what the translators could perceive.

Those strange minds had made what came to be known by humanity as the Malign, though of course, that name bespoke a human view. It was, all records said, a being embodied without need of inscribing patterns on matter. And it had proved malignant beyond measure.

The aliens who had made it vanished in its first, virulent actions. History did not record whether this was their goal, or their comeuppance. In time, the distinction scarcely mattered.

Then the true ferocity of their creation lashed across the galaxy. The witnesses to this era were few, for the Malign's energies erased all.

Seeker gave only one small example. Uncounted millions of years before, the Malign had directed a white dwarf into a Sol-type star. The dwarf carved its way through, and the star had turned into a thermonuclear furnace under the sudden, fierce compression of the dwarf's added gravitation. The gnawing dwarf ate its way through the fatter star, exploding into view on the other side, carrying forth like fruit of conquest a white-hot disk of incandescence, stolen from the Sol-star's matter.

An inhabited planet orbiting the Sol-star survived the initial seethe, still bound to its parent, but its atmosphere and then oceans boiled away within hours. The dwarf sped on, carrying its new disk like a brilliant skirt. Following it into the interstellar depths straggled most of the victim system's planets, borne into eternal chill.

And so the Malign had dealt with many civilizations throughout the hub of the galaxy. Star formation had begun eleven billion years before, at the galactic center.

Condensation into young suns propagated outward. Earth's ordinary star had been born 5.5 billion years before. The galaxy had rotated twenty-five times since the Earth was born, and nineteen since life appeared there.

So the oldest civilizations lay in the great spherical swarm that humans could not even see, through the intervening lanes of dust.

Beginning there, at the galaxy's hub, and raging outward for millions of years, the Malign had extinguished most of galactic civilization.

All this the Malign achieved with the great Talents that descended from a final theory of the universe. Only the Malign could master this. Indeed, many felt that this ability was the reason the alien minds and human helpers had created the Malign – a greatness beyond their knowing, who would finally understand the universe entire.

This had seemed to happen. Communications showed that the Malign had formulated a Theory of Everything, of infinite, supple nuance.

A long silence followed. Knowing the final answers to myriad questions that the best minds of humanity (and far more) had pondered for uncounted ages – knowing this in full – it moved to eradicate any intelligence that could do the same.

Through uncounted eons, it very nearly succeeded.

And no one knew why.

Humanity had suffered a single encounter with the Malign. A colonized star system, the boldest human venture into the galactic center, had attracted the destroyer's ravenous attention. Many of the bravest had died then, on the worlds they'd shaped with such loving care, and much of man's adventurous spirit died with them. Few escaped to tell of what had befallen them — fewer still with intact minds.

That trauma sent them reeling away, back to their stellar system, to hide. It also sent human minds fleeing from the analytical. If the Malign came from the quest for final knowledge, then such knowledge itself had to be abandoned.

Only a few had labored through that dark age. They kept the Library intact, moving it to deep caverns immune to even the vagaries of continental drift. Privation was common, but the greatest poverty was of prospect. Their horizons shrank. They kept their heads down.

No darkness endures forever. This one, the deepest, still did not extinguish the burning light of curiosity flickering in the human skull.

So another great human civilization came and ventured forth. In a mere few million years, it had spanned the stars again. It found ruins left by the Malign. And fugitives as well, most of them machine intelligences. A ramshackle alliance formed. The sphere of human endeavor expanded . . . and again met the Malign.

It was still foraging.

The tales of that time were now lost. A little came to light, long afterward, pieced together from survivors' accounts near-mythic in their scope. They were at least as accurate as what survived in the Library's records, purged of almost all mention of the Malign, by those fearful of another such monster's creation.

Only heroic struggle had managed to capture and restrain the Malign. To cage it firmly had been the work of billions, exhausting lifetimes. Billions more perished. Countless mortal minds had conjured up a counter to the

Malign. A guard was born, named the Multifold. Both dwelled in the depths of far space.

But with that last grand act some light had gone out of humanity. Later subspecies of humans had retreated yet again. They let their machines steal the variety and tang from their world. Their recessional took a million years to play out. Many resisted. But in time only the lights of Sonomulia burned in the sands that would one day overwhelm all.

Seeker sighed. 'There is more, but I cannot bear to say it.'

'You'd stop there? Why?'

'Vain pride,' Seeker said.

'Huh? Why? That makes no sense.'

'To think that humans were the pinnacle of creation?'

Cley grimaced. 'Oh. I see.'

Cley was subdued for most of the voyage to the moon. She had seen this fresh world hanging in her sky, known it was a fairly recent creation from a remnant of the original. Just as she had known a bit of Seeker's story, for fragments of it formed a tribal fable based on Supra lore.

But the Malign was older now than the mountains she had roved – far more than just a gauzy myth told by the Supras. They had spoken of the Multifold, too, but that equally tenuous entity was said to be strung like a veil among the crush of stars and radiant clouds.

Those stories had never seemed as immediate or important as the here and now of life in her Meta. Cley struggled to absorb that such a thing as the Malign could actually be real and have any connection to her. That it could want *her* dead, that it had destroyed all those she had loved, was almost beyond belief. But the myth still lived, raged, and ravaged, while her people's ashes blew on the winds. Those who had been her reality were now crumbling gray ash, slowly reclaimed by the woods she'd known.

The moon swam, green and opulent, as they looped outward. The Jonah's slight spin gave an obliging purchase to the outer segments of the great vessel, and Cley ventured with Seeker through verdant labyrinths to watch their approach. They spoke little. Cley sensed a momentum to their passage, a drama being played out beyond her understanding. And Seeker would say nothing more of this, for now.

The lunar landscape was a jagged creation of sharp mountains and colossal waterfalls. At the edge of the dusk line, valleys sank into shadows lit by reflected yellow from high peaks. Thick clouds, far higher than any on Earth because of the lesser gravity, glowed like live coals. Raw peaks cleaved the flowing cloud decks, leaving a wake like that of a giant ship. From these flashed lightning, like the blooming buds of blue roses.

These stark contrasts had been shaped by a bombardment of light elements, hauled sunward in comets. To kindle this, a rain had fallen for a thousand years in droplets the size of a human hand. Atop the lunar air sat a translucent film a few molecules thick, holding in a thick blanket of air. The film had permanent holes allowing spacecraft and spaceborne life access, the whole arrangement kept buoyant by steady replenishment from belching volcanoes. This trap offset the moon's feebler gravitational grasp so well that it lost less of its air than did the Earth. Intact, the moon swam like a single cell in the sun's warmth.

The fat, beckoning crescent moon hung almost directly sunward and so was nearly drowned in shadow until the Jonah began to curve toward its far side. For this passing moment the sun, moon, and Earth were aligned in geometric perfection before plunging back along their complicated courses. Cley watched this moment of uncanny, simple equilibrium and felt, as she had not in a long while, the paradox that balance and stillness lay at the heart of all change.

One of her Moms had taught that, using examples as humble as a bird's flight on rising warm winds. Cley had never imagined that the lesson could play out on such an immense scale, in silent majesty.

'See,' Seeker said. 'Storms.'

Cley looked down into the murk and whirl of the bottled lunar air. But the disturbance lay above that sharp division. In the blackness over both poles there snaked slow filaments of blushing orange.

'Damn,' Cley whispered, as though the helical strands could hear. 'Is that . . . ?'

'The Malign? I suspect so.'

'You've seen it before?'

'Not as directly, no. But whatever it is, I think it probes for us. I had thought the Malign would forage elsewhere first.'

Seeker did not explain further. It pointed with its ears at what seemed to Cley to be empty space around Earth. Seeker described how the Earth's magnetic domain was compressed by the wind from the sun, and streams out in the wake. Cley blinked her eyes up into ultraviolet and caught the delicate shimmer of a huge volume around the planet. She witnessed a province she had never suspected, the realm dominated by the planet's sturdy magnetic fields. They made a gossamer ball, crumpled in on the sun side, stretched and slimmed by the wind from the sun into a tapering tail.

Arcades of gossamer fretwork grew and died. In the rubbery architecture of this magnetosphere, roving violences were killing intricate fields, annihilating order. Suddenly, she knew that these crimes were the footprints of the Malign. That had been Seeker's point. A sullen dread she had been resisting fell upon her like a black weight. 'It's searching there, too.'

'It relishes the bands of magnetic fields,' Seeker said somberly. 'I hoped it would seek us only in that realm.'

'But it's spread here, too.'

'It is vast in a way that seems beyond description.'

'Huh? How?'

'There is mathematics our sort cannot comprehend.'

'Hell, there's *arithmetic* I had trouble with.'

'Oh?'

'Inboards have their limits.'

Though she chuckled, Cley felt a cold shudder. Immense forces lumbered through these colossal spaces. She was a woman born to pad the quiet paths of sheltered forests, to prune and plant and catch the savor of the sighing wind. These chilly reaches were not for her.

She stiffened her spine. 'It's able to punch through the air blanket.'

Seeker simply poked one ear at the lunar south pole. She shifted down into the infrared and saw faint plumes geyser below the hard curve of the atmosphere. Orange sparks worked there.

Cley felt her pulse quicken. 'Damn-all! It's already breached the air membrane.' She bit her lip and nearly lost her hold on a branch.

'And it can hunt and prey at will, once inside. It follows the lunar magnetic-field lines where it wishes.' Seeker cast off without warning, kicked against an enormous orchid, and shot down a connecting tube.

'Hey, wait!'

She caught up in an ellipsoidal vault, where an army of the clacking black spiders was assembling ranks of oval containers. In the dizzying activity she could barely keep up with Seeker. Larger animals shot by her, some big enough to swat her with a single flipper or snap her in two with a beak, moving in a blur − but all ignored her. A fever pitch resounded through the noisy mob. *So much life. So huge.*

Seeker had stopped, though, and was sunning itself just beneath the upper dome.

'What can we *do*?' Even to herself, her words sounded plaintive and lost.

'Do you wish to ride back to Earth?'

Cley bit her lip. 'I don't want to go back to the Supras with an apology in my mouth.'

'I agree.' Seeker grinned. 'My friend, I sense your foreboding. It is needless. Our deaths need no previews.'

'Thanks for the dollop of optimism.'

'Um. I had thought to catch the vessel now approaching.'

She saw first through the dome a smaller version of their Jonah, arcing up from one of the portal holes in the lunar air layer. Seeker had said that the Jonah was one of the indentured of its species, caged in an endless cycle between Earth and moon. The smaller Jonah dipped into the lunar air, enjoying some tiny freedom. She felt a trace of pity for such living vessels, but then she saw something that banished minor troubles. A great mass came into view, closing with them from a higher orbit.

'What's . . . ?'

'We approach a momentary mating.'

'Mating? They actually . . . in flight?'

'They are always in flight.'

'But . . . that thing, it's so huge.'

Seeker had found some small wriggling creature. It paused to bite it in half, chewed with an assessing look, and swallowed. Cley remembered the Semisent. Seeker smacked black lips and said, 'It is a Leviathan. The small Jonahs are its half-grown spawn. As it swoops closest to the sun, desires well in it, as they have for ages past. We shall simply take advantage of the joy of merging.'

'So we're part of a sex act?'

'An honor, yes.'

As the great bulk glided effortlessly toward them, she surveyed its mottled blue-green skin, the tangled jungles it held to the sun's eternal nourishing blare.

Cley could not help but smile. 'I think I prefer my lust in smaller doses.'

5

Editing the Sun

Grand beings communicate through emissaries. Slow, ponderous oscillations began to course through the Jonah. Cley saw a watery bubble pop into space from the Jonah's leathery skin nearby. It wobbled, seeking definition, and made itself into an ellipsoid.

'Hurry,' Seeker said. 'Departure.'

Seeker adroitly tugged her along through green labyrinths. When they came to the flared mouth of what seemed to be a giant hollow root, it shoved her ahead. She tumbled head over heels and smacked into a spongy, resilient pad. Velvet-fine hairs oozing white sap stuck to her. A sharp, meaty flavor clung in her nose. She felt light-headed and realized that the air was thick with a vapor that formed and dissolved and met again in billowing, translucent sheets. Seeker slapped away a rubbery blob as big as a man but seemed unconcerned. A shrill hissing began.

They were drifting down the bore of a narrowing tube. The walls glowed pearly and warm, and she felt the cloying sap cloaking her feet and back.

Seeker snagged a shimmering plate – a plant? – and launched it like an ancient discus toward her. The disk unfurled into a strand, and Seeker jerked on it at the right instant so that it spun around her. The sticky stuff wrapped about her twice, whiplash fast, then twisted away. Seeker caught it on the come-around, pivoted, and slapped the end against a prickly strand. 'This may be bumpy.'

Cley was tightly bound. They gathered speed in a swirl of refracting light. Cley held her breath, frightened by the rising hiss around them.

'What –' she began, but a soft, cool ball of sweet sap caught against her mouth when she breathed in. She blew it away and felt Seeker next to her as the wall glow ebbed. The ribbed tube ahead flexed, bulged with a hollow groan – and they shot through into the hard glare of space itself.

The Jonah had blown a rubbery bubble. A sap envelope enclosed them, quickly plumping into a perfect sphere.

'Our Jonah is making love to the Leviathan,' Seeker said, holding her firmly.

'We're seeds?'

'So we have misled it, yes.'

'What happens when something tries to sprout us?'

'We politely disregard the invitation.'

Such graciousness seemed doubtful. They were closing with a broad speckled underbelly, the Jonah already dwindling behind. The speckles were clusters of ruby-dark froth. The Leviathan was at least ten times the size of the Jonah, giving the sex act an air of elephantine comedy. As they approached, she felt fresh fear; this creature was the size of a small mountain range.

This time they donated momentum to their new host through a web of bubbles that seemed to pop and re-form as they plunged through the mass, each impact buffeting, slowing them. Cley bounced off the elastic walls of their own seed-sphere. Seeker seemed to absorb them and barely move.

When they came to rest amid a bank of green growths, a large needle expertly jabbed at their bubble. Ruby light from the walls gave a hellish, threatening cast to the approaching spiky point. The needle entered; Cley braced herself — but the bubble did not pop. The needle snout seemed to sniff around. The point moved powerfully and was quite capable, Cley saw, of skewering them both. She backed away from it — and Seeker raised a leg and urinated directly onto it. 'No, thank you,' Seeker said.

The needle jerked back and fled. Then their bubble popped, releasing them.

Again Seeker led her through a dizzy maze of verdant growths, following clues she could not see. 'Where're we going?'

'To find the captain.'

'Somebody guides this?'

'Doesn't your body guide you?'

'Well, I sure thought I was in charge.'

'Then please adjust your digestion so that you never fart again.'

'Is that a complaint? I'll work on it. Where's this Leviathan going?'

'To the outer worlds.'

'You think we're safe here for now?'

'We are safe nowhere. But here we hide in numbers.'

Cley dodged a wriggling, slick-skinned teardrop that had sprouted teeth. 'You figure the Malign can't be sure where I am? It tracked me pretty well so far.'

'Here there are many more complex forms than you. They may smother your traces.'

'What about this Talent of mine? Can't this mind pick up my . . . well, my Talent-smell?'

Seeker's mouth twisted judicially. 'That is possible.'

'Damn! I wish Kata hadn't provoked mine to activity.'

'She had to.'

Cley had been following Seeker closely, scrambling to keep up as they bounced from rubbery walls and glided down twisted passageways, deeper into the Leviathan. Seeker's remark made her stop for a moment, gasping in the sweet, cloying air. 'Had to?'

'You will need it. And the Talent takes time to grow.'

Cley wanted to bellow out her frustration at the speed and confusion of events, but she knew by now that Seeker would only give her its sardonic, black-lipped grin. Seeker slowed and veered into crowded layers of great, broad leaves. These seemed to attach to branches, but the scale was so large, Cley could not see where the gradually thickening dark brown wood ended. Among the leaves scampered and leaped many small creatures.

She found that without her noticing any transition, somehow this zone had gained a slight gravity. She fell from one leaf to another, slid down to a third, and landed on a catlike creature. It squashed like a pillow. Then, with a shudder, it died in her hands, provoking a pang of guilt. The cat had wings and sleek orange fur. Her heart ached at the beauty of it.

Seeker came ambling back along a thin branch, saw the bird-cat, and gruffed approval. 'You are learning.' With a few movements of its razor claws it had skinned the cat and plucked off gobbets of meat. Cley bit her lip, concentrated on the dripping leaves, and moved on.

The goal of finding the captain faded as she grew hungry. Seeker snatched at tubular insects and crunched them with relish, but Cley wasn't up to that . . . yet. It slowly dawned on Cley that this immense inner territory was not some comfortable green lounge for passengers. It was a world, intact and with its own purposes.

Passengers were in no way special. They had to compete for advantages and food. This point came clear when they chanced upon a large ribbed beast lying partly dismembered on a branch. Seeker stopped, pensively studying the savaged hulk. Cley saw that the fur markings, snout, and wide teeth resembled Seeker's.

'Your, uh, kind?'

'We had common origins.'

Cley could not read anything resembling sadness in Seeker's face. 'How many of you are there?'

'Not enough. Though the numbers mean nothing.'

'You knew this one?'

Seeker gazed at the mess pensively. 'Ummmm . . . yes. I mingled genetic information with it.'

'Oh! I'm sorry, I . . .'

Seeker kicked at the carcass, which was now attracting a cloud of scavenger mites. 'It was an enemy.'

'After you, ah, "mingled"? I mean . . .'

'Before and after.'

'But then why did you – I mean, usually we don't . . .'

Seeker gave Cley a glance that combined a fierce scowl with a tongue-lolling grin. 'Whereas we never think of one thing at a time.'

'Even during sex?' Cley laughed. 'Do you have children?'

'Two litters, which I bore with joy.'

'Seeker! You're female? I never imagined!'

'Not female as you are.'

Cley's mind whirled around this new, fulcrum fact.

Seeker had been looking after her, *like a mother.* At once came rushing in the memories of her own Moms, the warm force of her mothers and Meta. Somehow, she saw, Seeker had known this, how to make contact with Cley at a level below conscious understanding. The trust between them, given and received, had the same deep assurance as that she had shared, and then had wrenched away, with her Moms. Otherwise, Cley might never have gone along on this strange odyssey, no destination known. What else was going on beyond the powers of her observation?

She groped for words. 'Well, uh, you're certainly not male if you bear litters.'

'The choice is not always binary. Simple sex like yours was a passing adaptation.'

Cley chuckled. 'Seeker, sounds like you're missing a lot of fun.'

'You have no idea.' Seeker grinned. 'Literally.'

'It'll take a while to think of you as a she.'

'As it was for me with you. Humans are noted as sexual connoisseurs, and Originals especially so.'

Cley blinked. 'My . . .'

'With enlarged organs as a result of evolutionary selection.'

'Ummmm. I'll take that as a compliment.'

Out of nowhere she made another connection. 'That Semisent – you were acting like a mother. Protecting me.'

'I suppose there is some truth in that.'

A faint scurrying distracted Cley. She pushed aside a huge fern bough and saw a human shape moving away from them. 'Hey!' she called. The prospect of company lifted her heart; the last few days had made her miss terribly the comforts of simple humanity.

The silhouette looked back and quickly turned away.

'Hey, stop! I'm friendly.'

But the profile blended like liquid into the shifting greens and browns and was gone. Cley ran after it. After blundering along limbs and down trunks she stopped, listening, and heard nothing more than a sigh of breezes and the cooing calls of unknown birds.

Seeker had followed her. 'You wished to mate?'

'Huh? No, no, we're not always thinking about that. Is that what you think? I just wanted to talk to him.'

Seeker said, 'You will find no one. And you were sure it was male.'

She dipped her head in salute. 'I apologize for thinking you weren't female.'

'You humans do not enjoy the advantage of extra appendages beyond two, so you make binary choices.'

'But who was that?' She swung on a limb, spun completely around it in the light gravity of this place, and laughed with the joy of it. 'Say, that wasn't an illusion, was it? Like those who killed my tribe and that Rin said were just images?'

'No, that was the captain.'

Cley felt a surge of pride. Humans ran this huge thing. 'Hey, you said my kind was all gone except for me.'

'They are.'

'So this captain is some other kind? Supra?'

'No. I do not think you truly wish to explore such matters. They are immaterial—'

'Look, I'm alone. If I can find any kind of human, I will.'

Seeker tilted its massive head back, raising and lowering its brow ridges in a way that Cley found vaguely unsettling. 'We have other pursuits.'

'If you won't help me, I'll find the captain myself.'

'Good.' Seeker smiled.

Cley didn't understand this reply, but she was used to that with Seeker. She grimaced, thinking how hard it would be to find anything in this vast place.

Seeker said nothing more and seemed to be distracted, almost sleepy. Maybe this was routine for it – no, for *her*. They worked their way upward against the slight centripetal gravity and finally stood on a broad slope made only of great leaves. Sunlight streamed fierce and golden, framing the shrinking moon. Cley knew that when the Earth had come alive, over five billion years ago, it had begun wrapping itself in a membrane it made of tailored air and water, for the general purpose of tempering the sun's blast.

Buried deep in Earth's forest, she had never bothered to think much of other planets, but now she saw that the moon, too, had learned this skill from Earth. She was beginning to think of worlds as self-aware – larger entities with their own agendas. There was something fresh and vibrant about the filmed moon, and she guessed that it had not shared the long withering imposed by the Supras' bots. Where once *maria* had meant the dark blotches of volcanic flows, now true dappled seas lapped at rugged mountains with snow-dappled peaks. And once again, Earth's spreading voracious green could mimic its junior companion in exuberant disequilibrium.

'See there?' Seeker pointed, as if reading her thoughts.

She shielded her eyes against the sun's glare and looked that way. A barely visible circular film floated inward from Earth, glowing with refracted energy.

'It was put into place long ago, to deflect a fraction of

the sun's glare from our world,' Seeker said admiringly. 'It solved the problem of warming for you Originals.'

'Our kind made that?' She was feeling prouder of humans than ever.

'It is less thick than your skin. Of course it worked only for a while.' Seeker brushed her hands together, as if dismissing such obvious measures. 'Over there' — another pointed claw — 'is a later solution.'

Cley made out a swiftly moving mote. She judged angles and guessed that it came arcing in from the outer depths of the solar system, for it was moving fast with its infall velocity. The tiny twinkle of tumbling light was passing close in to the leading edge of Earth, breathtakingly close but also furiously fast. Suddenly, she saw the point — to tug the planet outward with this fleeting kiss, seducing it with gravity into a small step outward. Uncountable billions of such kisses, to flee the sun's growing wrath.

She was even more impressed. 'And it keeps working . . .'

'With the fine tuning of those we can hope to meet later.'

'People?'

'You mean humans? No, these crafters work in space itself.'

'All this to make the Earth work a little longer?'

'Editing the sun is not enough.' Seeker bent and pressed an ear against a purple stalk. She nibbled at the young shoots breaking through the slick bark but also seemed to be listening. Then she sat up alertly. 'The captain says that we are bound for Venus.'

Ignoring how the procyon knew this, she asked, 'The planet next out from Earth?' Her astronomy was shaky, though she had gazed at the night sky with longing.

'Yes, second from the sun.'

'Um. Can we live there?'

'I expect the question will be whether we can avoid death there.'

With that, Seeker fell asleep, as abruptly as ever. Cley, wary of the tangled jungle, did not venture away. She watched the Earth and moon shrink, twin planets brimming against the timeless blaze of the galaxy.

She knew instinctively that the moon was not merely a sheltered greenhouse maintained by constant outside management. Who would tend it, after all? For long eons humankind had been locked into its desert fastnesses. No, the ripeness came from organisms endlessly adapting. To imagine otherwise, as ancient humans had, was to see the world as a game with fixed rules – like human sports, strict and static. Yet even planets had to yield to the press of suns.

She had learned much in the Library, but seeing this silent grandeur made the points far better. The sun had burned hydrogen for nearly five billion years before Earth evolved a species that could understand that simple fact and its implications. Unlike campfires, solar furnaces blaze brighter as their ash gathers.

Earthlife had escaped this dead hand of physics . . . for a while. Long before humans emerged, a blanket of carbon dioxide had helped warm the Earth. As the sun grew hotter, though, life thinned that blanket to keep a comfortable clime.

But carbon dioxide was also the medium through which the rich energy of the sun's fusing hydrogen became transmuted into living matter. Thinning the carbon dioxide blanket threatened that essential reaction. So a jot of time after the evolution of humans — a mere hundred million years — the air had such skimpy carbon dioxide that this imperiled all the plant kingdom.

At that point the biota of Earth could have radically adjusted their chemical rhythms. Other planets had passed through this knothole before and survived. But the intelligences that thronged that era, including the forerunners of Seeker, had intervened.

Moving the Earth farther from the solar furnace would offset the steady banking of the inner fires. So came the era known as the Reworking. It led to the great maneuvers that rearranged the planets, opening them to fresh uses. All this lay buried in the Library's dusty records and crossed Cley's thoughts only as a filigree of myth.

The much-embellished stories her tribe had told around campfires taught such things through parable and grandiose yarns. Her kind were not studious in the strict sense of the term, but their forest crafts had needed an underpinning of sage myth, the 'feel' of why and how biospheres were knitted and fed. Some lore was even hardwired in Cley at the level of instinctive comprehension. She knew this, too, and was deeply grateful that she would never know which of her ideas came from those depths.

So the cloud-wreathed beauty of the twin worlds made her breath catch, her heart race with a love that was perhaps the hallmark of true intelligence. As Seeker slept, she watched specks climb above the sharp-edged air of Luna to meet other dabs in a slow, grand gavotte. Another Jonah approached from Earth. Attendant motes converged on it from eccentric orbits about the moon.

She adjusted her eyes to pick out the seeping infrared glow that spoke of internal warmth, and saw a greater cloud, a snapshot of teeming bee-swarm wealth. Streamers swung between Earth and moon — endless transactions of species. A thinner rivulet broke away from the figure-eight orbits that linked the twins. It trickled inward, and Cley — holding a hand against the sun's glare, shutting down her infrared vision entirely — saw that it looped toward a thick swarm that clustered about the sun itself.

She felt then both awe — that reverent fear of immensity — and a hollow loneliness. She wished her clan could see this, wished that there were other minds of her cut and shape to share this spectacle.

Her attention was so riveted on the unfolding sky that she did not hear the stealthy approach of scraping paws. But she did catch the jostle as something launched itself in the weak gravity.

The shape came at her from behind. She got only a snatched instant to see it, a thing of sleek-jacketed black and flagrant reds. It was hinged like a bat at the wings and slung with ball-bearing agility in its swiveling, three-legged attack.

Claws snatched at the air where Cley had been. She had ducked and shot sideways, rebounding from a barnacled branch. In a heartbeat she decided. Instead of fleeing into unknown leafy wilderness, where a pack of the attackers might well be waiting, she launched herself back into the silent, sleek thing.

It squawked. Thrashed. Plainly, this it had not expected.

Cley hit it amidships. A leg snapped; near-weightlessness makes for flimsy construction. She flicked two of her fingers into needles, usually used for the fine treatment of ailing creatures. They plunged into the flared red ears of the attacker, puncturing the enlarged eardrums. From their size, Cley guessed ears were its principal sensory organ. The creature jerked, yowled, and departed, a squawking blur of pain and anger.

Cley landed on a wide branch, hands ready. She trembled with a mixture of eagerness and fear, which a billion years of selection had still retained as fundamental to the human constitution. The foliage replied to her intent wariness with quiet indifference. Silence.

Seeker awoke, stretching and yawning. 'More food?'

VI
A Mad God

We are all in the gutter, but some of us are looking at the stars.

—Oscar Wilde, *Lady Windermere's Fan*

1

The Captain of Clouds

They sighted the Supra ship their third day out. It came flaring into view from Earthside, as Cley now thought of the aft layers of the Leviathan.

She and Seeker spent much of their time aft. They enjoyed the view of the steadily shrinking, cloud-shrouded moon as they rested among a tangle of enormous fragrant flowerpods. Seeker spotted the bright speck first. Near the moon a yellow star grew swiftly. It became a sleek silver ship balancing on a thin torch flame.

This had just registered with Cley when Seeker jerked her back behind an overarching stamen, whispering, 'Do not move.'

The slim craft darted around the Leviathan as though it were sniffing. Its nose turned and swiveled despite its being glossy metal. The torch ebbed, and fine jets sent it zooming beyond view along the long, coarse bulk of the Leviathan.

In her mind Cley felt a shadowy presence, like a sound just beyond recognition. A murmur of Talent-talk. The Supra ship returned, prowling close enough to the prickly growths to risk colliding with upper stems.

Seeker put both her large, padded hands on Cley's face. She had done this before, to soothe Cley when her anxieties refused to let her sleep. Now the pressure of those rough palms sent a calming thread through her.

She knew what the touch implied: let her mind go blank, so her Talent would transmit as little as possible. Any Supra aboard the ship who had come from Illusivia could pick up her thoughts, but only if they were focused clearly into perceptible messages. Or so Cley hoped. After all, she knew little of this.

The ship held absolutely still for a long while, as if deciding whether to venture inside. The cloud of space-borne life that surrounded the Leviathan had drawn away from the ship, perhaps fearing its rockets. Its exact cylindrical symmetries and severe gleam seemed strange and malevolent among the drifting swarms – hard and enclosed, giving nothing away. Suddenly, the yellow blow-torch ignited again, sending the life forms skittering in all directions. The ship vanished in moments, heading out from the sun.

'They must've guessed I was running this way,' Cley said.

Seeker took her paws away. 'They try every fleeting possibility.'

Seeker still seemed concerned, though Cley was seldom sure what meanings attached to her quick frowns, fur-ripplings, and teeth displays. 'I felt something . . .'

'They sought your thought-smell.'

'Didn't know I had one.'

'It is distinctive.'

'You can smell it?'

'In your species many memories are lodged near the brain's receptors for smell. Scents then evoke memories. Remember where you were as a child and first caught the wonderful bouquet of approaching rain?'

'Oh, yes. I was under a tree . . .'

'I do not share this property, but I had heard of it.'

'That's sad. So?' Sometimes Seeker's roundabout manner irked her. She was not sure whether the procyon was suggesting much by saying little, or simply amusing herself. Maybe both.

'A Supra can remember the savor of your thinking. This act of recollection calls up your Talent, resonates with it, makes it stronger.'

'Just by remembering and broadcasting, they make me transmit better?'

'Something like that.'

Cley could not match this idea with the odd, scratchy presence she had felt. 'Well, they're gone now.'

'They may return.'

'You've got the Talent, don't you?'

Seeker grinned. 'If you cannot tell, then I suppose I do not.'

'Well, yeah, I sure can't pick up anything from you. But—'

'Let us move away from here. The ship could try again.'

They left the flower zone, where they had foraged for a day, supping on thick nectar. Cley did not register a transition, but somehow they came into a region with little centripetal gravity. This place did not have as simple an inner geometry as the Jonah's. Internal portions of the Leviathan spun on unseen axes, and streams flowed along sloping hillsides that seemed to the eye uphill. The local gravity was never more than a subtle touch, but it gave shape and order to the rampant vegetation.

They came into a vast chamber with teeming plat-forms, passageways, tunnels, balustrades, antechambers, all thronged with small animals moving on intent paths. It was a central station for a system of tubes that seemed to sprout everywhere, even high up the walls. The moist air above was crisscrossed by great shafts of filtered sunlight rising from sources near the floor, up to a distant arched ceiling.

She could see no obvious biological point to this, or to the transparent membrane that brimmed with a view of the starscape outside. In the middle, the galactic center glowed brilliantly. Earth's sun had migrated inward from its original orbit, using swing-bys with other suns. Cley knew this from far history but could not imagine how people did it, or why.

Yet all the moist, busy grandeur of this place did not intimidate her; it was even inviting. The scurrying animals were intelligent, in their way, going about swift tasks without giving her more than a glance. Humans were apparently uninteresting, maybe not even unusual. She doubted that many Supras used Leviathans to journey, given their swift ships. She did not dwell on the Supra pursuit. As the momentum of events carried her farther from her lands, she had resolved to plunge forward rather than endlessly fret. Perhaps she could find Ur-humans somewhere out here, as Seeker had said.

It had taken a few restless nights truly to feel this, but now it held firm in her. She remembered the bright-eyed girl who had breathlessly sought the company of Supras, especially the men. That girl seemed very far away now. Yet she lay less than a single summer in the past, her inboards told her.

Her hunting skills reawakened as she followed Seeker in her foraging, unhurried but quick. Seeker ate a lot. She savored the pursuit of small prey and enjoyed the sport of it without remorse, though in fact she devoured mostly plants. She especially enjoyed ripping big feathery grass shoots to shreds, picking out packets of ripe red seeds. Cley watched and learned.

The ferment of tangled life around them, extending in all three dimensions throughout Leviathan, captivated Cley. It was so unlike the Supras' carefully tuned projects. As she immersed herself in this complex wealth, she finally understood what had irked and daunted her about the Supras. Their air of superiority had been tolerable, but in their grave manner she felt a cold brush with something she could not name . . . a distance.

Kurani, dear lost Kurani, had been intensely alive, astonishing. He had amused her, an ephemeral Original, by his need to exist in the moment. The other Supras were leaden and solemn. Kata had shown Cley their art, and it had been cloaked with images of decay. It was shaped by the weight of uncountable drowsy centuries, as if already a creeping tide of entropy had doomed the glowing stars.

Her spirit rebelled against this. Without the sun's abundance no light would have kindled life. The biota were like skilled accountants, living on the flow of energy, paying all required taxes but never neglecting a loophole. Burning fat in Cley's blood generated entropy, but she managed to excrete entropy even faster in waste heat and waste matter – a miraculous, improbable, but perfectly legal dodging of the second law of thermodynamics.

She, like whole planets, shed excrement and pollution. But in her home forest the pollution of one had been the meat of another. She was beginning to see that this truth worked on the interplanetary scale. Surely it worked a persistent magic in Leviathan, and would soon enough on Earth, with the return of the oceans.

No, she decided, the Supras had troubled her because they still resonated with the bleak, fixed compass of Sonomulia. Rin and the other Supras did not know *life,* that spark that hangs between two eternities. Not the way she saw it, anyway. In a deep sense the Supras were immortal, she decided, but not alive as she understood the term.

Then with a shiver she banished these thoughts. *Enough.*

They trekked through the light gravity of this inner vault, eating berries that swung from palmy trees. These were not mere passive trees, though; the berries were a lure. The sharp fronds could slice off an arm. Seeker showed her how to confuse the tree's ropy reflexes long enough to snatch a handful of berries.

There were even lakes. They hiked for two days along a broad beach, Seeker catching the yellow fish that thronged the shore. Through clouds Cley could see the lake curling over their heads, far away, describing the vast curve of a rotating cylinder.

'Why do we keep moving so much?' Cley asked when Seeker marched on resolutely, despite the gathering gloom. Glowing patterns of flickering, deep-reflected sunshine ebbed and flowed in the huge cylindrical vault like tides of light.

'We hide among life. Life moves.'

'You figure the Supras're still looking for me?'

'They have gone.'

'Your own mysterious wisdom tells you that?'

Seeker showed her sparkling fangs, recently cleaned by steaks of yellow fish. 'The Supras continue outward.'

'Great. Let's go back to Leviathan's skin, then. I liked the view.'

Actually, she wanted to search for the captain. She had glimpsed creatures that looked vaguely human near the Leviathan's transparent blisters. Each time they had seemed to evaporate into the humid jungle before she could pursue.

Seeker did not comment on her desire to find humans and would not help track them, though she suspected the procyon could sense the smallest animals that swung or padded through the layers of green. Why? She had learned to not ask too many questions; Seeker liked silence.

For three contemplative days they worked their way along the lake, stopping only to swim and, when the wind rose, to bodysurf. This zone of the Leviathan was spinning, driving curious spiral waves in the lake, which worked up and down the shore.

Two more days of hiking, by Cley's inner clock, brought them to the skin. Again Cley could not sense when they left the region of spin-gravity. Fogs had hampered their way, blowing into the Leviathan's recesses. They blew through wide shafts that admitted to the interior great blades of reflected sunlight.

Seeker taught her a favorite game. They perched in one of the translucent bubbles in the Leviathan's outer reaches, waiting. In the utter vacuum outside, a mere finger's width away, shelled silvery things like abalone attached themselves to the Leviathan's skin. From there, a steady perch, they could snag wandering prey.

But sometimes they mistakenly triggered a Leviathan reflex. In a convulsive gulp, the slick skin double-folded inward. Abruptly the predator became prey, crushed in a gassy world it had never known. Disoriented, it would flail about.

When one slipped inside, Seeker would snatch it, crack it open between her hardsoled feet, and gulp the shell's inhabitant with lip-smacking relish.

'Yes!' Seeker cried. Cley applauded and turned down any offered tidbits.

Long black creatures crawled over the Leviathan, grazing on the photosynthetic mats that grew everywhere. Cley could see these dark algae mottling the carbuncled skin, occasionally puffing out spores. The grazers slurped up the brown sun-worshipping goo of mat life and moved on, the cattle of the skies.

Seeker tried to entice one close to the translucent layer, whirling and grimacing to attract its attention. The vacuum cow turned its slitted dark eyes toward this display. Bovine curiosity brought it closer.

Seeker grabbed for it, stretching the tough, waxy wall with her clutching paw-hands and feet. Grunting, she managed to hang on to the grazer through the thin skin. Seeker was strong enough to pluck the struggling cow inward against the atmospheric pressure pushing the envelope out. For a moment Cley thought the growling Seeker would manage to drag the grazer far enough in, despite all logic, to trigger the folding instability and pluck it through. Smelling victory, Seeker yelped with tenor joy. But then the vacuum cow spurted steam, wriggled, and jetted away.

Seeker gnashed her teeth. 'Devilish things.'

'Yeah, looked appetizing.'

'They are a great delicacy. I have been trying to taste one for a very long time.'

'Pretty resistant, though. How long?'

'Three centuries.'

It took a while for Seeker to stop laughing at the expression on Cley's face. Before Cley could recover, she glanced to the side – and was startled to find standing there a human form. But only a form, for this was like nothing she had ever seen.

The face worked with expression – frowns and smiles and wild, flaring eyes, all fidgeting and dissolving. The thing seemed demented. Then she saw that she had been imposing her own need to find a facial expression, to find order. In fact, the skittering storms rippled and fought all through the body. Colors and shapes were but passing approximations.

The form took a tentative step toward Cley. She bit her lip. Could not breathe.

The body jiggled and warped like a bad holo image projected on smoke. But this was no illusion. Its lumpy foot brushed aside a stem as it took another step. The fidgeting skin seemed like a watercolor wash that blurred and shifted as the body moved.

She realized that she could see through the thing. Plants behind it appeared as flickering images. She heard a slight thrumming as it raised an arm with one unnaturally smooth motion – a swoop, not the hinged pull of muscles at the pivots of shoulder and elbow.

'Aurronugh,' it said – a sound like stones rattling in a jug.

Cley still could not breathe. She was frozen.

'It is imitating you, as it did before,' Seeker said.

A gasp. 'What – what is it?'

'You wanted to meet it. The captain.'

'But – it's . . .' All along she had just assumed that the captain would be human. She remembered Seeker smiling when she did . . .

'Not all of the captain, of course.'

'What does he – does it – want?'

'I do not know. Often it manifests itself in the form of a new passenger, as a kind of politeness. To learn something it cannot otherwise know.'

The shape said slowly, 'Yooou waaanteed by maaaany.'

Cley took a deep breath and made herself say, 'Yes. Many want to find me.'

'Yooou musssst lee-vah.'

'I, I can't leave. And why should I?'

'Daaaanger. To meeee.'

'You? What are you?'

The shape stretched its arms up to encompass all the surrounding growth. Its arms ended in stumps, though momentarily a stubby finger or two would sprout at the ends, flutter, and then ease back into the constant flow of the body.

'Everything? You're everything?' Cley asked.

'Wooorld.'

Seeker said, 'It is the Leviathan. Composite intelligence. This cloud-captain directs its many parts and lesser minds.'

Cley gaped. 'Every part of it adds to its intelligence?'

'Rin thought the phylum Myriasoma was extinct,' Seeker said. 'He would be happy to see that he was wrong yet again.'

Cley smiled despite her tingling fear. 'Supras don't like news like that.'

As she watched, the captain's legs dissolved into a

swarm. Each bit was the size of a thumb and swam in the air with stubby wings. The captain was an assembly that moved incessantly, each flyer brushing the other but capable of flitting away at any moment. The individual members looked like a bizarre mixture of bird and insect. Each had six eyes: two pairs on opposite sides of their cylindrical bodies and one each at top and bottom. Hovering. Each thinking, in its own tiny way.

Cley heard the captain then in her mind. The thrumming whisper of wings she had heard was echoed by a soft flurry of thoughts in her mind.

You are a danger to me.

'You? The ship?'

I am the World.

And so it must seem to this thing, she realized. It governed the entwined complexity of the Leviathan and at some level must *be* the Leviathan, its dispersed mind instead of merely its brain. Yet each moment, a flying thumb shot away on some buzzing mission and others flew in to merge with the standing, rippling cloud.

Beneath its clear message she felt the darting of quicksilver thought. She sensed this as a thrumming echo of the infinitude of transactions the Leviathan must make to keep so vast an enterprise going. It was as though she could listen to the individual negotiations between her own blood cells and the walls of her veins, the acids of her stomach, the sour biles of her liver.

Cley thought precisely, slowly, How can you be self-aware? You change all the time.

The shape let its right arm fall off, scattering into fluttering clumps that then departed on new tasks. *I do not need to feel myself intact, as you do.*

'So how do I know who's talking?' Cley countered aloud.

The captain answered, *I speak for the moment. A little while later I shall speak for that time. Only the I will change, not the me.*

Cley glanced at Seeker, who watched with bemused interest. Maybe in three centuries it all got dated. She thought, Will that be the same you?

How could you tell? Or I? I always find that your kind of intelligence is obsessed with knowing what you are.

Cley smiled. Seems a reasonable question.

The thing shook. *Not reasonable. Reason cannot tell you deep things.*

What can, then?

Those come through the body. Always the body.

Cley watched as the shape gradually, with pops and sighs and slow moans, decomposed into an oblong cloud of the thumb-things. It had made its polite gesture and now relaxed into a wobbly sphere, perhaps to bring its individual elements closer while lowering its surface area.

Are you afraid of me? she asked impishly.

My parts know fear. Hunger and desire, as well. They are a species, like you. I am another kind of being, able to elude attack by dispersing. I do not know fear for myself, but I do know caution. I cannot die, but I can be hurt.

Cley thought of the honeybees she had tended in the forest — satisfying, sweaty labor that now seemed to have happened a very long time ago. Bees had fewer than ten thousand neurons, she knew, yet did complex tasks. How much more intelligent would be a single arm of this cloud-captain, when its thumb-things united to merge their minds?

Not hurt by anybody like me, I assume?

The swarm churned. *Yes. I am not vulnerable to destruction of special parts, as are you. Merely by taking away your head, for example, I could leach life from you, rob you of all you know. But each part of me contains some of my intelligence and feels what a part of the World feels.*

Cley felt suddenly the strangeness of this thing. Hanging before her, bulging and working with sluggish energy, its misshapen head turned at impossible angles as it seemed to ponder the Leviathan's intricacies. Another phylum? No, something more – another kingdom of life, a development beyond beings like her, forever separated into inevitable loneliness.

In a way, she envied it. Each thumb-flyer knew the press of competition, of hunger and longing, but the composite could rise above that raw turbulence into realms she could not even guess. She glanced at Seeker again and realized that her expression was not truly of indifference but of reverence.

Seeker had not wanted her to seek the captain, because it was, even for Seeker, a holy being. Beyond even three centuries of learning.

I speak to you now because the World cannot tolerate you, the captain sent.

'How come you went away before? Dissolved?' Cley asked.

I needed time to speak to my brothers.

Other Leviathans? As she framed the thought, the captain's answer came lightning-fast: *Other Worlds.*

Is there something beyond Leviathans? Something—

Cley had never literally had a thought interrupted in her own mind. Running right over her own sentence-forming, the captain imposed, *I now grasp many recent events. Your connection with them. There is an entity called the Malign, and it reaches for you.*

I know.

Then know this . . .

In a flooded single moment a torrent of sensations, ideas, and conclusions forked through her. She had for an instant the waterfall perception of what the mind before her was truly like. The layers of its logic were translucent, like a building of softly lit glass. Every fact shone up through floors of stacked detail, breaking through to illuminate the denser lattice-lacing of concepts on a higher level. And that piercing light in turn refracted through the web of mind, shedding its fitful glow on assumptions lying buried in a shadowy weave beneath.

She staggered with the impact, trying to wrench away.

A realization came, a thin reed tossing on the crackling surge that swamped her. She sagged with the weight of what the captain had given her, stunned. She was dimly conscious of Seeker leaping forward to cradle her. Then the air clouded with ebony striations, and she felt herself dwindling, falling beneath a towering, dark weight.

2
Skysharks

'You can speak?' Seeker asked, her tilted chin and rippling amber fur patterns showing concern.

'I, I think so.' Cley had slept for many hours, awakening with only a groggy sense of herself. When she revived, Seeker had brought her a banquet of berries and fruits and thick, meaty leaves like slices of spongy bread. Now she tried to explain what she had sensed in the brief collision of minds. Like Kata, the captain sent information faster and at greater depth than Cley could handle.

'It was . . . thought without a human filter.'

'Um. I get that all the time.'

'No, I meant *really* strange, not like you.'

Seeker grinned. 'You truly have no idea, my dear human.'

'No, I mean, it was — like being licked with a rasping, wet tongue that *wouldn't quit*!' Her voice had gotten away from her at the end, letting out the brittle, heart-stopping fear she felt.

Seeker looked unimpressed. 'Humans are not good at diving into the pools of others' minds.'

'Especially Originals?'

'I was not going to mention . . .'

'Okay, and I'm not an Original anyway, right?' She

held up her fingers and extruded two bony tools. 'These don't look like anything that got worked out on the plains of Afrik.'

'Yes. You are as Original as humans get. The records are spotty.'

'Well, I guess. These fingers are tekky, not evolved. I'll bet the captain's a product of engineering, too.'

This, even little children learned. That rapid selection pressure operated on what already existed. It added capability to minds, layering rather than snipping away parts that worked imperfectly. The human brain was always retrofitted, and showed its origins in its cumbersome, layered workings. The captain had arisen from some engineering she could not imagine. Especially its mind.

'But didn't you feel it, too?' she asked.

'I do not have precisely your Talent.'

'What did the captain do after I fainted?'

'Scattered like a flock into which a hunter has fired a shot.'

'Huh. Maybe it didn't know how to tell me without overloading me.'

'Perhaps. I have seen captains before. This was different. *Ah—*'

Seeker snagged a ratlike creature that was passing, and bit off its fat tail. The rat squealed and hissed, and Seeker put it gently back down. As the rat scampered away, Seeker munched on the tail. 'A delicacy,' she explained. 'They grow tasty tails so that the rest of them is let go.'

'It'll live?'

'Within days it will sport another luscious tail.' Seeker smacked her lips over a morsel, holding out the last to Cley. 'Some of my kind cultivate them.'

'No rat's ass for me, thanks. You were saying something about the captain . . . ?'

'It was odd.'

'How?'

'I have never seen one worried before.'

Cley bit her lip, memories stirring. She had felt sour filigrees of the captain's anxiety. Yet already the sharp, vibrant images were trickling away. She suspected that her kind of intelligence was simply unable to file and categorize the massive infusion she had received, and so was sloughing it off.

'The Supras it could deal with,' she said. 'It fears the Malign, though.'

Seeker nodded. 'The Malign is fully arrived, then.'

'Fully?'

'All components knit together.'

'I caught something about that from the captain.' She frowned, troubled, eyes distant. 'Sheets of fine copper wire wrapping around blue flames . . .'

'Where?'

'Somewhere further out from here. Where it's cold, dark. There was a feeling of the Malign spreading over whole stars. Suns . . . like campfires.'

'It is expanding.' Seeker clashed claws together, a gesture of sly menace that somehow made her look more human.

Cley told Seeker what she had glimpsed in the captain's mind. In fading retrospect, much of it was a tapestry of rediscovered history.

The Malign's strange sentience had been confined to the warped space-time near a huge black hole. Only the restraining curvature there could hold it in place for long.

This had been done uncounted eons ago — a feat accomplished by humanity in collaboration with elements and beings she could not begin to describe. Around the black hole orbited a disk made of infalling matter, flattened into a thin plate, spinning endlessly. The inner edge of the disk was gnawed into incandescent ferocity by the compressive clawing of the hole's great tidal gradients. There the Malign had been held by the swirl and knots of vexed space-time. Matter perpetually entered the disk at its outer rim, as dust clouds and even stars were drawn inward by friction and the shredding effects of the hole's grip.

'Think of it as . . . well, like a bored god,' Cley added. 'Trapped for long enough to drive it insane, if it wasn't already.'

Seeker's eyes were veiled. 'Some say it was mad even before.'

Cley tried to describe the rest, awkwardly. By design, the Malign had been forced to swim perpetually upstream against this flux of matter, caught in the thick disk. If it relented, it would have been carried by the flow to the very inner edge of the disk. There it would have been sucked farther in, spiraling down into the black hole.

That had been the prison and torture of the Malign. It had been able to spare nothing in its struggle to survive. And that is all that had saved the rest of the galaxy from its strange wrath.

'But it escaped,' Seeker said.

'It . . . diffused.' The odd word popped into her head, summoned by the fading images from the captain. 'It is made of magnetic fields, and they diffused across the conducting disk. That took a very long time, but the Mind managed it.'

'Now it has reformed?' Seeker frowned. 'Where was the hole?'

'It was the biggest humanity could find – at the center of the galaxy.'

'So legend says,' Seeker said pensively.

'I *think* it was humanity that did it, but the captain used another word, something about the Singular.'

'Um. Another legend. The Singular is a construction, emerging from an event the Ancients termed the Singularity. First the Quickening precipitated changes in what some humans made of themselves. The Singularity was one of the more successful of those leaps, and it created the Singular.'

'What is it?'

'It is what part of humanity became. A structure made of folded space-time itself. Some humans augmented themselves to beyond the others' – your – perception. Then they, with others from far stars, made the fold.'

'Sounds . . . well, *difficult* is too mild a word.'

'It was an act that transcended our space-time. Somehow those Ancients went beyond our infinities. They were – or are – both part of the Singular and its cause. I admit I do not follow these matters well.'

'Maybe nobody can.'

'The Singular helped to make the Multifold. How, no one any longer knows. But no alliance against the Malign could have succeeded without the Multifold to counter its powers. We do not even know exactly how the Multifold did so.'

'The Library was crammed with history—'

'But not enough,' Seeker finished for her.

They both looked out through the transparent pressure

membrane. The vibrant glow of a million suns wreathed the center of the galaxy in its bee-swarm majesty. Yet at the center of all that glare dwelled an utter darkness, Cley knew. Ten billion years of galactic progression had fed the hole. It sucked dust from passing clouds. Stars that swooped too close to it were stripped and sucked in. Each dying sun added to the compact darkness, the dynamical center about which a hundred billion stars rotated in the gavotte of the galaxy.

Cley whispered, 'But we're so far from there.'

Seeker said, 'We could have fled. Outward, into the galactic fringes.'

'Ummm. Wouldn't it be safer to get as far away as possible?'

'Yes. But not responsible.'

'So now it's loose?'

'And has been moving outward, bringing catastrophe, over twenty-eight thousand light years. One possibility is that its malignancy is being played out, to weaken it as it travels so far into the hinterlands of the galaxy.'

'It knows that the Quickening, and then the Singularity—'

'Both were human-made, yes. But they also contained the workings of others, of alien forms. And the Quickening was a very long time ago. The galaxy has rotated four times since then.'

'How can we defend against it?'

'With difficulty.'

'That's one possibility, you said. What's another?'

'That we were placed here as a sentinel, to warn others.'

'Who?'

'I do not know.'

Cley grimaced. 'Hard to warn somebody when you don't know who that might be.'

'There is yet one more possibility.'

'What?'

'That we are here as a sacrifice.'

Cley said nothing. Seeker went on. 'Perhaps if the Malign finds and destroys us — humanity and its consorts, whom it thinks of as its imprisoners — it will be content.'

The offhand way Seeker said this chilled Cley. 'What's all this *about*?'

'My phylum believes that the Malign wants to hasten the era when another universe, on another brane, collides with ours.'

'How can that happen?'

'Our brane moves like a flat plate along a string, in a higher dimension. Another brane is approaching along that string. When they collide, matter and energy annihilate.'

'Leaving nothing?'

'Leaving fields. And magnetic fields, which comprise the Malign, will survive to dominate whatever comes to pass after the collision.'

Cley rolled her eyes. 'How in hell can this Malign move the branes around?'

Seeker licked its black lips. 'Here you exceed my knowledge. Except that it can, and the Multifold could prevent this. But to truly use all its powers, in concert with others, the Multifold must access its primordial elements.'

'Uh-oh. Elements that were put into place by Originals.'

Seeker shrugged. 'Perhaps the Supras know.'

'Well, then, let them fight the Malign. I want out of it.'

'There is no way out.'

'Well, moving further from the sun, out to Venus, sure

doesn't seem so smart. That's where the Malign is accumulating itself.'

Seeker studied the stars, bright holes punched in the pervading night. 'Your Talent made you too easy to find on Earth. Here you blend into the many mind-voices.'

Cley opened her mouth to disagee and stopped, feeling a light, keening note sound through her thoughts. She blinked. It was a hunting call, she knew immediately – a flavor that eons had not erased, as though from some fierce raptor swooping down through velvet air, eyes intent on scampering prey below.

She glanced back at the smoldering glow of the galactic center. Against it were black shapes, angular and swift, growing. Not metal, like Supra ships, but green and brown and gray. 'Call the captain!'

'I have,' Seeker said.

As Cley watched the approaching sleek creatures, she saw that they were larger than the spaceborne life she had seen. It was far too late to avoid them, even if the Leviathan could have readily turned its great bulk.

Skysharks, Cley thought, the word leaping up from her buried inboard vocabulary. The term fit, though she did not know its origin. They were elegantly molded for speed, with jets for venting gases. Solar sails gave added thrust, but the lead skyshark had reeled in its sails as it approached, retracting the silvery sheets into pouches in its side. Cupped parabolas fore and aft showed that it had evolved radar senses. These, too, collapsed moments before contact, saving themselves from the fray.

Cley gasped as they dove straight in. The first of them came lancing into the Leviathan without attempting to brake. It slammed into the skin aft of the blister that held

Seeker and Cley. They could see it gouge a great hole in the puckered hide.

Shrieks came through the foliage. Cley's ears popped. Outside, the sleek skysharks banked and fought small defenders. A great head bit deep into a small opponent. Muscular, powerful jaws worked. Throats swallowed. Cley watched the first few plow headlong into the mottled hide of the Leviathan and wondered why they would risk such damage merely for food. But then her ears popped again, and a *whoosh* rushed by.

'They're breaking the seals!'

'Yes,' Seeker said calmly, 'such is their strategy.'

'Shouldn't we run?'

'Where?'

'But they'll kill everything aboard.'

'Not all, no. They penetrate inward a few layers. This lets the outrushing air bring to them the smaller animals.'

'Then, let's—'

'No time. Watch.'

Cley watched a skyshark back away from the jagged wound it had made. A wind blew the backdrop of stars around, the only evidence of escaping air. Then flecks and motes came from the wound, a geyser of helpless, wriggling prey. The skyshark caught each with its quick, wide mouth, seeming to inhale them.

Cley had to remind herself that these gliding shapes with their cool, soundless, artful movements were actually carrying out a savage attack, remorseless and efficient. Weightless vacuum gave even death a quality of silent grace. Yet the beauty of threat shone through, a quality shared alike by the grizzly, falcon and rattler. Her ears popped again. 'If we lose all our air . . .'

'We should not,' Seeker said, though plainly she was worried, her coat running with swarthy spirals. 'Membranes close to limit the loss.'

'Good,' Cley said uncertainly. But as she spoke, a wind rose, sucking dry leaves into a cyclone about them.

'That should not happen,' Seeker said stiffly.

'Look.'

Outside, two skysharks were wriggling into older gouges. Waves rippled along their sleek torsos. Air had ceased to stream from the holes, so the beasts could enter easily. Others withdrew from the rents they had torn after only a few vicious bites. They jetted along the broad sweep of skin, seeking other weak points. In their tails were nozzled and gimbaled chambers. She saw a bright flame pucker and flare. Her inboards told her this was hydrogen peroxide and catalase, combining in shaped rear chambers. Puffs and streamers pushed the muscular bodies adroitly along the rumpled brown hide. It was a mad harvest. From the gaping gashes where skysharks had entered came fresh puffs of air. Some carried animals tumbling in the thinning gale, and skysharks snapped these up eagerly.

'The sharks that went inside – they must be tearing up those membranes,' Cley shouted against the rising shriek. 'That vacuums out the protected areas.'

Seeker braced herself against the gathering winds. 'A modified tactic. Even if those inside perish, their fellows benefit from the added game. Good for the species overall, despite the sacrifice of a few.'

'Not much consolation.' Already it was getting harder to suck in a breath.

'I am becoming concerned, yes.'

Seeker's calm exasperated Cley. 'Yeah, but what'll we *do?*'

'Come.'

Seeker launched herself away, paws spread wide. Cley followed. The air was alive with cross-currents that plucked at her. Between bounces off trunks and bowers, Seeker curled up into a ball to minimize the pull of the howling gale. Cley copied this, narrowing her eyes against the rain of leaves and bark and twigs that raked her.

Seeker led her along a zigzag path. They bounced from bower to vine, just beneath the Leviathan's skin. Over the whirling winds she heard the yelps and cries of animals. Nearby a yowling catlike creature lost its grip on a tubular root and pinwheeled away. A triangular mat with legs caromed off Seeker and ricocheted from Cley, spitting, before whirling into the madhouse mist.

They came twirling toward a system that looked like a blue-green heart, with veins and arteries stretching away in all directions. Fluids gushed here, fraying away into the thinning air. The wind moaned and gathered itself here with a promise of worse to come. The open wounds behind them were probably tearing further, she guessed, evacuating more and more of the Leviathan. For the first time it occurred to Cley that even this colossal creature could die, its fluids and air bled into space.

She hurried after Seeker. A gray cloud streamed by them, shredding, headed toward the sighing breezes. Cley recognized them — a flight of the thumb-sized flyers that had made up the captain, now streaming to defend its ship. There might even be more than one captain, she realized, or an entire crew of the anthology-beings. Or perhaps the distinction of individual entities was meaningless.

Ahead was a zone of gauzy, translucent surfaces lit by phosphorescent streaks. Seeker grabbed a sheet of the waxy stuff, sinking in her claws. The flapping sheet seemed to be a great membrane for catching pollen. Even in the chaos of drifting debris Cley could see that this was part of an enormous plant.

They were at the tip of a great pistil. Seeker was wrenching off a slab of its sticky walls, clawing energetically. Above this was a broad transparent dome, which brought sunlight streaming into the leathery bud of the plant. Its inner bulb had mirrored surfaces that reflected the intense sunlight into bright blades, sending illumination deep into the inner recesses of the Leviathan.

She took this in at a glance. Then Seeker yanked her into position on the bulb wall, where her feet caught in sticky goo. The wind lashed at her, but the goo held.

'We're better out than in,' Seeker said.

'Huh? How . . . ?'

Seeker barked orders, and Cley followed them. They fashioned the tough sheet into a pyramidal shape. Seeker stuck the edges together with the wall adhesive. She turned down the last side, leaving them inside the pyramid.

Cley got her bearings. They were drifting toward the transparent ceiling, moving on an eddy of the shrieking, building winds. Their pyramid smacked against the outer skin of the Leviathan.

Seeker crouched at an apex of the pyramid. She touched the ceiling and quickly twisted the wall. 'Here – help . . .'

Cley grabbed a waxy fold and torqued it in the opposite direction. The Leviathan's hide puckered and parted

— and *pop!* — they passed through, into naked space. The pyramid drifted in the slight breeze of escaping gas from the pucker, which was closing like a quick smile behind them.

'We're out!' Cley cried, delighted.

'This will last for only a while,' Seeker said.

'Till we run out of air?' Cley said.

'If that long.'

The advantage of living construction material was that it grew together, if encouraged by an adhesive, becoming tighter than any manufactured seal. One side of their pyramid was so thin, Cley could see out through it, yet the film held pressure. Nature loved the smooth and seamless. She and Seeker helped it along with spit — Seeker had a lot of faith in her own fluids — and some muscle work. Soon their pyramid held firm and snug.

They drifted away from the Leviathan. Cley hoped the skysharks would ignore them, and indeed the predators were nuzzling greedily at the raw wounds amidships. Around the Leviathan swam debris. Into this cloud came spaceborne life of every description. Some were smaller predators who scavenged on whatever the skysharks left. Others spread great gossamer sheets, eager to catch the air that poured forth from the Leviathan's wounds. Small creatures billowed into great gas bags, fat with rare wealth. Limpets crawled eagerly along the crusty hide toward the rents. When they arrived, they caught streamers of fluid that spouted irregularly into the vacuum.

This was a riotous harvest for some. Cley could see joy in the excited darting of thin-shelled beetles who snatched at the tumbling fragments of once-glorious ferns. The wounds created fountains from the Leviathan's skin. These geysers shot motley clouds of plant and animal life into a gathering crowd of eager consumers, their appetites quickened by the bounty of gushing air.

'Hope they don't fancy our taste,' Cley said.

Her mouth was dry, and she had long since passed the point of fear. Now she simply watched. Gargantuan forces had a way of rendering her pensive, reflective. This trait had been more effective in the survival of Ur-humans, she had long suspected, than outright aggression or conspicuous gallantry. It did not fail her now. Visible fear would have attracted attention. They drifted among the myriad spaceborne forms, perhaps too strange a vessel to encourage ready attack – even hungry predators wisely select food they know.

'Do you think they could kill Leviathan?' Cley asked.

'Mountains do not fear ants,' Seeker answered.

'But they're gutting it!'

'They cannot persist for long inside the mountain. For the spaceborne, air in plenty is a quick poison.'

'Oxygen?'

'It kindles the fires that animate us. Too much, and . . .'

Seeker pointed. Now curls of smoke trickled from the ragged wounds. The puffs of air had thinned, but they carried black streamers.

'The skysharks can forage inside until the air makes their innards burn.' Seeker watched the spectacle with scholarly interest, blinking owlishly.

'The sharks die, so that others can eat the Leviathan?'

'Apparently. Though I suspect this behavior has other purposes, as well.'

'All this pillaging? It's awful.'

'Yes. Many have died. But not those for whom this raid was intended.'

'Who's that?'

'Us.'

3

The Living Bridge

They waited out the attack. Wispy shreds of smoke thinned as the Leviathan healed its internal ruptures, damming the torrent of air. The remaining skysharks glided with easy menace over the Leviathan's skin but did not rip and gouge it. They ignored the periodic rings of plant life around the Leviathan's middle. Apparently, these thick-skinned, ropy growths had developed poisons or other defenses. They were left in peace to spread their leathery leaves to the sun, oblivious to the assault on the Leviathan's body.

The skysharks fed first on debris. Then Cley felt ominous, silent presences in her mind, like the sudden press of chilled glass on her face. She recoiled at the bitter sensation. 'I . . . think I can . . . feel them.'

Seeker said, 'Hate them.'

She could now capture some fragments and knew that they sensed Cley and Seeker's presence. The sleek shapes began trembling with eager hunger. They milled about, drifting toward the pyramid. Their thoughts converged to a knot of menace. Cley looked out at them through the transparent film-wall. Their mouths gaped, showing spiky blue teeth.

'Hate them,' Seeker said again.

'You do?'

'No, *you* hate them. That will protect us.'

'I . . .'

'They have a rudimentary Talent.'

'But—'

'*Now.*'

She let go some of her bottled-in emotions, envisioning their energies as a sharp spear lanced directly at the nearest skyshark. This time she felt her transmission as a bright spark of virulent orange. The skyshark wriggled, turned, fled.

Seeker gave a malicious chuckle. 'Good. You have a Talent, strong enough to be a weapon, as I suspected. Do that whenever one approaches.'

'Why doesn't Leviathan keep them off this way?'

Seeker floated free of the wall, flexing her claws. 'In their packs they have some defense. They can damp and defend against Leviathan thought patterns. But it taxes them greatly, for they are not very intelligent. When foraging among the helpless outgushed life, that defense mode is shut off.'

Already the skysharks were roaming farther from the Leviathan, catching up with creatures and plant shreds blown away. Their angular bodies bulged, bellies still throbbing with the struggles of their ingested banquets.

Fore and aft on the skyshark bodies, appendages unfolded from their warty hides. Parabolic antennae blossomed and scanned the volume around the Leviathan with patient, metronomic vigilance. Cley suspected there were species that preyed on these sleek hunters, too, though to look at these mean, moving appetites, she could not imagine how they could be vulnerable.

'So you think they're after us?'

'They seldom assault a Leviathan; the losses are too heavy. Usually it is a tactic of desperation, when pickings elsewhere are lean.'

'Well, maybe it's been a bad year.'

'Their bodies are not thinned by hunger. No, they were directed to do this.'

'By the Malign?'

'It must be.'

Cley felt an icy apprehension. 'Then it knows where I am.'

'I suspect it is probing, trying whatever idea occurs.'

'It killed a lot of creatures, doing this.'

'It cares nothing for that.'

Their jury-rigged bubble was clouding with moisture. Cley rubbed the surface to see better, forgetting the skysharks. She was beginning to wonder how they could survive for long out here, Malign or no. And it was getting cold. Seeker seemed unbothered. She spread her hindquarters, assuming the hunched posture that meant she intended to excrete, and Cley said, 'Seeker! Not now.'

'But I must.'

'Please. Look, we're going to suffocate out here unless—'

Seeker farted loudly and shat a thin stream directly onto the nearest wall. Smiling daintily, she said, 'Take a deep breath.'

Cley caught just a taint of the smell – and then her ears popped. Seeker's excrement had eaten a small hole in their protection. Vacuum sucked the brown slime away.

Cley grabbed for the nearest wall as a gathering breeze plucked at her hair. Sudden fear darted through her, and she sucked in air greedily, finding it already thinner. The small hole screamed its banshee protest. The wind drew her toward the wall.

She struck it and rebounded in the sudden chill. Seeker's fur abruptly filled her face, and she clutched a handful. She would have demanded an explanation, but that would have taken air. Seeker surged, carrying her along with muscular agility. Her ears felt as though daggers were thrust into her eardrums. Seeker dug claws into the walls, wedging the two of them into a corner. She struggled to see what was happening.

Their draining air made a thin, screaming rocket exhaust, thrusting them back toward the Leviathan. Seeker lurched around the pyramid, dragging Cley, to direct their temporary missile. Cley smacked into the walls, got disoriented, yelped for Seeker to stop. Seeker didn't.

Whirling, they passed into the Leviathan's shadow. She saw a raw wound in the skin nearby. A pale pink membrane slid out from its edges. The gouge looked like a majestically closing eye, hurt and red-rimmed. They were headed almost directly toward the slowly narrowing rent.

Seeker lunged away. This momentarily altered the direction of the jetting air. Then Seeker slammed against the far wall, and the jet swung again. This midcourse correction took them straight through the closing iris of the gouge.

They struck a large, soft fern and bounced among a confusing tangle of branches. The pink membrane sealed shut above them, puckering along the seam. Seeker extended razor-sharp claws and tore open the membrane, releasing them from its collapsing folds. They fumbled outward in an awkward parody of birth, comically mismatched twins.

Cley could hold her breath no longer. She exhaled, coughed, and sucked in thin but warm air. She breathed greedily. Just panting was a profound pleasure.

'How . . . how'd you do that?'

Around them small scurryings and slidings began. The Leviathan had already begun to secure and revive itself.

'A simple problem in dynamics.' Seeker yawned.

They lived for two days in the segmented chambers, snuggled into this zone of the Leviathan. Armies of small insectlike workers thronged everywhere, patching and pruning.

The pink membrane thickened just enough to keep in air securely but allowed in beams of sunlight, which hastened regrowth. Cley found food and rested, watching the crowds of hurrying workers. Through the transparent membrane she could see the spaceborne life outside, and at last understood their role.

Small crawler forms healed the torn skin with their sticky leavings. Others seemed to ferry materials from distant parts of the Leviathan to the many lacerations. Strange oblong creatures scooted in from distant places, trailing bags of fluids and large seeds.

She slowly caught the sense of the Leviathan, its interlocking mysteries. The carcass of a skyshark, gutted by its own internal fires, became food for the regrowth of myriad plants. The armies that distributed skyshark parts showed no malice or vindictive anger as they tore the body to shreds, sometimes stopping to eat a morsel. They were intent upon their labors, nothing more. Nature, she knew, could be cruel but not malicious.

Though much could be repaired, clearly the great

world-creature was badly hurt. Long chasms yawned where skysharks had ruptured enclosed pressure zones, spilling moist wealth. Whole regions were gray with death. On the second day, the reek of bodies drove Cley and Seeker from the once-tranquil groves of ropy banyan-like trees.

But the true sign of the enormous damage came when Cley felt a slow, steady gravity pushing her toward the aft layers. 'We're moving,' she said.

'We must.' Seeker was carefully picking the briars from a pretty bunch of red berries. She had assured Cley that the thorns were quite tasty, whereas the berries were poison; the bush was a master of sly deception. Cley passed.

'Where to?'

'Jove.'

'Not Venus?'

'Events accelerate.'

'Who says?'

'The captain. That rodent who passed by brought word.'

'If you trust a rat. Is the Leviathan dying?'

'No, but its pain is vast. It — the captain, if you must personify — seeks succor.'

'From this Jove thing?'

'No, though the Leviathan expends its fluids to take us there. It can receive the aid of its many friends as we travel. The point is for the Leviathan to rid itself of us.'

'Us? Um. We brought the pain . . . ?'

When Seeker said nothing, Cley scrambled away impatiently. So much was going on that she didn't know about. She recalled the clubby way small girls had kept secrets from her out of spite. Try as she did to be more mature, through all this, she felt the same way now: irked, rejected, angry.

Better to go find out for herself. But nobody would talk to her. The sticks-and-stones workers swarming everywhere ignored her. Very well, she would explore. After getting lost three times, she found a translucent bubble that gave an aft view.

Long, pearly plumes jetted from the Leviathan. They came from tapered, warty growths that Cley was sure had not poked from the Leviathan before. They had been grown with startling speed and somehow linked to a chemical system, one fed in turn by the Leviathan's internal chemistry. Her nose prickled at the scent of peroxide, and the thunder of steady detonations made nearby boughs tremble.

She tuned in her inboards and let them free-associate on what she saw. She had never been a big fan of inboards, preferring to learn from the rub of experience. But she knew now that she was hopelessly outclassed out here in the wild and woolly, too. The inboards filled in whispery knowledge, keyed to what her eyes took in.

Even as the immense bulk accelerated, Cley could see groups of space life detach themselves and spurt away. Some species seemed to be abandoning ship. Perhaps sensing that something dangerous lay ahead? They spread broad silvery sails, which reflected images of the shrinking sun.

Others had sails of utter dull black, and Cley guessed that these might be the natural prey of skysharks. Reflections would attract unwanted attention, so these oddly shaped creatures deployed parachute-shaped sails to absorb sunlight. They gained security at the price of getting only half the propulsion of their reflective brothers. They were also warmer. Some of them contrived to shed the buildup of heat through thin, broad cooling vanes. In space, without the warmth of air about them, their infrared images would draw predators, too.

Such adaptations led to every conceivable arrangement of surfaces. Creatures like abstract paintings were quite workable here, where gravity had no hand in fashioning evolution's pressures. There was no price for size, so creatures of apparently arbitrary extent flourished. Their living struts, sheets, tubes, and decks made use of every geometric advantage. Pivots as apparently fragile as a flower stem served to turn vast planes and sails. Transparent veins carried fluids of green and ivory.

Yet as these fled the wounded giant, others flocked in. Great arrays swooped to meet the Leviathan — things that looked to Cley like no more than spindly arrays of green toothpicks. Nonetheless, these unlikely assemblies decelerated, attached themselves to the Leviathan, and offloaded cargoes. Some brought their dead. All moved with a springy energy born of zero gravity and a billion years of crafting by blunt nature.

It struck Cley that the Leviathan played a role with no easy human analogy. It cycled among worlds, yet was no simple ship. Fleets of spaceborne life exchanged food and seeds and doubtless much more with it. All shaped their existences by intersecting the Leviathan's orbit, hammering out biological bargains, and then returning to the black depths where they eked out a living. The Leviathan was ambassador, matchmaker, general store, and funeral director, and many other unfathomable roles as well.

Now the vast beast was deeply damaged, and panic ran

through the labors outside. As well, a fretful tang layered the air around Cley. She turned away from the sunlit spectacle of the aft zones just in time to glimpse a small, ruddy disk coming into view. Then the hackles on her neck rose and she whirled, already knowing what she would see.

You brought this upon me, the captain sent.

The restless shape towered above her. Its thumb-sized components hovered as thought full of repressed anger, buzzing, buzzing. Their fevered motions, like caged birds, gave the stretched shape the appearance of a warped statue. Across the humanoid figure the fluttering was like dappled light, as if it were made of leaves stirred by fitful breezes.

Cley felt her throat tighten. 'I didn't know the skysharks even existed. You've got to understand, I—'

I understand much. Toleration requires more.

It made a sound like dry winds blowing through palm fronds. The head of the thing was a blob – no eyes, no mouth – that stirred as if small crabs ran beneath the skin. The whole mass of it fidgeted. As the blob-head turned, it exuded a yellow vapor with a cutting smell.

Cley ached to flee. But how could she elude this buzzing, manic swarm? Better to keep it talking. 'It wasn't my idea to come here.'

The elongated human form bulged. Its left arm merged with the body. She sensed a massive threat behind these surges, underlined by spikes of anger that shot through the murky Talent-voice of the captain. *Nor mine.*

'I – I'll leave as soon as I can.'

I shall rid myself of you.

She backed away, despite herself.

The Malign sends tendrils everywhere.

'I know, it's . . .' What to say? That it was after her? Not likely to win this thing over.

They snake into me.

Throw herself on its mercy? That was a human category. At least try to get some information. 'Do you think it can find me?'

The constantly shifting form curled its fat legs up into the body, as though its components had to be brought closer to ponder this point. *Soon, yes. It probes me.*

'How much time do I have left?'

This set off an agitated dance of the thumb-birds. They whirled around each other, spun, hovered with tiny wings abuzz. *It would have tracked you by now.*

'Why hasn't it come here?'

It is opposed by another of similar skill.

'What? Who?'

The buzzing changed to a hiss. *I cannot predict the outcome of such large collisions.*

Cley tried to make herself think of this thing as a community of parts, not simply an organism. But the moving cloud seemed to purposefully make itself human-like enough to send disturbing, atavistic fears strumming through her. And she wondered if that, too, was its intention. She sensed a certain holding back, to avoid flooding her again.

'What other "skill"? Another magnetic mind?'

The hiss became like a liquid fire. *Similar in power, and winging on the flexings of the fields. It is called the Multifold.*

'Is it dangerous to you? I, I am sorry if it is . . .'

Despite herself Cley edged away from the shifting fog of creatures. She resolved to stand straight and undaunted in the slight pseudogravity of the Leviathan's centrifugal acceleration, to show no sign of her inner fear. But how much could the captain sense from her unshielded thoughts?

I do not know. I despise all such human inventions.

'The Multifold?'

In typical human fashion, as a corrective to your earlier error – the Malign.

'Look, even Leviathans must make mistakes,' Cley said giddily.

Ours do not remain; we winnow. Ours do not keep, encased in the lace of magnetic fields, while the galaxy turns upon itself again and again. Our errors die.

The cloud-captain hummed and fretted. Its head lifted into the air. Suddenly, it had a mouth, gaping like a huge bullet hole that ran completely through the head. Cley could see the vegetation beyond. Angry waves roiled up and down the torso.

This thing could kill her in seconds. Showing fear wasn't going to do any good. All right, then, do the opposite.

'So we build things to last.' Cley shrugged with airy abandon. Damn it, she was not going to let this talking fog intimidate her. 'Can't blame us, can you?'

Why should we not?

'We don't last long ourselves. Not Ur-humans, anyway. Our creations have to do our living for us.'

Nor should you endure. Time once honored your kind. Now it drags you in its wake.

Despite her fear, this rankled Cley. 'Oh, really? You seem pretty scared of stuff we made.'

The captain lost its human shape entirely, exploding

like shrapnel into the air. Components buzzed angrily around Cley. She stood absolutely still, remembering the time on Earth when she had sealed her nostrils against clouds of mites. But that would be of no use here.

She stared straight ahead and kept her mind as steady as she could. Small and limited her brain might be, but she wasn't going to give the maddened cloud any satisfaction.

The captain's flyers came swarming. They brushed her like a heavy, moist handclasp – insistent, clammy, repulsive. She shut her eyes. Wings battered across her face. Tiny voices shrieked and howled in her mind. Slapping her hands over her ears would be no help.

Panic struck. Flyers covered her face, her nostrils, started to smother her. She frantically shoved several away, trying to clear breathing room, and dozens took their place.

She opened her mouth to scream. A humming thing flew into it. She did not dare bite down. It fluttered against her teeth, her tongue; she tried blowing it out and felt herself beginning to vomit . . .

'You will kindly go about your tasks,' Seeker's voice came cutting through.

Cley jumped backward, startled by the smooth, almost liquid quality to the sound. The thumb-bird scooted out of her mouth. She clamped her jaw down, opened her eyes.

Seeker hung by one claw from a strand, peering at the center of the fog. *'Now,'* she added.

A long moment passed. Silence.

Slowly the components steadied, whirling in a cyclone about both Seeker and Cley, but keeping a respectful distance. Then, *I suffer agony for you!*

'As you should,' Seeker replied evenly, 'for you must.'

Be gone!

'In due time,' Seeker said.

Now!

'You know we are your hope,' Seeker said, peering sharply at it, 'in the long run.'

In the long run we shall be dead!

With that the thumb-birds streaked away. Cley felt a spark of compassion for the strange things, and their even stranger sum. She supposed that in some way she was also an anthology being, and that her cells suffered in silence for her. But the captain was a different order of thing, called by numberless tasks. It was more open to both joy and agony, in a way she could not express but had felt deeply through the Talent.

'Thanks,' she said in a whisper, her throat still tight.

Seeker coasted to a light landing near the transparent bubble. 'Even a great being can harm in a moment of self-loss.'

'Getting mad, that's self-loss? Funny term.'

'For Leviathan, the pain is of a different quality than you can feel.'

Quietly Cley said, 'I think I got some of that.'

Seeker shook her head. 'Never think that you can sense its sacrifice.'

Cley did not know what to say to that. She had seen the terrible damage, the shriveled zones, the creatures that had died as their blood boiled, and worse.

'Meanwhile,' Seeker said in the way she had of abruptly changing the subject, 'enjoy the view.'

Ahead, the ruddy disk was much larger now. It was a planet of silver seas and rough, brown, cloud-shrouded continents. As they approached, Cley saw that a circle hung over the equator like a belt. It seemed to be held above the atmosphere by great towers.

These thin stalks were like the Pinwheel she had ridden, but fixed. With feet planted in the soil, their heads met the great ring that girded the planet. Each tower could remain erect by itself, and perhaps they had stood alone once. Now the ring linked each to the others, making the array steady.

The Leviathan intended to sweep by the great circle, Seeker told her. Cley relaxed and let the slow energies of this approaching world steal over her. Even at this distance she could see twinkling, tiny compartments sliding up and down the towers, connecting the spaceborne to the worldborne. And larger shapes shot along the grand ring itself, bringing their stores around the planet. At the tower nearest their eventual destination, goods got off-loaded.

This was how the Leviathan and its myriad passengers merged their fortunes with the spreading emerald of the world below. Some towers plunged into the silver seas, while others stood at the summits of enormous mountains. All were wedded into a slow symphony of patient metabolism.

Close-upping her eyes, Cley could make out the texture of the towers now. With surprise she saw that they were made of the same woody layers as the Pinwheel – indeed, that the entire ring system was like a living, balanced suspension bridge, cantilevered out into the great abyss of vacuum.

'What is this place?' Cley asked.

'Mars,' Seeker answered.

'What about Venus?'

Seeker gestured at a blue-white dot. 'Nearby. We do not need it now, so I directed the captain to bring us veering close to Mars. We shall gain momentum, stealing from the planet's hoard, and hasten on.'

'Either we're moving very fast, or these places aren't very far apart.'

'Both. All the ancient worlds are now clustered in a narrow habitable zone around the sun, each finding its comfortable distance from the fire.'

'And we moved them?'

'Yes. A later form, not you Originals. The work required a particularly long-sighted human form, the Staple Dons — alas, now extinct.'

'How'd they do it?'

'By cycling asteroids, passing them by worlds over many millions of years. The Dons emerged from their labyrinths — for they preferred living underground, no one knows why — to regulate these slowly building outward tugs.'

'Umm. This Mars looks better off than Earth.'

'True, for no humans have meddled with it for nearly a billion years. Once it, too, was desert.'

This Cley flatly refused to believe, for Mars was a carpet of rich, many-colored convolutions. Earth might have been like this, she imagined, without the endless tinkering by the human forms that came before the Supras, and the eras of desert-loving bots. 'Can we live there?'

'Oh yes — but we must pass on. It is too dangerous for us.'

Seeker pointed. Along the ring, filaments of orange and blue twisted. They shot up and down the towers, as though seeking a way in.

Cley whispered, 'Lightning.'

'It searches,' Seeker said.

She could see magnetic storms rolling in from beyond Mars, blowing against the ring like surf from an immense ocean. 'Can it damage the ring?'

'It may destroy all of that great creature, if it thinks you are there.'

'Damn! The Malign is everywhere!'

'Spreading, always spreading. When we left Earth, it had penetrated sunward only momentarily, and at great cost. Now it hunts amid the worlds. It roves and probes. This Leviathan must have seemed a likely target.' Seeker's brow crinkled with concern. 'It has even learned to muster packs like the skysharks.'

Cley bit her lip in exasperation. 'Things are getting worse fast.'

'This is as we wish,' Seeker said mildly.

'Huh? Why?'

'If it hid among the stars, we could never be sure of its demise.'

Cley shook her head. 'You think you can kill it?'

'Not I.'

'Who can?'

'Everyone, or no one.'

4

Continents Alive

Cley awoke with a start, uneasy, almost as if something – or someone – had been watching her . . . That nebulous disquiet vanished as she saw they had company. A furry thing was sitting on Seeker's shoulder, whispering. Seeker answered in a whisper, glanced at Cley. The furry thing went on talking, and Cley admired the elegance of it, the sculpted head and graceful body. Then it glanced her way, eyes widened – and it was gone in a flash.

'What was that?'

Seeker said, 'One of the intelligent cats.'

'I heard they were wiped out in a war with us.'

'They were – on Earth. So they fled here.'

'Housecats in space. Sorry I spooked it. I'd have liked to hear it talk.'

'They do not speak to humans, ever.'

'Why?'

'You tried to render them extinct.'

'Not me. And they're just pets, after all.'

'They are major figures in the intellectual life of Leviathan.'

'Cats? Say, what was it telling you?'

'About another Original.'

Cley blinked, startled. 'Here?'

'Not far.'

'Let's go!'

The cat was correct in how close the other Original had been. The hiding place he or she had used, in a dense, snaggy stand, must have been within sight of her and Seeker. Cley had no idea how they'd evaded the procyon's nose and ears. Whoever it was had obviously left recently and hastily – the leaves crushed by his passage still wept slow, pearly tears from broken edges. And he was moving fast, away from her and Seeker. Fleeing? Why?

The pursuit took hours, and she was sweaty and tired when she found him. A man, tall and leanly muscular, and he didn't want to talk. He was definitely running *from* her – his speed only increased when he glanced behind. Cley pursued him through the foliage, leaving Seeker behind. She cornered him in a bower behind a slow-tumbling waterfall. 'Hey! I'm one of you!' she called.

He glowered and stayed silent.

He looked vaguely like others in her tribe and Cley tried to compare her own face to his. Could this be . . . ? 'We're Originals, you and me – I can tell! I'm Hard River Meta.'

'I won't discuss my origins.' He edged away from her, eyes darting, looking for a way out. 'We, we should not meet now.'

'Huh? Why?'

'You must . . . keep focus,' he said reluctantly, eyes averted.

'My Mothers—'

'No! You shouldn't be talking to me – it's too danger-ous! Leave me alone!' He seemed suddenly scared, maybe even angry, but he didn't seem angry at her. He gathered himself, tensing . . .

'But—'

'I do not want to know. You're with' – a jerk of the head toward the hull – '*them,* Supras. Can't stand them; that's why I came out here in the first place. They're coming. That's all I need to know.'

'Well, why? What's wrong . . . ?'

'Logic doesn't always rule our hearts. But here it should.' To this odd statement he added a sudden look of warm longing, gazing into her eyes. His mouth moved, but no words came out.

'Why can't we –' she started.

And he was gone, diving headlong into the waterfall. She went after him but quickly lost sight of his brown body in the spray and churn.

They arced outward.

Cley fretted about the man – why had he run away? – but then, despairing of making any sense of it, made herself put the memory aside. Instead, she struggled to understand the incessant activity around her. Her inboards prompted her with darting whispers. She stitched together some understanding of what she had seen in the days that passed.

The original solar system had been a hostile realm, with all worlds but Earth ranging from the dead to the murderous. Then came the fabled, eon-long Reworking by the Dons. That great crafting had left Earth as the nearest child of the sun, Venus next, and then Mars. All were ripe gardens now.

Beyond Mars lay the true center of the great system,

the Jove complex. Its gargantuan hub had once been the planet Jupiter. The swollen, simmering superplanet that now sat at the center of Jove glowed with a wan infrared shine of its own. It had been fattened by gobbling up the masses of ancient Uranus and Neptune. The collisions of those worlds had been the most legendary of all the spectacular events in human history.

She could find no images of those gaudy catastrophes. They lay so far in the past now that little record remained, even in the Library.

After its deep atmosphere had calmed, bulging Jupiter's steady glow had warmed the chilly wastes of its moons. Then Saturn, cycled through many near-miss passes around Jupiter, had been stripped of much of its mass. This gauzy bounty was spread among the ancient moons. A shrunken Saturn of cool blue oceans now orbited Jupiter. After all this prodigious gravitational engineering, the long-lost Saturnian rings were replaced, and looked exactly like the originals.

The baked rock of Mercury had arrived then, spun outward from the sun by innumerable kinetic minutes. Light liquids from Saturn pelted the hardpan plains of Mercury for a thousand years, and now the once barren world swung also around Jupiter, brimming with a curious pink and orange air. Seeker remarked that a particular highly prized delicacy of winged life flew in the russet cloud decks there.

All this had come about through adroit gravitational encounters over millennia. Carefully tuned, each world now harbored some life, though of very different forms. The Jove system hung at the edge of the sun's life zone. Swollen Jupiter added just enough ruddy infrared glow to make all the salvaged mass of the ancient gas giant planets useful. Beyond Jove wove only the orbits of rubble and ice and, farther still, comets slow-blooming under cultivation.

Cley watched with foreboding the approach of the Jove system's grand gravitational gavotte. Just as they were drawn to the true vital center of the solar system, so would be the Malign.

About her the Leviathan regrew itself, moist mysteries abounding, but the springlike fervor of its renewal did not lighten Cley's mood. Seeker was of little help; she dozed often and seemed unworried about the coming conflict. To distract herself, Cley peered out from the transparent blisters, trying to fathom the unfolding intricacies outside.

She had to overcome a habit of thought ingrained in all planetborne life. Space was not mere emptiness, but the mated assets of energy, matter, and room. Planets, in contrast, were inconvenient sites, important mostly because on their busy surfaces life had begun.

After all, unruly atmospheres whip up dust, block sunlight, rust metals, hammer with their winds, overheat and chill, rub and worry. Gravity forced even simple land-roving life forms to use much of their bodies just to stand up. Even airless, rotating worlds robbed their surfaces of sunlight half the time. And nothing was negotiable: Planets gave a fixed day and night, gravity, and atmosphere. Life had to adjust to the iron rule of inertia.

In contrast, constant sunlight flooded the weatherless calm of space. Flimsy sheets could collect high-quality energy undimmed by roiling air. Cups could sip from the light rush of particles spewed out by the sun — a wind that fluttered but never failed. Asteroids offered ample mass without gravity's demanding grip. Just as an origin in tidepools did not mean that shallow water was the best place for later life, planets inevitably became backwaters, as well.

Biological diversity demands room for variation, and space had an abundance of sheer volume to offer the first spaceborne organisms. Apparently, humans had crafted the first of these, then lost control as evolution took charge. These earliest forms had sported tough but flexible skins, light and tight, stingy with internal gas and liquids. Evolution used their fresh, weightless geometries to design shrewd alternatives to the simple, cylindrical guts and spines of the Earthborne.

Cley expected to see fewer of the free-roving space-forms as the Leviathan glided outward. Instead, the abundance and pace of life quickened. Though sunlight fell with the square of distance from the sun, the available volume rose as the cube. Lessening energies traded off against more free volume in which to experiment.

Evolution's blind craft had filled this swelling niche with myriad forms. Spindly, full-sailed, baroquely elegant, they swooped around the Leviathan.

But inside, the great being teemed with an even greater profusion of life, or 'animated water,' as Seeker put it. Her explorations took her into odd portions of the Leviathan. She ambled along shallow lakes and even across a shadowy, bowl-shaped desert. She found a chunky iceball the size of a foothill, covered with harvesting animals. The Leviathan had captured this comet nucleus and was paying out its fluid wealth with miserly care.

She paid a price for her excursions. Humans had not

been privileged among species here since well before
Sonomulia was a dream. Twice she narrowly escaped being
a meal for predators that looked very much like animated
thornbushes. The second one was a damned near miss.
Cley turned back, or rather, completed her circumnavi-
gation of the Leviathan. Somewhat the worse for wear, she
found Seeker just where she had left her days before, and
the beast tended to her cuts, bites, and scratches.

Cley had done some thinking. Not having a soul to
talk to actually helped, somewhat to her surprise. 'Why
are you helping me, Seeker After Patterns?' she asked as
Seeker licked a cut.

Seeker took her time answering, concentrating on pressing her nose along a livid slash made by the sharp-leaved
bushes. When she looked up, the cut had sealed so well,
only a hairline mark remained. 'To strengthen you.'

Cley laughed. 'Well, it's sure as hell working.
Weightlessness has given me muscles I didn't know I had.'

'Not your body. Your Talent.'

She blinked in the pale yellow sunlight that slanted
through the bowers. 'I was wondering why I keep hearing things. That last thornbush—'

'You caught its hunt pleasure.'

'Good thing, too. It was fast.'

'Can you sense any humans now?'

'No, there aren't . . .' Cley frowned. 'Wait, something
. . . Why, it's like . . .'

'Supras.'

'How'd you know?'

'The time is drawing close.'

'Time for what?'

'The struggle.'

'You weren't just giving this li'l Talent of mine a chance to grow, were you? You're taking me somewhere, too.'

'To Jove.'

'Sure, but I mean . . . Oh, I see. That's where it'll happen.'

Seeker lounged back, tongue lolling. 'Humans have difficulty in understanding that Earth is not important now. The system's center of life is Jove.'

'So the Malign has to win there?'

'There may be no winning.'

'Well, I know what losing will be like.' Cley thought of the ashen bodies of all the people she had ever loved.

Seeker shook her big head – a human gesture, a politeness she recognized now. 'It is because we do not know what losing would be like that we resist.'

'Really? Look, it stomped on us as if we were bugs.'

'To it, you are.'

'And to you?'

'Do not insects have many uses? In my view they are far more seemly in the currents of life than, say, just another species of the Chordata.'

'Cor what?'

'Those who have spinal cords.'

Irked, Cley said, 'Well, aren't you just another spinal type?'

'True enough. I did not say I was more important than you.'

'You compared us Ur-humans – me! – with insects.'

'With no insects, soon there would be no humans.'

Exasperated, Cley puffed noisily, sending her hair up in a dancing plume. 'The Supras sure got along without them, living in their dear, dead old Sonomulia.'

'The Supras are not of your species.'

'Not human?'

'Not truly.' Seeker finished ministering to her wounds and gave her an affectionate lick on the chin. 'Nor as tasty.'

Cley eased her blouse gingerly over her cuts. 'I have to admit, I pretty much felt that way myself. Except the taste part.'

'They cannot be true companions to you.'

'They're the only thing left.'

'Perhaps not, after we are done.'

Cley sighed. 'I'm just concentrating on avoiding that Malign.'

'It will not care so greatly about you after you have served.'

'Served? Fought, you mean?'

'Both.'

She felt a light trill streak through her mind. At first she confused it with warbling birdsong. But then she recalled the sensation of blinding, swift thought, conversations whipped to a cyclonic pitch . . . 'Supras. They're coming.'

She felt their presence now as several tiny skittering notes in the back of her mind, mouse-small and bee-quick. 'What'll we do?'

'Nothing.'

'They're getting close.'

'It is time they did.'

'Should we hide?'

'Not necessary now. Events make their own momentum.'

Seeker gestured at the intricate whirl of light visible

through a high, arching dome above the tangled green-ery. They were coming in on a sunward orbit, and the Jove worlds lay beneath them like jewels on a black carpet.

Beyond Jupiter's original large moons there now circled rich, russet-clouded Mercury and shrunken, blue-oceaned Saturn. These radiant dabs swam among washes of bright magenta and burnt gold. Spinning very slowly, these washes were single life forms larger than continents.

Seeker had described some of these in far more detail than Cley could follow. They all seemed to be complex variations on the age-old craft of negotiating sunlight and chemicals into beautiful structures. Seeker implied that these were intelligences utterly different from Earthborne kinds, and she struggled with the notion that what appeared to be enormous gardens could harbor minds superior to her own. Or at least different.

Cley lay back and listened to the steadily waxing burr of Supra talk. She could not distinguish words, but a thin edge of smoldering worry and ice blue alarm came through clearly.

Languidly she dozed and listened and thought. The smears of light that swung throughout the great orbiting globe of Jove reminded her of sea mats formed at the shorelines of ancient Earth. She had learned of them through tribal legend, much of which dealt with the lean perspectives of life.

Sandwiched between layers of grit and grime, even those earliest life forms had found a way to make war. Why should matters be different now? Some microbe mat three billion years before had used sunlight to split water, liberating deadly oxygen. They had poisoned their rivals by excreting the gas. The battle had raged across broad beaches bordered by a brown, sluggish sea. The victorious mats had enjoyed their momentary triumph beneath a pink sky. But this fresh gaseous resource in turn allowed new, more complex life to begin and thrive. Their heirs eventually drove the algae mats nearly to extinction.

So it had been with space. Planetary life had leaped into the new realm, first using simple machines, and later, deliberately engineered life forms. The dead machines had proved to be like the first algae. Instead of excreting oxygen, they brought life — inadvertently at first, then with deliberation. Compound forms arose.

In time the space-dwelling gray machines, adapting solely through unliving self-evolution, retreated. They were driven into narrow enclaves, like the early algae mats.

Out here, bordering the realm of ice, machines had finally wedded with plants to make anthology creatures. This desperate compromise had saved them.

The alliance of the gray mechanical and the living green drove a cornucopia of new forms. Once allied with the virtues of dead mass, synthesis life seethed across the vast volumes with prodigious invention. Nothing could stop — though some tried — the creative destruction of Darwin from fashioning human designs into subtler instruments. For a billion years life had teemed and fought and learned amid harsh vacuum and sunlight's glare. This opera in the sky played out with little aid from the planets.

Cley had seen several synthesis creatures enter the Leviathan — beings that looked to her like mossy, unfolding furniture or animated blue-steel buildings.

Some time long ago, spaceborne life had begun to compete for materials with the planetary life zones. After all, most of the light elements in the solar system lay in the outer planets and in the cometary nuclei far beyond Pluto. In this competition the rocky worlds were hopelessly outclassed.

From the perspective of space, Cley thought, planetary life looked like those ancient algae mats – flat, vulnerable, trapped in a thin wedge of air, unaware of the great, stretching spaces beyond. And now the true ancient mats survived only in dark enclaves on Earth, cowering before the ravages of oxygen.

Cley referred to her inboards and let the sliding presences of history come into her mind. Given a billion years, planetborne life had done better than the mats. Slowly the planetary biospheres forged connections to spaceborne life through great beasts like the Pinwheel, the Jonah, the Leviathan. But was this only a momentary pause, a temporary bargain struck before the planets became completely irrelevant?

Or – the thought struck her solidly – were they already?

5

Homo Technologicus

The Supras boarded the Leviathan after protracted negotiation. The captain had appeared before Seeker and Cley, humming and darting madly, alarmed for some reason Cley could not understand. She had to reassure the captain three times that she was indeed the primitive human form the Supras sought.

Only then did the captain let the Supras board, and it was some time before Rin appeared, alone, thrashing his way through the luxuriant greenery. He was tired and disheveled, his usually immaculate one-piece suit stained and dirty.

Then Cley saw that his left arm was missing below the elbow. 'What – how . . . ?'

'Some trouble with a minor agency,' Rin said, his voice thin and tight.

She rushed to him, instinctively wanting to help, then felt embarrassed. She felt the stub of his arm. The flesh at the elbow was deeply bruised and mottled with livid yellow and orange spots.

'A little snarly thing,' he said, sitting carefully in a vine netting. 'Came at me . . . in space . . . as we entered this enormous beast.'

'An animal?'

'A concoction of the Malign.'

'What . . . ?'

'I killed it.'

'What can I do?' The recovery arts of Supras were legendary, but *this* . . . 'Didn't you bleed? How . . . ?'

'Let it go,' he said, waving her away, mustering more strength in his voice.

'But you're hurt. I—'

'My arm will take care of itself.' He grimaced for an instant but then recovered with visible effort, his face pale.

She moved to help him, but he turned to keep the severed arm away from her. She frowned with concern. 'Well, at least take something for the pain.'

'I have released' – a twinge shook him – 'my own metadorphins. Or I can use more powerful agencies . . . if I chose. But that . . . would slow regrowth.'

'What do you need?'

'I? Rest. Fluids. But mostly I need you.'

'Me?'

'You we came to take, but there is . . . little time. Let me recover. Best to stay here. It . . .' He faded off.

'The Malign?'

He revived with effort. 'It destroys our ships, so . . . best . . . we stay here . . . hide.'

'Sleep.' She patted his brow, and his eyes closed.

She couldn't keep her eyes off the stump. It had already formed a protruding mass of pale cells at its tip. Wheezing, he lay back in a matting of vines and closed his eyes, but she did not believe he slept.

And she felt none of the old surge, the – she had to admit to the word itself – *desire* for him, for his . . . Supraness. Good; now she understood. Rin had never inspired her oddly free-floating lust, but he had been the exception. Something missing in the chemistry, somehow.

There, she thought. She had, at last, to admit that she had come out of her girlhood with minimal sexual skills but enormous passions, directed at the Supras. A Supra man fitted neatly into her needs. Her blazingly vivid affair with Kurani had firmly set that nascent pattern, and his loss had left her aching, empty, craving the consolation of the nearest substitute she could find. And it could have been pretty much any Supra man, in the end. Except Rin. It was good to know that there were exceptions.

Kurani had indeed been extraordinary, the best man and Supra she had known. What had been, with him, had been true. No matter how blind or misguided, it had still been true. Small wonder, really, that her heart had been shaped to his mold . . .

But substitutes for him weren't enough anymore. She knew them for the pale ghost echoes they were.

And now, only now, could she see her own patterns. Watch that part of her taper away in the rearview mirror of life. For she was finally beyond it. Distance helped. Relief flooded her. She sighed.

Cley watched Rin's flesh slowly begin to extrude from his elbow. Oily secretions seeped to the surface as the arm seemed to build itself layer by layer, bulging outward. Stubs of bare white bone first inched forth. Then ligaments and tendons accumulated along the bones, fed by swarms of migrating cells like moving, busy lichen. A wave of denser cartilage followed, cementing attachments with muscle fibers that wove themselves as she watched. Then layers of skin fattened in the wake of growth — first a column of pink and then darker shades. Already Rin's arm was longer by the length of her little finger. Sweat drenched his clothes, but he clenched his teeth and said nothing, muscles standing out in his neck. Then he slept.

Cley sat beside him, fetching water when he awoke and asked. She had taken weeks to recover from her injuries. This man was regrowing a limb in a single, fitful sleep. The gulf between them was quietly impressive.

A long while passed. Seeker had vanished. Rin ate some red nuts when she offered them but refused any more food. He seemed to summon up the materials and energy for regrowth from his own tissues. His strong legs seemed to deflate slightly, as though flesh was dissolving and migrating to his wounded arm. His entire body turned a ruddy brown, flushed with blood. Muscles jerked, and filigrees of color washed over his skin. He moaned occasionally but managed to contain his torment, breathing shallowly.

His hand formed from matted gray cells. Sheets of them made quick rushes, like an invading army, over the muscle and membrane that in turn cloaked bare bone. These invasions flowed directly from his circulatory system, she saw, moving to the working surface and making greasy mats that cured in the sunlight. Over hours they gathered into the fine network of muscles that made the human hand such a marvel of evolution's art.

She watched as though this were a living anatomy lesson. Bones grew to their fine tips, followed by a wash of cloaking cells. Blue waves of cells settled into place as muscle. Stringy, yellow fat filled in spaces, then got eaten for other uses. Fresh skin had begun to wrap the thumb and fingers before Rin blinked and seemed to be returning to full consciousness. White slabs hardened to make his fingernails, their tips nicely rounded.

She felt a long, slow body-murmur from him through her Talent. Low, like a moan, it seemed to come from a dispersed web, as though she were sensing his entire neuromuscular network. Shared relief flooded her, echoing his near-audible exhalation of tension, as she sensed his sharp pain finally ebbing away. The quiet here made it apparent, growing as she concentrated. Laboring, quickening. Rin's breath came faster, and his eyes opened at last.

'I . . . I never saw such,' Cley said.

Rin yawned. 'Hmmm . . . Usually we would take more time.'

'You must be exhausted. I could see your body stealing tissues to build your arm.'

'Borrowing.'

'My people have some ability like that, but nothing nearly so—'

Rin waved his new hand dismissively. 'We must talk.'

Seeker appeared nearby. Where had she been all this time? Cley wondered.

Rin seemed to shake off the torpor that had possessed him in a single shake of his head. He stretched his arm experimentally, and joints popped in his wrist and fingers, crisp and sure. For a moment he reminded Cley of a teenager testing his newfound strength. Then he darted a glance at Seeker and said, 'So . . .'

'So what?' Cley countered. She felt, at the very edge of her perception, thin striations of darting Talent-talk.

Rin shook his head and said to Seeker, 'You promised you would help keep her safe.'

Seeker yawned. 'I did.'

'But you did *not* have permission to take her away from

us. And certainly not to escape into the system solar.'

Cley had expected anger from Rin, not this air of precise displeasure. Both he and Seeker glanced at her, as if she were the most likely to explode. Not so, she realized suddenly. She was not truly surprised that Seeker had struck some kind of deal with them back on Earth. Their escape from the Library had gone far better than it should have, as if the Supras had never realized she might leave, let alone have aid in doing so.

Seeker said, 'I did not need permission.'

'I should think—'

'After all, who could give it?' Seeker asked lazily.

'She is of our kind. That gives us species rights.'

'You are Homo Technologicus. She is Ur-human, several species removed from you.'

Rin pursed his lips. 'Still, we are more nearly related than you.'

'Are you so sure?' Seeker grinned devilishly. 'I span the genetic heritage of many earlier forms.'

'I am quite confident that if I read your helix I could easily find many more differences in—'

'Listen, you two,' Cley broke in. 'I wanted to get away from that Library. From Supras. So I left. Seeker was just along for company.'

Rin blinked, looked at her for a long moment, and then said calmly, 'At least you are safe and have made the journey to where we need you.'

'You intended to bring me here yourself?' Cley asked.

Rin's mouth played with amused shapes. 'Yes, in a ship. Comfortably.'

Cley's temper flared despite her efforts to maintain the easy calm of a Supra. 'What? You planned to bring me here? I could have zipped out here in a ship?'

'Well, yes.' Rin seemed surprised at her question.

She whirled to confront Seeker. 'You made me go through all this?'

Seeker worked her mouth awkwardly. 'I perceived that as the correct course.'

'Correct? More like damned dangerous. And you didn't even consult me!'

'You did not know enough to judge,' Seeker said uncertainly.

'I wanted to get away from the Supras, sure, but—'

Seeker backed away. 'Perhaps I erred.'

'Perhaps?'

'I believed you needed the journey.' Seeker smiled, though to Cley's eyes, her expression seemed more uncertain than usual.

'Do not be hasty,' Rin said mildly. 'This animal is clever, and in this case it showed foresight.'

'How?'

'It was lucky for you that I did not convey you outward by our planned route. We thought it intact. Yet several craft carrying needed Ur-human passengers were destroyed after leaving Earth, and you could well have been among them.'

'What?' Cley's flare of anger guttered out. 'My people?' Cley was so excited, she lost her grip on a vine and had to catch herself.

'Not exactly. We grew them from your helix.'

'You mean they're – they're me?'

'Some, yes. Others we varied slightly, to get the proper mix of abilities.'

Cley had feared that the Supras would do this. Would

such cooked-up Ur-humans be zombies, shorn of culture, mockeries of her kind? Such disquiets had propelled her to escape before.

'Did any survive?'

'Some.'

'I . . . I want to see them.'

Rin waved his new hand. 'You can when all this is over.'

'Why then?'

'They are dispersed, as a precaution.'

'No! I have a right to be with my own kind.'

'Are you not content with our company?' Rin gestured languidly to his left. Cley saw that while she was so intent, a group of Supras had quietly infiltrated the bowers around them. Kata stood nearby, one eyebrow cocked, studying the leafy cascades with evident distaste. Her clothes had been torn and blackened – in the same engagement as Rin? Already the rips were healing. Smudges dissolved, digested by the glossy fibers. And her Talent-talk trickled into Cley's back-thoughts . . .

Cley sighed. 'I'm out of my depth with you Supras. You aren't human, not the way I know people.'

We are more than human, in your manner of speaking, Kata sent.

Cley ignored her. 'If you have any sense of justice, you'll let me see my people.'

Justice will come in time, Kata sent with a tinge of blithe unconcern.

Cley looked at Seeker, who seemed to be absorbed in picking mites from her ruddy pelt. 'How long will that be?' she asked, sticking to old-fashioned Original speech.

'Our struggle has already begun,' Rin said. 'It is best that you stay with us for the time being.'

Cley blinked. 'The fight's already going on?' *And best for whom?* she thought.

'In a way, it has been going on since long before the rebirth of Originals,' Rin said, coolly gentle.

Cley saw the chinks in his armor now, though — a wounded tilt of his solemn mouth, a refractory glint to his eyes. 'Where?'

'The final engagement has begun on the outer rim of the solar system. It now converges here, where the strength of the Jovian magnetic fields can shelter us somewhat, and our reserves are greatest.'

Seeker said, 'I suspect the Malign has many tricks we cannot guess.'

Rin nodded. 'We are minor players, but some are crucial nonetheless.' He gazed solemnly at Cley. 'Especially you.'

6

Blue Barnacles

Cley opened her mouth to interrogate Rin some more, and her ears popped. Seeker sprang upward, where something was rattling down through the canopy.

'Surround her!' Rin called, and Supras were gliding everywhere. Cley had no idea what to do. Wind whispered in her hair.

A big blue patch shot out of a mossy bank and smacked into her. Instantly it wrapped itself around Cley's arm.

'Barnacles!' someone shouted.

She fell backward from the impact, hit a branch, and extruded her punch finger tool. It hardened at the tip into a fingernail now needle-thin. Acidic pain shot up her arm. A slurping noise came from it. *Eating my skin?* She stabbed into the thick blue thing. It just grabbed her tighter. At the edge of it a thick, moist mat crept up from her elbow.

The air filled with flying barnacles, slapping themselves onto the Supras. Tumbling chaos. Cley heard a woman scream – not her, she was pretty sure – and men shouting. She kept stabbing, short jabs that met thick resistance. A sheet of pain shot up the arm and froze her throat.

She gasped for breath. Was it injecting some poison . . . ? The air got fuzzy, and sounds hollowed out; motion slowed . . . Her arm felt so heavy . . .

She was still trying to breathe, but it took longer and longer. And her finger wouldn't come unstuck from the thick mat. Purple dots danced in her eyes, blocking her view of the turmoil all around her. But somehow, it did not seem to matter, not now that time was getting slower and slower and . . .

A bristling bundle fell on the mat, and her arm sagged with the weight. It was Seeker – with impossibly long razor claws out. They did not sink into the blue mass but around it, under. Cley toppled backward, carrying Seeker's weight into a bower of vines. Seeker's claws jerked upward, yanking, her mouth spitting anger – and the mat went into seizure. It rippled, flapped, and was free, wriggling in Seeker's paws.

Cley rolled away. She choked on pollen, and when she could look back, the blue mat was in three pieces. Seeker seemed bent on making it a much larger number, shredding the thing.

Beyond the snarling, rolling fight, Cley saw something else in the air. The captain.

'Leave! You cause . . . cause . . . all this!' It was speaking to her, ignoring the Supras, who were cutting and shooting the barnacle-mats. The captain birds hovered and cheeped and darted in a whirl. Its hands and legs blurred, reformed, then lost themselves in a new frenzy. The body barely kept a human shape.

Rin had finished with his and came toward her, then saw the captain. 'You! Damn! I said to stand aside.'

'I be . . . not part . . . of this . . . evil.' The voice was reedy, wavering.

'You're of us. *We made you.*' Rin glared.

'A looong time . . . ago.'

'If we lose, it will eat you.'

'Not . . . my . . . my . . . quarrel.'

Rin gestured to a Supra woman nearby. 'Do it.'

A thin stream of green gas came from the Supra woman's tubular weapon. It did not spread but instead wrapped itself around the captain. Cley expected the birds to zip away, squawking, but instead they fell silent. In a sudden quiet she could hear the whirring of their wings. The captain's body solidified, taking on detail – cheek, fingers, ears – she had never seen before. It was the face of an old woman, eyes watery, her face racked by emotions that flitted away with each new second. The mouth worked anxiously, the sum of many flutterings. Tendrils of gas curled up into her nose and tightened about the body. In a moment the old woman was a mummy in a green shroud.

Rin said quietly, 'You will sail on. Afford us your provinces and give us succor.'

'I . . . yes. Yes.'

The captain seemed to fade back into the green background, keeping its shape yet somehow vanishing, as if the living body of the Leviathan were digesting it.

In a moment only silence hung over the bowers. The Supras were tending to their wounded. Seeker was wrapping big moist leaves around Cley's arm, as Cley finally noticed. The entire arm was red and oozing blood.

No one remarked on the strangeness that had passed by. Cley realized that it was just another skirmish to them.

Cley felt strongly the skittering, frayed skein of Talent-talk that flitted among the Supras from Illusivia. She could pick up nuances, grave worries, a burn of high excitement. Time and practice had enlarged her ability, and she could shield her own thoughts somewhat. She could now trace faint threads of flittering ideas, currents, and implications that came and went in gossamer instants.

The captain's betrayal, the clumsy assault using the barnacles — all quite expected, the Supras seemed to feel. Not all life forms were united into one coherent front. Even in an alliance, they seemed to say, one occasionally had to rap knuckles.

Later, as they recovered, Cley found Rin among the clumps of Supras. Some had lost sheets of skin to the barnacles. The bodies of dead barnacles showed them to be evolved for the light-gravity regions of Leviathan. Their name came from their habit of sticking to plants and taking flight only when they had prey well positioned. Earthside barnacles, her inboards told her, didn't attack anything. These, though, were a pack-hunting species, not like any birds Cley had ever seen. In different circumstances, she would have found them elegant and beautiful.

Then she remembered the maroon ray-birds they fought in the Tubeworld. Had evolution converged on the shape? Or did they have a common origin?

She felt the muscular flesh of a dead barnacle-bird. Rin seemed almost glad that the captain had launched them on its ill-considered attack and now was under Supra control. 'One more potential trouble out of the way,' he said, lips pale. 'We are willing to ally with different life forms, but we enforce loyalty to humankind.'

'Ummm,' Cley said, eyeing the barnacle carcasses. The Supra teams were all working with portable instruments, monitoring, ordering resources into place. The Leviathan was a refuge now, and the battle would center on it.

'What can *I* do in all this?' she asked Rin.

He smiled. As if years of preparation had focused on a single instant, an answer leaped through her mind. Kata was the channel for this, Cley felt, but she had a sense of a chorus of booming voices behind the massive intrusion. A wedge of thought drove itself through her. They were telling her much, but again, it was like trying to take a drink from a fire hose.

'I . . . I don't understand . . .'

'It will take a while to unsort itself in your mind, I'm told,' Rin said.

'So much . . . What's this thing, this black brane?'

Rin said slowly, 'An ancient term. It is a . . . a membrane, in a way. Our universe lives upon one. There is another, extending in a higher dimension that is effectively infinite—'

More than infinite, Kata sent. It is a dimension which itself spreads into other dimensions. It transcends, it transmutes, it is—

'Transfinite,' Seeker said dryly. 'We have had such discussions before, of the categories of thinking beyond infinity. I do not think them profitable at this time.'

Kata looked insulted, sniffed, sent nothing.

Rin gave Seeker a cautious look, as though recalculating the equations for this conversation. 'The other membrane houses many intelligences, of course. They learned quite a long time ago – nearly a billion years back – how to transcend dimensions. To come here.'

Cley brightened. 'Seeker and I went through that Tubeworld – was that their work?'

'Undoubtedly – and Fanak agrees. The Morphs live on the other brane. This fits the ancient texts.'

Seeker asked, 'Why ancient? Why have we been out of touch so long?'

Rin looked uneasy. 'It's a whole other *universe* on the black brane. Societies rise and fall there, just as here. For a while – perhaps not long, by their standards – they fell silent. They do not explain. Or apologize, for that matter.'

'For kidnapping us?' Cley asked.

'They were probably perfecting their methods,' Rin said. 'I am unsure if they will even act today.'

'How about *that,* then?' Cley pointed out the dirty transparent dome above them.

A column of twisting sheets was roiling around in the vacuum outside. Luminous, they turned amber, purple, gold. They broke into slices. An intricate geometric artifact spun and wove outside, as if looking for an opening.

But the makers were of another, higher dimension, she reminded herself. They must mean something by this.

'The Morphs at work,' Rin said.

Then Cley remembered suddenly the way Kurani had been cut into sections so exactly – his guts hanging in air, arteries pulsing one last time, a convulsion working down his sweaty skin – and gasped, her pulse pounding. *They do not explain. Or apologize.*

'They are finding their way,' Rin said. 'Remember that they are strange beyond description.'

'I cannot guess what they mean to do,' Seeker snorted, crossing her several arms.

'Nor can we.' Rin smiled ruefully.

I hope for a collaboration, Kata sent. We cannot engage the Malign without the help of the Multifold. Hopeless! And this black brane – it is a strangeness of another sort. Does it know the Singular?

Cley felt a dizzying confusion rise in her. Altogether too much was happening, coming at her so fast – bugs splattering on her conceptual windshield . . . 'What was that, about whether the black brane knows the Singular?'

'We believe so, but we do not know.' Rin carefully chose his words, obviously talking down to Cley. 'Our legends held that the Malign was imprisoned in gravitational stasis – the Time Sink, some call it – in the black hole that sits at the galactic center.'

'Time Sink?' She tried to visualize such a thing.

'There is no reference on that. A flaw in notation, apparently.' His earnest precision reminded her that his first love had been Sonomulia's Library. 'History was correct about the Malign's devastation, though. It knows a way to eat the plasma veils which hang in the galactic arms, leaving great rents where suns should glow. It is a master of diffusion. It levered its way out of the warp of the black hole, using that fulcrum.'

Cley had little idea what this might mean, and little prospect of learning more. This was not her area. 'So it's out in the open and came all this way?'

Rin grimaced. 'Yes – twenty-eight thousand light-years. Stories say that the Malign and the Multifold would meet among the corpses of the stars. That will occur when the red dwarf stars die.'

'Which is . . . ?

'About a hundred billion years from now.'

'Somebody miscalculated.'

'Indeed. The Malign apparently knows more than our Speakers of Astrophysics. Apparently, it feels that the collision must occur here, near Earth, where matters started and must finally end.'

Cley blinked. 'Now . . .'

'That is why we brought you here.'

Cley shook her head, trying to clear it. 'I can't possibly amount to much in all this.'

'So I would have said as well, once.' Rin had settled on a branch, and even in the low spin-gravity the lines in his face sagged. 'But you do matter. You Ur-humans had a hand, along with more advanced human forms and alien races, in contributing to both the Malign and the Multifold.'

'Us? Originals? Impossible.'

Rin looked rueful. 'I admit it seems extremely unlikely. Yet the deep records of the Library are clear, if read closely.'

'How could we make something like smart lightning?'

'Oh, it is far more than that. You may come to understand how in the fray that approaches.'

'Well, even if we helped make the Multifold, what's that matter now? I don't know anything about it.'

Rin looked at Seeker, but the big creature seemed unconcerned. Cley got the feeling that all this was running more or less as Seeker expected, and the procyon was never one to trouble herself with assisting the inevitable.

Rin spread his hands. 'Deep in the Multifold lies a set of assumptions, of worldviews. They depend on the kinesthetic senses of Ur-humans, upon your perceptual space.'

Cley found a piece of ruby fruit and bit into it. 'Um. What's that?'

Rin looked at her solemnly. 'What matters is that we cannot duplicate such things.'

'Come *on*,' Cley said. 'I know I'm dumber than anyone here, but that doesn't mean you can—'

We do not delude you. Kata gazed at Cley somberly. The makeup of a being circumscribes its perceptions. That cannot be duplicated artificially. We tried, yes – and failed.

Rin said, 'We find communicating with the Multifold exceedingly difficult. We have struggled for centuries to no avail.'

'Centuries?' So this was not a new problem, Cley realized. 'I thought you people could do anything.'

We cannot transcend our worldview any more than you can, Kata sent, speaking aloud as well. True courtesy, or soothing noises to a necessary, nervous animal? Cley wondered.

'That is always true of a single species,' Seeker said casually.

Rin's forehead knitted with annoyance. 'And you?'

'There has been some tinkering since your time,' Seeker said.

'This *is* our time!' Rin said sharply.

Seeker leaned back and did not reply.

'Look,' Cley said, 'how do you talk to the Multifold?'

'Badly. To reach it we must step through the thicket of the Ur-human mindset.'

'Thicket?' Cley asked.

Rin shifted uncomfortably. 'A *swamp* is perhaps a better term. A morass ingrained in the Multifold's being.'

'It has some of us, dirty old Originals, in it?' Cley laughed and felt a spurt of elation. This was at least some mark her kind had left in the great ruined architecture of time.

'In the growing struggle, speed is essential. To link our own abilities with the Multifold requires connections only you and your kind can make.'

Cley's eyes narrowed. 'Those Ur-humans you manufactured?'

Rin could not cover all his signs of unease. 'Yes, they

will be used. If we can. Kata and the others of Illusivia have schooled them in the Talent – a labor of great difficulty in such a short time.'

'You're manufacturing us, *using* us like, like—'

'Of course.' Rin was unbothered. 'That is in the nature of the hierarchy of species.'

'You have no right!'

'And we have no wrong.'

Seeker made a rude noise and twisted her mouth into an unreadable shape. 'There is no moral issue here,' Rin went on, casting an irritated glance at Seeker. 'These matters transcend the concept of rights. Those ideas attach to strategies societies use to maintain order and station. As concepts they have no validity in the transactions across the gulf that separates us.'

Cley's mouth twisted in unconscious echo of Seeker's grimace. 'Which means?'

'Ethics are nothing compared to the implications of the Malign's mere existence.' Rin smiled with his mouth but without any change in his eyes, as though he knew this facial gesture was the sort of thing Ur-humans did to take the edge off a stark statement.

Cley said, 'That's incredible. We have an obligation to each other, to treat everyone as holding natural rights.'

Natural to what? Kata sent.

Cley answered, To anything and anybody who can think.

Kata sniffed derisively. Think what? These are not times like those in which your kind evolved. Now there are many beings, large and small, who carry self-awareness. And think very differently, my dear Original.

Cley covered her own inner confusion with Then they have to be accorded their own dignity.

Kata gave Cley a look of concern, but in her striations of quick thought there was an underlayer of annoyed impatience. Dignity does not mean they can step outside the inherent ordering ordained by evolution's hand.

'Look, I have to think about all this.' Cley reverted to speech in self-defense.

Rin said, 'There is no time for the kind of thinking you do. The moment is upon us.'

Cley turned to Seeker. 'What should I do?'

Seeker smacked her lips hungrily. 'I do not subscribe to their ideas. Or to yours. Both are too simple.'

'Damn it, Seeker, I need support from you.'

'Your actions I can assist, perhaps,' Seeker said.

'Gee, thanks.' Cley considered stalking off, and then thought better of it.

Seeker held up a cautionary paw. 'As these Supras say, your core abilities are much needed.'

'No, I didn't mean help with their fight. I want you to – well, tell them they're *wrong*. That they're treating my people like, like animals!'

'I am an animal. They do not treat me as you.'

'You're not an animal!'

'I am not remotely human.'

'But you're, you're . . .'

Seeker gave her a wolfish grin. 'I am like you when I need to be. But that is to accomplish an end.'

'What end?' Cley asked, her confusion deepening.

'To bring you here at this time. You are essential to the struggle. And to unite you with Ur-humans, as I promised – eventually.' Seeker glanced at Rin and Kata and gave a slow – maybe mischievous? – blink. 'I knew the Supras would probably fail to.'

Across Rin's face flitted an expression Cley could not read, but the nearest equivalent was a mixture of irritation and surprised respect.

Rin said warily to Seeker, 'It would have been simple to bring her here, had the Malign not managed to learn how to enter our ships. And you could not have known it would understand that so quickly, correct? Much less that it could find the Ur-humans among all the ships we have.'

'I could not?' Seeker grinned.

Cley felt something pass between Seeker and the Supras of Illusivia—a darting note of complex thought. She couldn't catch what it meant, but . . . 'Seeker, your Talent is showing again.'

'I try not to entangle my mind with others',' the procyon said guardedly. 'And mine is not like your Talent, no. But no matter.' Seeker turned decisively to Cley. 'I believe this issue must be resolved now, so I shall do it.'

Rin said sternly, 'I cannot allow so crucial a matter to—'

'Do as they say,' Seeker said to Cley.

'But I—'

'If you wish to think in terms of the structure of rights, then consider a point.' Seeker brought a nut toward her mouth but fumbled and dropped it. Her eyes brimmed with a strange sorrow. 'These others of your kind – and I do not believe they are your 'people,' for they are not yet people at all – will certainly die if you do not act.'

Rin scowled. 'You can't be sure of that.'

Seeker did not immediately answer. Instead, she pulled the carcass of a small rodent from a snag in her pelt and casually began to gnaw on it. The Supras all looked askance at this. Cley remembered how delicate and rarefied their own food had been, like eating clouds. Seeker was making a point, though Cley did not quite grasp it.

Seeker licked the carcass. 'You remember the era of simple laws?'

Rin frowned. 'What? Oh, you mean the age when science discovered all the laws governing the relations between particles and fields? That ancient time is of no relevance now.'

Seeker closed one eye and let one side of her face go slack, as if she could slip halfway into sleep. Cley wondered if this was some arcane joke. The Supras shifted uneasily.

Seeker said, 'The Ur-humans found all such laws – the work was that elementary. But to know how gravity pulls upon a body does not mean even in principle that you can foresee how many such bodies will move. The prediction of any real system is beyond the final, exact reach of science.'

Rin nodded, but Cley could tell that he did not see where this subject led. Neither did she. And through her Talent she felt skittering anxieties. Time was running out, while these two argued over grand principles.

Rin said, 'But that is ancient philosophy. Quantum uncertainty, chaos – these forever screen precise knowledge of the future from our eyes.'

Still with one eye closed, Seeker said, 'And what if this were not so?'

'Then we Supras would have discovered that long ago,' Rin insisted. 'Such knowledge would reside in the lore of the Library of Life.'

Seeker blinked with both eyes, and animation returned fully to her face. At the same moment Cley felt a burst of Talent-talk, long and strong like unrecognizable bass notes. Some Supras stirred. Seeker had sent some sort of message while carrying on this lofty discussion.

Seeker said, 'Much has been discovered since strata of learning were laid down like fossils. But not by you.'

Rin looked around at his fellow Supras, who seemed distantly amused by this conversation. Rin, though, was getting slowly angry. 'Beast, are there higher orders which know science?'

Seeker said, 'None you can readily see standing before you.'

'Magnetic minds, then? The Singular? Even they merely *use* science,' Rin said. 'They do not truly comprehend it.'

'There are other methods of comprehension.'

Rin leaned forward, his lips working. 'What, then?'

'The sum of species can know more. Together.'

Rin's head jerked with surprise. 'But we are discussing the fundamental limits on knowledge!'

'This "knowledge" of yours is also a category,' Seeker said, 'much like – what was Cley's term? – oh yes, "rights." It does not translate between species.'

'I cannot understand how that can be,' Rin said primly.

'Exactly,' Seeker said.

'What's that?' Cley pointed out a transparent bubble nearby. Planes of ivory laced with burnt orange were appearing in the space outside. It was as though some invisible giant were slicing a fruit, leaving only the sections visible.

Rin said, 'You two should recognize them.'

Seeker frowned. 'The higher dimensions. They have manifested again.'

Let's hope they're on our side,' Rin said, eyes grim.

Abruptly a wobbly pattern snapped into being, amid the vine tangle. It pulsed in chromed yellow and smelled like vinegar to Cley. She shrank from it. The Supras stayed still, but Seeker swung over to it and poked a paw at it. The thing jerked away.

'Maybe it remembers us,' Seeker said.

'Want to try to grab it?' Cley said with some bravado, wondering if the others could hear the quaver in her voice.

Seeker cocked an eyebrow at Rin, who shook his head. A Supra nearby, nearly hidden in foliage, said, 'It seems to have trouble telling us apart.'

Rin said, 'We might have the same difficulty distinguishing one ovoid from another in two dimensions. I suspect it seeks . . . you.' A quick glance at Cley, as if not to draw the four-D thing's attention to her.

'No point in running,' Seeker said. 'Let us hope it does not drop us into one of its Tubeworlds again.'

Cley backed away. 'I'll say.'

Seeker studied the air carefully. 'Or perhaps by now they know that was a failed experiment.'

Rin gave quick orders to nearby Supras. 'Our attempts to speak with them failed, back at the Library. Now they return. Not a good sign.'

Cley said, 'What do they want?'

Rin shrugged. 'Perhaps they do not wish our troubles to make theirs worse.'

Cley asked, 'Worse? How can we?'

Seeker said, 'I suspect, by breaching the equilibrium between dimensions.' Then she laughed at herself. 'Not that we can see how . . .'

The slices shaped into a disjointed surface, glowing golden. It flexed and rippled and tracked along beside them. Cley got the impression of something powerful and pensive, waiting.

The chrome-bright bubble abruptly vanished with a gonglike clang.

Rin looked sober. 'I would like to laugh, as you do, animal. But I fear you are right.'

VII
Malign Attentions

The greatest good for the greatest number must mean the longest good, since the majority of humanity is yet to come.
—Jack McDevitt

1

The Prison of Time

Sometimes it can be a relief to be ignored. The strange, darting conversation between Seeker and the Supras wound on. They had found a pleasant place amid hanging vines, chirping animals, and stringy tree trunks. A bower, echoing humanity's primate origins. Cley curled up, arms around her knees, and tried to think.

In the end she saw that she had no choice. She had to take part in whatever was to come, no matter how little she knew to do against the gargantuan events. Already her folk, her Meta, had begun to fade in memory, crowded out by the jarring, swift events . . . since, Cley reminded herself forcefully, all she had loved had been burned into oblivion by the Malign.

So much had happened! She had fallen in love with a Supra — reckless of her, sure, blind, even worshipful, and foredoomed — and then seen him die. Had barely survived, then been saved, learned a lot, lived a lot — was it *always* going to be like this? How about that serenity that maturity brings? Would she never get it all straightened out? *Aaaahh!*

One thing at a time, then.

She felt now the totality of what that single, vicious act had meant. To murder not merely people but *a* people, a species.

Was she becoming more like the Supras now? That such an abstraction could touch her, arouse what Rin would no doubt term her 'animal spirits'?

An animal that liked abstractions? Maybe that wasn't all that bad a definition of being human.

Still, she *knew* that the Supras and their cosmic games mattered to what she still thought of as 'real' people, her own. Maybe this attitude itself was a symptom of her kind – but if so, then *so be it,* she thought adamantly. A species has to know its limitations.

So she said, 'All right. I'll do it.'

The Supras seemed pleased with her decision. Seeker gave no sign of reaction.

After all her agonizing, she was surprised that nothing dramatic happened immediately. Most of a battle lies in the preparation. The Leviathan swooped in toward the disk of life and worlds that was the Jove complex. Trains of space biota came and went from the Leviathan, carrying out intricate exchanges.

In the moments when Rin and Kata were not occupied with tasks, she learned more from them. She recalled the moments when Kata and others had let go of their constraints, dancing, especially at their festivities – flooding Cley's mind with unsorted impressions and thoughts. Cley had then slept long hours – fitfully, sweating, letting her brain do much of the unscrambling. She had learned not to resist. And to avoid.

So it was now. She got much through the Talent-talk, staggered from its impact . . . and slunk away. Slept. Each time she awoke, surprises awaited, fresh ideas brimming within her. But it was hard work and drained her.

She spent some time watching the scintillant majesty

of Jove. It was a blessing, as some in her Meta used to say, simply to *be*.

She now also understood that this grandeur was not the outer limit to the living solar system. She had been misled by her own eyes. Knowledge Kata sent through the Talent told her of provinces she had not guessed.

Earthborne life saw through a narrow slit of the spectrum. Time had pruned planetary life to take advantage of the flux that most ably penetrated Earth's obliging atmosphere. Earthlife preferred the ample green light. But that tiny slice of the spectrum was blind to bigger, more subtle events.

No Earthbound life ever used the lazy, meter-long wavelengths of the radio. So none could witness the roil of immense plasma clouds that fill the great spiral arms. Seen with a large radio eye, the abyss between suns shows knots and puckerings, swirls and crevasses. The wind that blows outward from suns stirs these slow fogs. Only an eye larger than Leviathan itself could perceive the incandescent richness that hides in those reaches. The beings that swam there gave forth great booming calls and lived through the adroit weaving of electrical currents.

Cley realized this after a long sleep, the knowledge coming to her almost casually, like an old memory. She would never see these knots of ionized matter trapped by magnetic pinches, smoldering and hissing with soft energies beyond the seeing of anything born in flesh.

Yet now she recalled, through Kata, the vast flaring of plasma veins, the electromagnetic arteries and organs. Plasma structures had formed within the first eons of the universe, passing through many generations before mass began to fuse and flare in the first stars. Evolution had begun its workings on those naturally driven energies, long before suns had thundered forth their full, mature radiance.

Light required a week to span these beings the size of solar systems. Bodies so vast must be run by delegation, so the intelligences that had evolved to govern such bulk resembled parliaments more than dictatorships.

She caught a glimmer of how such beings regarded her kind: tiny assemblies powered by the clumsy building up and tearing down of molecules. How much cleaner was the clear rush of electromotive forces . . .

But then her perceptions dwindled back to her own level, the borrowed memories faded, and she understood.

'Seeker!' she called. 'The Malign – did the Ur-humans contribute much in shaping it?'

Seeker was quiet for a long time, her long face mysteriously sober. 'No, they were drawn into a later . . . well, *modification* is the wrong term, but it is the closest in your worldview.'

'I caught pictures from Kata, confusing ones. Of magnetic things that live naturally.'

Seeker smiled. 'Strange, yes, but they are our allies.'

Rin spoke from behind her. 'And ones we desperately need.'

Cley demanded, 'Why didn't you tell me about them?'

'Because I did not know, not fully. The knowledge . . .' Rin's normally strong voice faltered. He looked more tired and pensive than before. 'No, it was not knowledge. I discounted the Multifold's testimony when it told us of these magnetic beings. Our Keeper of Records said there were none such. After all, there were no references throughout all of the Records.' He smiled wanly. 'Now we are wiser. It was smug legend that I knew. The arrogance of Sonomulia, as vast as its truths.'

Cley said slowly, 'Humans somehow trapped one of those magnetic creatures?'

Rin chuckled dryly. 'Mere humans, you mean?'

'Well . . . yes.'

Rin settled onto a sloping, crusty branch, his shoulders sagging. 'Humans have a reach which somehow always exceeds our grasp.'

'The Malign got away?'

He nodded ruefully. 'And somehow, from its associations with humans and other intelligences, it learned to perform feats which no other magnetic being knew. It ravaged enormous territories, marauding along the dust lanes. It slaughtered the native magnetic structures.'

'Until someone trapped it again. This galactic civilization I keep hearing about?'

She shot him an impish grin to cover her feelings. This talk was unsettling. She started a small fire to cook supper.

'Galactic civilization was once majestic,' Rin said. 'Compared to what we know, at least. It made the higher forms of the pure magnetic mentalities – stately beings, grand, though they led to the Malign. Humans carry some of that guilt as well.' Rin seemed sobered, but then he visibly took heart. 'Seeker, what do you think of galactic civilization?'

'I think it would be a good idea,' Seeker answered very softly.

'But it exists!'

'Does it? You keep looking at the parts – this or that species or phylum, fleshy or magnetic. Consider the whole.'

'The whole what?'

Seeker shrugged. 'One of your own philosophers remarked that nothing that is worth knowing can be taught. You must live *through* your world.'

Cley said, 'I'll never have the perception of Rin, of the Supras—'

Seeker laughed heartily, her legs scrabbling for purchase, so that she did not fall off her perch. 'Supras? They are like other people, only more so.'

Rin shot Seeker a sour glance. 'We like our lives orderly, free of the messy way the Originals and other early forms thought.'

Seeker laughed again and ignored Rin, looking at Cley. 'The messiness of life *is* your life, which you hope to shape with a perceptible narrative line.'

Rin's nostrils flared, and he said icily, 'We are wasting time – waiting for the Malign to descend upon us.'

'So?' Seeker licked her black lips with the red tip of her tongue. 'Your ships and magnetic inductors and all the rest – they are ready?'

'Um, yes.'

'Then we might as well talk. It's therapy for you super-smart primates. And procyons.'

Rin nodded ruefully. 'As nearly as we can tell, the precipitating event in galactic history was the Quickening. Humans and others, aliens – they all passed through this stage. Some termed it the Singularity. But later historians believe that it was only when they all came together and became the event historians term the Singular that the true amplitude of the deed became clear. They transcended horizons we cannot even sense, among them, the higher dimensions.'

Cley said, 'The Singular disappeared from our known universe, leaving . . . what?'

'Leaving room for newer forms to grow,' Seeker said. 'Very polite, I would say. It was certainly no tragedy.'

Rin frowned. 'For humans it was. We were left behind, almost like, well, *leftovers*.'

The sudden anger in his voice was daunting. Cley had never considered that Supras might be insulted by history itself; certainly the thought had never occurred to *her*.

'And the Multifold,' Rin continued vehemently, 'it is a wonder, but still a shadow of the Singular. Most vexing . . .'

She stopped listening, taking shelter in the familiar rituals of cooking. Something in the human mind liked the reassuring order of repetition, she supposed. Rin kept talking, explaining facets of sciences she could not even identify. She let him run on. The man was troubled, hanging on to his own image of what human action meant. It was better to let his spill of words carry frustration away from him — the most ancient of human consolations. She skinned and blackened up three large snakes — caught using a forked stick, a trick she learned as a girl — then roasted them with a crust of spices and offered Rin one.

To his credit he did not hesitate. 'A curious custom,' he remarked, after biting into a muscular yellow chunk. Its savor seasoned the air. 'That such a simple procedure brings out the raw power of the meat.'

'You've never cooked before?'

'Our machines do that.'

'How can machines know what tastes good?'

Rin explained patiently, 'They have something better — good taste.'

'Ha!' Cley snorted. She bit off a mouthful of snake and chewed ferociously. Originally.

Rin looked offended. 'Sonomulia has programs handed down from the greatest chefs.'

'I'd rather stir the coals and turn the meat myself.'

'You do not trust machines?'

'Only so far as I have to.'

'But it was an Ur-human subspecies that set us on the road of technology.'

She spat out a piece of gristle. 'Has its limits, though. Think technology's done you a lot of good?'

Rin looked blank. 'It kept us alive.'

'Those bots? They kept you in a bottle, like a museum exhibit. Only nobody came to see.'

Rin frowned silently, lost in thought.

Cley liked the way the flickering firelight cooked tangy flavors and heat into the air, clasping them all in a smoky, perfumed veil. Something deeply human responded to this wood-smoke redolence. It touched even Rin, smoothed his face. The play of firelight tossed shadows across them all. Seeker sucked in the smoky bouquet, licking the air.

Cley said softly, 'Did you ever wonder why nobody ever came to visit the museum?'

Rin looked startled. 'Why, no.'

'Maybe they were too busy getting things done,' she said.

'Out here?'

She could see that no matter how intelligent these Supras were, they also had values and associations that were virtually hardwired into them. 'Sure. Look at that' – she gestured at the translucent bowl above, where Jove spun like a colossal living firework – 'and tell me dried-up old Earth was a better idea.'

Rin said nothing for a long time. Then, 'I see. I had thought that human destiny turned upon the pivot of the home world. Still.'

'It did, oh, yes,' Seeker said brightly. Rin twitched as though something had prodded him; Cley suspected he had forgotten that Seeker was there. 'But that is only a partial story.'

Rin looked penetratingly at Seeker. 'I have long suspected that you represent something . . . unknown. I extensively interrogated the archives of Sonomulia about your species. You evolved during a time when humans were relatively unambitious. When the Artificials ruled.'

The firelight danced across the odd expressions on Seeker's face as she said softly, 'They did great damage, those early bot culture forms. Remorse tinged them, yes, but only for a while.'

Rin nodded. 'Still, our records did not show such a high intelligence among the procyons as you display.'

'You still think of traits lodged in individuals, in species,' Seeker said.

Rin looked irritated. 'Well, of course. That defines species, very nearly.'

Seeker asked, 'And if a trait is shared among many species simultaneously?'

Rin shook his head. 'By a Talent, like that of Illusivia?'

Seeker's luminous eyes peeked out from beneath heavy lids. 'Or more advanced.'

Rin considered. 'Well, that might alter the character of intelligence, granted.' His face took on his librarian's precise, pensive cast, his cheeks hollowing as though he contracted into himself. 'I wonder if such Talents could arise naturally.'

'They do,' Seeker said. 'I am a member of a larger system. So are you. But you do not communicate well — a typical characteristic of early evolved intelligences.'

Rin's thin mouth turned up in an irked curve. 'People seem to feel I speak fairly clearly.'

'People do, yes.'

Rin smiled stiffly, peering down his long nose at Seeker. 'We re-created you ourselves, remember? Made you whole from the Library of Life. Sometimes I think we erred somehow.'

'Oh no!' Seeker barked happily. 'It was your best idea.'

'The records say you were solely suited for Earth.'

'Wrong,' Seeker said. 'Libraries can lie.'

'That would explain why you move so easily in space.'

'Not entirely.' Seeker's eyes danced.

'You have other connections?'

'With everything, approximately. Do you not?'

Rin shrugged uncomfortably. 'I don't think so.'

Merrily Seeker said, 'Then do not think so much.'

Cley laughed, but at the back of her mind a growing tenor cry demanded attention. 'Say, something's . . .'

Seeker nodded. 'Yes.'

She felt the Supras of Illusivia now, Kata's just one among many cascading voices. They formed tight links, some in their ships, some in this Leviathan, others dispersed among Jonahs and Leviathans and the churning life-mats of the Jove system. A long, soaring chorus. Yet anxious, trembling.

They all sensed it. Something coming.

'How quickly does it approach?' Rin asked urgently.

The earlier mood was broken, his doubts momentarily dispelled. Now he was all cool efficiency.

'I can't tell.' Cley frowned. 'There are refractions . . . Is it possible that the Malign can move even faster than light?'

'That is but one of its achievements,' Rin said, concern creasing his forehead. 'We humans attained that long ago, but only for small volumes in warped geometries – for tunnels, for ships. The Malign was limited, as are the magnetic beings.'

'But it broke out . . . using what?' Cley pressed. 'Its final theory?'

Rin nodded. 'Somehow, yes. Until then, a single great fact – that the speed of light was a true limit, for the Talent and all else – ordained that the linking of the natural magnetic minds proceeded slowly, all across the galaxy. Nothing large can move faster than light. Or so we thought. The Malign found a way. Somehow.'

'That's how the Malign finally got out of the galactic center, isn't it?' Cley asked. She caught thin shouts of alarm in her mind.

'It used the quantum vacuum,' Rin said. His cheeks hollowed again with a cast of relief. He found it comforting, Cley guessed, to be secure in his knowledge.

Rin leaned forward, his eyes soft as he peered into the dying firelight. 'On average, empty space has zero energy. But by enclosing a volume with a sphere of conducting plasma, the Malign prevented the creation of waves with wavelengths larger than that volume. These missing waves gave the vacuum a net negative energy and allowed formation of a wormhole in spacetime. All such processes are ruled by probabilities requiring great calculation. Yet through that hole the Malign slithered.'

'To our solar system,' Cley concluded.

'Never before has a magnetic mind done this,' Rin said. 'It escaped from the prison of time – a feat on such a scale that even the Singular did not anticipate.'

Seeker whispered, 'Coincidence, Rin?' This was the first time Cley had ever heard Seeker use his name. There was a tinge of pity in the beast's voice, or what she took for that.

Rin's head jerked up. He flicked a suspicious glance at Seeker. 'The thought occurred to us, too. Why should the Malign emerge now?'

'Just as you're getting free of Earth again?' Cley asked.

'Exactly,' Rin said. 'So we studied all the physical evidence. Observed the path of damage the Malign has wreaked as it left the galactic center . . .' He hesitated. 'And made a guess.'

Seeker said, 'You found something, and your discovery had unforeseen effects.'

Rin's eyes shifted away from the waning fire, as though he sought refuge in the gloom surrounding them. 'So you guessed. Yes, I was in the expedition that found the Multifold.'

Cley whispered, 'And . . . ?'

Rin's voice came to them in the twilight glow as a slow, solemn dirge. 'The exuberance of the Multifold was so great at being discovered! We arrived in wormhole craft, arrowing in on the suspected location. What a moment!' His eyes filled with remembered awe.

'It greeted you?' Seeker whispered.

'Too mild a word. Peals of salutation!' His face clouded.

'But those magnetic shouts sent enormous magnetosonic twists echoing through the whorls of an entire galactic arm. These reached the Malign in its cage. To see its ancient foes reuniting again sent it into a rage, a malevolence so strong that it exerted itself supremely – and forced its exit.'

They sat silently for a long moment. Cley looked up and out, in search of some consolation. The inky recesses of the Leviathan were unrelieved by the distant promise of stars.

Rin said hollowly, 'If I hadn't been so curious . . . hadn't searched the Library's records, the plots of magnetic fields throughout the galaxy . . . hadn't sent the signals . . .'

Cley said finally, 'You didn't know. Curiosity is built into us humans. And all the lore of the Library of Life did not warn you.'

He smiled mirthlessly. 'But I did it. All the same.'

Cley said, 'That Singular of yours might have troubled their mighty selves to make a jail that held.'

Rin shook his head. 'There is none better in this space-time.'

'Well, damn it, at least they shouldn't have just left it as a problem to be solved by us.'

Seeker lifted her sniffing snout, seeming to listen to something far away. She said, 'Shoulds and mights are of no consequence. The problem has arrived.'

2

Closed Curves of the Timescape

In the end it was like nothing she had expected or feared.

She lay on a thick brownvine mat deep in the Leviathan, alone, eyes closed. She felt nothing of the rough cords, or of her body. All carefully arranged, Supra-supervised. A circuit element, awaiting the currents.

And then she suddenly could not face the confrontation. 'Aaargh!' she muttered, eyelids fluttering open. Not this way. Not as a mere doormat.

She got up and fled the comfy confines. Moved silently through the Leviathan's ropy jungles, using the light-footed forest ways she had learned as a girl. She probed ahead with her Talent. Avoided a hovering swarm that looked like a partial captain. Sneaked by a few preoccupied figures, hunched over their devices.

Where was Seeker? The Talent could find nothing.

Softly she moved through fretted shadows. One of the transparent blisters hung on the Leviathan's pebbled wall. They were a lot like the pyramid she and Seeker had used to escape into vacuum. She felt along the capsule's waxy surface, found an edge. After some fumbling she unzipped the inner skin. It pried open like tough old skin, and a smartvoice said, 'Welcome. Which use do you —' and she cut it off as she squeezed in.

Lay back. Made her breathing regular.

The Supras had been wrong about her safety before, after all. So many of them clustered together would make an inviting target for the Malign – with her smack in the middle. And the Leviathan itself was not secure; it could always make another captain, enlist its species against humans – and especially, Cley.

Better to be on her own.

Still . . . The Talent brought her the brewing battle. The struggle raged red through the landscapes of her mind.

Her Talent now linked her with the Supras, yes – she could feel those coiled, slinky passages. Minds were moving somewhere. A seethe of thoughts, sensations, and something deeper . . . Ideas grown rank with time and experience, powerful, overbearing . . .

This cauldron of sensations was only a fragment of the broadening perspectives that the Supras said would open for her in the hours and days of the conflict. She shuddered at the thought.

These rode in the background of her mind. She had to ignore them. *Fly,* part of her said. Only by being *out of control* – their control – could she feel that this was part of her work. Her Original self would enter into this strange moment *as herself,* not as a Supra component. She might not survive this, but she would keep something – simple dignity.

Back to work. She struggled to get the bubble to let go of the Leviathan hull. The touch-signals were complex, and having watched Seeker call them up was not enough to get her through it easily. She tugged and tweaked and then had to bang on the walls even to get the bubble's attention. She got the sequence right but had no chance to savor the satisfying *pop*. She was among the roiling abundance of life and had to learn to navigate. Jove's amber scowl peered over her shoulder as she skimmed away along the Leviathan's skin.

The skysharks did not notice her, but something small and bullet-shaped did.

It arrowed at her, a spike emerging at its nose. This lanced through the bubble in an instant. Orange mist puffed from it. The cloud's mere touch ignited flares in her nerves. Grinding hurt reverberated in her nervous system in a searing echo.

She frantically hacked at the spike with a hastily extruded augmentation, a pitifully inappropriate data reader. It broke, but so did the spike. Spaceborne life was light, quick, and fragile. More of the orange fog spurted. Her skin shrieked. The stench was awful. The spike wavered, turned toward her as if it could see – and abruptly jerked back, slipping through the hole it had punched.

Her ears popped. The vacuum draft sucked most of the orange mist away, and then the bubble self-sealed, a thin line zipping shut. She was drifting outward from the Leviathan into a swarm of life.

And ahead, suddenly, came a glistening yellow soap bubble. It looked like some of the shapes she had seen on the plain of the Library – twisted signatures of something trying to manifest itself in a lower dimension.

It drifted closer, now inside her own bubble. Mere three-D barriers meant nothing to a four-D intelligence. Her skin still itched and twitched from the orange cloud. Pain, she remembered a wise old woman in her Meta once saying, was the world's way of letting us know that we were really alive, and always playing for keeps.

The burnt-yellow bubble wrapped itself around her, stifling all sound, all motion, and yet letting her mind fly free.

She shut her eyes, opened her Talent . . .

Kata sent, The Malign is near. It wants you. We are sending you to time isolation.

'What?' But something swallowed her . . .

Falling, whirling — and she was in another place.

On a barren brown landscape, dancing.

No hurry, no sense of the dance ever ending.

She spun on one toe, elegant, whirring, and yet the movement was . . . static.

She was not dancing, but . . . in the state of dance. She now understood something of what Kata and the others might feel when they did their mad, entranced dancing. Did they come to this frozen place? And what was it?

Somehow, she could hold in this state of *being dancing* and still think. Better, think with swift, new clarity.

Ah, yes, she thought. Someone had said that the higher dimensions did not need to be spatial. There could be two dimensions of time.

Along one time axis, matters were simple — only forward motion was allowed. In two dimensions loops can form. A simple circle in time could wrap around into the past. Or cycle — endlessly.

Moments of future time are as fixed, immutable, as those of the past. The knowledge came to her all at once. But then, everything *was* all at once, when she looked at it right.

She saw that she had lived in the illusion of sequential time. Her whole lifetime came into being at once, in 'an instant' — she was at her birth and at her death and all points in between, seeing them all.

Hello, Cley. Here she came from the womb fresh and wet, and there she lay dying on fresh white sheets.

The scroll of life did not unwind but rather stood like a painting of a complex landscape, seen at once.

Peer deeper and you will witness more. But she did not merely see the painting; she *was* it, both in and outside the timescape, standing granite-hard, unmovable in . . . what?

Only darkness surrounded the timescape, until — she turned her head — there were the others, too, an infinite array of slices parading off into the distance, each a life, a scape, stacked in like folios, in space-time on edge.

For all her life she had moved in her own solid slice — narrow, blind, never sensing the others except when they cut across hers. And the intersections were immutable incidents, also fixed firmly and unshakable. Unavoidable, invariant.

All actions in her life — right/wrong, good/bad — were at one with each other. Knowledge diffused from one act to another just as the contour of a hill knows the slope above, the gravitational and hydrostatic pressures shaping it, and then passes on such pressures to the next point in the grade below. The slant between carried information that shaped static events. Outside time, but alive.

The revelation came arrowing into her, hurting in its simplicity.

She saw that this geometry itself was a measure of the capacity of some channel — *yes,* a conduit through which information flowed from past to future and was *the area of a surface.*

So that geometry was not the basis at all but was instead *derived,* a mere thing like the way temperature measured the average energy of some particles. So in turn the shape of space-time was itself a measure of something more fundamental,

Space-time is just another building block.

Her awareness of her own awareness was also an event, frozen. She was *all these Cleys,* backward to birth, forward to . . . what?

To the end of the timescape she could not see, somehow, for it lay shrouded in a fog with dark striations, churning, not static in the landscape but a moving storm of . . . possibility. Not the end, not truly fixed yet . . .

And the landscape snapped away, dwindling, as if she were rising above it. Above all the other stacked lives. Flying, up and out of the space-time universe, into . . .

The moment. Again. And again. Again.

She – *whoosh* – whirled into another place. The pain of it riveted her, impaled her, left her in a spinning instant.

Out of time-fixed. Into time-flowing.

This was not the brown plain but instead a canyon of shimmering rock. Silent. Within the translucent stone, slow blades of shadow descended, as if a sun were setting somewhere deep within the foggy reaches. Radiance danced within it, like summer's promise lancing into a watery cavern.

Her mind still spun with the experience just past – or was it happening now? Eternally? – and she frowned and concentrated.

She walked across a rocky shelf and looked down into an abyss that had no end. It tapered away into infinity. And from beyond infinity came toward her a trilling sense of the . . . *spongy* nature of things in this place.

Air, rock – all had a *give* to them. Moments seemed slippery, too, each sliding into the next. Softly, in absolute silence. Her own footsteps were silent. Her heart thumped faster, but at least she could hear it.

Shards of emerald emerged from the rock, like living presences breaking free. In the air they dissolved into scattershot blue, birds flapping into an opal sky. Without warning, a cliff above twisted in scraping agony, laboring to be born. A sheet of it peeled off, cracking and booming, curling into air like a petal of a huge flower.

She ran, trying to get clear. But the sheet did not fall.

The layer compressed, thinning, complaining in loud *aaaawwwwkkkk*s. Yellow flame shot from it as if a fire baked inside – roaring virulence. Its edges turned crimson and then curled back, blackening. Flares ran along its edges, and – *crack!* – it vanished.

A sharp concussion knocked her flat. She got up against a slight gravity, feeling as if a stick had smacked her in the forehead.

A phrase came into her head: . . . in anxious equilibrium along the axis of duration . . .

And she felt the presence of someone, a Supra – yes, Kata. Somehow she had penetrated to this place. Was this crazed landscape part of the battle?

Maybe, she thought, there was no place to flee the struggle. The strangeness would find her even here.

A color like chalk meeting rust flooded around her. The rock sublimes into a cloud, but do not breathe it.

She held her breath for a long, aching time. Her arms would not move; her lips seemed solid from the cold. The cloud blew by, and she could see again that she was still in the rock canyon. But it had altered.

This is an abode of the Singular, Kata sent. They have folded space-time itself until it serves as mass. The two are equivalent, after all. But only at the Quickening did this possibility come into play. It makes a fine haven, yes?

Above her, towers of the stone popped and grew, shivering the pale night above and wrenching the stars apart with restless chaos.

You were right to come here.

'To run away?' Cley spoke.

The Malign has searched for you and now attacks the Leviathan.

She called, Seeker! Rin! They did not answer. Were they still in the Leviathan?

She caught a quick sensation of searing fire, unbridled fury. It invaded her, even at this remove. Her sphincters clenched so hard, she gasped. A jumping nervous electricity wormed across her skin, as if seeking an opening.

'I can't . . . take this . . . for long,' she whispered in her pain.

You must. We all must.

3

The Meta-Universe

She had anticipated great flares of phosphorescent energy, climactic storms of magnetic violence. There were some, but these were merely sideshow illuminations dancing around the major conflict, like heat lightning on a far horizon.

For Cley the struggle called upon her kinesthetic senses, as Rin had said. He knew what was coming: She would be overloaded and strained and fractured, splitting into shards of disembodied perception. He had told her no more because this was certainly enough, all she was capable of grasping.

Her own perceptions were somehow . . . bridging. She felt her mind divided, one side focused on a realm of abstractions, the other embedded in her body. Information flowed between them, modulated, *used* – by some agency she could dimly sense, far back in the shadows. But large and slow and massive.

Experience – that was the bridge. Each splinter intensely lived, vibrant, encompassing.

She felt herself running. The pleasant heady rush of sliding muscles. Of speed-shot perspectives dwindling, of slick velocities – and then she was in cold, inky oblivion, her sun blocked by moving mountains. These moist shadows coiled with acrid odors. Harsh, abrasive air thrust up her nostrils.

The ground, like a plain of lead-gray ball bearings, slid by below her invisible feet, tossing like a storm-streaked, grainy sea.

The ground was not dirt. It was alive. Like a lesser dimension beneath her running feet, a carpet of intelligence. She plunged forward, feet pounding, each step making a fluorescent ivory light spray up into the air. Synapses completing.

She was moving ideas between minds utterly different. The carpet was a layer not of stuff but of thought. Hammering feet opened connections. Kinesthetic circuits closed . . .

Sweetness swarmed up into her sinuses, burst wetly green – and she tumbled into another bath of rushing impressions. Of receding depths. And then of oily forces working across her skin. It went on and on, a river run she could not stanch or fathom.

But at times she did sense pale immensities working at great distances, like icebergs emerging from a hurricane-racked ocean. Dimly she caught shreds of a child-like mind, incomparably large, and recognized the Multifold. It had prowled the solar system, she saw, blunting the attacks of the Malign. She owed it her life, for surely the Malign would otherwise have found her on her outward voyage.

Malign attentions, Kata sent. Cley could think of no reply, could not think at all. It took all of her to focus her puny self upon the river run of events that engulfed her.

Beneath the ragged waves that washed her she felt infinitesimal currents, tiny piping voices. Minds in the oceanic Talent-space, adrift. She recognized these as the recently grown Ur-humans. They floated as howling, unformed personalities, nuggets speckled by dots of kinesthetic tension.

They were all like elemental units in an enormous circuit, serving as components that relayed messages and forces they could no more recognize than a copper wire knows what an electron is.

And Seeker was there. Not the Seeker she knew, but something strange and many-footed, immense, running with timeless grace over the seamless gray plain.

Or was it many Seekers? The entire species, she saw now – a kind that had come long after the Ur-humans and yet was equally ancient now. A race that had strived and lost and strived again, endured and gone on silently, peering forward with a hollow barking laugh, still powerful and always asking, as life must, and still dangerous and still coming.

And something more. She glimpsed it then, a corridor of ruin stretching back to the Ur-humans and lined with the dead who had stood – single minds, alone and finally afraid – against the fall of night. They had died to imprison the Malign, and now their work lay in shreds as down that long passage of a billion years there now sped a vast shaggy shape, now compressing itself into this narrow inlet of a solar system . . .

'That's it, yes,' she said to herself. For she did not know what this place was, transcending the dimensions of her world, skating somehow outside the brane of the ordinary. She was lofting now, high above a seethe that smoldered red and black.

'You want to make it come for me, to focus here,' she said.

It is our only hope. You are the only one who has a mature Ur-human mind. The younger ones . . .

'Don't work, right?' The floating minds in Talent-space had felt adrift, panicked.

They do not sense the world well enough. Apparently, that must be learned over time.

Cley reached out and suddenly felt Seeker. The huge shape was engaged somehow at levels she could only glimpse. Seeker struggled in what seemed to Cley to be a crystal sphere – luminous, living. Yet the mote glaring at the sphere's center was a star.

She felt the plasma beings then. Nets of fields and ionized gas slipped, fishlike and silvery, through blackness. They converged on the Jove system. Great slowtwisting blue lightning worked through the orbiting rafts of life there.

Silent slaughter. She felt a horrible screaming through the Talent – and shut it off. Seeing this was enough.

The mere backwash of this passing struggle scorched broad carpets of space life. Lances ruptured wispy beings the size of whole worlds.

The biting pain of it made Cley twist and scream. Her eyes opened once to find her fingernails embedded in her palms, crimson blood streaking her arms. But she could not stop.

Dimly she knew that the Supras were protecting her body – mere body! – in real space. There she floated in a bubble. Here . . .

Her eyes squeezed shut against her will. A swelling seized her. She felt herself extended, warping the space around her as though she were herself a giant sun, bending rays of light.

She knew this meant she had somehow been incorporated into the Multifold. But instantly another presence lapped at her mind. She felt herself tucked up into a cranny, snug — then yanked out, spilling into hot, inky murk.

The Malign had her. It squeezed, as though she were moist fruit and would spit out seeds — an orange, crusty with age, browned and pitted, covered by white maggots sucking at the inner wealth . . .

She saw this suddenly, hard and vivid. Her mouth stung.

I see it now. She had to cleanse the slimy maggots before she could eat. She sent down fire and washed the orange in burnt-gold flame. Screaming, the maggots burst open.

And the orange was a planet.

Seared and pure and wiped free of the very atmosphere that had sustained the soft maggots. Slugs singed to oblivion. They had been scaly, quick of mind. But not quick enough. They had barely comprehended what rushed at them out of the maw at the center of the galaxy.

I have to live it all. Cley was the orange and then the fire and then the maggots and then, with long, strangled gasps, the fire again.

It was good to be the fire. Good to leap and fry and crackle and leap again. Forking its fingers up at a hostile sky.

Better *by far* than to crawl and mew and suck and shit and die.

Better, yes, to float and stream and tingle with blue-white fires. To hang in curtains between the stars and be greater than any sun that had ever flared. To roar at the jeweled stars. Better to smell and shimmer and reek. To rasp against the puny clots of knotted magnetic fields, butt into their slow waltzes. To jab and hurt and keep on hurting, *because it is right they obey,* when the magnetic kernels had been ground beneath you, broken, and were dust.

Better to be a moving appetite again, an intelligence bigger than a galactic arm.

Pleasure seethed in its self-stink. Excess demanded more of the same . . . Yes, this was the Malign she sensed. More raw and muscular with every gathering moment.

Eyes closed, her mind saw.

Along the length of a Leviathin, hot fires raged. The living craft writhed like a great beast. Sharp spokes of hellish light blazed and jetted from ruptured ports. Creatures came forth in spouts, twisting in agony as they met vacuum. Flames lived and died along its enormous flanks as their oxygen burned out and space itself claimed them. A great beast died in the eternal night. No sounds could carry its last wails.

A Pinwheel. Turning, ceaselessly turning, but now to no avail. A great hammer had struck through it, bending the long, woody shaft. Now the Pinwheel spun unbalanced, unleashing vibrations that tore at its mahogany ligaments. It turned with majestic energy, one end slipping into the air of a green world — but its centrifugal poise was wrong. Great waves swept from tip to tip. Fragments of brush and branch peeled away. The huge creature was dying of a thousand small subtractions as the fevered wind stripped it. Those aboard launched themselves forth from the topmost tip, seeking higher orbits like passengers jumping into freezing waters from a doomed ocean liner. Along the huge length a shudder ran, as if the very core of the Pinwheel knew what was coming. Yet it must gyre onward, for it knew no other destiny but to kiss the air again and again. Even if the kiss meant death.

Memories.

The Malign loved these hideous memories.

And she broke away from the massive hating presence for a moment, into what seemed to be cool open space, empty of the skittering violence.

Oh! she thought with buoyant relief.

But no – this was another part of the Malign.

Oily and slick and snakelike, it slid over her. Into her ears. Up her vagina. A long, deep, snub-nosed probing for her ovaries. Down her throat, prodding with a fluid insistence. A scaly stench rose and bit into her. Its sharp beak cut deeply, and that was when she understood a flicker of what the outside struggle was about.

Suddenly, she could *feel* abstractions. The partition between thought and sensation, so fundamental to being human, was blown to tatters by the Malign's mad gale. Trapped, she understood.

The Malign held that this universe was one of many expanding bubbles adrift inside a meta-universe. Ours was but one of the possibilities in a cosmos beyond counting. The great adventure of advanced life forms, it believed, was to transcend the mere bubble that we saw as our universe. Perhaps there were civilizations of unimaginable essence, around the very curve of the cosmos. The Malign wished to create a tunnel that would prick a hole in our universe-bubble and extend into others.

And against it came the Singular. For they had ventured into the higher dimensions, learning to fold spongy space-time itself and make mass, to build castles beyond imagination.

They knew the Malign well, and came to kill it.

But somehow, in all this, she mattered . . .

Slimy blackness crept like oily fingers. Easeful ideas soothed into her.

Here are my works. So . . .

Bodies crushed and scorched.

Leviathans boiling away their guts into vacuum.

A burnt-red corkscrew boring into the pole of Jupiter. The magnetic pressure forced its way down, to the core. Found the metallic hydrogen trapped there. Released it into sunlight, where it fizzed into liquid, into gas, a hard flare cutting the sky.

Gray moons melted to slag.

Ships sliced and spilling blue-green fluids.

Bodies punched and seared and tumbling away into vacuum.

The Malign told her. Forced her to see through its eyes:

The Galactic Empire, she saw, had been a festering pile of insects. When she stopped to see them better, they were of all shapes, chittering, filled with meaningless jabber.

Long ago some of these vermin had slipped away, she remembered, through the veils beyond the galaxy. Out, flying through strings of galaxies, across traceries of light. Spanning the great vaults and voids where few luminous sparks stirred.

The Quickening led them to the Singular, beyond the grasp of the Malign.

Those Empire maggots had vanished, leaving dregs to slump into petrified cities: Sonomulia. Illusivia.

And elsewhere in the spiral arms, other races had dwindled into self-obsessed stasis.

But should the holy, enduring fire follow the Empire across the curve of this universe? Should the Malign pursue? Watch the Singular's last agonies?

She knew instantly that such goals were paltry. *The stuff of maggot minds.*

No — far grander to escape the binds of this universe entirely. Not merely voyage in it. Not simply skim across the sloping warp. Learn from the Singular — and finally kill it, of course.

Follow those who had already leaped free of the brane, into dimensions beyond the paltry infinity of this place. *Ah.*

Cley struggled but could find no way through the cloying hot ink that oozed into her throat, that seared her bowels. Faintly she felt that these turgid sensations were, in fact . . . ideas. She could not comprehend them as cool abstractions. They reeked and banged, cut and seared, rubbed and poked at her.

And on this stage ideas moved as monstrous actors, capable of anything.

She understood now, as quickly as she could frame the question, what the madness cloaking her wanted.

It desired to create deep wells in space-time. Compression of matter to achieve this in turn required the concerted efforts, willing or not, of many magnetic minds — for in the end, only intelligence coolly divorced from matter could truly control masses and their warps.

So the Malign digested those magnetic immanences. And forced their energies to its own desires.

Such a venture risked the destruction of the entire galaxy. Fresh matter had to be created, carved, and compacted. This could curve space-time enough to trap the galaxy into a self-contracting sphere, cut off from the universe even as it bled downward into a yawning gravitational pit.

Only in this way could the Malign escape the brane, as the Singular had done. Join the Singular, which in turn desired the death of the Malign.

In joining it, the Malign would find the means to kill the Singular. Somehow.

The galaxy could not accept such danger. The magnetic minds had debated the wisdom of such a venture while the Malign was confined. Their discussion had been dispassionate, for they were not threatened by the destruction of the galaxy. Magnetic intelligences could follow the Malign beyond such geometric oblivion, since they were not tied to the fate of mere matter.

But the galaxy brimmed with lesser life. And in the last billion years, as humanity slept in Sonomulia, life had integrated.

Near most stars teemed countless entities, bound to planets or orbiting them. Farther out, between the shimmering suns, the wisps of magnetic structures gazed down on these chemical agencies. Scarcely more than packets of moving water, but the magnetics watched them with a slow, brooding spirit. Their inability to transcend the speed of light meant that these most vast of all intelligences took millennia to speak across the chasms of the galactic arms.

Yet slowly, slowly, through these links a true galactic mind had arisen. It had been driven to more complex levels of perception by the sure knowledge that eventually the Malign would escape.

The Magnetics became the highest form – but not the

only part – of the galactic mind. The Chemicals still had a role to play. They were quick, vibrant, mortal. They were fascinating and vivid to the Magnetics, whose pace was at best glacial.

Suddenly, Cley realized, *They mean us. Chemicals. Me!*

So the magnetic beasts could not abandon the matter-born to extinction. They had ruled against the Malign's experiment before, and now they moved to crush the new-risen malevolency before it could carry out the phased and intricate compression of mass.

Cley saw this in a passing instant of struggle, while she swam in a milky satin fog – and then immeasurably later, through sheets the colors of bloody brass. She was like a blind ship adrift, with her senses the sole gyroscope of any use.

The pain began then.

It soared through her. If she had once thought of herself and the other Ur-humans as elements in an electrical circuit, now she understood what this could mean.

The agony was timeless. Her jaws strained open, tongue stuck straight out, pink and burning. Her eyes bulged. She shook with terror and then went beyond that to a longing, a need for extinction simply to escape the terror.

Her agony was featureless. No tick of time consoled her. Her previous life, memories, pleasures – all dwindled into nothing beside the flinty mountain of her pain.

She longed to scream. Rin! Seeker! She could feel a faint murmur of Rin's body-net . . . but it was fading.

Muscles refused to unlock in her throat, her face. Excruciation made her into a statue.

And through her came a bulge, thickening in her, a blunt momentum. She felt what it needed, and *pushed*.

Gave, letting the deep recesses of her mind gush out, letting the Multifold have the substratum of her Original self. It needed to know how her worn old mental machinery clanked and ground and slogged forward. To use her as an ancient tool.

Something huge came seeking. She sent the Multifold her skills, shaped in ancient days: The only way to turn the tide is to be embedded deeper than it is.

She felt herself and the Multifold merge. It was the same sensation she had felt back on Earth, when she and Seeker had sunk into the forest and eluded the Supras. Here the span was vast, but her instinct played out through the Multifold – damping its salients, making it invisible to the Malign.

A moment later, an inspecting pressure wave swept through – probing, prodding, sensing the slight perturbations of dissonance and movement that would have revealed their presence. All the Malign's energies mounted behind the pressure . . .

And the wave washed on. It had missed them. Now she sent. The Multifold snapped out of the state she had sent it to. It coiled, struck.

The sensation was not like orgasm but like what came after. The knowledge of something gainfully lost.

But the cost . . .

The pain was now exquisite. It sucked the strata from her. Her cramped way of seeing the world was a language in itself, and she finally gave it forth. The *her* of her blew outward, was sponged up. Gone.

Without this, we could not traverse.

It was not Kata or any Supra. The voice strummed low and certain. She sensed a distant presence that was embroiled in a terrible vast struggle. A tiny fraction had come to her and taken what she could yield, what she could birth, and now went back into the fray.

The Malign's agony was terrible. She gave the Multifold her fierceness, then the ancient blood rage that humans carried. That helped. Her pent-up angers arced with purpose, animating the Multifold. She was only a part, but a vital one.

The Malign was coming apart. Its stored energies turned against itself, searing and cutting.

It went on a long time and left her limp. In the end came not a sense of triumph but of tragedy, of gray exhaustion.

Thanks to you. We leave you as we found you. Enjoy your simple self and do not try to be more. To be like this, ancient and quick, is enough. There are times when we wish we could be so again.

She heard a scream. Not aloud, but in the Talent.

It was a human. A Supra. She caught the sweeping away of life. Dying. Rin.

And then, without transition, she was standing, water cascading all over her, soggy hair bunched atop her head, her shoulders and breasts white with soapy smears.

She felt this, but it was somehow abstract. An imposed moment.

Her prickly flesh shimmered and melted, and her nipples were fat spigots. They snagged bubbles and dripped rich drops. The air eagerly lapped these teardrops as they fell. Her eyes closed, but she could still somehow sense a pulse fluttering in her throat. A satin moistness slithering over her tender breasts.

She screamed. Coming at her suddenly, this assault was close, intimate – horrifying.

She screamed again. The splashing waterfall vanished in an instant.

She knew that this – this place, this state of mind – it, too, was part of the Malign.

Or a last, brushing kiss from it. For it was genuinely mad and contained within it a skein that humans would see as love, or hate, or malignant resolve. But these were categories evolved for a species. They no more described another class of being than violins and drums describe a storm.

Some of its madness was human. Lodged in magnetic helices lay the mentality of man. Several races had been digested by the Malign, and each left a signature.

Its ambition, to escape the bands of the brane itself, was born in part of humanity. Mankind had helped build the Malign, in arrogance and the need to know, and those qualities had been reflected in what they made. Many species throughout the galaxy, and many of man's finest and bravest, had fallen – subsumed in the long-ago fight to stop their creation. Many species throughout the galaxy had built the Malign. Lacing through the pain were streaks of ancient guilt.

Rin had known this, she saw. That was some of the weight he carried. Curiosity was never simple.

The Malign had a substrate of magnetic beings, too. She felt them now, ponderous and eerie. They brimmed throughout the solar system. Focused here, they fumed with red anger. Their intelligences were neither higher nor lower than humans', for they were not born from the evolutionary forces that had driven humanity to solve problems. They had survived by altering their perceptions. How this happened, Cley could not fathom.

She hovered above a bubble of frayed light, a star at its center. A sphere, alive with racing darts of luminescence. It was the most beautiful thing she had ever seen.

And suddenly, Seeker was there. With her.

Seeker's ears flexed and changed from cinnamon to burnt yellow. It gestured at the sphere. 'I think it best to call all that the System Solar.'

'What . . . what . . . ?'

'She gave birth to humankind. She is a third as old as the universe itself. She is a source of life everlasting.'

Cley knew not where she was or what had happened, but . . . 'And you, Seeker, you're her agent, aren't you?'

Seeker nodded and laughed. Or at least Cley thought this apparition did. She was never really sure what Seeker meant, and perhaps that was for the best. 'From the beginning. We procyons were made for such tasks.'

'I . . . I suppose it's reassuring, being part of something so large.'

Seeker said, 'It is the foundation of my being.'

Cley *felt* this, a jolt of calm certainty. As though now, here, she could enter into Seeker's mind.

Seeker waved a paw and went on. 'Rin knew of her. But he described her as endless chains of regulatory messages between the worlds, of intricate feedback, and so missed the point.'

'What point?'

'Rin saw only metabolism. He missed purpose.'

'Ah. I—'

In a withering instant, Seeker dwindled down a deep fault line, falling away.

Gone in a moment. Utterly. 'Wait!'

But Cley was in the grasp of something else now.

For a sliding instant she caught a glimpse of humanity, from *their* view. The procyons, yes, but something larger, behind them, *in* them.

The grip of something else tightened around her. She blinked and was in another place. A foreboding sense coursed in her, and she felt real panic – *Run!* – but could not move.

A great eagle hung in black space, near a sulfurous planet.

Its wings flapped, long and lazy. Diamond-sharp eyes glinted. The beak hung slightly open, as though about to call out a booming cry. She watched the flex of the immense feathers for a while as muscles bulged beneath the wings. Only then did she see that the bird flew between the planet behind it and a sun in the distance – a star, red and hairy with immense chromatic flares.

And across the span of the immense wings nestled small, fevered mites. At one wingtip rose pyramids. Mountains capped in white framed broad plains, which in turn led to silvery, spiky cities. Across the wingspan lay ages of greatness and long nights of despair. But always the ferment, the jutting towers of boundless ambition, the dusty ruins brought by wear and failure. At the far wingtip a fogged land lay, just beyond her ability to make out detail. *So much history – no Library could know this . . .*

Humanity in its timescape. All who had ever carried the gleam kindled behind searching eyes – they abided there.

Mites. Pests.

Gathered in time's long tapestry, on the back of the eagle. They milled and fought and saw only their limited moment. They did not know that they flew between unreadable spheres, in the perfumed air of vast night.

As the bird flapped past her, it turned. The glinting black eyes looked at her once; the beak opened slightly. Malignant.

Then it turned away and flew on. Intent. Resolute.

Cley raged.

She sent torrents of herself – *age-old fury, the stuff of the species, an anger out of Afrik so long in coming* – she sent it forth, her own tiny part of the exploding battle . . .

And she was *in it* at last, in a single fractured eyeblink, caught up in hard momentum, her own small self *linked* to something far larger, but *a part* and now knit fully in, the entire huge moment acting through her as she *felt* the kinship of her kind, of all kinds hominid together and still coming, her very self extracted and sucked into the moment, her inner way of seeing the world somehow uplifted into a big shadowed thing she only glimpsed as it passed – larger than the eagle, more ferocious and yet more kind . . .

There came a moment like an immense word on the verge of being spoken.

And then it was over.

She sat up. Vines holding her were like rasping, hot breaths. Her wrists were rabbed raw.

'Where's the bubble? I thought I escaped.'

No answer. A woody, moist smell. She was back inside the Leviathan, feeling . . .

She vomited violently. Coughed. Gasped.

Brown blood had caked, thick and crusty, at her wrists. Her fingernails had snapped off. The tips were buried in her palms. Numbly Cley licked them clean.

Someone came scrabbling down a vine. 'Have a rat,' Seeker said, and held up a green morsel on a forked stick.

4

The Heresy of Humanism

R *in!* No answering murmur of his body-net. Nothing. She shook her head and was sick again.

'It's done,' Seeker said.

'I . . . Who won?'

'We did.'

'What . . . what . . . ?'

'Losses?' Seeker paused as though listening to a distant song. 'Billions of lives. Billions of loves, which is another way to count.'

She closed her eyes and felt a strange, dry echo of Seeker's voice. This was Seeker's Talent. Through it she witnessed the gray, blasted wastes that stretched throughout the solar system. Worlds blistered, atmospheres belched into vacuum, countless lives gone.

'The Malign?'

'Eaten by us,' Seeker said.

'Us?'

'Life. The galactic mind.'

'I was with it. Horrible . . .' She shook herself to throw off the memory. Her Talent caught frayed strands of Seeker's ebbing vision. 'You . . . see it all, don't you?'

'Only within the solar system. The speed of light constrains.'

'You can sense all life? On all the worlds?'

'And between them.'

'How?'

Seeker pricked up her outsized ears. Waves of amber and yellow chased each other around her pelt. 'Like this.' More ear flicks, and a grin.

'Well, what's that?'

'*This.*'

In a glimmering she saw fragile, lonely Earth, now among the blighted worlds. But it had been diminished by humans, she saw; the Malign had not injured it. Humans had hemmed in its horizons. Sentinel Earth had played its role and now could return to obscurity. Or to greatness.

'What will happen to it?' Cley asked quietly. Her body ached, but she put that fact aside.

'Earth? I imagine the Supras will dream on there.' Seeker nipped at the rat with obvious relish.

'Just dream?'

Seeker shook one paw. She had just burned it on the cooking stick, and whimpered in pain. Cley saw the hollows beneath Seeker's eyes. There was a weathered, wan look to the age-old raccoonlike face – older, worn gray. Cley sensed that the creature had suffered much since she last saw her, but there was no hint in her speech. 'Human dreams can be powerful . . .' a breath, wheezed out. '. . . as we have just witnessed.'

A moment hovered between them. Cley saw that they would never be quite the same, she and Seeker. They had each been through something that they could not speak of, or know from the other's perspective. So it was with differing intelligences.

Maybe that was how it should be. Anyway, it was.

Cley then saw, through Seeker's strangely bounded Talent, the Earth shrinking into insignificance. It became a speck inside a great sphere – the same glowing ball she had seen in the struggle.

'What is it?'

'An oasis.'

'The whole solar system?'

'An oasis biome, one of billions strewn through the galaxy. Between them live only the magnetic minds. And passing small travelers bound upon their journeys, of course.'

'This is your "higher cause," isn't it?' Cley grimaced. Compared with pain, abstractions were nothing. 'I mean, when Rin asked if you would help defend human destiny?'

Seeker farted loudly, grinning. 'He was guilty of the heresy of humanism.'

'How can that be heresy?'

'The narcissistic devotion to things human? "Man is the measure of all things"? Easily.'

'Well, he has to speak for his species.'

'His genus, you mean, if you would include yourself.'

Cley frowned. 'I don't know how close to them I am. Or what use they'll have for me now.'

'You share the samenesses of your order, which are perhaps the most important.'

'Order?'

'The order of primates. A useful intermediate step. You possess the general property of seeing events in close focus. Your ears hear sounds proportional to the logarithm of the intensity. Otherwise you could not hear a bee hum and still tolerate a handclap next to your ear. Or see both by moonlight and at high noon – your eyesight adjusts.'

'Those are all damn useful,' Cley said defensively. She could not see Seeker's point.

'True, but you also consider time the same way. Your logarithmic perception stresses the present, diminishing the past or the future. What happened at breakfast clamors for attention alongside the origin of the universe.'

Cley shrugged. 'Hell, we have to survive.' And saying it, she knew that was not enough. She had to grow through all that had happened. She was just a kid, after all. Maybe all humans were.

'Yes, and hell is what you would bear if you had continued with your heresy.'

She shot Seeker an inquiring look. These were grave words, but Seeker rolled lazily and swung from two vines, using them to cavort in midair with flips and turns and airy leaps. Had the Supras moved her back into the Leviathan? Or the extradimensional Morphs? Maybe it didn't matter. Plenty had happened without her understanding. Right now, that was perfectly fine. She was content just to feel air whispering in and out of her lungs.

Between her huffs and puffs Seeker said, 'You humans would have prevented our oasis biome from integrating, with your grandiose plans.'

Cley felt a spurt of irritation. Who was this animal, to deride humanity's billion-year history? 'Look, I might not like Rin and the rest all that much, but—'

'Your trouble is that contrary to the logarithmic time sense, evolution proceeds exponentially. And the argument of the exponent is the complexity of life forms.'

'And what's that mean?' Cley asked, determined to sail through this airy talk on a practical tack.

'One-celled organisms take billions of years to learn

the trick of marrying into two or more. From dinosaurs to Ur-humans took only a hundred million. And then intelligent machines — admittedly, a short-lived experiment — required only a thousand.' Seeker did a flip and caught herself on a limb, her tongue lolling.

'You don't seem all that advanced beyond us,' Cley said.

'How would you tell? If my kind had evolved into clouds, I could not have the fun of this, could I?' Seeker gulped down the rest of the fat green rat.

'Or the fun of dragging me all the way across the solar system?'

'There is duty, too.'

'To what?'

'To the System Solar. The biome.'

'I—' she began, but then a piercing cry burst through her mind.

It was Kata. Her Talent-wail broke like a wave of hopeless grief. Shards of sound.

Cley scrambled away through raspy vines, driven by the mournful, grating power. She nearly collided with a man in the foliage. He gazed blankly at her. She recognized something in that face . . . 'Who're you?' she asked.

'I have . . . no name.'

'Well, what . . . ?' And then she fully sensed him. A tiny speck of Talent-talk purring in him. Ur-human, yes.

You were one of those links I felt, she sent.

Yes. Those of us here . . . have gathered. We are afraid. His feelings were curiously flat and without fervor. Unformed.

Cley sent carefully, You're like a . . . child.

I am like us. The Talent-voice carried no rancor, and his face was smooth and unmarked, though that of a full-grown man. But no comprehension. No experience. He didn't even take offense at being compared with a child.

She looked beyond him and saw a dozen like him, men and women of the same height and body type. Her eyes widened. You're me!

In a way, he sent mildly.

From the Ur-humans came a tide of bland assent. They were untouched by time and trouble, she saw. Conjured up in some Supra process, from her DNA. Fast-grown, stamped with some nominal learning and skills. Yet she could not despise them.

The struggle – how was it? she asked.

A woman sent, We had never done anything like that.

'Well, you won't again,' Cley said aloud. She preferred concrete speech to the sensation of dropping stones down the deep well of their emptiness.

A man stepped forward, and she recognized him. From the Leviathan – the one who had fled. He said, 'They worked well, after all.'

He was tall and thin and handsome in a way that tugged at her memory. 'I was there, some way. And you?'

He grinned, and lines crinkled around his eyes. 'They sure hadn't planned on my being there, and I was a last-minute addition, but yes, I was there, too. The Supras needed the help. You were the core of it, but they needed all the Originals they could get. They tried to get some from a higher dimension – humans who had gone into the Singularity, they were that desperate – but it didn't work. So they were stuck with us, the home-grown.'

'You're, you're . . .'

'Your father.'

She embraced him silently, her world falling silently

away. He was lean and weathered and somehow smelled right. In his high cheekbones and wary eyes she saw something of herself. *So much to learn.*

'Wait, you . . .' She made a guess. 'Hey, Seeker!'

The procyon was right there, as if she knew she would be called. Cley asked her, 'All the talks we had about my father — you've used a lot, been behind a lot, haven't you?'

Seeker blinked, and Cley rushed on. 'This isn't any kind of coincidence, is it? You agents of the biome — did you arrange this? My father being *here,* of all the unlikely places, I mean?'

'Of course.' She blinked, slow and heavy-lidded. 'He was bound to be a wanderer, like you. And the Supras needed Originals to connect with the Singularity. So I arranged for him to be brought to the Leviathan.'

'Huh!' Cley turned back to her father. 'Then why did you run away when I saw you?'

He smiled. 'You were disturbed enough already. The connection the Supras wanted to make between you and the Multifold — it would have been made more . . . noisy.'

She admired his understatement. 'Noisy?' More like the big bang, speeded up.

'But I needed to at least see you, y'know? The procyons sure weren't happy when they found out.' His smile edged into a grin — a kid sharing a secret. 'They like to think they're in control, as much as the Supras do. They had a fit about my sneaking off and maybe messing with "the Plan," Tough.'

Back to Seeker. 'He was my *backup,* right?'

Seeker's silence and features were almost unreadable, but there seemed a trace of discomfort in them.

'Too strong a term,' her father said. 'But yes, I was there to help.'

'So much was going on behind my back!' She didn't like it, but could they be right? Maybe ignorance had helped simplify? She had always thought that knowing was better, but looking into her father's warm eyes, she was not so sure.

And Seeker — 'You led me by the nose, all the way!'

'And not an easy task — your nose is tiny compared with mine. I wanted you to survive what I suspected was coming.'

The simplicity of this somehow brought Cley some peace.

Afterward there was a long inward-looking time she could not remember. Inside her, doors opened and soft breezes blew her thoughts around, high and light. No talk, only a quiet. At the end of it she said to her father, 'You went away from the Meta . . .'

'To see all these things, yep.' His smile was broad but rueful. 'Out here. Figure out where we stand in it all.'

'Where do we?'

'Part of the flow. That's all anybody is. Even Supras.' His disdain colored the name, but he did not lose his smile. She knew there was a whole story lurking there.

And it was . . . *him. So much to know.* Her heart seemed to swell, tightening her throat. The little girl still in her began, 'But look, what—'

Then she saw the body. Some Ur-humans carried it between them in the light gravity. 'Rin!'

Kata followed the corpse, her face stony, body stiff, emitting no Talent-trace at all now.

Cley asked a man-child, 'What happened?'

'He . . . gave . . . too much.' The man-child's throat sounded raw and unused, as though he had seldom spoken before.

Cley gazed into Rin's open eyes. A rosy pattern of burst veins gave them the look of small, trapped seas. Blood lakes. Ruin at a cellular level.

Cley sighed. Kata put a hand on Cley's shoulder but said and sent nothing.

Cley looked at Rin's troubled, fractured eyes and tried to imagine what he had finally faced. She remembered that she had sensed him, that he had somehow helped her when she was in the Malign's grip.

She had been the conduit, and he the guardian. And his cost had been to have his own mind burned away, the brain itself fused.

Yet his face held a calm dignity in death. She felt a pang of loss. He had been strange but majestic, in his way. Seeker was wrong; the Supras were still essentially human, though she would never be able to define just what that meant.

In a heartbeat she sensed something beyond the kinesthetic effects she had ridden, beyond the explanations she had glimpsed. The coiling complications of ambition, the crazed scheme to tunnel out of their own space-time . . .

That was part of it, yes.

But she remembered, too, the algae mats of Earth's first oceans, billions of years ago. They lived on in the guts of animals, hiding in dark places where chemistry still kindled without oxygen. She recalled that her own tribe had used such yeasty agents in the brewing of beer. If such an organism could think, what would it make of the frothy spume of beer? As catalysts they were certainly taking part in processes transcending themselves, yielding benefits they could not imagine. If they could somehow know, they might well feel immeasurably exalted.

But to those who brewed beer's casual delights, yeasts were unimaginably far beneath the realm of importance, mere dregs of evolution. And whatever dim perceptions the yeasts could muster would hardly resemble the talk and laughter and argument that swirled through the minds that felt the pleasant effects of that beer.

Her own understandings of what the past struggle had been about — could they be similar? Valid, perhaps, but dwarfed by the unknowable abyss that separated her species from the purposes of entities enormously removed.

Could that bear somehow on what Seeker meant about logarithmic time and exponential growth? That she could not even imagine such a gulf?

The thought caught her for only a single dizzying instant. Then it was gone, and she was back in the comfortable, linear progression of events she knew.

She turned away from the body. The Ur-humans milled uncertainly around her. Her father stood silently, letting her work on this herself. 'Seeker, I . . . these people. My people.'

'So they are,' Seeker said noncommittally at her side.

'Can I have them? I mean, take them back?' She gestured up at the transparent dome where the tired but receptive, pale Earth still spun.

'Of course. The Supras could not raise them alone.'

'I'll try to bring up just a few of them at first,' Cley said cautiously. Leave some in a stasis bubble, somehow?

Bring them out gradually, to be reared? The enormity of becoming mother to a race struck her.

'No one tests the depth of a river with both feet,' Seeker said.

Her father said mildly, 'I can help. I did it before.'

That meant so much to Cley, she could not speak.

Kata had gone on, moving with a forlorn gravity, solemn and silent, not looking back. Cley wondered if she would ever see her again. Perhaps not – Supras had their own ways.

Her father said, 'Let's get some food for you kids. Tend to business.'

One of the Ur-human men said experimentally, 'Sure . . . Dad.'

They moved off, her father leading them with a natural authority. She admired the way he simply took charge; she could learn from him. The others – her children! – followed. Full of potential. 'Do you think there'll be a place for them?' she asked.

'If you make one,' Seeker said.

'And you?'

'This is my place.' She fanned a greasy claw at the quiet immensities around them.

'The – what did you call it? – System Solar?'

Seeker produced another rat, yellow this time, and began to eat.

'Was it "her" – your System Solar – that really destroyed the Malign?'

'Of course.'

'What about the Supras?'

'They did as they must. We helped sculpt their uses.'

'Which is it: "she" did it, or "we" did it?'

'Both.'

Cley sighed. 'Well, did we humans matter at all?'

'Of course. Though not as you imagine.'

'You did so much, for all of us. For me. But . . . you helped me because of your biome, didn't you?'

Seeker caught the disappointment in her voice. 'Truly. You are an element I had not comprehended. I chanced to pass nearby, felt the resonance, and stayed with you. You were the first Original I had met. So different! And I came to love you.'

Ah, Seeker, she thought. Cryptic, rarely solemn, never gushing, but sincere in what she did say. To cover her emotions (*a very human mannerism,* she thought wryly) Cley said, 'Just doing your part in the System Solar.'

Seeker said with a grave scowl, 'As you did.'

'Hey, c'mon, I did have other motives.'

'They were incidental.' Seeker lunged at a passing bird, missed, and tumbled into a tangle of vines. Cley laughed. Was this the superbeing she had seen roving among the planets during the battle? The same creature that now wrestled with vines, sputtering in irritation? Or was there really a contradiction?

'This biome – how come you're so loyal to it?'

'It is the highest form which can evolve from this universe – so far. Far more complex than the Magnetics, in depth of interactions.' Seeker kept twisting around in the thick vines to no avail. Even so, she continued in an even, measured tone, 'The biome has been implicit in the governing laws since the beginning, and arose here first as intricate networks on ancient Earth.'

'So Rin had part of it right after all.'

Seeker thrashed around, getting herself caught tighter. 'Only a narrow view.'

'You said once you had contact with everything.'

Seeker shook her head in frustration. 'Everything and the nothing.'

'What's "the nothing"?'

Seeker bit into a vine and tore it loose. 'When a thinking being chooses to not think for a while.'

'The unconscious?'

'The transconscious. Separation into isolated beings was a feature of evolution in the human era and before. I am a fragment of the self-awareness that arose from that early web – after all, life was once confined just to Earth, and now grows apace.'

'Sounds pretty exalted, Seeker After Patterns.'

'You are part of it, too,' Seeker said softly.

'I don't feel all that cosmic right this minute,' Cley said, beginning to notice her many aches. Her palms throbbed. Her joints felt as though someone had popped them open, blowtorched them, and snapped them closed. She wondered if the Supras had any medical miracles handy.

'The biome is ordinary. Not a big abstraction.' Seeker wrestled free of the vines.

'And you're a housekeeper for the, uh, System Solar?' Cley smiled ruefully.

'In a way. I voyaged once to another biome, and—'

Cley was startled. 'Another star?'

'Yes. I journeyed to speak with that far biome. Quite different, it was.'

'What's a biome say to another?'

'Little, at first. I had difficulties.'

'I thought Seeker After Patterns could do anything.'

Seeker made her barking laugh. 'Only what my planets allow me.'

'They sent you?'

'Yes. Eventually the biomes strewn through the spiral arms will connect. There is much work to be done, to understand those strange beings.'

'Biomes are conscious?'

'Of course. Evolution proceeds beyond the scope of individuals now, or of species and phyla. Biomes are different orders of beings.'

As she said this, Seeker no longer looked like an amiable pet. Cley sensed quiet, eerie powers in her.

'Seeker, you speak as if you are the System Solar.'

'So we do.'

Cley chuckled and cuffed Seeker beneath her ample, matted chin. 'Well, so much for words. Whatever won this, and at whatever cost, we're alive.'

Seeker gazed at her soberly. 'Far more important that the biome lives.'

'Yes, thank God.'

'You are welcome,' Seeker said.

That night the surviving humans, Supra and Original alike, did an ancient human thing: drank alcohol. No matter how many millennia of research had come and gone, something about that elementary organic compound still resonated in times of mourning and celebration, deep in the human soul. The consolations of chemistry.

Cley did not mingle much with the Supras. They kept largely to themselves anyway, looking a bit uncomfortable. They looked as if they wanted to help but hadn't a clue. Child-rearing had to be learned from experience, and Supras lived so long, they seldom needed the art. The clones had some social skills, but Cley could tell from her

Meta experience that they needed much work. They were pseudobabies, really — full-grown bodies, with all the hormonal/physical demands those would put on them, but with child minds and no social context. Making presentable adults of them would be a wild animal-taming act.

Unlike at every other party she had ever attended, she felt no need to go over and try to work herself into conversation with the Supras. Even the Supra men had no particular gravitational attraction for her. It felt good.

Instead, the Ur-humans drew her. They were equally curious about her, and their innocent, friendly chatter she found touching. Not much alcohol for them, of course — they had no experience to brace them against it. She monitored that. Their gaiety came from within — amusing, quick, light as a breeze. In turn their humor provoked her own giggles, and it was not just the alcohol.

Cley looked around the room — actually, a bower the captain had ordered to be worked forth from a vine cloister in the Leviathan — and felt an odd feeling creep over her.

She knew humanity's role in the biome. Knew it in her gut. The mighty Supras did not; somehow, she could tell. She very well might be the only person in the room who *felt* the meaning of that.

And her own retinue of her genetic identicals — they knew little.

Neither had she, until now. Until the long struggle with the Malign — a battle that had lasted seven days, someone said. It had felt like years. Cley could feel the fatigue like an ache in her bones and knew that she would sleep for a week, once she closed her eyes. But not yet. Not yet.

Seeker came by, sipping suspiciously at a cup of a Supra

punch. Cley fell upon the procyon with glad cries. 'You made all this happen! I've got a family. And I never thanked you.'

'Not necessary. I was following my nose.'

Cley tweaked the long snout. 'That must be easy; it's so big.'

'With your kind, you are happy in a different way,' Seeker said pensively.

'You never saw me with my Meta.' Cley made a sweeping gesture. 'Now I've got all of my kind there are, right here.'

'Not all.'

'Huh? But you said my kind were gone.'

'Gone into the Singular, some of them.'

'There are Originals in those branes of yours?'

'Yes, they made the leap into the branes, after all. But they are not mine, the branes.' Seeker eyed Cley. 'Nor yours, either. The higher-dimensionals have incorporated humans in ways we cannot know.'

'Wow. And I thought the Supras were the best ever.'

'Evolution meanders; it seldom climbs directly.'

'Originals in four-D? What do they look like?'

'I do not know. Perhaps they are Morphs. Or so we would call them.'

'Oog.' Cley wrinkled her nose. 'Maybe I don't want to find out.'

Seeker said soberly, 'Those, too, fought in the battle with the Malign.'

'My kin, though. How can I reach them?'

'That expedition would be more difficult than the one we have just finished.' Seeker raised a skeptical eyebrow. 'Are you willing?'

'Huh? Hey, first I have to get these kids back, find a place to live, make—'

'I know. There will be time for that. Shall I come calling for you?'

'Uh, sure. But wait – last time we spoke, you owned up to being, well . . .'

'God?'

'Yes. How . . . ?'

'But so are you.'

'What?!'

'Of course, you need some polishing. But you show definite promise, and there is work remaining. I shall see you in a while.'

Seeker walked away, still sipping.

'Wait! I don't understand!'

'Welcome to our society of the happily ignorant,' Seeker called back as she disappeared into some flowering foliage. Her passage left behind a spray of pollen like a quick puff of ivory smoke.

As usual, Seeker left leaving more questions than answers. Cley had to take all this in. Above, through a transparent membrane, hung one of those nights when the silence, and the trumpet-clear beauty of light spilling across darkness, echoes with something as primal as a heartbeat. Back in her Meta she had never understood people who didn't look up – didn't they hear that singing? She stood there for several minutes, just being, the Leviathan's warm, moist wind and the night swirling around her as if their pull could send her flying, dancing without moving a muscle. Sublime.

There was so much to do now.

The young versions of herself milled around, working

on their social skills, and tipped back their crystal glasses – after all, they were her, and she was doing a lot of that, too. All blithely adorable. Hers.

'We're going back together,' she said to one of the young men. 'Tomorrow.'

'Really? Where?' he asked, blank-faced.

'Earth. Home.'

'I dunno, we were all speed-grown in tanks, fast-taught, had a lot of time in the crucibles . . .'

'You need bringing up,' Cley said softly.

'Do we?' His face was open and could take any impression, she realized. The imprint of a soft touch.

A strange form of adulthood beckoned to her. She would take these back to Earth and bring them up. They were of her kind, and she had to honor that. She would make a home for them, and for herself.

And then, too, there was her father. He would help, sure – but she already had a gut sense about him. He was a rover, like Cley, and would be off to the great reaches of the sky in the long run.

Hell, in the long run, she would go, too. It was in the genes.

Cley felt a dawning wonder and joy. She finally had a place, somewhere she belonged, a home to build. In emerald forest or broad, dry plain, a spinning cocoon in high vacuum, no matter – a home.

Afterword

Prediction is always difficult, especially of the future.
—Danish saying, often quoted by Niles Bohr

Years ago a friend, David Hartwell, used the term 'transcendental adventure,' and I thought about what that might mean. This novel may be an example. Another contribution that might fit is my 1984 novel, *Against Infinity*. I suppose there's a pattern here. I wonder what I could title another such tale, should I write one.

This novel emerges from a novella, *Beyond the Fall of Night,* that I published in 1990, together with Arthur C. Clarke's *Against the Fall of Night*. That novella was a continuation of Clarke's, and I shaped it to fit the length (though not the style) of his original. It was fun, especially the give-and-take with Arthur. Writing is lonely work, which explains many collaborations. Science fiction is unusual in the number of collaborations, probably because it is easier to share ideas than characters, and ours is an idea-intensive genre. I'm told that I have written more novels with others than any other SF writer, so my opinion in this is somewhat biased.

Still, after *Beyond the Fall of Night* I finally felt that the result was unsatisfactory, cramped, full of shorthand – but did not then see how to fix it.

This novel attempts to remedy that. Plainly, the ideas needed more air to breathe, so I have expanded the novella to about three times its original size and retitled it. Trappings of Clarke's far future I have dropped or rearranged. New ideas, principally those of extra dimensions in our universe, I have used from the latest theoretical physics. Centuries of speculative writing have shown us that often our principal sin lies in not being daring enough, and the idea that our universe has more dimensions – tucked away, hidden but significant – is too luscious to resist.

Many people helped with the myriad angles and perspectives the book required. I thank Jamie Levine especially for her editorial help. Elisabeth Malantre and Naomi Fisher made many useful suggestions.

Yet once again I find that there are more ideas in here than I could do justice to. Perhaps I will eventually write a sequel, to explore the avenues opened by this larger version. After all, I haven't finished the sequel to *Against Infinity* yet.

The far future is a big place. This is a snapshot of where I think evolution and technology might take us. No doubt the reality will be far stranger.

Gregory Benford
August 2003

MARTIAN RACE

Gregory Benford

March, 2015. NASA's first manned voyage to
Mars is about to launch.

But disaster strikes. The rocket explodes, killing
the entire crew, and the US government
abandons the project. What they come up with in
its place will change the nature of space
exploration for ever.

Businessman John Axelrod and his consortium
have every intention of winning the $30 billion
Mars Prize for the first successful mission to the
red planet. He knows that it will involve far
higher risks than the one NASA had planned.
But he has no choice. He has to win.

The Martian Race has begun.

ARTIFACT

Gregory Benford

In a 3500-year-old Mycenaean tomb an artifact
has been unearthed. An incomprehensible object
in an impossible place; its age, purpose and
origins uknown.

Its substance has scientists baffled. And the
miracle it contains does not belong on this Earth.

It is an enigma with no equal in recorded history
and its discovery has unleashed a storm of
intrigue, theft and espionage that is pushing
nations to the brink of war.

It is mankind's greatest discovery . . . and
worst nightmare.

It may have already obliterated one world.
Ours is next.

FOR THE LATEST NEWS AND THE HOTTEST EXCLUSIVES ON ALL
YOUR FAVOURITE SF AND FANTASY STARS, SIGN UP FOR:

ORBIT'S <u>FREE</u> MONTHLY E-ZINE

PACKED WITH

BREAKING NEWS
THE LATEST REVIEWS
EXCLUSIVE INTERVIEWS
STUNNING EXTRACTS
SPECIAL OFFERS
BRILLIANT COMPETITIONS

AND A GALAXY OF
NEW AND ESTABLISHED SFF STARS!

TO GET A DELICIOUS SLICE OF SFF IN <u>YOUR</u> INBOX EVERY MONTH, SEND YOUR
DETAILS BY EMAIL TO: <u>ORBIT.UK@TIMEWARNERBOOKS.CO.UK</u> OR VISIT:

 WWW.ORBITBOOKS.CO.UK
THE HOME OF SFF ONLINE